D0123961

Acknowledgments

Thanks to my Bywater Books family:
Marianne K. Martin, Salem West, Ann McMan,
Kelly Smith, Nancy Squires,
and Elizabeth Andersen

and to Veronica Flaggs, AJ Head, Renee Bess
and Marcia White.

And, thanks to Detroit for my roots, tenacity
and swagger.

"Got nowhere to run to, baby
Nowhere to hide."

Nowhere to Run
Martha and the Vandellas
Brian Holland, Lamont Dozier, Edward Holland Jr.
Motown Records
1965

Cast of Characters

Charlene "Charlie" Mack
Partner in Mack Investigations,
a Detroit-based Private Investigations firm

Don Rutkowski
Partner in Mack Investigations, former police officer,
and Homeland Security trainer

Gil Acosta
Partner in Mack Investigations, attorney,
and former Marine

Judy Novak
Office Manager, Mack Investigations
Hoyt Timbermann, Lin Fong, Carter Bernstein, Josh Simms
Mack Investigations freelancers

Scott Hartwell, Irwin Cross, Tommy Kozol, Oscar Acosta
Board of the Detroit Auto Dealers Association (DADA)

Mr. Kwong, Amy Wu, Yu Chenglei
Guí Motors employees

Geoff Heinrich
CEO, Spectrum Security

Cynthia Fitzgerald
Operations Director, Spectrum Security

Bernard Dudiyn
Spectrum Security employee

Tyson Pressley
Cobo Center Communications Staff,
liaison to the Mack partners on the Auto Show case

Elise Hillman
Cobo Center Director of Food Services

Dennis Calhoun
Cobo Center Facilities Supervisor

Garry Jones
Cobo Center Food Services Supervisor

Tony Canterra
Senior Agent, Department of Homeland Security (DHS)
liaison to the Mack partners on the Auto Show case

Jim Routledge
Assistant Regional Director, Department of
Homeland Security (DHS)

Mandy Porter
Grosse Pointe Park police officer, freelancer on Cobo case,
and Charlie's lover

Chapter 1

Thursday, December 29, 2005

Charlie wore three layers of clothing and thick socks, but it was all she could do to keep from shivering. Gil slumped unmoving in the driver's seat; a knit hat covered his ears, and his hands were pushed deeply into the pockets of a four-hundred-dollar parka. No doubt his military training helped him in this kind of situation. They were parked on a narrow residential street in Ferndale after following the subject of their surveillance to a house across the street from their position.

"Aren't you cold?" Charlie asked.

"Of course, but it doesn't do any good to talk about it. Judy told you to pack those hand warmers."

"My hands are fine. It's my toes and legs I think I'll have to leave behind. You got any Navy Seal tricks on how to stay warm?"

"I do, but since we don't have access to steaming animal entrails, I guess we'll have to man up."

Detroit was in a deep freeze-thaw cycle. Each day, the sun melted huge piles of snow into dirty mush mounds, which at nightfall froze into depressing, otherworldly ice sculptures. The house they watched had grimy half-walls of snow on each side of a short driveway, where the subject's late-model sedan was parked behind another vehicle.

Charlie aimed warm breath at the window, then cleared a circle

1

in the condensation to peer out. "How long have we been sitting here?"

Gil tapped a gloved finger on the dashboard clock. "Fifty minutes and counting. Did you get enough pictures of the house?"

"Yep, and I got a few shots of her getting out of the car and going into the house."

"By the way, there's a lady in the house behind me who's peeking at us through her drapes," Gil announced.

Charlie turned to look. "I don't see her."

"She's looked out at least three times that I've noticed."

"We should probably move the car soon. We don't want her to call the police."

"Given the city's budget, I doubt they'll bother with a loitering call."

Charlene Mack Private Investigations had been hired to keep an eye on a runaway daughter who had taken up with an older man. It was a small case, not the kind the agency liked to handle, but the client was paying the going rate, with a deposit up front, and the end of the year was always their least busy time.

Seventeen-year-old Jennifer Cashin suddenly appeared on the porch, followed by a man wearing a blue hoodie and a bulky, black jacket. He supported Jennifer's elbow as she made her way down the steps.

"That must be our guy," Gil said, sitting upright.

Charlie pulled out the camera and snapped three quick pictures. "Damn, these are no good; the windshield has a glaze of ice."

Gil hit the down button on the passenger window, and Charlie quickly stuck her head out the vehicle, lifting the camera in time to catch the pair in a long embrace. Jennifer started the car and began backing out of the driveway.

"Should we stay with her?" Gil asked.

"Yeah, we better. We're on the clock for two more hours."

The man looked their way, shouted something to the girl, and pointed at their car.

"Uh oh. We've been spotted," Charlie said. "Let's get over there."

Charlie and Gil jumped from the car together, but Jennifer was already moving and her face was a pale blur as she sped past them. The guy took off running in the opposite direction.

"I'll stay with him," Charlie shouted. "You follow her."

"You sure?"

"Yes. Go. If she gets to the freeway, we may lose her."

"Be careful," Gil hollered over his shoulder.

Charlie ran in the middle of the street to the corner where she leaped atop a snow mound, and caught a glimpse of the man she was chasing. She darted back into the street holding up her hand in apology to a driver who pumped his horn. The sidewalks and streets were dry, ashy gray from heavy salting, but the layers of clothing slowed her down. She was grateful she'd worn her sneakers instead of boots, and thankful for her daily mornings at the gym.

Ahead, the man was beginning to lose steam. Most people could do a quick dash, but when it came to a distance run, stamina was key. He'd begun to look over his shoulder which was a time waster, and then he turned into an alley. Charlie followed, slowing her pace a few steps in. Then stopping to gauge her next move.

The alley was narrow, a dead end, and the high-rises on either side blocked most of the light. A truck idled on the left, and halfway into the alley on the right, melting snow and natural light poured from a space between the buildings. The runner was nowhere in sight. Charlie didn't usually carry her gun, and today was no exception. She pulled her ID from her back pocket, zipped her jacket to the neck, and hugged the wall of the alley as she inched forward. She reached the truck, but no one was visible in the cab, so she crept to the rear where a worker was stacking boxes of lettuce onto the tailgate. She displayed her PI credentials, but without even glancing at them, he pointed in the direction of the alcove.

Charlie had no authority to detain, or apprehend this man she was chasing, but she did need to speak with him. She stopped and scanned the surroundings. It was a small loading area—

empty except for the piles of snow around its perimeter. Iron steps on the left and a concrete ramp on the right led to a dock and the freight elevator. The young man huddled under the steps in a vain attempt to hide.

"You're not in trouble," Charlie said loudly. "I just want to talk to you."

"Are you the police?" he asked.

Charlie knew her answer would take the conversation to a different level. "No, Sal, I'm a private investigator."

The boyfriend peeked his head out from his crouching space. He sized up Charlie who held out her ID with her left hand, and kept her right hand at her waist so he'd think she had a weapon. After fifteen seconds, he stood erect, his hands by his side. He was about six-foot-one. She knew he was a runner, but maybe he was also a fighter.

"You know my name? Did Mr. Cashin send you?"

"He's my client. He wants to meet with you and Jennifer."

"Where's the guy that was with you?"

Charlie pondered the motive of the question, and stashed her ID. "Guarding the entrance to the alley."

"Hmm. I don't think that's true," Sal said taking a few steps toward Charlie. "I think maybe he went after Jenny."

Charlie assessed the boy. He was lanky, handsome, with curly, brown hair. He was trying to look menacing, but couldn't pull it off.

"Salvatore, let me tell you something. I'm not going to chase you anymore, and I don't want to hurt you."

The boy chuckled at the suggestion, and took another step closer. Charlie put her hands on her hips, and the posture stopped him in his tracks. Charlie watched the boy weigh his chances to overpower her.

"You have nothing to lose by coming with me and having a conversation with Jenny's dad. I can see you're not a bad kid, but Jenny is only seventeen, and her father has a right to bring his daughter home."

"We tried talking to him," the boy said. "He hates me."

"How old are you?" Charlie asked.

"I just turned twenty-one." His eyes pleaded for understanding. "I know Jenny is young, but we love each other. We want to get married."

"I don't doubt that, Sal."

"Do you know, he threatened to have me arrested?" The boy's hands began to shake, so he shoved them into the pockets of his jeans. "For rape."

"I think Mr. Cashin regrets saying that," Charlie said. "Now he just wants his daughter home."

"How do I know you're telling the truth?"

The Dodge minivan pulled to the curb, and Charlie hopped into the passenger seat.

"Where's the guy? Did he get away?" Gil asked.

"He's gone."

"Gone where?"

"I'm not sure."

Charlie and Gil shared a look. They had been recruited together to Immigration and Naturalization services from their law school and, later, had resigned together from Homeland Security, troubled by the agency's profiling tactics. Gil merged into traffic and made an illegal U-turn that pointed the minivan in the direction of their downtown office.

"What did Cashin say when you dropped off Jennifer?"

"He barely spoke to her. He asked me about Sal, and about his car."

"She didn't bring back the car?"

"I forced her off the road and made her get into the van. The girl is terrified by the whole situation, I feel kinda sorry for her."

"Yeah. I know what you mean." Charlie stared out the window.

"What?" Gil's tone revealed he already knew the answer.

"Hmm?"

"You let Sal go, didn't you?"

"He's just a kid. A student. They're in love."

"Right. And you let the guy go."

When they arrived at their three-room office suite, Judy was packing up for the day. She had a commute to Livonia where she lived with her husband of thirty years, and three of her five children.

"You were right about the hand warmers," Gil said, passing Judy's desk in the reception area.

"Nobody ever listens to me," Judy said, feigning hurt feelings.

"I listen to you, Novak," Don hollered from the inner office.

"You least of all, Rutkowski," Judy hollered in return. She stopped Charlie for a question.

"So did you guys find the girl?"

"We found her," Charlie said.

"What about the older man?"

"He wasn't that old."

"So you caught them both. We can bill for another eight hours, right?"

"Uh huh. Maybe. It's a bit complicated. I hate these stalking assignments," Charlie announced.

"Yeah, well at least on this case, you're doing the stalking, and not the other way around."

Judy's point was well made. Only a few months ago, while investigating a missing person case in Alabama, Charlie had been followed by a murderer who cold-cocked her and left her for dead in an empty lot. It was only luck, and Judy's knack with phone ringtones, that had saved Charlie.

"Oh, and we got a call today from someone at the auto dealers association. Don took the call. He says we may have a new case."

"I hope it doesn't involve following anyone's wife, mistress, or boyfriend."

"How *was* the surveillance?" Don asked, his feet propped on his desk.

"Cold."

"Didn't you take the hand warmers, Mack?"

"The next person to mention those damned hand warmers is fired."

The four-person agency bore Charlie's name because she was the principal investor. But things were actually much more egalitarian. Now, into the second year of their business, they had a reputation for hard work and good results. Like Gil, Charlie had met Don at DHS where he was a trainer. Judy had been inherited from the previous occupants of their office, and had made herself invaluable by managing their administrative work with the ferocity of a mother cougar. The agency's success was built on their diverse experience, networks and mutual respect for each other.

"What did the auto dealers want?" Charlie asked.

"DADA called us?" Gil looked up from his desk with interest.

Gil's uncle was a respected member of the Detroit Auto Dealers Association, and owned three car dealerships in the metro area. Gil had been a top salesman for his uncle on and off for a dozen years, and still benefited from the relationship by driving the latest model car every year.

"Their executive board wants to see us. They have a problem of a sensitive nature and want a private meeting," Don reported.

"What do they mean by private?" Gil asked.

"They don't want us to reveal that we're meeting with them."

"And what's their problem?" Charlie asked.

"There was a murder last week at Cobo Hall. A Chinese national. The police say it was a robbery gone bad. DADA thinks there might be more to it."

"Why do they think so?" Gil asked.

"The dead guy was a member of the advance team for a Chinese auto exhibitor. The Chinese have a delegation at the auto show for the first time this year."

"When do they want to meet?" Charlie asked, looking at her calendar.

"Tomorrow, and they want to come here."

"Well, give them a call and tell them to come sometime after lunch," Charlie said.

"I already told them two o'clock would work," Don said, stacking the papers on his desk.

"Okay. That means we need to finish up our paperwork tonight," Charlie said to Gil. "If we get the info on the Ferndale house early enough, I'll include that in the report, then drive out to Cashin's place tomorrow morning and give him the photos and the report, and close out the case."

"Works for me. Hand me the camera. I'm going to start downloading those pictures," Gil said.

"Should I make a pot of coffee before I leave, folks?" Judy asked from the door.

"No. Go on home. Gil and I will order in dinner if we have to."

"Okay. Good luck. Call me at home if you need anything."

Ernestine had visited the art museum earlier in the day, traveling on a bus with her building's seniors club dubbed the WOLF pack, short for Wild, Old Ladies on Foot. They met weekly for a group walk and once a month for a bus outing. She looked forward to these activities because they gave her a chance to dress up, socialize, and leave her apartment. Charlie looked forward to the outings, because they gave her mother the opportunity to flex her short-term memory muscles.

"How was the museum today, Mom?"

"I already told you, the new exhibit is not my cup of tea."

"I know. But what didn't you like about it?"

Mandy was in the kitchen making tea for the three of them. She peeked around the corner to give Charlie a look of chastisement.

"I'm sorry if I'm nagging. I'm just interested in what you do with your days."

"What you mean, Charlene, is that you're concerned about my dementia."

Ernestine rarely mentioned her disease. She'd been a respected high school principal and civic activist, but the diagnosis of early-onset Alzheimer's was affecting her lifestyle and outlook.

"Do you guys want me to leave?" Mandy asked carrying out a tray.

"No. I want you to stay," Ernestine said. "I have something to say to both of you."

They gathered around Ernestine's dining-room table. It was stacked with books and newspaper articles she'd clipped to share with friends. She was still a stunning woman. Her softly curled, salt-and-pepper hair complemented high cheekbones, clear brown eyes, and a complexion that defied her sixty-three years of age. She cupped her mug of ginger-spice tea, blew at the steam, then pointed to one of the books on the table.

"That book has some of the latest research on Alzheimer's. I've been reading up on it. Checking to see what I'm in for."

"You're still managing pretty well I think." Charlies' eyebrows formed a "V."

"I know. But I've never been one not to have a plan, and a contingency."

Charlie looked over at Mandy who was dipping a sugar cookie into her tea. Then her mother picked up a cookie and dipped hers.

"I know you're worried, Charlene. You're a worrier, you always have been. Did you know that, Mandy? My daughter has been a worrier since she was a little girl."

"I'm not too surprised to hear that, Mrs. Mack."

"What do you want to talk about, Mom?"

"Charlie, I don't want you to be alone. It's not good for your mind, body, or soul. Or your heart either. I want you to know I'm glad you've found someone like Mandy. I know I've criticized you over the years for leaving Franklin, but I understand more now."

"What do you think you understand?"

"I've been doing some reading about LGBT issues. I've read about Stonewall and Barbara Gittings, and I read this book of essays by Audre Lorde. Now I'm reading that book over there."

Mandy lifted the hefty volume about activist Bayard Rustin and held it up for Charlie to see.

"The history is fascinating, and now I'm looking at the paral-

9

lels between the gay rights and the civil rights movements. You know I love that stuff."

Charlie took a deep breath, and grabbed a cookie.

"Anyway, I don't understand much about what it means to be a lesbian. But I do know you seem happier and more relaxed than you have been for years, and I think it has a lot to do with Mandy."

Mandy and Ernestine beamed at each other, and dipped their cookies again. Charlie rounded the table to sit next to her mother and put an arm around her.

"I'm not as comfortable with, uh, this lifestyle as Mandy. But I *am* happy. She's very important to me."

"I can tell."

"I was never fully myself with Franklin. That isn't the case with Mandy."

"You guys know I'm here, right?" Mandy asked.

"I appreciated the things you said about me to your mother."

"Surprised?"

"A little. She's a fine woman, Charlie. I see where you get so many of your good qualities, and also your independence."

"Uh-huh."

It was a cold night, the kind where the air chapped your lips and stung your skin. They walked quickly through the parking lot to Charlie's Corvette, and as they settled into the warming car shared a kiss.

"Your mom doesn't want to be ruled by her disease, and she doesn't want to be a burden."

"I know. It was her decision to try an assisted-living facility."

Mandy slipped her hand through Charlie's heavily layered arm. "Your instinct is to be protective of your mother, but you have to let her be in charge of her life for as long as she can."

"I know."

Charlie navigated West Grand Boulevard, passing the iconic Fisher Building and the St. Regis Hotel, and turning south on Cass Avenue. This was familiar territory. She'd received her undergrad degree from Wayne State University, and she silently noted the buildings she'd roamed as a student. Despite the cold, there were plenty of pedestrians on the sidewalks. People coming or going into the area bars, students leaving evening classes, people waiting on buses, and New Center residents making their way home.

"Are we going back to your place?" Mandy asked.

"I thought maybe you would spend the night, and I'll take you home tomorrow."

"Didn't you say you had an early appointment?"

"Shit, I forgot."

"It's not like you to forget appointments."

"It's because I hate this case we're on."

"And because you're worried about your mom."

"True."

"Okay, so drive me home. Come in for a little while, and I'll make you a hot toddy."

"You *are* a hot toddy."

"You're such a flatterer, Ms. Mack."

Chapter 2

Charlie saw the four men in business suits around the conference room table when she entered the Mack offices, one of whom she recognized as Oscar Acosta, Gil's uncle. She had purchased her Corvette from Mr. Acosta last spring.

"What's up? Did they come early?" She asked Judy.

"They arrived ten minutes ago, looking nervous. I made them coffee and Gil is doing his best to keep the small talk going, but I think you should go right in," Judy said. "Are we done with the Cashin case?"

"Not quite yet. I'll explain later," Charlie said, dropping her purse on Judy's desk. "I'm going to the ladies' room to freshen up. I'll only be five minutes."

"Okay, I'll let the others know."

Charlie stared into the mirror. The sunlight from the windows mixed with the fluorescents, and her skin was radiant. *Not bad for thirty-four.* She brushed her fingertips through her short hair and freshened her neutral-colored lipstick. Her blue tweed suit and cream blouse contrasted nicely. She washed her hands, checked her nails, and put on a dab of lotion. "Dressed for success," she said aloud.

The men in the conference room rose when she entered the

room. All except Don, whose scowl and folded arms announced he was already upset about something.

"This is our partner, Charlene Mack." Gil made the introductions. "You remember my uncle, Señor Acosta."

"I do. *Que bueno verte, señor*." Charlie practiced her Spanish.

"It's also good to see you again, Ms. Mack. I hope you're still enjoying your convertible," Oscar Acosta said.

"Charlie, this is Irwin Cross, Scott Hartwell, and Tommy Kozol," Gil said, pointing to each.

"Glad to meet you all. Please, let's sit," Charlie said. "Do we need more coffee?"

"We've had enough coffee," Don said curtly.

"Uh, Ms. Mack? I'm afraid we've gotten off to a bad start with your partner," Irwin Cross said. "We have a very, uh, sticky problem, and we wanted to wait until you arrived to discuss it. We've come to you because of your reputation in Detroit's business community. Your agency is also highly recommended by Mr. Acosta, who has been a member of the DADA board for many years."

Cross was a youthful fiftyish, handsome, fit, well-dressed, with salon-styled, salt-and-pepper hair. Don was irrationally annoyed by men he labeled dandies, since his own style leaned toward corduroy and short-sleeved shirts. Cross sent a blue-eyed glance toward his companions, which was met with silent authorization to proceed with presenting their case.

"We have a very troubling situation that requires imagination, fearlessness, and good instincts," Cross said.

"And utmost secrecy," Hartwell added.

"Yes. That's crucial," Cross agreed.

"Please explain, Mr. Cross. When you called yesterday, you mentioned someone had been murdered?" Gil asked.

"That's right."

Cross nodded at Kozol, who produced three manila folders from his briefcase and slid them across the table to the Mack partners. The folders were stamped "confidential" in red stencil.

Inside were three photographs: one of a body lying on its side, a close-up of the victim's face with a bullet wound at the forehead, and the last, an enlarged photo of a passport. The man's name was Yu Chenglei, a resident of Beijing.

"This man was a member of the delegation from Guí Motors. It's the first year the Chinese have exhibited with us, and their team arrived five weeks ago to meet with their U.S. counterparts. Mr. Chenglei is credentialed as a design engineer. The police report—you'll find it in the folder—says he was murdered in an attempted robbery four nights ago," Cross said.

"It says here, witnesses saw this Chenglei being chased by a man wearing a mask who cornered him in an alley, and a few minutes later shot him at close range," Don noted. "Seems like a robbery to me, maybe gang-related. You think something different from the police?"

"Yes, Mr. Rutkowski, we do. We've been told by Homeland Security that Mr. Chenglei was in their database as a person of interest."

"Did they say they were investigating him?" Don asked.

"No. And we've had no follow-up with Homeland Security. They said the notification to us was just a courtesy."

"What do you suspect?" Charlie asked.

"We have reason to believe Mr. Chenglei was planning, um, a disruption during the auto show, and we believe he was not working alone."

"Do you have evidence to confirm your suspicions?" Charlie asked.

"One of our longtime vendors reported an Asian man offered him $100,000 for his exhibition permit. When the vendor refused, the man paid him $10,000 for a copy of the exhibitor planning guide, which includes maps, security information, and the names and numbers of key Cobo Hall personnel."

"You haven't shared this information with the police?" Don was still irritated. In addition to a stint in the Marines, he'd been a Detroit police officer for nine years, and he still had lots of friends on the force.

14

"No."

There was an uncomfortable pause in the conversation. Gil exchanged a nervous glance with his uncle. Scott Hartwell was sweating. He was a slight man, younger than Cross, and he reminded Charlie of a nervous cat. His head turned with every movement in the room. When the coffeemaker gave a final, exhausted gasp of steam, he almost sprang from his chair. Kozol, on the other hand, was a cool customer, fastidious in his dress and grooming. He wore a half smile throughout the meeting, and his elbow rested casually on the chrome suitcase in the chair next to him.

"Ms. Mack, we want to hire you and your partners to discover whatever Mr. Chenglei and his cohorts were plotting. The Auto Show opens in nine days, so time is of the essence, and we're prepared to pay you handsomely for the work."

"Well, I don't know, Mr. Cross. There's not much to go on. It's really just speculation that there even *is* a threat." Charlie looked at her partners for their concurrence. "That means we have to talk to a lot of people, in a short amount of time. We're a small firm, and this sounds like a big job."

"If we had more time for planning, we could do it," Gil said.

"Or, if we could rely on help from the police or the FBI," Don added.

"People carrying badges and wearing uniforms would just upset people. We're downplaying this incident because we don't want negative publicity for the show. We like it that you're a small firm. We prefer a low-profile investigation," Cross said.

"Really? For a potential terrorist attack?" Don asked incredulously.

"We haven't used the word terrorism," Cross said.

Don looked disgusted, and pushed his chair back from the table loudly. He refolded his arms across his ample stomach.

"You must understand how important this event is to Detroit's economy and its reputation, Mr. Rutkowski. This is a very big year for us."

Don wasn't impressed.

"It's the Super Bowl," Gil said matter-of-factly.

"What?" Charlie asked.

"You're worried about the Super Bowl, right?" Gil asked, looking at his uncle, and then scanning the faces of the other men.

Cross went silent. So did the others. Kozol lifted the chrome suitcase into his lap. Gil's question hung in the room.

"A lot is at stake. The success of the auto show is critically important to us, but if we somehow jeopardize next month's Super Bowl, Detroit won't host another important cultural, political, or sporting event for decades," Scott Hartwell responded.

Charlie began reading the brochure in her folder. "The auto show brings in three-quarters of a million people? That's amazing."

"That's more visitors than we expect for the Super Bowl," Cross said. "This year, the show is fifteen days. We'll introduce sixty new cars and host journalists, auto manufacturers, suppliers, dignitaries, and car lovers from all over the world. The media preview begins next week."

"What do you expect we can do in such a short time without the assistance of federal or local law enforcement?" Don pushed the point.

Sr. Acosta spoke up. "We hope you can find the source of our threat, neutralize it, and do it all . . . discreetly."

Charlie and Don shared a glance. Gil stared at his uncle, and the three other DADA members kept their eyes locked on the table.

"Tio?" Gil asked.

"*Es muy grave y peligroso, sobrino*," the elder Acosta said, then switched to English. "There's been no major terrorist attack in this country since New York City on 9/11. Detroit doesn't want the distinction of being the next location."

So there was the word. *Terrorism*. Kozol lifted the heavy briefcase onto the table, opened the lid and turned it toward the Mack partners. The case was filled with neatly stacked packets of twenty-dollar bills.

"There's twenty-five thousand dollars here. We prefer to pay you in cash. It's for your expenses and the like. Just a down payment, but it will get you started," Kozol said.

The partners gathered around Judy's desk to discuss their options. This was the most unusual case they'd been offered. It would require them to bypass their usual sources of information, and tax all the firm's energy and resources.

"I don't like it. We can't consult with the police," Don said. "It makes no sense. If this really is a terrorist cell, everyone should be involved."

"If Homeland Security knows about the dead man, you can bet they've already done some investigation of their own," Gil said.

"That's right. So we'll just make it clear to the suits in there, that working on this case is contingent upon our cooperating with DHS," Don said. "Otherwise, they can find other investigators."

"Agreed," Charlie said. "But I'm not convinced we should even be involved. Suitcases filled with money don't sit well with me."

"Suitcases of money?" Judy's face lit up.

"They brought twenty-five thousand in cash for our startup expenses," Charlie said.

It was now open-and-shut for Judy. Among her office manager duties, she was the firm's conscientious bookkeeper, helping Charlie keep an eye on expenses and pay the bills. She'd been warning Charlie for weeks that their cash reserves were under duress.

"We only have the Cashin job to close out," Judy said. "The rest of our cases involve legal hearings and such, and they're on hold for a couple of weeks. Right, Gil?"

"That's right, but this DADA case is going to be grueling work for all of us. We'll likely need to hire a dozen or so subcontractors. We gotta have more feet on the ground."

"We'll probably need to use Judy in the field, too," Charlie said.

"I don't think it's a good idea to use Novak in the field," Don said. "What would she do?"

Judy was creative, and could charm the rubber from a Goodyear tire. It was, however, one of Judy's less obvious skills that had won her a place in Charlie's heart. Like Charlie herself, Judy was a champion liar, a skill that often could make or break a private investigation.

"People open up to Judy. Besides, we'll need her fibbing talents."

"*I* can tell a whopper when it's needed, and so can Acosta," Don argued.

"Yes. But Judy can weave three fabrications in the time it takes you to come up with one," Charlie said admiringly.

Judy smiled at the compliment, and sang: "*Anything you can do I can do better, I can do anything better than you.*"

"You and your blasted musicals," Don said with agitation. "Look, are we ready to go back in there and take this job, or what?"

"Wait a minute," Gil said shaking his head. "Are we *absolutely* sure?"

"What's on your mind, Gil?" Charlie asked.

"My uncle. He doesn't worry easily."

"What did he say in there? I couldn't make it out."

"He called it a grave situation and said it was very dangerous."

Judy's smile faded.

The Mack team returned to the conference room and listed their conditions for accepting the case. Kozol took notes. First, something in writing that would serve to explain their arrangement with the auto dealers. It would be token protection, but at least a line of defense if laws were broken in the course of the investigation. The fee would be one hundred thousand dollars, plus expenses. The number didn't seem to faze the four business owners. There was only one sticking point, and after initially refusing, the men reluctantly agreed to allow the Mack partners to brief Homeland Security.

"It's a deal-breaker," Don stated, with Charlie and Gil nodding their assent.

"I guess we'll just have to trust your judgment, and discretion, in how you handle your former colleagues at Homeland Security," Cross finally acquiesced.

Kozol left the conference room with Gil to draft a letter of agreement. With Judy, they also established a process for billing and receiving payments. Charlie and Don brainstormed with Cross and the other DADA execs about the best cover for the partners as they began their investigation.

"Perhaps the easiest thing to do would be to give you Cobo security credentials. Earlier this year, we hired a private security firm for the show. You could use their offices, and you'd have access to the entire building."

"That's a possibility," Charlie said. "Can we also use their manpower?"

"Uh, that probably won't work," Cross said, his brows tightening into a furrow. "The new security chief is a man by the name of Geoff Heinrich. We haven't told him about hiring you, but obviously he would have to be in the loop on this."

"You haven't even confided in your own security guy?" Don asked.

"Mr. Heinrich tends to be a bit heavy-handed. He stepped on a lot of toes, including one of the mayor's security team, when the police investigated Chenglei's death."

Charlie was aware of the chasm in the relationship between the city's business community and the second-term mayor. Kilpatrick's flamboyant confidence and political pedigree had at first won over voters, especially the city's disenfranchised black working class, but reports of cronyism, abuse of power, and questionable use of public funds had gotten the attention of the FBI. DADA had been very vocal in their assessment that the mayor's negative publicity was bad for the city's economy.

"We're pretty good at balancing the power dynamics," Charlie said.

"So we've heard, Ms. Mack. We're relying on that, and your agency's networks, to provide us a positive resolution," Cross said.

Gil, Kozol, and Judy returned with the letter of agreement,

which everyone tweaked until they had an acceptable version. Judy produced two originals, which were signed by all parties.

"We'll need a point of contact. Someone we can call day or night if we need something, or run into trouble," Don said.

"That'll be me," Scott Hartwell said.

Charlie's eyes narrowed. Hartwell seemed the least likely to be helpful under pressure. Cross read the body language and offered a defense of his colleague.

"Mr. Hartwell is a third-generation auto dealer. He knows the business in and out, and has been the president of DADA for seven years. He has the full cooperation of DADA's executive committee, and we'll stand by any decision he makes."

"On *this* matter, we'll have to trust *your* judgment, Mr. Cross," Charlie said.

It was three o'clock. The Mack team was in full throttle in the office bullpen. Judy had ordered in corned beef sandwiches, and the room smelled of meat and pickle brine.

"What time is tomorrow's appointment with DHS, Don?" Charlie asked, taking a large bite of dill pickle.

"They just confirmed for 5 p.m."

"They don't care that it's New Year's Eve?" Judy asked.

"To Homeland Security, it's just another day," Don said.

"Okay. I'll email Hartwell and tell him we want to meet with the Cobo security guy first thing in the morning," Charlie said. "Judy, add Josh Simms to our list of subcontractors. How many does that make?"

"Eleven. We just need one more. What about Mandy Porter?"

"Let me think about that. I'll let you know tomorrow morning."

"Do we know anybody who speaks Chinese?" Don asked. "Might come in handy."

"Remember that geeky kid from the community center, Charlie?" Gil asked. "His mother enrolled him in your martial arts class because he was being bullied in school."

"Oh, right. Lin Fong. He spoke Mandarin. But I haven't seen him in four years. He might not even be in the area."

"Would his mother remember you?" Judy asked.

"I'm sure she would. I worked with Lin one-on-one several times. She came around to thank me after he finally got the better of one of his bullies. I think she said he'd been accepted to U of M, so he *may* be in the area."

"Give me a couple of days and I'll find him," Judy said.

"We don't have a couple of days," Charlie said, swallowing the last chunk of thick homemade bread smeared with mustard and meat juice. "I'll call his mother."

"I'm going to start contacting the subs," Gil said. "We'll need them to start no later than Sunday. Judy, will you copy that list for me?"

"Sure. I'll also draw up a freelancer's contract you can use."

"While we're talking about calls: Everybody should call their mothers, wives, husbands and significant others," Charlie said. "Because this year we won't be counting down the clock on New Year's Eve; we'll be *on* the clock."

"Charlie, didn't you say you had some follow-up with Mr. Cashin?" Judy reminded.

"Damn, that's right. He wants us to do a background check on the boy. Judy, send him a final invoice. I'll tell him to find someone else to harass his daughter."

"And somebody has to take that cash to the bank before it closes." Judy continued the reminders.

"I'll take care of that," Don said, taking his gun from the desk. He adjusted his shoulder holster, put on his tweed jacket to cover his firepower, and buttoned his fifteen-year-old raincoat. He picked up the chrome suitcase and the bank deposit slip Judy had prepared, and headed to the door. "I'm a man with a gun, a car, and twenty-five thousand dollars in cash. Maybe you'll see me in the morning, and maybe you won't."

Skinny snow chips, too cold to hold together as flakes, fell and then bounced around with the wind. A sweep of stars glinted to be admired, but those walking in Greektown held their heads down and leaned into the bracing gusts. Charlie and Mandy walked arm-in-arm to the parking garage, and Charlie stiffened each time they passed someone.

"No one's looking at us," Mandy said, reading Charlie's body.

"I didn't say anything."

"You didn't have to. You tensed up as soon as I grabbed your arm."

"It's cold, that's all."

"Uh-huh, frigid."

Their cars were parked side by side, and Charlie pulled Mandy as close to her as their padded parkas would allow. They kissed a long time.

"Did that feel frigid?"

"No. I can't say that it did." Mandy smiled, and played with the zipper of Charlie's coat. "But you wouldn't do that if anyone were around."

Charlie began to protest, but Mandy stopped her with another kiss. When they released each other, Mandy pointed in the direction of the elevator. "Smile."

Charlie turned to see the oversized surveillance camera mounted above the elevator doors. It blinked.

"Why didn't you tell me? Get in," Charlie said ducking into the car.

"You've got to get over this. It's irrational fear. Nobody cares that we're lesbians; they really don't." Mandy's voice revealed frustration.

Charlie was five years older than Mandy. That gap, along with her upbringing, accounted for the discomfort she had with being labeled a lesbian. Mandy had been out to her family and friends since high school, but Charlie was still closeted, and it had caused many awkward moments in their six-month relationship.

"It's easier for you, Mandy. Black folks have a harder time accepting gay people. It's the church thing and . . ."

"I know. You've told me that before. And some people have a problem with an interracial couple, but you knew all that when you said you wanted to be with me."

"I *do*. I introduced you to my mother, didn't I?"

"Yes. But we're still hiding the truth from your partners."

"Judy knows. And I'm pretty sure Don knows, too."

"You know what I mean. You haven't told them we're a couple. If we're going to be working together on this case, I don't want to have to pretend we're not lovers."

Charlie shook her head. "It won't be an issue. I promise."

Mandy responded with a hurt look.

"Are you absolutely sure you want to freelance on this one? It might be dangerous."

"You're changing the subject."

"No, I'm not."

"You are."

Charlie ran a fingertip across Mandy's chin, and up to her lips. "You're beautiful," Charlie said.

"That won't get you off the hook."

"Can I come over and stay the night?"

Mandy didn't answer. She turned toward the passenger window, drawing the collar of her parka closer to her.

"I'd have to leave early tomorrow," Charlie said. "I need to go home and pack some clothes, because I'm checking into a hotel close to Cobo for the duration of this case. Tonight could be the last time we get to sleep together until this is over."

"You really believe there's a threat to the auto show?"

"I know our clients believe it, and they don't seem like alarmists. I hate an investigation like this, where you don't have any real clues to follow so all you can do is ask questions and wait for someone to show their hand."

"Terrorism is an awful burden for the modern world to bear. Even after four years, I'm angry about 9/11. I think about it almost every day," Mandy said.

"Well, that's understandable, since your brother died that day."

"It's not just that. It's how much our lives have changed and how that terrible day still makes us feel so vulnerable."

"We've had terrorism in this country since the Revolutionary War. Only the form has changed."

Mandy gave Charlie another look of exasperation.

"I'm sorry. I didn't mean to be so academic about it. C'mon, don't be mad."

Charlie leaned over and buried her face in Mandy's hair. Mandy responded by turning her lips toward Charlie's hungry mouth.

"Okay, come over. When you get to my place, let yourself in. I'm going to stop for champagne so we can celebrate New Year's early."

"Why don't I just follow you?"

Mandy smiled provocatively. "Anywhere?"

"I'm beginning to think so."

Chapter 3

Saturday, December 31, 2005
Auto Show: 8 days

At 6:30 a.m., Charlie, Don and Gil were escorted by a sleepy uniformed security guard to a stairwell that led from the Cobo lobby to a lower-level office wing. The stenciled letters on the glass double doors read "Spectrum Security Services," and above the name was the logo of a satellite dish riding on a beam of light. A red beacon flashed above the door and turned green when they were buzzed in. It was clear that Spectrum was not your grandfather's security company.

The interior continued the high-tech theme. The floor plan was open, with a maze of low cubicles and conversation pods. The subdued lighting was punctured by a splash of illumination at each work area. The massive room had a carpeted walkway on each side, and a glass and steel catwalk stretched overhead. In the middle of the cubicle configuration was an elevated glass-walled room where a row of fifty-inch video monitors hung above a streamlined counter. Charlie counted a half-dozen men and women seated at the counter observing the various views of Cobo Hall. Attached to the catwalk were two mega-screens. One displayed time zones for cities in the U.S., Europe, Africa, Asia, and South America; the other had a panoramic view of the Detroit River.

There was no receptionist, so the Mack partners moved off to the side of the double doors where an orange rug provided the perimeter of a visitors area. The space was completed with a round, white marble pedestal table and contemporary white stools. Spectrum employees wore white shirts, black ties, and green blazers. A few looked curiously at the visitors, and one or two nodded a greeting. Within a minute, a tall brunette wearing the company attire stepped out of a door along the nearest walkway and approached the group.

"Ms. Mack, Mr. Rutkowski, and Mr. Acosta? I'm Cynthia Fitzgerald, Mr. Heinrich's executive assistant. We've been expecting you. Won't you follow me?"

Cynthia had short-cropped hair and wore a black pencil skirt with three-inch black heels. Charlie noted Gil and Don's attention to her legs as she led them along the corridor, and Charlie took a good look, too.

Irwin Cross and Scott Hartwell sat in sleek, gray chairs across from Geoff Heinrich who was seated at a pretentiously large desk. Cross and Hartwell popped up when Charlie and the others entered the room, but Heinrich didn't bother lifting himself from his black leather chair. His mouth was a tight line, and his stare unnerving.

"These are the people I was telling you about, Geoff," Irwin Cross said.

Charlie moved toward Heinrich's desk to offer her handshake, but he abruptly stood and gestured toward his stainless-steel conference table. He was tall, maybe six-five, and wore a charcoal pinstriped suit with a cobalt blue silk tie. He was tanned and fit, and Charlie was sure his Italian shoes had cost no less than eight hundred dollars.

"I'm going to have some breakfast; may I offer you some?"

"Coffee would be fine for me," Charlie said.

"Same here," Gil said.

"Help yourself," Heinrich said pointing to the open pantry. "There are a variety of grains, dried fruit and nuts. There's yogurt in the refrigerator, and greens and fresh fruit for the juicer," Heinrich listed.

26

"Do you have any Danish or a muffin?" Don asked.

Heinrich looked at Don as if he were in a specimen tube. Don returned the glare. The two were sizing up each other—a rhinestone-collared tabby versus a scrappy alley cat.

"I can't offer you any pastries. We only serve whole foods in the office. We're extremely health conscious," Heinrich said, opening a sliding door to reveal an espresso machine.

"Would you like me to go to the Starbucks upstairs, Mr. Rutkowski?" Heinrich's assistant, Cynthia, asked. She was hovering, always keeping one eye on Heinrich. She carried an electronic tablet and had a phone bud in one ear. Heinrich seemed to dislike her offer of hospitality.

"That's nice of you." Don finally shifted his eyes from Heinrich. "But I'll just have a couple of pieces of fruit and some bottled water."

"Actually, we only have filtered water. I'll get you a glass," Cynthia said.

Heinrich had taken a seat at the head of the conference table with a bowl of granola and strawberries in front of him. Irwin Cross made a cup of espresso, while Hartwell watched the dynamics from his seat near the desk.

"Shall we get down to business," Hartwell said, standing. "As I told you, Geoff, I need you to provide staff credentials to Ms. Mack and her colleagues. They need to have access to every space in the building, and a complete report on security measures. They will sit in on any event-related meetings, and they need a private office space with a conference room."

"We'll also need copies of any reports you've compiled on Mr. Chenglei, as well as a list of your employees, Mr. Heinrich," Charlie said.

"Why do you need my employee list? They've all been fully vetted. Credit reports, background checks, and drug tested. The works."

"Mr. Heinrich personally hand-picked most of his staff, Ms. Mack, and I spent a good deal of time investigating Spectrum, including checking all their references," Hartwell said from across the room.

"It's just part of the protocol. It's a system of exclusion, which we've used before at Homeland Security. It's quite effective when looking for the proverbial needle in a haystack," Charlie said.

"Geoff, I want you to provide your staff records to Ms. Mack, and I want you to give her, and her colleagues, your full cooperation. If you have any concerns, bring them directly to me," Hartwell said, receiving a hard look from Heinrich.

"Can we get our credentials and office today?" Charlie asked.

"Yes," Heinrich said, pouring a green concoction from a pitcher into a large glass and returning to his desk. "Cynthia will show you to your office suite and handle your credentials. We have four levels of security clearance. You'll have level three clearances, the same as my department heads."

"Who has the top clearance?" Charlie asked.

"Only me," Heinrich said, staring adamantly.

Charlie smiled and turned slightly toward Don and Gil to discourage any pushback they were about to offer. "Well, we better get to work. Thank you for your cooperation." Charlie's words dripped with sarcasm.

There were no goodbyes from Heinrich for the Mack Partners. Hartwell shook hands with the trio and stayed behind, while Cynthia and Irwin Cross escorted them to a large two-room corner office nearest the main entrance.

"I think you'll have everything you need here—copiers, fax machines, desktop computers. I've made extra keys for the Spectrum doors and your office suite; and the door to your conference room has a separate lock. They're in the envelope on the table. There is a phone card at each desk with Mr. Heinrich's office number and cell phone. My private number is also on that card. You can reach me there day and night." Cynthia's last statement seemed to be directed at Gil. He responded with a smile.

"Ms. Fitzgerald, we'll need access to your email server and databases, and the names and contact information for the companies and people handling the auto show, like registration, vendor licensing, and the technical setup for the show," Charlie said.

"And blueprints of the building," Don added.

Cynthia punched notes into her tablet, keeping pace with the requests.

"We also need the contact information for all the unions working the show. I bet there must be a half-dozen," Gil said.

"That's about right," Cynthia said, punching in more notes. "Anything else for now? Will you need an administrative assistant?"

"No. Actually, our office manager will be here soon, and you'll be seeing a lot of her," Charlie said.

"Okay, we'll also get credentials for her, and I'll get her a set of keys. Will you have other associates using the office?" Cynthia asked.

"We're hiring contractors. They'll all need credentials. We hope that won't be a problem," Gil said.

"No. We'll just need to discuss their clearance levels with Mr. Heinrich. If you come with me, I can get your ID cards made now," Cynthia said.

"If you don't mind I'll wait here, Ms. Mack," Cross said. "Scott and I would like to speak with you and your team before we leave."

Spectrum had a full-service photo and biometrics lab. The staffer who took their pictures and made their chip-based security badges was cheerful and efficient. An optical technician, wearing a lab coat, used a piece of equipment with a long, black tentacle to scan their retinas. He had a more reserved personality, but was very professional. Cynthia chatted amiably with Charlie, Don, and Gil about the capability of the lab as she waited with them to receive their credentials. Within fifteen minutes, the Mack Partners had level-three security status, and Cynthia guided them back to their temporary office space. Cross and Hartwell were having a heated argument in the conference room when they arrived.

"I'm not interested in his pride, Irwin. He works for us, and if he doesn't like it, I'll fire his ass," Scott Hartwell yelled.

"Well, I'll leave you to your work," Cynthia said pausing just inside the outer door.

The shouting in the conference room stopped. Cross appeared at the door with a flushed face, just as Cynthia turned to go.

"If you need anything, please don't hesitate to call," she said over her shoulder.

The tension in the conference room was noticeable as Charlie, Gil, and Don took their places around the conference table. Hartwell was fidgeting with his shirt cuffs, and Cross opened and downed a small bottled water. Don, who had been unusually quiet during the credentialing process, was ready to speak his mind.

"Your security chief is a Nazi," he announced to Cross and Hartwell.

"Don, please," Charlie said. "Forgive my partner. He can be very blunt. What he means is . . ."

"What I mean is, the guy's a prick. He's obviously pissed off that we've been brought in over his head, and despite your pleas, he's not going to cooperate with us."

"Heinrich *will* be cooperative, Mr. Rutkowski," Hartwell said emphatically.

"I'm telling you now, the guy will be trouble, and the moment his interference jeopardizes our ability to work this case, you're getting a call from me," Don shouted.

"That's fair enough," Hartwell said looking sideways at Irwin Cross.

"His assistant, Cynthia, seems nice enough. She's been very accommodating," Gil said to bring the energy level down.

"Yes. But don't be fooled. Her full loyalties are with Heinrich," Hartwell said.

"How did Spectrum come to work for DADA? Did you put out bids for the security work?" Charlie asked.

"That's right," Cross replied. "Last year, we realized we should have a full-time security agency. The auto show requires a twelve-month planning cycle, and we have security needs all year long. We did a request-for-bids process, and Spectrum was one of twenty firms to respond."

"The company had contracts with the federal government and a dozen multinationals, and their references were impeccable," Hartwell continued. "Everyone I spoke to mentioned Heinrich's healthy ego and militaristic management style, but they also had high praise for his use of technology and his results."

Don was unimpressed. He folded his beefy arms on the table. Charlie leaned forward to parrot Don's gesture.

"The way I see it," Charlie said to Hartwell, "Heinrich isn't our problem, he's yours. We have enough constraints to overcome. If he gets in the way, we won't be successful."

"We won't let him get in the way," Hartwell promised.

By 10 a.m., Judy had set up her desk in the office suite and was coordinating the Mack team's needs. Gil might already have the attention of Cynthia Fitzgerald, but Judy would get to know the other support staff at Spectrum and in the Cobo administration offices. Her internal relationships would make their work easier. She had already procured a larger conference room for a meeting with the freelancers who would help on this assignment; they'd arrive at Cobo Center in two hours ready to work. Meanwhile, Gil had called Cynthia with a request for a person who could give them a tour of the Cobo complex. In less than a half hour a junior staffer from Cobo's General Manager's office stepped into the office.

"Hi. I'm Tyson Pressley," the young man said. "I'm going to give you the twenty-dollar tour."

"I thought someone from Spectrum would show us around," Gil said.

"All I know is my boss said we had VIPs who needed a tour, and I would find you here," Tyson said.

Charlie, Don, and Gil exchanged looks. Heinrich's obfuscation was already beginning.

"Is there a problem?" Tyson asked.

"Not with you," Charlie said. "We're not VIPs. We're, technically, Spectrum staff, but we have a special assignment. You'll be seeing a lot of us in the next few days, and we need to familiarize ourselves with everything real fast."

Tyson made quick work of measuring the situation. He was tall and skinny with a shaved head and a neatly trimmed beard. He looked to be in his mid-twenties, but without the beard he could pass for a teenager. He wore a red polo shirt, dress khakis, and a blue blazer. He exuded a sureness that was just short of arrogance.

"Let me guess? You got the Heinrich maneuver."

"What?" Don said.

"Geoff Heinrich. He's an ass," Tyson said without flinching.

Charlie scowled. Gil rested his forehead on his fingers, and Don allowed the "I told you so" look to take over his entire face.

Charlie chided Tyson. "It's totally unprofessional to speak of a colleague that way in front of strangers. We're Spectrum staff."

"No, you're not. You're private investigators working for Mr. Hartwell. He told me all about you. I'm to be your inside man."

"*You're* our inside man?" Gil asked.

"Don't be fooled by my good looks and youth. I practically grew up in Cobo Hall. My grandfather was part of the original crew that built this place, and my father is the president of the local electrical workers' union. Hartwell said you would need to be familiar with the infrastructure, and he thought I could be helpful because of my background, and because I have a degree in mechanical engineering."

"Where from? MIT?" Gil guessed.

"No. That place is for geeks. Do I look like a geek? I got my degree right here at Wayne State," Tyson said with pride. "But my MBA is from Wharton."

"See," Don said to Charlie. "He should know an ass when he sees one."

"I apologize, if what I said offended you," Tyson said to Charlie. "But nobody here likes Heinrich. He thinks he's some kind of genius or something, and better than anyone else in the building."

"Okay, you're our inside guy, so why don't you show us around?" Don said, putting his arm around the young man and leading him out of the office followed by a skeptical Gil and Charlie.

Tyson pointed to a four-seater golf cart outside the Spectrum glass doors. "That's our transportation. It's a big place and you're going to need one of these. Should I requisition one for you?"

"You can do that?" Don asked.

"Sure. I should have one for your use by tomorrow. Maybe I should get you two."

Don grinned his affirmation. A walkie-talkie squawked, and Tyson opened his blazer to lift the unit from his belt. He motioned for the Mack partners to take a seat in the cart, and stepped down the hall outside of earshot. Don sat behind the wheel. As usual, Gil and Charlie were to be passengers. Tyson motioned for Don to bring the cart up.

"I see you like to drive."

"Better you should know that about him now," Charlie admitted. Don had a penchant for anything with wheels and was an expert driver. Charlie had seen his skills firsthand in a high-speed car chase or two, but it drove her crazy that he insisted on driving whenever they were in the field.

"Wait 'til you see some of this year's concept cars. A few of them are already here, and they are sweet," Tyson said with feeling.

"Where are they?" Don said excitedly.

"On level two. But first I want to show you the rest of the ground floor."

The use of a golf cart was the only practical way to tour Cobo in a few hours, and it didn't hurt having the expertise of a guide like Tyson in the front passenger seat. He had an immense knowledge of the complex, and was on a first-name basis with everyone they passed in the halls. There was no door that was inaccessible to him including the lower-level areas for the water supply, electric and HVAC, all of which required key access.

"Mr. Hartwell didn't tell me the exact nature of your assignment, but I assume he has some concern about the show. So you'll probably want to examine these areas in more detail," Tyson said.

"Where's the retina-scanning access used?" Gil asked.

"So far, Heinrich has it installed in the IT server room, and in some of Spectrum's offices."

"Do you have access to those spaces?" Charlie asked.

"No."

"What's *your* opinion of Cobo's security, Pressley?" Don asked.

"Oh, you can just call me Ty; everybody does."

"Don only uses last names. If he doesn't like you, he won't talk to you at all," Charlie said.

"Got it," Ty said, glancing at Don. "We have relatively good security, but this is a 9/11 world now, so we needed to ratchet up our game. Heinrich's people seem capable, but they spend too much time looking at monitors instead of moving around the place. The auto show isn't the only thing we do at Cobo, and on any given day there are probably three thousand people coming and going. Some are attending meetings, having lunch, parking in our garage, doing maintenance and construction. Or they could be employees working in our administrative departments on sales, accounting, and hospitality."

Cobo Hall had four public levels. The ground level had exhibit and meeting space, access to the Cobo Arena, and a food court. The remainder of the ground floor was taken up by parking garages and loading docks. The second level was dominated by the exhibitor showroom and meeting space, and the huge Joe Louis statue was a permanent fixture in the concourse. Level three had more meeting space plus administrative offices. The fourth level had the entrance to the People Mover, downtown Detroit's above-ground rail system, and executive meeting areas with amazing views of the city.

Charlie had spent a lot of time in Cobo Convention Center during her stint as a public relations executive. She'd been either an exhibitor or attendee at many events in the facility. But that had been two careers ago, and today she paid attention to things she wouldn't have cared about then, like closed doors, security cameras, and utility access panels. On a 300-foot expanse of wall in the service area of the ground floor, Charlie counted seven windowless metal doors with plain silver doorknobs.

"What's behind those doors?" Charlie pointed.

"Maintenance offices, HVAC systems, electric and cable wiring, water and sewer pipes, equipment storage, internal stairwells, venting that traverses all four levels of the building, access panels for the escalators and elevators, you name it," Ty said.

"You thinking what I'm thinking?" Charlie asked Gil.

"Probably. Were you thinking we're screwed?"

"Yeah. Something very close to that. There are too many nooks and crannies. Places where someone up to no good can hide themselves, contraband, or worse."

There were many options for lunch at Cobo and in Detroit's downtown, but Charlie's suggestion of White Castle burgers received quick agreement from her partners. Gil swept a finger through his wallet. "Okay, I'm good to go."

"You buying, Acosta?" Don asked.

"Uh. No. Just wanted to make sure I had Tums," Gil said. "I love those little square beauties, but within an hour of eating them, I'll have either gas or indigestion."

Don leaned into the speaker at the drive-through window. Fourteen dollars later they had two bags of burgers, fries, and three cokes. He pulled his five-month-old Buick to the curb near one of the parkscapes along Michigan Avenue and left the car running. It was raining lightly, and temperatures were in the mid-thirties, a heat wave for December. The warmer temperatures brought out all strata of humanity and wildlife, and the trio ate in the car observing the daytime drama of the homeless and the hapless. A squirrel and a couple of pigeons inched toward the car, as did a boy under sixteen who was probably selling drugs. The rodent, birds, and boy lined up at what must have been an agreed-upon boundary, eyeing the occupants of the idling car. Within thirty seconds they each went their own way, determining they would not be rewarded with a transaction.

"I don't know if we have enough guys for this job, Charlie," Gil said, tearing open a packet of mustard with his teeth. "We may also need to call in some of our informals."

"Let's figure that out after we orient the freelancers. Then we can fill in the missing skills."

"That Pressley kid's kinda sharp," Don said, plopping a whole slider into his mouth.

"I'm still on the fence about Ty," Charlie said.

"Well, he sure knows his way around," Gil said. "His panache makes up for what he lacks in judgment, I'd say." Gil prided himself on assessing people quickly.

"I like him. He speaks his mind without a lot of pussyfooting around," Don said, drawing the last of his Coca-Cola through a straw. "Now that was a good meal."

"I just hope the conference room has windows that open, or good air conditioning," Gil said, letting two Tums melt onto his tongue.

Judy greeted each freelancer with a one-page, work-for-hire agreement. When all eight men and four women were seated, Gil, flanked by Charlie and Don, rose from his chair at the head table.

"Let's start by having everyone introduce themselves," Gil instructed.

Ty Pressley had been invited to join the meeting, and when it was his turn to speak up, Charlie interrupted the process. "I also want to introduce Tyson Pressley. He's on staff at Cobo Center, and extremely knowledgeable about the behind-the-scenes activities and relationships. He'll be our go-to guy for all situations involving Cobo's protocols."

Ty looked surprised at the announcement that he was part of the team. As the introductions continued, he shot Charlie a look, and she nodded affirmatively.

"Each of you has been hand-picked for this assignment. Most of you will work twelve-hour days, and be on-call the other twelve hours," Gil said. "It will be eight days of work, starting today."

Grumbles and moans floated through the conference room, and Gil held up his hands for quiet. "I'm aware that it's New Year's Eve, and I know those are long hours, but I've personally seen some of you play poker for three days straight with no sleep. So I don't want to hear it." The quiet slowly shifted to laughter. "The paperwork you signed spells out your specific duties and compensation. We'll want you armed at all times. You'll need to carry your weapons registration, and we'll need the serial numbers," Gil continued. "There's also a confidentiality agreement in front of you. I want you to read it, and sign it. The work we're doing is highly sensitive, and the general public cannot get wind of any potential problems with the auto show."

Mandy raised her hand with a question: "Are the local police aware of our operation?"

"Don is our liaison with area law enforcement. And we'll be coordinating with the local Homeland Security office," Gil responded. "But we don't want any of you to talk to your police contacts. We've been asked to keep a low profile on this case. Casual talk, even with people we know and trust, can blow this thing wide open."

There was another round of buzzing. Don stared straight ahead, and Charlie gave Mandy a look that said *don't push it*.

"Is everyone clear on confidentiality?" Gil asked, watching heads around the conference table nod, and waiting until each person had signed the agreement.

After the housekeeping tasks were completed, Charlie began the team briefing with an explanation of the general concerns of DADA, and the specifics of the murder of Yu Chenglei. Don provided an overview of Cobo's general security protocols, and Gil distributed a folder containing floor plans and infrastructure blueprints.

"We don't really know what, or who, we're looking for, so question anything or everything that doesn't feel right to you. If you step on toes, we'll handle it," Charlie said. "Questions?"

A half-dozen hands raised at once. The freelancers around the table were good at what they did. Each had been selected for a particular skill, and most, like Mandy, had police backgrounds. Within a few minutes the Q & A had turned into a brainstorming session.

"Hey, won't we need someone who knows Chinese?" Hoyt Timbermann asked. He'd served on the Metropolitan Police Department with Don, and had gone private after several excessive force complaints. Still, Don said there was no one better at search work than Timbermann.

"You're right, Hoyt, and we've got that covered," Charlie said.

"I've heard the people at Spectrum are hard-asses," Hoyt announced.

Don and Ty locked eyes and shared a smug smile.

"They may be more of a hindrance than a help," Charlie conceded, "but we need them, and our clients have assured us of their cooperation. In fact, the head of Spectrum will join us sometime during this briefing."

"Are there other questions or ideas?" Gil asked, pausing a few beats. "Okay. You've all met Judy Novak. She's the real brains of the operation. I'm going to turn the meeting over to her."

Judy was a logistics guru. She had the group line up for photographs, distributed folders explaining each investigator's assignment for the case, and passed out laminated cards with the phone numbers of key team members. Judy asked Don to record the serial numbers of the freelancers' weapons, and she distributed a new BlackBerry phone to each member of the team. Judy and Gil had become fans of the devices when they partnered with the FBI on a missing persons case. The 2006 Berry could be used for calls, messaging, and to check email, and had an exceptionally good camera.

"You probably already have a personal mobile phone, but this is the phone you will use for this assignment. Keep it on your person at all times," Judy said. "You've each been given an email address and we've leased a proprietary server for our communications. You'll be able to download pictures, data, maps, and other documents. Don't worry, we'll teach you how to do everything."

Most of the freelancers looked overwhelmed by the phone's capabilities. Only Ty was completely at home with the device, and he shot a question to Judy.

"Do these units have the GPS chip?"

"Yes, they do. We'll be able to locate each of you through your phone."

For the next half hour there was a discussion of logistics. Five two-person teams would patrol Cobo, keeping an eye on exhibitors, staff, vendors, visitors, construction teams, and deliverymen. Others were assigned to research and interviews. They would work in shifts: twelve hours on, four off, and start again. Judy had reserved rooms for the freelancers at hotels in proximity of Cobo, because Charlie wanted them to be able to respond to any situation within minutes.

At 4 p.m., Geoff Heinrich, Cynthia Fitzgerald, and two Spectrum security guards who could have passed for Greek gods entered the conference room. Heinrich oozed European chic. The cost of his pocket square and socks was the equivalent of a week's worth of groceries. Cynthia was the only one of the four who might blend into a drugstore without undue attention. Charlie asked Heinrich to join them at the presenter's table. Cynthia took a seat with the freelancers, and Atlas and Helios flanked the table like pillars.

"This is Geoff Heinrich, president of Spectrum Security and responsible for all security for the auto show," Charlie said. "Mr. Heinrich is aware of our work and has offered his full cooperation. The badges you've received are Spectrum IDs, so we wanted him to meet all of you and share any words of advice he might have for us."

Charlie introduced each freelancer to Heinrich, while he looked bored. He pulled a speck of lint from his expensive jacket sleeve and examined his manicure. He only looked up from his grooming to take in the four women who were introduced. Then Charlie invited Heinrich to speak.

"Spectrum is a world-class security agency with access to state-of-the-art surveillance and investigative tools. My employers have chosen to supplement our work by bringing in outsiders." Heinrich glanced sideways at Charlie, Don, and Gil the way he might at a waiter who had delivered a tea service. "However, I doubt your efforts will be of any demonstrable help to our overall operations. I wanted to meet each of you, to issue a caution. The Spectrum credentials provided to you do not give you unbridled authority, nor license, to interfere in the day-to-day work of the auto show."

The room was silent for nearly thirty seconds. Charlie cleared her throat and was about to speak when Ty gave a cough behind his hand with a muffled message: "Asshole." Charlie and Heinrich glared at him.

"I have a question." Mandy Porter raised her hand. As she did, auburn hair fell across the shoulder of her simple white collared shirt. Charlie noticed the reactions of the men in the room with a twinge of jealousy. Mandy was aware of the attention her looks garnered, and in business situations she tried to counter by dressing plainly. The ploy, as was the case now, rarely worked.

"Yes?" Geoff Heinrich's voice no longer had an edge, and he squinted his eyes seductively. "Ms. Porter, isn't it?"

"That's right. Given the critical nature of this threat, why wouldn't you want to include us as full allies? If your employers, as you call them, believe this might be a serious threat, I'd think you'd want all the help you can get."

Charlie was still getting used to the fact that Mandy didn't know the meaning of the word timid. As a rookie at the Grosse Pointe Park police department, she'd been shot three times when responding to an attempted bank robbery. She'd received a second commendation last year when she'd pulled a pregnant woman from a burning car. Heinrich was momentarily dumbstruck by Mandy's question—and her green eyes.

"Perhaps you're right. I'd be happy to hear your ideas about how we can work more efficiently together."

"Well, for one thing . . ." Mandy began.

Charlie stood, stopping the banter before it began. "Good. We're making progress. We'll be sure to follow up with you on Ms. Porter's ideas, Mr. Heinrich. Thank you for coming. We've made a dossier of each of our freelancers for your review."

Heinrich was clearly annoyed by Charlie's interruption, but he stood also, his slacks unfolding in a wave of soft wool. His guards moved closer to the table. Heinrich glanced at Cynthia who thumbed through the dossiers and nodded to him that all was in order. He fastened the caramel-colored leather buttons of his sports coat and moved to the door, aware of the myriad eyes giving him the once-over. He hesitated at Mandy's chair, but she didn't look up. She was busy punching the tiny keyboard of her new phone.

"Heinrich is going to be trouble," Gil said.

The Mack partners were gathered in their borrowed office. Don had already swept the room for bugs, a precaution learned from the experience of a previous case. He intended to check every day for the ultra-tiny cameras and audio devices used in modern surveillance. Judy's temporary desk was quickly becoming a clone of her desk in the Mack offices, piled high with folders and color-coded file labels.

"He's quite something, isn't he? With his mannerisms, accent and elegance," Judy said. "But there's also something disturbing about him. I can't quite put it into words."

"How about, 'Demons'll charm you with a smile for a while . . . ,'" Charlie offered from *Sweeney Todd*.

"That'll do it," Judy said.

Charlie looked toward Don. "Nothing to say on the subject?"

"I've already said what I have to say about the guy. Is Fong in place yet?"

When Charlie had reached out to her former martial arts student, he'd been very willing to help out. They'd met briefly, and she'd filled him in on the work. Lin had changed a lot. He was handsome, sure of himself, no longer the nerdy kid. In addition to speaking Mandarin and Cantonese dialects, Lin was an expert programmer with a degree in computer systems analysis. Gil had learned from Cynthia that Spectrum had an immediate need for a multilingual programmer, and it had been his brilliant idea to embed Lin Fong in Heinrich's staff.

"Lin met with Heinrich this morning. Spectrum called the

fake references we set up, and he got an immediate job offer. He starts Monday. He'll do some programming and be one of Spectrum's liaisons to the Chinese auto delegation," Charlie said.

"Perfect," Don said.

"Did you tell him the work might be dangerous?" Judy asked.

"No. I told him it was an undercover assignment, which he thought was thrilling. There's very little chance of Lin being in danger; he's just in place to have eyes and ears inside Spectrum."

"Maybe we can also use Heinrich's interest in Mandy to our advantage," Gil said, checking signatures on the confidentiality agreements.

Judy looked at Gil. "That *was* pretty obvious, wasn't it?"

"I don't think Mandy would go along with that," Charlie said.

Don and Judy looked at Charlie and then away. Don had discovered Charlie's romantic interest in Mandy Porter on their last case. Judy knew because of Mandy's frequent calls to the office. The awkward silence got Gil's attention.

"What's going on?"

"Mandy and I have gone out a few times."

Gil had heard the rumors at their law school that Charlie swung both ways, but his attitude was live and let live. He dated a lot of women himself. From time to time, he considered settling down, but only yesterday he had received a florist's delivery from Sonia with a card that read: "Thank you for a delightful evening." Gil smiled at the memory of the voluptuous Puerto Rican beauty—a cross between Jennifer Lopez and Rosario Dawson. "That's it? You've dated a few times, and that's all there is to it?" Gil asked.

"I'll find out what her comfort level is for interacting with Heinrich," Charlie said, clearing her throat, and changing the subject. "Okay, so let's spend some time looking at the schedules and tomorrow's assignments."

"Maybe Pressley should join us if we're talking about the Cobo assignments. It'll be helpful if he knows what everyone is doing," Don said.

"You really do like that kid," Charlie remarked.

"I do. He seems to have a good head on his shoulders. He strikes me as someone who can be counted on."

"I agree," Judy said in rare solidarity with Don. "He's already been very helpful to me."

"Okay, let's get him in here."

"I'll message him," Judy said using her thumbs to pound on the BlackBerry keyboard. "Don, you need to start practicing with yours."

"Get off my back, Novak." Don held the phone in his palm as if it were an injured baby bird. "How do you turn this thing on?"

"It's already on," Judy said. "At night just charge it up like you do your regular cell phone. The charger is in that bag I gave you. There's also a cool belt holster in there."

The holster piqued Don's interest. He pulled the various BlackBerry accessories from his bag, thumbed through the operating manual, and then clipped the holster to the left side of his belt. The right side was reserved for his 9 mm Ruger.

Ty arrived out of breath. "Hi. I got here as soon as I could. Some of the network television crews arrived today, about fifty of them, and I had to make sure Spectrum had all their info."

"We'll need all their names and credentials too," Charlie said, "and we should make sure there haven't been any recent substitutions to the TV crews. We'll also need a list of their equipment."

Ty nodded. "I got it."

The group spent two hours discussing assignments. Judy had purchased a giant wall calendar that helped with the task. Don and Gil would interview auto show manufacturers, vendors, and Cobo staff. Charlie would be the primary liaison with Homeland Security, DADA, and Heinrich. Hoyt Timbermann would be team leader for the freelancers, who would form round-the-clock security patrols, starting tonight. Carter Bernstein would be in charge of research, and Judy would work the office.

"We'll need to work closely with the rent-a-cops at the information desks and the security personnel at the loading dock and parking areas," Don said.

"Ty, can you arrange a group meeting for us with all the

managers at Cobo? How many people would that be?" Charlie asked.

"Including Spectrum?"

"No, excluding them, but every other department. Payroll, food services, engineering, maintenance, custodial staff, parking operations, even your sales and communications staff."

"That's something like thirty people if you want directors and their managers," Ty said. "Some of them work different shifts, so we may need two meetings."

"Look, I know it's a lot of work, but let's schedule the meetings for Monday."

"That's gonna be tough. Monday is officially the New Year's holiday," Ty reminded the group. "My boss will have to call each of them into the office."

"Well, work with Judy on it, and get as many of them in here as you can. It's very important. We don't want to scare anybody, but we need managers aware that we have a heightened level of security for this year's event. We'll need everyone looking out for breaches in security, protocol, or routines. Nothing's too small," Charlie said.

Ty appraised the serious faces of the Mack partners. His head was full of questions. "So, you mean even Cobo employees are under suspicion?"

"Not necessarily, but we can't rule anyone out. Most people are creatures of habit, if they change their routine, it's usually innocent, but sometimes not," Charlie said.

"A manager may notice something that would be helpful to us, and not even realize it," Don said.

"Like if an employee has had a recent personal problem," Gil picked up the lesson. "Or a vendor has made a big change in their standard setup, or one of the admin assistants has recently come into a lot of money, or the regular cleaning crew has new staff. Anything like that might be significant."

"Wow. I'd never even think of stuff like that," Ty said, pausing to take in all the examples.

᯽ ᯽ ᯽

Charlie, Don and Gil arrived at the regional headquarters of the Department of Homeland Security at six o'clock. The entrance was ordinary, with only a small square plaque announcing the building's business. On the roofline, three cameras performed sentry duty as the evening visitors passed through the narrow alcove. The young woman at the information counter was also ordinary, except she was likely packing heat.

"Hello, I'm Charlene Mack. This is Donald Rutkowski, and Gilbert Acosta. We have a meeting with Assistant Director Routledge and Agent Canterra."

"You're expected."

Charlie searched for a name tag, but saw none. The woman pushed a sign-in sheet forward, and placed three visitor tags on the counter. She'd noticed Charlie's stare. "I'm Estella Morales. I'm an agent-trainee. Once a week, we rotate through the various job assignments, and tonight I'm on the desk."

"I remember." Charlie smiled.

Morales reciprocated. She looked to be in her early twenties. Her full, dark hair was pulled back in a ponytail and she wore the gray trousers and black jacket with the DHS insignia that were standard issue for trainees. "Of course you know all that," she said.

"I see our reputations precede us," Don said.

"Yes, we've heard all about you."

Don was suddenly taken aback, not sure if the woman was insulting him or not. Don and Charlie had been actors in an unfortunate training incident involving a firearm. No one had been hurt, but Don's fellow trainers had teased him mercilessly about the mishap, and he was sure he'd never live it down.

"We tried not to burn bridges when we left," Charlie said.

Agent Morales nodded graciously.

They were escorted by the third-floor receptionist to the assistant director's office. As they entered, Jim Routledge pointed in the direction of his small conference table, and continued a personal call. "I'll only be away a few days. I know I promised to take him to the zoo tomorrow, but the director asked me to fill in for him." Routledge turned his back for a modicum of privacy.

Charlie studied the photos on the wall. Routledge had been a senior agent when Charlie and Gil trained at the DHS academy. In the five years since the inception of DHS, he had moved up the ranks quickly. Like Don, he was a former police officer, but he'd also been a U.S. Army intelligence officer. Charlie remembered Routledge as even-keeled, fair, and well liked throughout the agency.

"How the hell are you three?" Routledge pulled his six-foot-five frame up from his desk chair, striding to the conference table in three steps. He shook hands all around and was immediately joined by Agent Anthony Canterra.

"Look what the cat dragged in." Canterra grinned, shaking hands with Don, giving Charlie a friendly hug, and engaging in a ten-second soul handshake with Gil. "Haven't seen you on the court for a while, Acosta. You scared to come out and play?"

Gil had been an All-City high school basketball star and was still known to dominate some of the pickup games on Detroit's inner-city courts. Gil unbuttoned his suit jacket, sat down and leaned back in his chair. "Man, I could wear this suit and tie and still beat you in a fifteen-minute game." The trash talk continued, while at the other end of the table, Don and Routledge compared photographs of their sons and talked about their Lions season tickets.

Charlie poured a glass of water from the pitcher on the table and enjoyed the man banter. She actually had more male friends than women, and preferred this kind of conversation over discussions of shopping and manicures. She appraised Tony, who was animatedly making a point about the Pistons' chances for a playoff slot. They had been a short-time item after she left ICE. He was handsome, squared-jawed with steel-gray eyes. She had dated men of all races, and Tony fit her cultural criteria for any man she'd dated: He had to know who John Coltrane was, have read at least one book written by a woman, and could sit through a Broadway musical. She'd reported to Mandy that Tony got a check mark on each criterion.

Routledge looked at his watch. "Look, I have a family gathering at my house tonight, and I'm already in trouble with my wife, so we better get going on this meeting so I can get home by seven-thirty."

"We have a case that involves the murder of a Chinese national you investigated. His name is Yu Chenglei, and the auto dealers seem to suspect his death may be tied to terrorism," Charlie initiated.

"Yes, we did investigate him. He's not on our watch list, and has no ties to Al Qaeda or any other terrorist group, but he is associated with government-backed disruptions of information systems."

"Come again?" Don said.

"You know, those widespread computer hacking attacks?"

Don nodded. Pretending he understood.

"We've been interested since before 9/11 in how the Net is being used to support terrorist activities—moving money, triggering campaigns and attacks, even recruiting new fighters. There's a lot more emphasis in our work these days on the nexus between cyber threats and the activities of fringe groups."

"How was Chenglei involved?" Gil asked.

"Our experts think he may have been focused on industrial espionage," Routledge explained. "We know a Yu Chenglei was once employed by the People's Republic of China to penetrate the computer firewalls of American companies."

"Well, that's a relief, really," Don said.

Charlie had been listening and observing. Tony Canterra was unusually quiet, and as Routledge spoke, Tony stared down at the table.

"What else is going on, Jim?" Charlie asked.

"What do you mean?"

"I mean, are you telling us everything?"

"We don't think there's a threat to the auto show." Routledge paused to look at Tony, who was now staring wide-eyed at his boss. "But we do have chatter around what could be a credible threat to the Super Bowl."

"What's the nature of *that* threat?" Charlie asked.

"I'm sorry, I can't give you any details."

"But you will give us some help?" Don asked.

"Well, of course. We'll help all we can, but our chatter isn't about the auto show. What kind of help do you think you'll need?"

"Maybe manpower," Don said.

Routledge shook his head no. "I can't promise that. There'd have to be overt evidence of a pending attack."

Charlie's sixth sense nagged at her. "What if, there's no real threat to the auto show, but it's a dry run for the Super Bowl?"

"Now that's an interesting question," Gil said.

"A city like Detroit rarely hosts two back-to-back, high-profile international events. An infiltration of the auto show would be a way for someone, or some group with sinister intentions, to learn the city, test transportation options, build, buy or rent space for equipment and people, recruit staff, and embed operatives. Could that be the case?" Charlie asked.

Routledge wasn't buying it. "Like I said, the chatter doesn't support that. If we find something definite that spells out a threat to the auto show or points to your theory, we'll shift gears. That being said, the death of this Chenglei character is certainly a smoking gun, and we're relieved you all are involved in following the leads."

Routledge excused himself, leaving Tony Canterra to arrange the mechanism for sharing information between DHS and the Mack Partners. Later, Tony escorted them to the front lobby, and as Don and Gil moved toward the exit, he touched Charlie's elbow to slow her stride.

"So, how are you doing?"

"I'm doing well. I have no regrets about leaving the agency, and the partnership with Don and Gil has worked out even better than I thought."

"Any regrets about us?" Tony lowered his voice and glanced at Agent Morales, who was paying attention to them.

"You know it wouldn't have worked out, Tony. I can't settle down with any man. I was upfront with you about that, wasn't I?"

"You were. But sometimes I think about us. You still look good, Charlie."

"You look good, too. You're the best-looking white man I ever dated." Charlie laughed. "Look, can you tell me *anything* about this Super Bowl threat?"

"No. Not really. The FBI picked up email and Facebook chatter. They're taking it seriously, and they've asked us to help. Most of the detail hasn't yet trickled down to my pay grade."

"You'll let me know if we need to duck, won't you?"

"I'll try to tell you everything I can." Tony paused and pushed both hands into his pockets. He stared at Charlie earnestly. "Look, are you seeing anyone now?"

"Yes. I'm in a serious relationship. Happy New Year, Tony."

"Happy New Year to you, too."

Tony watched Charlie walk to the front entrance. Her heeled boots clicked along the marble floor, and her jacket swayed with the rhythm of her gait. After she'd gone, he continued staring at the glass door until he felt Morales's stare.

"Everything going well this evening, Agent Morales?"

"No problems to report, sir. Except, I didn't retrieve Ms. Mack's visitor pass."

"Where to?" Don asked as he pulled out of the DHS parking lot.

"We may as well go back to Cobo. We can start going through the personnel files and get organized for the staff meetings," Charlie said. "Jeez, how soon before we have some heat?"

"Give it a minute and I'll turn on the blower. It would only be cold air now," Don said. "What are we going to eat?"

"We'll get some food on the way in," Charlie said.

"We're not too far from Buddy's you know," Don said.

"Okay, pizza it is. I already knew nutrition would go to hell during this case," Charlie complained.

"Judy just emailed. We have late check-in status at the Woodward Hotel," Gil said from the back seat. "Apparently, she was able to get a block of rooms for us, and most of the freelancers."

"Okay, email her that we're heading back with deep-dish and salad."

"Will you be seeing Mandy to convince her to help us with Heinrich?" Gil asked, punching on his BlackBerry.

"No, but I'll get her on the phone."

"Hi. I wondered if you'd have time to call," Mandy said

"We just left DHS, and now Don and Gil are ordering pizza from Buddy's."

"Ooh. That sounds good. I'm having a not-so-fresh iceberg lettuce salad with seven chunks of chicken breast in one of those plastic containers. The best part is the sleeve of honey-mustard dressing."

"Yummy. Where are you?"

"The Woodward Hotel. I checked in a couple of hours ago. I'm on patrol with Hoyt Timbermann at ten o'clock."

"I'm staying at the Woodward too, but who knows when I'll get there. We're on our way back to Cobo after we get the pizza. I called to ask you something."

"You want my room number?"

"Ha-ha. Yes, eventually. But look, we may need you to cozy up to Heinrich. We want to know what he's thinking, and he was obviously smitten with you."

There was a pause. Charlie had never formally worked on a case with Mandy. It wasn't fun to be in a position where she had to weigh her personal interests against the interests of a case. If Mandy weren't her lover, she wouldn't have a moment's hesitation asking her to use feminine wiles to get information. Now, Charlie couldn't help hoping Mandy would be outraged at the suggestion.

"Oh, sorry. I had a huge piece of lettuce in my mouth. Sure, I'll find out what he's up to. I got a call from his office this afternoon inviting me to have breakfast with him. I said 'no,' but if you need me to play him, I'll call back and accept the invitation."

"Thanks," Charlie said without much appreciation. "It'd be helpful to the case."

"Anything else?"

"No. nothing. I saw Tony Canterra tonight."

"Oh, yeah. How's he? Still good-looking?"

"Yep. But he's not you."

"I know, and don't you forget it. Happy New Year, baby."

"I'll be tied up all week on this case, Mom. So, if you call and I don't pick up, don't worry. If there's an emergency, let Gloria know, okay?"

Charlie looked up when she heard the knock at the car window, and she pushed the unlock button. Don and Gil ripped at the car doors, and tumbled into the Buick's warmth. The car quickly filled with the smells of cheese and pepperoni.

"I've got to go now, Mom. I love you, and I'm sorry we can't spend New Year's Day together. Bye."

"How's your mother doing?" Don asked.

"Okay, but she doesn't venture out alone much. She still talks about those guys who robbed her."

"I'm sure it's a traumatic memory for her," Gil said.

Don pulled into the Saturday evening traffic heading east on Michigan Avenue. There was more volume than usual as people traveled to New Year's Eve festivities, including a Red Wings game. The dashboard readout said the temperature was thirty-five degrees, but the wind chill said otherwise.

"Mandy is in," Charlie informed her partners. "Cynthia had already called her for a breakfast meeting with Heinrich to discuss ideas for working closer together." Charlie formed quotation marks with her fingers to emphasize the last words. "She initially declined, but she's calling back to accept the invitation."

"That's good. Right?" Don asked.

"Sure. It's great."

∽ ∽ ∽

While the Mack team devoured two six-square, deep-dish pizzas, green salads and soft drinks, they discussed the work still to be done. Don and Gil departed Cobo at ten to check into their hotel rooms, and Charlie and Judy sat at the table with shoes off. Over the two years they'd worked together, they'd become friends, and Charlie sometimes sought out Judy's advice, which was always grounded in common sense.

"Maybe we should set up a cot here in the conference room so you, or I, can be here all the time," Judy suggested.

"You trying to get a break from the husband and kids?"

"Not really. I told them not to expect to see me much this week. They're all old enough to fend for themselves, and I'll call them at midnight to wish in the New Year. How's Ernestine doing?"

"She's a bit less interested in the world these days, and that worries me."

"Who's keeping an eye on her this week?"

"Gloria, who works at the front desk. But Mom doesn't feel she needs anybody to check in on her and, besides, she thinks Gloria is too nosy."

The two women chuckled and shook their heads in unison. Then Judy slid into her shoes, and Charlie donned hers.

"Are you worried about Mandy playing up to Heinrich?" Judy asked. "I wouldn't blame you if you were. He's clown creepy."

"Mandy can handle herself."

"I know. But you don't mind?"

Charlie didn't answer the question, so Judy padded around the table gathering plates, cups, and food containers to dump into a trash bag she'd retrieved from a cabinet. "It's good to have a small refrigerator and microwave. That's Cynthia's doing. She's been very accommodating of every request I've made."

"She does seem to want to help," Charlie agreed.

"Well, it's getting close to midnight. We may as well just take one car to the hotel."

"Right."

They turned off the conference room lights and exited the

suite, into the dim hallway. Several staffers were seated in the glass room staring at the monitors, and light spilled from Cynthia Fitzgerald's office, but Spectrum Security was otherwise closed for business.

"I like to keep my private life, private," Charlie said out of the blue. "That's why I haven't said much about Mandy." Charlie swiped her key card at the outer door and held it open for Judy.

"I understand."

They moved to the elevator and watched the red blinking camera over the Spectrum door. Charlie turned to face the elevator. "Mandy and I have agreed to be in an exclusive relationship."

"That's great, Charlie. Now maybe you won't be so lonely."

"You sound like my mother."

"Has Ernestine met her?"

"Yes, a few months ago. She likes Mandy and thinks she's good for me."

"I do too. She's full of fighting spirit."

The chime on the elevator sounded, and the door opened to Hoyt Timbermann hurrying out.

"I was just coming to see you," he said to Charlie. "Are you leaving?"

"Yes. Is there a problem?"

"No. I just have a question for you."

"Come on; ride up with us, Hoyt," Charlie said, blocking the closing door.

"I wanted to verify with you that Mandy Porter can leave her shift a bit early. She says you've given her another assignment?"

"Oh, sorry, Hoyt. I should have told you about that. Can you get one of the others to come in early?"

"Sure, that's easy to do."

Cynthia watched the three enter the elevator, and the door close. She picked up her phone and punched a few numbers. Heinrich was a despicable man but he was her boss, and he'd made it clear her job was to keep the Mack team at arm's length from Spectrum business. She wasn't sure what he was up to, but the off-the-calendar meetings, the secret files he kept locked in the wall safe, and the calls to and from the extra mobile phone he carried suggested he was keeping secrets.

"Tom, I'm leaving now. Everything looking good?"

"Nothing out of the ordinary, Ms. Fitzgerald, except the patrols by those investigators. There's a lot of action at the loading dock tonight, but our man down there hasn't reported any problems."

"Okay, Tom. I'll see you tomorrow."

Cynthia gathered a couple of files, moved to the closet, and pushed the button on the video recorder.

Chapter 4

Sunday, January 1, 2006
Auto Show: 7 days

Charlie called Judy's room at 6 a.m. to get a time for the ride back to Cobo, but Judy was already awake and dressed.

"Who could sleep with the drunks rolling into their rooms all night long?"

"Yep. I forgot how crazy it is on New Year's Eve if you're not drinking along with everyone else."

"Would you mind if I went home for a few hours this morning? Gary's complaining that he doesn't know what he'll make for dinner if he's on his own for the full week. So, I thought I'd go home and prepare a few meals he can freeze."

"No problem. I'll meet you in the lobby in five minutes and take you to your car."

The hotel lobby showed the wear and tear of New Year's Eve revelers. Confetti was strewn around the floor and on the three sofas. The desk clerk from the night before was still on duty, and was making the rounds of the room picking up plastic glasses and party favors. He held a pair of panties at arm's length before dropping them into his trash bag.

"Tough night?" Charlie asked the clerk.

"You don't know the half of it, ma'am. I had to mop up vomit a couple of times last night, our security guy went to the hospital for stitches after a guest hit him with a bottle, and the police were here twice. But we won't really have the full story until the housekeeping staff arrives," the man said, shaking his head.

Charlie watched Judy get into her car in the underground garage at Cobo, then moved the Corvette to a parking space close to the elevators. When she pushed through the door of the temporary office, Don was doing a sweep for electronics, and Gil sat at his desk cradling his head in crossed arms.

"Good morning. You two are in early," Charlie said.

"Yeah. You know that old adage about the things you do on New Year's Day are the things you'll do all year? Well, I hope that's not true," Don said.

"Except for the part about making money all year. I can handle that," Charlie said.

"Where's Novak?" Don asked.

"She went home for a few hours to cook for Gary and the kids. She'll be back later."

"How'd you sleep?"

"Not well. Too many partygoers."

Gil sat up and rubbed his hand through his hair. He was unshaved and his eyes were red. "I need some coffee."

"I'll make the coffee," Charlie said. "And not because I'm the woman in the room. I need some, too."

"We got here about five," Gil said, yawning. "There was some guy in the hall on my floor who begged his wife all night to forgive him."

"I don't remember ever being that young and stupid," Don said.

His two partners stared at him, until he was forced to add: "I know I probably was. But, I just don't remember it."

"You bring your colored notes?" Gil asked.

"You know me too well," Charlie said, measuring for six cups of coffee.

Charlie had developed a personal process for her brainstorming, using three-inch color Post-it notes. There were usually two sets of notes, red notes with questions and green with facts and data. For the auto show investigation, she'd added a third color, blue, for conjectures. Gil was particularly helpful with the conjectures because he was imaginative. Don was more literal, and helped the process with solid questions framed in bias and gut feelings. Charlie's gift was in being able to connect the dots.

Don loved controlling the white board, and they went at it for several hours. At 10:30, Judy arrived with breakfast sandwiches from McDonalds, and a load of hash browns.

"Okay," Charlie said, looking at the board filled with green, red, and blue sticky notes. "What have we got?"

"There sure aren't a lot of green notes," Don said, taking a bite from his second sandwich.

"And the ones we have are more assumptions than facts," Charlie said. "I'm hoping we'll have more hard data to work with after we meet the managers and review staff files."

"I have another green note we can add," Don said. "Heinrich is a pain in the ass that won't go away."

"Can we look at the conjectures?" Gil asked, ignoring Don's remark. "Let's move them off the board."

It went on like that for a while. At noon, the freelancers for the midday patrols dropped by the office, so Judy ordered in Domino's pizza. At 3:00 p.m., Charlie suggested they break from the brainstorming.

"Sometimes it helps to shift to another task, use a different set of muscles, and then an idea will just hit you. That happens to me all the time."

"I'd like to take a look behind some of the doors we saw with Pressley yesterday," Don said. "He said the infrastructure guts were in there."

"Good idea," Charlie said. "According to the blueprints, one of those rooms holds a panel of circuit breakers as large as this conference room."

"I'll grab one of the golf carts. You coming, Acosta?" Don asked.

"No. We haven't done a perimeter check today, so I'll get the car and cruise through the neighboring streets, and drive by the loading dock and parking garages to see what I can see."

"Sounds good to me," Don said.

"Okay. Let's meet back here around six," Charlie said.

Don steered a golf cart along the service circulation area behind the ground level meeting rooms. In the passenger seat was a stack of Cobo blueprints. This corridor was off-limits to all but authorized personnel, and on a Sunday the only sounds were of surging water and electricity. Don stopped the cart in front of a door marked "Mechanical Room. Authorized Entry Only." Another cart was parked twelve yards ahead. Don's Spectrum ID, on a chain around his neck, was tucked into his shirt pocket. He placed the ID on the card reader until he heard the click, pushed the door open, and stepped into a massive room with giant boilers humming. A metal catwalk traversed the ceiling, and two lifts were parked in the corner. There was an array of panel boxes, cast-iron pipes, and wheel-shaped shut-off valves along the wall. Warning signs and fire extinguishers were prominent every hundred feet.

He stepped farther into the chamber and followed a path marked by fluorescent paint and pedestrian walking signs that ended at an office. The door was ajar, and half-drawn mini blinds showed a lighted interior. Don paused at the entrance. An engineer Don had seen when Ty guided the team through Cobo's levels, sat on a stool in front of a panel board. Don knocked. The man turned at the sound, but wasn't startled.

"Hey, remember me? Don Rutkowski? Pressley introduced us."

"I remember you. Come on in," he said. He turned back to his panel to press and hold a button, and then grab a clipboard that hung on a wall hook next to the console. "I'm monitoring the climatological data, and I have to time-stamp my reading."

The room was a high-tech maze of circuit boxes, gauges, illuminated buttons, and electronic circuit diagrams. The fluorescent lights and aluminum-paneled ceiling gave the place a science-fiction feel. Don felt he'd entered a scene from the movie *Alien*.

"I see you're checking out the building innards," the man said. His name tag read "Fletcher."

"I am. We've been studying the blueprints, and I wanted to get a firsthand look. Is this the main room for Cobo's engineering?"

"No. For a facility of this size, we have two control centers for redundancy. We call them MEEP rooms, short for the mechanical, electrical, energy, and plumbing systems."

"What can you control from this room?" Don asked. "For instance, can you turn off the heating systems and lock down the elevators?"

"Oh, sure. There are security codes I need to enter, but with those codes I can do lots of things."

"Like what?"

"Well, I can control the hot-water circulating systems, turn the exhaust and sprinkler systems on and off, lock the escalators, turn lights on and off. Those sorts of things."

"So, if someone got in here, they could really do some damage to Cobo."

"Well sure. Is that what you guys are worried about?"

Don hesitated. He wasn't sure how to answer that question without compromising the confidentiality DADA wanted.

"You don't have to answer the question. But it must be some big deal, 'cause I have to come in for a meeting tomorrow morning—on my day off," Fletcher said with emphasis. "Well, I'll tell you what *I* know. Somebody would really need to know what the hell they're doing to mess with any of our systems. We're state of the art. I'm only using that clipboard so the chief engineer can come in here and see that I'm making my rounds. Any system that is touched is tracked on a computer program. When I pushed that button to test the temperature in the People Mover corridor, the computer knew what I was doing, why I was doing it, and that it was a routine protocol. If I tried to do something out of the ordinary, like turning off the HVAC systems, I'd have to input my personal security code to do that."

"But what if someone had the personal codes?"

"We have many fail-safes. If an operation is initiated that is contradictory to the protocols, the computer will begin an authorization check. If there's an emergency, depending on what it is, the computer can call the fire department, the police department, the water treatment plant, the power company, even the People Mover control desk."

"Got it," Don said.

"Did you see the camera when you came into the mechanical room?"

"I saw the ones in the corridor."

"Well, they're 360 cameras. As soon as you activated the outer door with your ID, that camera took a picture of you. Since it's Sunday, the door also sounds an alarm here in the control room, and at Spectrum. I saw you come in on this camera," the man said pointing to one of the small monitors atop the console.

"So that's why you weren't surprised when I knocked at the door."

"Correct. Other cameras and alarms are triggered if someone enters the mechanical room from one of the other doors. The computer knows we're here, Spectrum security staff know we're here, and the engineer in the west control room knows we're here."

"That gives me comfort," Don said.

"Me too."

Gil returned to the Mack Team's temporary office a few minutes before six. Charlie was studying Cobo blueprints at her desk, and freelancer Carter Bernstein was staring at the white board in the conference room.

"Where's Judy?"

"She's with Tyson in the General Manager's office. They're still trying to contact all the managers for tomorrow's meetings."

"Anything interesting in the blueprints?"

"Only that there are so many hallways, corners, and recesses in this building that even if we had a hundred guys we'd still be at a disadvantage," Charlie said, sighing.

"I know what you mean. It'll be sheer luck if we can stop any organized threat," Gil said. "I took a slow drive around Cobo's exterior, then stopped at the loading dock. It's closed for deliveries today, but a trash truck was doing a pickup, so I watched them empty the trash bins. There were a few cars in each of the parking garages, but nothing that looks suspicious. The problem is, I don't know what suspicious looks like."

"Exactly. I was saying to Mandy a couple of nights ago that this is the kind of case where our usual investigative techniques are limited."

Gil gave Charlie a smile. "So you two are an item, huh? Mandy. She's really beautiful."

"Let's stick to the business at hand, shall we?"

"I, I'm sorry. I didn't mean to overstep. I didn't mean anything by it, really." Gil stammered, struggling to apologize.

"Forget it, Gil."

Gil sidestepped his embarrassment by turning toward the conference room. "What's Carter doing in there?"

"I'm not sure. He's been playing with my notes and staring at the whiteboard for almost an hour."

Gil entered the conference room, followed by Charlie and Don, who had just returned. Gil put on a stank face. "Pizza again? Oh, well, guess I'll have a slice." He reached over the table to select a large piece with ground beef and green peppers. "What's shaking, Carter?"

"Not much, Gil."

Charlie sat across from the board, curious about how Carter had organized her Post-it notes. "You got something, Carter?"

"Not yet, Ms. Mack. Nothing's popping out at me."

Don grabbed the nearest box of pizza and took it to the far end of the table. "Well, I just spent an hour in the mechanical room. This place is really a masterpiece of engineering."

"There are two mechanical rooms aren't there, Don?" Charlie asked.

"No, just one huge one. But there are two control offices. Connected by more than a mile of pipes, ducting, electrical wiring, and catwalks. But they have all kinds of security precautions, so I'm a lot less concerned about a threat to the infrastructure."

"Well, that's good news," Charlie said brightly.

The conversation turned to Cobo's intricate layout until Judy and Ty joined the group. They reported that two managers' meetings were scheduled for the next day. Hoyt, Mandy, and freelancers Josh Simms and Barbara Burnett checked in before their evening patrol shifts. While Judy offered pizza, Charlie pulled Mandy aside to ask about the Heinrich breakfast meeting.

"I got nothing from him at breakfast, except he wants to sleep with me," Mandy said.

"He said that?"

"He was pretty direct."

"Damn, I'm beginning to hate that guy," Charlie said, her voice rising. She saw Don look her way.

"No worries. I had things under control."

"I know you can handle yourself. I guess I'm just . . ."

"Jealous?" Mandy winked.

Charlie felt her cheeks burn. "Did he say anything about the investigation?"

"He says there's absolutely no threat to the auto show."

"Are you seeing him again?"

"That didn't come up."

When Charlie and Mandy returned to the conference room, Don assessed Charlie's demeanor with a glance, then continued his advice to Hoyt Timbermann.

"Remember, just keep moving, chatting with the guards, checking doors, stairwells, and the parking structure. We might even put a permanent team outside, riding the perimeter from time to time. Gil did that today."

"Yep, I covered both garages, checked all the entrances, and spent some time at the loading dock. I got out of my car and just walked around down there," Gil said. "I don't think anyone even noticed me."

"Okay, I'll step up the patrols in the loading dock area," Hoyt said. "That reminds me, shouldn't we have one of our people be with the Spectrum guys who monitor the cameras?"

"I don't think that's necessary," Charlie said. "Cynthia has said if they spot anything, she'll call us right away."

"Okay," Hoyt said, taking notes.

"Don't follow any particular routine, and don't hesitate to be in touch if something feels wrong to you." Don gave more instructions. "If anyone sends a message on the BlackBerry, it comes directly to us, right?" he asked, glancing at Judy.

"That's right."

"So, if we get an SOS, we'll come running," Don said, sweeping his eyes across the group.

At 10 p.m., Hoyt and the freelancers left the suite to start their patrols, and Judy started packing up for the night. She pushed the carts filled with files to the side of the room, and shoved the extra pizza boxes in the refrigerator.

"We got a lot done today," Charlie said. "I could use a few hours of sleep."

"Me too," Gil said, stacking folders on the table. "I must have looked at a hundred files."

"Did Mandy have anything to report about Heinrich?" Don asked, yawning.

"Nope. Not much." Charlie turned away from Don's further questions. "You ready, Judy? Should we take one car again?"

"Yep. That's good. Looks like we'll have a full house for tomorrow's meetings."

"I'm going to stay here tonight if that's okay," Carter announced.

"Appreciate your dedication, Carter. The cot's all yours if you need it," Charlie said, grabbing her parka.

The Mack team padded along the deeply carpeted corridor. In

the glass room, video monitors glowed on the faces of three Spectrum employees. The scene reminded Charlie of the images she'd seen of the NASA control room at Cape Canaveral. When they reached the exit, Gil stepped forward to hold the door, and Charlie was surprised to see Cynthia Fitzgerald standing in her office doorway watching their departure.

"She works late, doesn't she?" Don observed.

Chapter 5

Monday, January 2, 2006
Auto Show: 6 days

"What do you think of this one?" Ty pointed out the Aston Martin Rapide concept car.

Don had asked Tyson to give him an early morning tour of the concept car installations. They'd already visited BMW, Audi, and Mitsubishi's display areas, where engineering techs were molding temporary materials to mock up features of their concept cars, and design teams were standing by to add finishing touches.

"That's the James Bond car, Pressley. You really think that's your type?"

"Yeah. It's long, lean, and dark like me. I could see myself in this ride. Either this one, or that 2007 Lexus LS460 over there."

"Your tastes run to luxury I see. But I have a wife and kid, so I don't have luxury car money. I'm more interested in seeing the American brands. Where are they?"

Ty pointed the way, and Don maneuvered the golf cart through the showroom areas for Lamborghini, Kia, Nissan and Toyota. When they got to the GM display, Don slowed the cart and let out a long whistle.

"Now that's a car," Don said admiring a shiny bronze Buick.

"Yep. It's a looker alright. It's one of GM's new sports utility vehicles. You want to take a closer look?"

The workers staging the General Motors vehicles knew Tyson, and exchanged friendly greetings with him as he introduced Don. These were not the stuffy business suit guys of GM's executive offices. The men wore khakis and open collared shirts; the women were comfortable in slacks, or skirts with black tights, and wearing boots or stylish flats. Don nodded quick hellos, but saved his smile for the shiny cars around him that glistened like loose pearls. He opened the driver's door of the Buick Enclave concept car and swept his hand across the console, then opened the back hatch and leaned inside. When he closed the door, he glanced across the showroom to the Dodge/Chrysler area. His face froze, and mouth parted.

With no thought of Ty, Don glided across the gigantic exhibit hall as if beckoned by the pied piper. Ty saw Don on the move, bid his farewells to the designers, retrieved the golf cart, and tracked after him. He parked near the restroom, and walked over to where Don stroked the racing stripe on the Dodge Challenger prototype.

"So, you like the muscle cars."

"This baby is a beaut."

"I thought you said you had a wife and kid?"

"There's room for them," Don said defensively. He opened the driver's door with reverence, and sank into the contoured black leather seats. "Now this is how a man should sit."

Ty was studying the specs on the display sign. "She has a 6.1 liter, Hemi V-8," he said with approval.

"I see you know a little something about *real* cars," Don said as he lifted himself out of the Dodge and circled it. "Look at those beefy wheels and tires."

"Yep. Nice. And I like the grille work too. It's a sweet ride."

Don and Ty moved next to the new Chrysler Imperial, trading their ideas about the pros and cons of American luxury cars. Later, they spent some time admiring Chevy's new Camaro. Don's BlackBerry had vibrated on his belt a couple of times, but he ignored it. When Tyson's phone rang, he answered.

"Oh hi, Ms. Mack. Yes, he's with me. We're on the exhibitors' level. Oh, sorry, we lost track of time. We'll be right there."

"It's time for the meeting with the department heads. The rest are already there," Ty said, moving back toward the Challenger.

Don looked at his watch. "Damn. Did you move the cart?"

"Yep. It's over here. We can be there in two minutes if I drive."

"Okay, Pressley. But I need to come back later to see the new Lincoln."

"And you definitely need to see the Jeep display. They plan to drive a Wrangler right off the showroom floor and through one of the front windows."

"You're kidding me," Don said, jumping into the passenger seat.

"No. I'm not kidding," Ty said as he sped up the corridor to the service elevator.

"There are always security concerns about the auto show. What's so important this year that we had to come in on our day off?"

The question came from a manager in the Cobo Hall food services division. She was a middle-aged black lady with an ego as large as her hips. Charlie dealt with women like her all the time because, in truth, they ran the unofficial tier of power in Detroit. She respected these women, who were smart, outspoken, and skeptical for a reason. But today Charlie was short on patience for the woman's head-wagging, and she rose from her seat at the front table to address her. Ty, who was sitting to Charlie's right, pointed to a name on the sheet of paper between them.

"Well, that's a fair question. Mr. Heinrich and the show sponsors are simply experimenting with new protocols this year. It's good to shake things up from time to time, don't you agree, Ms. Hillman?" Charlie asked, smiling.

Charlie was immediately aware her charm tactics had no effect when the woman added harrumphing and eye-rolling to her act. She glanced sideways to see, too late, that Ty had written "don't mention Heinrich" on the paper. She looked to Gil for help and slid the paper toward him. He stood.

"I think what Ms. Mack means is, the success of an event as

important to Cobo as the Detroit Auto Show should not be left solely in the hands of a few people who think they have all the answers. Even a company as experienced as Spectrum."

Hillman uncrossed her arms and leaned forward in her chair to look at Gil. Charlie took a seat.

"Ms. Mack, Mr. Rutkowski and I used to be agents at Homeland Security. The best tips in our investigations never came from the so-called experts. The best intelligence came from those people who were on the front lines. That's why we wanted to meet with you and the other managers, to seek your advice."

Hillman slowly revealed a wide gummy smile. Her eyes batted, and she stood to give her testimony. "Well, first of all, the Spectrum folks ought to pull themselves away from those TV screens and that high-tech stuff. They act like they're in one of them Tom Cruise movies. Not once, since they got here, have they asked Bernie, the daytime guard, his opinion about anything. I run food services, and I have to sign off on every food vendor that comes in the door. But this year, some out-of-town vendors have been asked to provide food at the VIP events. I don't know these folks from Adam, and when the food inspectors make a spot check, you won't see *my* name on their work orders."

Her remarks were met with a chorus of "hmm-hmm," "I know that's right," and "You tell 'em, Elise."

"Well, that's just the kind of information that can be useful to us," Gil said, smiling with enthusiasm. He had purposely dressed in his brown slacks, peach shirt, and suede jacket. He laughingly called the outfit his "suit of amour."

Suddenly, the room was animated, as hands shot up to offer information and suggestions. At the end of the hour-long meeting, Mrs. Hillman came up to the head table to offer Charlie a handshake.

"I knew your mother. She was the principal at my high school. That was back in the day," she said, smiling in memory.

"I'll be sure to remember you to her," Charlie said.

"Is she doing well?"

"Mostly yes. But there are early signs of Alzheimer's."

"Oh, I hope they find some kind of pill or shot for that soon. It is such a mean disease," Hillman said with accustomed authority. She then joined the small group of women and two men who had enclosed Gil in a semicircle of appreciation.

"That went well," Charlie said to Ty. "We got some good tips."

"Yep. I got it all down. Your man Gil is pretty smooth."

"That he is, Ty. Here he comes now."

"Well done. I almost botched it," Charlie said to Gil.

"We all have our roles to play. Where did Don get off to?"

"He had appointments to interview exhibitors."

"Uh oh. That can take a soft touch. I better go and find him," Gil said.

"I could help him," Ty offered. "I already know a lot of the exhibitors."

"We'd appreciate the help," Charlie said. "Check with Judy to see who he's meeting with."

Ty stepped over to Judy for a brief conversation, handed her his meeting notes, and hurried out of the room.

Lin Fong felt someone's presence and looked up from his laptop. Cynthia Fitzgerald was standing at the entrance to his cubicle. He was working on a program that would link the automated visitor system to the security cameras so that any Spectrum employee could click an entry in the visitor database to pull up the camera view of the appropriate door and check-in desk.

"How's the work going?" Cynthia asked.

"Oh, fine. It's more tedious than difficult. I just have to isolate each security camera and designate a proprietary code, then do the same thing with the computer terminals at the three visitor entrances. The cameras don't record continuously, so I may need to do some programming to trigger recording when an entry is made at any one of the terminals. It's simple stuff."

Lin swiveled his chair toward Cynthia and smiled. He was twenty-two, but had an eye for older women. He might have held the smile a bit longer than he should have because her demeanor changed, and she shifted her weight to one leg and crossed her arms.

"Mr. Heinrich wants you to join him for a meeting tonight. Actually, a conference call between the operations manager and owners of Guí Motors in Beijing. The only catch is you'll need to stay late."

"How late?"

"The call is at eight. Beijing is twelve hours ahead of us."

"Right. Any idea how long it will be?"

"No. Maybe an hour or so. We'll give you a cash advance for dinner, and you can take the day off tomorrow."

"Well, okay. That's great."

Cynthia turned to leave, then stopped. "To kill some time until the call, maybe you and I could grab dinner. Say, around six? I'd like to hear more about the work you've done."

"Oh, I'm afraid you'd be pretty bored by my shop talk. But I'd like to know more about you," Lin said. "I mean, you know, what brought you to Spectrum, that sort of thing. I really don't know much about the security sector, but I'm fascinated by it."

Lin smiled again. He'd been told by more than one woman that he had boyish charm. He was a bit skinny, but it didn't hurt that he was six-foot-two. He crossed one long leg over the other, giving her full view of his large feet.

"Where are you calling from, Lin?" Charlie asked.

"I'm in the cafeteria. Don't worry, no one's paying attention to me."

"What's this meeting about tonight?"

"I don't know. Cynthia, I mean Ms. Fitzgerald, said Heinrich wanted me there to do some translation."

"Will the Chinese advance team be at the meeting?"

"I think so."

"Okay. Don't go to the hotel after the call. I don't want anyone to see you coming or going there. We may need to move you to another place."

"I could go to my aunt's house. She lives in Palmer Woods."

"That's a possibility. One of us will pick you up after the meeting. Just leave when the others do and walk toward the parking elevators like you're going to your car. Send me an email that says OTM and one of us will meet you on the top level," Charlie instructed.

"OTM?"

"On the move."

"Wow, just like Jason Bourne," Lin said lowering his voice as two businessmen approached a table near him.

"See you tonight, then."

"Oh, by the way, I'm having dinner with Cynthia. Uh, you know, Ms. Fitzgerald."

"How'd that come about?"

"She suggested it. She wants to learn more about my work."

"Do you have your phony resumé memorized?"

"Yes."

"Be sure not to say anything that might blow your cover or associate you with us."

"I'll be careful. I think maybe we're just flirting with each other, you know."

Charlie recalled the gangly teenager who took a beating from his class bullies once a week. In just a few years he'd become socially adept and extremely confident.

"When did you become so sure of yourself?"

"It was right after you taught me how to kick ass, Miss Mack. Nobody's messed with me since. I've got to go."

Charlie turned to Judy. "Lin has a dinner date with Cynthia Fitzgerald tonight."

"Hmm. Gil will be sorry to hear that."

"Really? He has eyes for her?"

"It seemed that way to me. I've been thinking some more about Cynthia. She's very helpful, but she keeps a pretty close watch on our comings and goings."

"I'm sure Heinrich has told her to keep tabs on us."

"Yeah, but I think, just like Heinrich, there's more to her than meets the eye."

Charlie trusted Judy's instincts. She could be a worrier, like Charlie, but also an innovative problem solver. "Maybe we could plant some information with her and see how she responds."

"I think I have just the thing," Judy said.

Don welcomed Ty's offer to help with the exhibitor interviews. Most were repeat customers, car manufacturers who used the auto show as a platform to show off their latest models, and their setup processes had been honed over dozens of years. The interviews had been low-key, focusing on a few questions to determine any major fluctuations in their standard operating procedures.

"So far things seem normal, right?" Ty asked.

"So far. Who's next?"

Ty looked at the schedule Judy had emailed. "We've got a tire manufacturer, Guí Motors, and three more after that."

"Let's save the Michelin folks for last. This Chinese group is new, right?"

"Yep. They're not very friendly with peons like me. They're VIPs, and the general manager has been meeting with them on logistics and such. They've been very demanding, and ever since that worker of theirs was murdered, I've been told to stay away from them."

"Why?"

"Because they believe everything they've read about Detroit, and they think their guy was killed by some black dudes. Enter me."

"Well come on, they're going to have to deal with a black dude today," Don said, leading the way.

Guí Motors was a diversified company that had been in the auto manufacturing business in China and Eastern Europe for a dozen years. Their small, fuel-efficient cars were characterized by workhorse chassis and practical accessories; they wanted to make a splash in Detroit by revealing a new luxury model that could compete with Hyundai's Sonata sedan.

The Chinese automaker's three-room office suite was on

Cobo's third level and was lavishly decorated in teak and jade. A receptionist with her hair swept up in a bun recognized Tyson with a smile, and nodded politely at Don. She stood to greet them. The plaque on her desk read: "Amy Wu."

"May I help you?"

"Amy, this is Mr. Donald Rutkowski. He is a special security liaison for the auto show," Ty said.

Don took over. "Would it be possible to meet . . . uh, Mr. Kwong?" he asked, looking at his clipboard. "He's the team leader, I understand."

Amy entered the door that led to an interior office, and closed it behind her. The anteroom was decorated with traditional Chinese furnishings. Two red screens flanked high-backed wood chairs at a black-lacquer table. On the tabletop were three small jade boxes. The modest reception desk sat in front of a six-foot-high, ornately carved wood cabinet with brass hardware shaped like dragons. Within a minute, the inner door opened and Amy appeared, the smile still pasted to her face. "Mr. Kwong will see you."

Don and Ty entered the office and met the stares of Kwong and Geoff Heinrich. Heinrich sat on a red satin bench with copper nail heads along the base; Kwong sat on a matching bench opposite him. Between them was a low rectangular black table inlaid with mother-of-pearl. Both men's faces were strained in seriousness. Kwong stood while Heinrich turned his attention to the crease in his slacks.

"How do you do," Kwong said, holding out his hand to Don. He nodded to Ty. "I understand from Mr. Heinrich that you have some concerns about the death of Chenglei?"

Don glared at Heinrich, who showed his unabashed contempt for the two visitors. Don took an involuntary half-step toward the man, then stopped. "Actually, I'm surprised he's shared any such information with you, since he is aware that the nature of our inquiry is confidential."

Kwong averted his eyes, signaling his distance from the conflict brewing between these two Western men. "Please sit," he said, pointing to the other two benches that completed the set. Don was uncomfortable on the seat with his knees almost parallel to his chest. Ty admired the satin covering on the bench and rubbed his hand along the decorative nails.

"Mr. Kwong. Can you tell me your understanding of Chenglei's murder?" Don asked.

Kwong looked at Heinrich, who gave a stare that was difficult to read. Kwong sat straight-backed on the bench and placed a palm on each knee. His dress was formal, a navy-blue suit with a red tie. His black socks peeked above highly polished shoes. Don thought Kwong must be the most well dressed of those overseeing the construction of their company's exhibits. The dress of the other advance teams consisted primarily of jeans, boots, and flannel shirts.

"The Detroit police told us Chenglei was in the wrong place at the wrong time. He left the hotel after dinner to take a walk. He was accosted by a group of . . ." Kwong looked at Ty then averted his eyes. "He came upon three men who beat him, and then one of them shot him. Chenglei was a recent addition to our company; he didn't follow all the rules," Kwong said.

"What rules are those?" Don asked.

"Our group had several weeks of training to acclimate ourselves to American culture and customs. We also familiarized ourselves with Detroit. Chenglei was aware that he was not to travel outside of the hotel alone, but he disregarded that rule. He was a foolish boy."

"How old was he?" Don said, looking at his notes. "Oh, I see it now. He was twenty-three years old. What was his job, Mr. Kwong?"

"He was part of our engineering team. We have a piece of new technology we plan to introduce at the show."

"Oh, that's interesting. What is it?"

Heinrich lifted his eyes from examining his herringbone trousers. He gave Kwong a look of warning and shifted in his seat.

"I'm not at liberty to say, Mr. Rutkowski," Kwong said. "Ours is a very competitive business and often requires secrecy."

"Sounds mysterious," Don said.

Heinrich rose from his bench, and spoke to Kwong. "I'll leave you to your discussion. I'll be in touch with you on that other matter." He shared a brief look with Don before leaving the office.

The afternoon Cobo managers' meeting went smoothly. Following the formula of the first meeting, Gil took the baton while Charlie played second fiddle. When they were done, they had twenty leads that needed follow-up, and the promise from each manager to contact Ty if they had any other ideas or incidents to report.

Don was still doing exhibitor interviews, so the next order of business was to complete the check of personnel records. Judy had three file carts stacked high with folders for Cobo employees, Spectrum staff, and contract workers. Charlie, Gil, Judy, and Carter Bernstein were systematically going through each.

"What are we looking for again?" Judy asked.

"Anomalies," Gil said. "Five years of good performance evaluations, and then the last one sucks. Anyone who has been employed with Cobo for less than six months, or someone who recently returned from an extended sick leave. Things like that."

The group worked through lunch, munching on chips, soft drinks, and M&M's. As dinnertime arrived, so did Don.

"You guys thinking about food?"

"Not yet," Charlie said. "Did you and Ty finish the exhibitor interviews?"

"We did today's list, but we have a few more for tomorrow. Nothing much to report so far, except the Chinese delegation may be in cahoots with Heinrich." Don dug into the bowl of M&M peanuts and popped a few in his mouth.

"What makes you say that?"

"Heinrich was sitting with the head of the Chinese group when we got there, and they're keeping secrets about something."

Don pulled a couple of brochures out of his pocket and leaned back in his chair to read.

"You and Ty went to see more concept cars, didn't you?" Charlie accused.

"Only the new Lincoln SUV. It was developed with the Volvo designers. It has 20-inch chrome wheels and a 4.4 liter V8 with a six-speed transmission."

"Is that the one with the transversely mounted engine?" Gil asked.

"Yeah, man. It's a good-looking car, and it's got all-wheel drive."

"What's transversely mounted mean?" Judy asked.

"Don't you have some work to do, Novak?"

"Don't I have the right to ask questions?" Judy retorted.

"If you open the hood of your car, the engine will be mounted parallel to the windshield," Gil explained in lay terms. "A normal rear-wheel drive engine is mounted the long way, perpendicular to the windshield."

Gil's explanation was to keep the peace. But he needn't have bothered. Judy was still confused, so she let it go. Don was hungry, so he did the same.

"What about dinner?" Don asked.

"Those are the personnel files we've flagged." Charlie pointed to a stack of folders next to the M&M's. "We need to follow up on those tomorrow, but we still have more files to review, and I want to finish them today."

"I think I've got something here," Carter said abruptly, and all eyes turned to him.

"What is it? You were looking at the TV crews, right?" Gil asked.

"No, I finished those a while ago," Judy said. "He's going through the Spectrum staff files now."

"Spectrum hired a new technician six months ago to install and test their retina-scanning gear. The guy's name is Bernard Dudiyn. He seems to have the right skills, but his references don't work."

Carter paused to down a bottle of water. His face was unremarkable, a good quality for an investigator, but his attire screamed attention. His tortoiseshell glasses looked very expensive, as did his wristwatch. His white shirt appeared to be tailor-made and Charlie thought the jacket which hung on the back of his chair was probably Armani. With a less flashy wardrobe, he could pass for an accountant.

"What's wrong with his references, Bernstein?" Don said impatiently.

"Oh. I'm sorry. Uh, it's this company called Bantom Biophysics in Tel Aviv. He says he worked for them from 1998 to 2002 but they don't hire Americans."

"How do you know that?" Gil asked

"I did some work for them."

"Aren't you an American citizen?" Don asked.

"Yes. But I also have an Israeli passport."

"Hmm," Don responded.

"Maybe this Dudiyn guy also has dual citizenship," Gil said.

"Maybe. But there's only a copy of a U.S. passport here," Bernstein said, flipping through the folder, then picking up another.

"Anything else?" Charlie asked.

"Well, maybe. They just hired a programmer. Name's Lin Fong. His resume looks too perfect to me, and I never heard of the companies he says he worked for."

"You can pass on that one. We've already checked out Mr. Fong," Charlie said.

"I don't know. He speaks Mandarin, like the guy who was killed, and he just got hired. That's a lot of coincidence to me."

"Just forget about Fong," Don's voice was raised. "We already have him on our radar."

Bernstein looked perplexed, but nodded. "Okay, should I just do some more checking on Dudiyn?"

"Yep. Good idea, Carter," Charlie said. "Meanwhile, Don, why don't you go out and pick up something for dinner?"

"Sure. Maybe Chinese carryout? What's so funny? Oh, I see. No, really, I didn't make the connection. I just have a taste for shrimp egg foo young."

Kwong pushed the intercom button and Amy appeared at the door. She was the American granddaughter of an important man in China. He'd agreed to take her on for the planning and execution of their auto show launch—a six-month job. She was respectful, obedient, and attractive. "I want a scotch and water." He watched as she moved to the bar hidden in the cherry bookcase. Her calves were well defined; her small hips moved in a languid sway. He imagined how she might feel against him. Amy placed the drink on a black coaster on his desk and bowed slightly.

"I've told your grandfather that you are doing an excellent job," Kwong said.

"Thank you, Mr. Kwong. I've enjoyed the work. Except, of course, the horrible incident with Chenglei."

"Of course." Kwong held Amy's gaze until she looked down.

"Is there anything else I can get for you?"

"No."

Kwong's eyes followed Amy's exit, and he felt a tremble in his loins. He took a long sip of his scotch. That foolish boy's death had jeopardized his plans, and intensified the already heavy scrutiny of his delegation. He'd contained the police investigation, and thought he'd assuaged the concerns of the auto dealers group, but now they'd hired private investigators because of their continued suspicions.

At tonight's teleconference, he would have to listen to his bosses' complaints about the diplomatic fallout. He, in turn, would report the programmer's death as an unfortunate, but random, act in a city with a reputation for violence. He would tell the Guí owners that by the time the show opened next week, the launch would be a success. On the other matter, he'd report that another young programmer was already in place, and the job was almost complete. Kwong buzzed the intercom a second time.

"Would you freshen my drink, Amy?"

"Yes, Mr. Kwong."

When she leaned over to place his drink on the napkin, Kwong thought about touching her hand, but didn't.

"Thank you, Amy. Is the presentation ready for tonight's meeting?"

"Yes, everything is ready. I put the finishing touches on the presentation this afternoon as you instructed. I emailed the reports to Beijing an hour ago, and called to confirm they had been received."

"Thank you. You're very efficient. Why don't you go get yourself some dinner?"

"Can I bring back anything for you, Mr. Kwong?"

"No, I'll be fine. I had a late lunch."

Amy Wu gathered her purse, coat, and keys. Mr. Kwong's late lunch had consisted of a scotch on the rocks. She jotted the word *Dewar's* on her calendar as a reminder to replenish the supply in his cabinet. Kwong was an odd man. Hardworking, but very secretive, and unable to disguise his lustful thoughts. Amy was sure he would have made a pass at her long ago were it not for her grandfather's reputation on the mainland.

She portrayed the demure young girl at work because that's what Mr. Kwong required, but she was a second-generation American. Away from the traditional environment of this office she was a modern woman. She didn't dislike all black people the way Mr. Kwong and Mr.Heinrich did. She'd overheard the derision they used when talking about Chenglei's assailants. She would never repeat those conversations, filled with the N-word, to her mother or father who were both professors at the University of Michigan. Kwong and Heinrich had only slightly more respect for white Americans. They called the U.S. hypocritical and laughed at what they called the softness of America.

Amy pulled her late-model Chrysler Sebring up to the exit gate and pressed her badge against the electronic pad. When the gate opened, she eased into traffic heading away from downtown. There was a light rain, so she turned on her windshield wipers and her radio. "Oh, this is my jam," she shouted, and punched the up button on the volume until Beyoncé's "In Da Club" reverberated through the car.

Lin Fong tapped his foot nervously under the counter in the control booth. His orders from Mr. Heinrich were to appear to provide technical support for the videoconference in the next room. He followed the directions of the Spectrum technician who was doing audio checks, adjusting the table cameras, and monitoring the satellite feed from Beijing. The third person in the booth was Amy Wu, who worked for the head of the Chinese auto manufacturer. She was observing, and a couple of times Lin caught her staring at him. She was an attractive girl, but a bit too young and buttoned-up for his tastes. He preferred Cynthia, who had seemed even more seductive after he'd downed a glass of wine during their dinner.

Cynthia had asked about his family, and his childhood, and his experiences growing up as an Asian-American in southeast Michigan, and she marveled that he had such an impressive work background. A half hour into their dinner, Cynthia discarded her Spectrum blazer and he was rewarded with flashes of cleavage through her white cotton shirt. He might have talked too much after that. When his BlackBerry vibrated in his pocket, he waited until she visited the ladies' room to check the message from Ms. Mack—a reminder that she'd pick him up from the top level of the parking garage.

"Okay, we're ready to begin," the Spectrum tech said into the microphone that fed Heinrich's earpiece.

"Keep an eye on the audio levels," the tech reminded Lin, who squared his chair to the console. "I'm opening the feed to your guys," the tech said in Mandarin to his counterpart in Beijing.

Kwong began the transcontinental meeting by introducing Geoff Heinrich. He then switched to Mandarin and began reading his report. Within five minutes, one of the executives in Beijing closed his copy of the report with a slam, and began firing questions at Kwong. Lin Fong picked up a pen and began writing. Geoff Heinrich was nonplussed, and he leaned back in his chair and clasped his fingers on the table.

"The boss is pissed," the technician said to no one in particular.

When the meeting was completed, Lin left the control room to hand Heinrich a few pieces of folded paper. Lin noticed Amy watching. She remained in the conference room as her boss debriefed with Heinrich. Lin helped the technician pack the microphones and portable cameras, then said his good-byes. At 9:30 p.m., he punched the button on the parking elevator and tapped a message into his phone. As the elevator doors were closing, he caught a glimpse of Amy Wu stepping into the corridor.

The Mack team was still hard at work reviewing the personnel files. Charlie's BlackBerry buzzed, and "OTM" appeared on the screen.

"OK, I've got to go pick up Lin and drive him to his aunt's house," Charlie said.

"You want me to go with you?" Don asked.

"No, I can handle this solo."

"Then I'll go check on the night patrols. You coming back?"

"No. When I'm done, I'll try to get a few hours of sleep. See you in the morning."

Heinrich slipped out of the olive green silk sheets and into a deep blue brocade robe. He tightened the belt around his muscular waist, eased onto his chocolate-leather chaise, and lit a small cigar. The slight burn in his throat, and the sound of running water, made his abs tingle with the memory of sex with the girl in the bathroom. He smiled, leaned back on the chaise, and watched the snaking smoke. He sat up when the nude girl tiptoed from the bathroom door onto the deep, gray shag carpet. Tonight's annoying conference call with Kwong's people had driven him to this tryst, against his better judgment. He looked at his watch and beckoned her over.

"I have a business meeting tonight. You'll have to go now."

"You want me to leave?"

"That's what I said."

"It's after midnight," the girl protested. "And it's raining."

"I'll call you a cab. Get dressed."

The girl's disappointment quickly shifted to anger. She spun, grabbed up her clothing from the floor, and returned to the bathroom, closing the door with a slam. He ordered a cab, lit another Italian cigarillo, and leaned deeper into the chaise, thinking about Mandy Porter.

Her sensuality sprang, he believed, from a complete disregard for limitations. She was not likely to be caught up in romantic notions, like the girl in the loo. He should have absorbed her flirtations, rather than responded to them. He then considered Charlene Mack—all caramel skin and sinewy limbs. Charged and unpredictable like the air before a thunderstorm. "Hmm." But it was Mandy he couldn't shake from his thoughts.

Yesterday, she'd come to his house for breakfast and deflected his not-so-subtle proposal with complete confidence. He hadn't forced the issue, because the power was in having a woman offer herself to him.

"You're flirting with me."

"No."

"Then what?" Mandy asked.

"I want sex with you."

"You're very sure of yourself, aren't you?"

"I know what I want. I believe you're a woman who shares that trait."

"I know *exactly* what I want, and right now that's your full cooperation in thwarting this threat to the auto show."

"There is no threat."

"How can you be so sure?"

Mandy's dossier described her as a hero. Three bullets had lodged in her back, one barely missing her spine, when she'd traded gunfire with bank robbers. He tried to imagine how she'd react to the touch of his cigarillo against the scar tissue on her body. Three beautiful wounds—fleshy, disfiguring, erotic. He felt the rise pushing against his silk robe and inhaled deeply, then released the smoke, following its path as it curled and rose toward the cathedral ceiling. He looked at his watch and swung his legs to the floor. He needed to be on time for his late-night meeting.

Charlie was awakened by a sound, and she shifted to her back on the hotel's king-sized bed. She splayed her legs across the cool sheets as if making a snow angel. The phone vibrated again, and she turned toward the nightstand to see the phone's green light blinking. The red display on the clock showed 1:30 a.m.

"Hello?"

"Mack, it's me."

"Don, what is it?"

"Josh Simms has been shot."

"What?"

"He and Hoyt were walking the parking levels and spotted activity at the back of a white van. They went over to investigate, and someone started shooting. Josh was hit twice. He's dead."

"Oh, no, Don."

Charlie jerked herself to a sitting position and her stomached lurched. The dark, unfamiliar room brought a flash of an empty, debris-filled lot where she'd been bound and left to die. Charlie shook the memory from her head.

"There's something else, Charlie." Don only called her Charlie when he was worried or sentimental.

"My God. Mandy. Is she okay?"

"It's not Mandy. She's fine. She was on patrol on the other side of Cobo. But the white van. It was filled with electronics."

"You mean like TVs and stereos?"

"No. Like circuit boards, wiring and batteries," Don said. "We've got to get back to Cobo."

"I'll be ready in two minutes."

Chapter 6

Tuesday, January 3, 2006
Auto Show: 5 days

It was three in the morning. Tyson had returned to Cobo, and Tony Canterra and Scott Hartwell also joined the sullen group in Heinrich's office. He sat at his desk with the air of a king holding court. The Detroit police commander who had left a few minutes ago was livid when he learned the auto dealers had kept the department out of the loop on the auto show security investigation.

"I'll speak with the Commissioner," Hartwell announced to the room as he paced the office. "I'll make him understand the sensitive nature of this situation."

"Look, to hell with the politics," Don yelled. "I don't give a damn about your PR issues anymore. One of our guys was killed last night, and the contents of that van suggests there's some crazy terrorist shit going on."

"I don't think we can jump to conclusions about that," Tony said. "The police know DHS is claiming jurisdiction over this shooting because of the van's contents, but our preliminary search didn't turn up any explosives or residues. It's not against the law to have wiring or circuits, but the van is stolen, and there were plenty of fingerprints that we're checking out."

"What were those guys doing in that garage in the middle of the night anyway?" Gil asked.

"It's a good question," Charlie said. "Maybe meeting someone. A half-dozen exhibitors had crews working here overnight."

"You have surveillance cameras in all the parking areas, correct, Mr. Heinrich?" Tony asked.

"Yes. But after hours, that particular garage is only for our monthly parkers, and the van was in one of our blind spots."

"How convenient," Don said bitterly.

"If your people knew what they were doing, and had called for backup before moving in on a situation they didn't understand, this might not have happened," Heinrich countered.

Hoyt Timbermann had been sitting quietly in the corner. He'd tried to resuscitate Josh and, when he realized his partner was dead, had followed a blood trail from the van into the northeast stairwell before he was stopped by three Spectrum security guys moving up the stairs. The police had grilled Hoyt for two hours, and he was haggard and despondent. Now he lifted his head to glare at Heinrich.

"Why you contemptuous little . . ." Hoyt was rising from his chair to confront Heinrich, but Don interceded by putting a hand on his shoulder.

"I know you feel like smacking this prick, but it won't do any good. I promise you we'll find out who shot Simms."

Charlie noted Heinrich's posture. He wasn't at all intimidated by Don or Hoyt, but he shriveled a bit under the glower of Scott Hartwell. Like Charlie, everyone had dressed hurriedly before coming to Cobo, and it showed. But Heinrich hadn't hurried. He was dressed casually, but neatly, and was freshly showered. He offered an apology.

"We're actually very sorry about your team member's death. It's a tragedy." Heinrich glanced at Cynthia who obediently nodded her agreement.

There was ten seconds of quiet while the group assessed the sincerity of Heinrich's apology. It gave Scott Hartwell the opening he needed to get the players refocused on the safety of the auto show.

"We have five more days. What are our next steps, Ms. Mack?"

"Two murders in two weeks at Cobo Hall is no coincidence. Whoever's behind this is getting reckless," Charlie said. "We need your approval to add more security cameras. Temporary ones that can take care of the blind spots in the building. These guys seem to know the terrain."

"We should also add cameras at the entryways of every exhibitor office," Gil added.

Heinrich objected. "Our international automakers are strident about their privacy, and they've paid a lot of money to be here." Heinrich looked toward Hartwell for help, but received none. "These people think of their offices as extensions of their embassies. They won't allow us to put cameras in those areas."

"We need those cameras," Charlie stated emphatically.

Hartwell was pacing again his face heavy with worry. "You'll have them." He stopped to give Heinrich a "this is not negotiable" look, and returned to his walking. "What else do you need, Ms. Mack?"

Charlie understood now why the auto dealers had chosen Hartwell to represent them. She had mistaken his catlike alertness for nervousness. But, in fact, he made decisions with the agility and speed of a cheetah.

"I have a call to make," Heinrich said in Hartwell's direction, and popped up from his desk. "Cynthia can authorize anything else you need."

Hartwell left the office a few minutes after Heinrich, and Tony excused himself to check his messages. The rest reconvened around the conference table in the Mack team's suite, and were joined by the freelancers to map out a new game plan. Judy made fresh coffee and put doughnuts out on a platter, but the atmosphere in the conference room was too sober for eating. Now they were one man down.

Hoyt was the first to speak up. "I know we should have called for help, but everything happened so fast. We didn't even have our guns drawn. Josh just called out to the people behind the van, and they opened up on us." Hoyt ran his hands through his short-cropped hair and coughed.

"We probably need to establish specific protocols for the situations we run into," Mandy said. "And, when we're on duty, we should wear jackets marked with the word *security*."

Charlie nodded to Judy, who wrote down the suggestions. "Any other ideas?"

"It might make sense to get bulletproof vests since people are shooting at us," Gil said.

Mandy had another request. "Also, the BlackBerry phones are fine, but let's get some walkie-talkies for the patrol crews. They're not new-tech, but they work."

"We have walkie-talkies and the vests, too, if you want them," Cynthia offered. "We can also help install the security cameras."

Cynthia's suggestion set off a full-fledged disagreement among the team.

"I think we should have the monitors here, Mack," Don said. "Spectrum can still keep an eye on the cameras they have in place, and we can monitor the new camera locations. That's the practical thing to do. The more eyes on Cobo, the better."

"It might be a waste of manpower to have people sitting around in front of monitors," Gil offered.

"I can take a monitor shift," Judy said.

"So can I," Carter Bernstein said. He had commandeered the conference room cot as his new home away from home, and he had traded his suit for a T-shirt and jeans.

"That's fine," Charlie said, "but I agree with Gil. Spectrum can continue the camera monitoring. We should be moving around."

"We can set it up so you can see the output of the new cameras on a laptop. Or two laptops. It's just like the new security monitoring systems you can get for your house," Cynthia said.

"We accept," Don said.

"Okay. That's a good compromise," Charlie agreed. "We also

accept your offer to have Spectrum install the cameras in Cobo's blind spots. But we'll supervise the camera installations at the exhibitor offices."

"Whatever you say," Cynthia replied, taking notes on her tablet.

"I'll rework the schedule to keep most people on patrol, and have one or two people monitoring the cameras," Hoyt said. "I have to do a new shift schedule anyway."

Remembering Josh, the mood in the room shifted to sober again.

"Please, keep me in the field, Hoyt?" Mandy pleaded. "I'd be useless to everyone watching a monitor."

"I know that, Mandy."

"Did you determine where the guys in the van escaped to?" Gil asked Cynthia.

"We spotted three people fleeing the parking garage, and sent our guys to intercept them, but we lost them."

"I'd like to take a look at the camera footage from the parking lot," Gil said. "Did DHS already take it off-site?"

"No. It's all digital. I'll send it to you as a link," Cynthia said.

Tony Canterra burst into the conference room. "I've got news," he said. "The fingerprints in the van were in our national database. Three sets. American. Small-time crooks. Theft, arson, aggravated assault. But, obviously, now also armed and dangerous. A fourth set of prints was found on three cash labels discarded on the floor of the vehicle. Not in our database. We're working with Interpol to see if the prints are in the international databases. We're trying to trace the blasting caps and wiring, but they're easily bought online and, in the case of the phones, you can get them at any mall kiosk. We also retrieved information on the van. Get this, the van was leased three months ago to an employee of the Chinese Consulate in Chicago."

"The Chinese again," Charlie stated the obvious.

"I guess now DHS will step in to take charge of the operation," Gil said somberly.

"No. We'll stay on last night's incident, but we want you guys to continue as lead on the threat investigation. If we step in, we'll have to notify every other security agency and the State Department. We've informally spoken to the FBI, but since we don't have a specific threat to the homeland, we'll stay in the background. Otherwise, the auto show might be canceled, and the Super Bowl would be put on high alert. Both options are still on the table. A lot depends on what you all dig up in the next thirty-six hours."

Don and Charlie didn't talk much in the idling car. Lin Fong had stayed at his aunt's house overnight, but today they were moving him to Charlie's apartment on East Jefferson, where he would stay for the duration of his assignment.

Lin bounded down the stairs with a large duffel bag, and a backpack thrown over his shoulder. It was raining and in the mid-thirties, but he wore a University of Michigan sweatshirt, knee-length shorts, and sneakers with no socks. White earbuds hung from under his hoodie.

"So, Charlie tells me the executives in Beijing mentioned trade secrets?" Don spoke over his shoulder as Lin settled into the backseat.

"What? Did you say something?" Lin said pulling the right bud from his ear.

"Would it be too much to ask, for you to focus your attention on the people you're with?" Don said angrily.

"Don't mind him." Charlie smiled at the embarrassed boy. "We had a really rough night."

Charlie looked at Don, whose jaw was set hard. They'd agreed not to tell Lin about Josh Simms. They didn't want to scare him, and Charlie was still convinced Lin was in no particular danger.

"Tell Don what you told me about the videoconference."

"The Guí motor guys were upset with Mr. Kwong. They badgered him about some new navigation system they want, and one of them told Kwong that his family's well-being was connected to his success in Detroit. Kwong told them he was being careful, because their efforts had already been spotted by General Motors techs."

"Did you tell all this to Heinrich?" Don asked, keeping up with the traffic heading east.

"Yes."

"How did he respond?"

"He didn't seem surprised or concerned. He asked if anyone asked about the investigation of Chenglei's murder."

"Did they?" Charlie asked.

"Mr. Kwong brought it up, but that was it."

"Anything else we should know?" Charlie asked.

"Well, like I told you last night, I think Kwong's assistant may have guessed that I speak Mandarin. I think she noticed me taking notes, and I know she saw me give my notes to Mr. Heinrich. Also . . . well, you know, Cynthia Fitzgerald asked me a lot of questions when we had dinner."

"What kind of questions?" Don was scrutinizing the boy in the rearview mirror.

"About where I grew up and things like that."

"Is there more to it than you already told me?" Charlie turned toward the backseat.

Lin squirmed. "Well, I remembered more about it this morning." Lin paused, looking at Don's eyes in the mirror, then shifting quickly to Charlie. "I had a glass of wine. Cynthia said it was okay, you know, because Spectrum was paying for our dinner. She seemed real understanding about how I was bullied at school, and, you know, I may have mentioned that I took self-defense classes when I was a kid and that you were one of my instructors."

"Oh, for God's sake," Don said with exasperation.

"Did she want to know more about that?" Charlie asked.

"No. But, I realized I shouldn't have said it as soon as it came out of my mouth, and I . . . you know, glossed over it, and just started talking about how college was much better for me than high school. She was drinking wine, too. So I don't think she even noticed."

Charlie exchanged a glance with Don. Lin's cover was probably blown. They'd just have to see how Cynthia responded. She had, so far, passed the loyalty test Judy had devised. It involved a handwritten note planted, in full view, on Judy's desk. The note said: *Heinrich. Foreign national, temporary visa?* The number at the bottom, connected to a voicemail on one of the extra Berrys. Cynthia had seen the note, but the number hadn't been used.

"Nice place," Lin said, surveying the contemporary décor of Charlie's high-rise apartment.

"Yeah, and it's all yours for a few days. There's food in the refrigerator, high-speed internet, and cable TV. Don't have any wild parties, don't bring in any drugs or prostitutes. Don't answer the phone, and, oh, don't go through my dresser drawers."

Lin blushed.

"Are we clear?"

"Yes, Ms. Mack. Thanks."

As expected, a few exhibitors were livid about the new security cameras, and they filed formal complaints with DADA about privacy infringements. Although foreign cars were being assembled in the U.S., and vice versa, manufacturers were still very competitive, and leaks of proprietary information were always a concern. New technologies, engineering breakthroughs, even innovative accessory designs, could give an automaker an edge resulting in tens of millions of dollars in annual sales.

Charlie and Don were making personal visits to the holdouts, and Don maneuvered a cart nimbly through the second-floor exhibit areas, where equipment and construction crews prohibited a straight course. Charlie held tightly to the grab bar on the canopy and leaned with every turn.

"Guí and Bavarian Motor Works have refused the additional cameras. Tesla Motors pulled out of the show altogether, but they had an electric car prototype they were skittish about, and might have dropped out anyway."

"What kind of leverage do we have?" Don asked.

"If any exhibitor refuses the cameras, they'll be suspended from the show. The DADA board members will visit, in person, to make it official. Hartwell means business."

"The guy's got more balls than I gave him credit for," Don said. "Agreed."

"Believe me, we wouldn't be so insistent if we didn't have major concerns," Charlie told the BMW operations director, who finally acquiesced at the mention of Homeland Security.

"Will the show be safe?" a member of the design team asked nervously.

"Yes," Charlie answered with unwavering eyes and as much certainty as she could muster.

The Chinese weren't as easy to convince. Kwong sat behind a large cherry desk. The emblem of the People's Republic of China was affixed to the wall behind him. Heinrich stood near a bookcase; he'd been invited by Kwong to help his case. Don and Charlie were seated on the uncomfortable benches.

"We understand your concerns, Mr. Kwong," Charlie said. "But we're taking orders from the dealers. We think there is a credible threat to the show, low-level, but a threat, nonetheless. Mr. Hartwell says if you refuse, your company will be suspended from the show."

"He can't do that," Kwong said, looking toward Heinrich who cleared his throat as if he might say something, then shook his head in resignation. Kwong's fists tightened on the desktop and his face flushed with rage. Suddenly, in an amazing metamorphosis, Kwong's skin paled and his hands began to tremble. Charlie thought he might be having a heart attack, then realized he was willing himself to be calm. She watched with fascination.

"Are you in or out, Kwong?" Don asked impatiently.

Kwong couldn't help but show the disdain he felt for Don's incivility, but his thoughts quickly drifted to his family in Nanjing. His two sons would be sleeping, their bed sheets thrown aside, with sweat clinging to their foreheads. His wife, Jiaying, would be lying near the open window allowing cool air into their small room. She was depending on him to reverse their fortunes. This job was their second chance, and an opportunity to prove his worth to the Central Committee.

"I have no choice but to agree to your conditions," Kwong said. "But I do so under great protest. I must check in with my superiors who will, no doubt, be in touch with your State Department."

"That's your prerogative, Mr. Kwong. Technicians will be around this afternoon to install the cameras," Charlie said, rising.

Charlie and Don paused in front of Amy's desk in the reception area, and she looked up from her work with a shy smile. When Heinrich followed through the door, she feigned concentration on her computer keyboard.

"If you don't mind. I'll have a couple of my techs assist in installing the cameras in Mr. Kwong's space," Heinrich said to Charlie. "He's a VIP this year, and I've been asked to show him every consideration."

"That's fine," Charlie said. "But we'll be there to supervise, and we need to put cameras on the entrance to this suite, as well as in their staging areas."

Heinrich left without another word. Amy picked up her phone in response to the intercom buzz. "Yes, Mr. Kwong." She reached under her desk and retrieved a canvas bag that rattled with the sound of bumping bottles. She stood and looked patiently at the two visitors, waiting for them to leave.

"We'll be going now," Don said.

Amy gave a slight bow, stepped around the desk, and passed into the interior door.

"Uh, Ms. Mack. I need to speak with you." Carter Bernstein had come into the office from the conference room as if being chased, and now he hovered over Charlie's desk.

Charlie and Judy had just returned from an emotional visit with Josh Simms's widow. Bonnie Simms was surrounded by family. She had three small kids, and the two youngest had clung to their mother as she moved about the house being attentive to

93

all her visitors. Bonnie's mother had followed her daughter's movements with eyes filled with worry. "She's being very brave. She and Josh were devoted to each other, and I don't know how she'll be able to go on," her mother had said. The oldest boy, J.J., was almost eleven and had sat sullenly in the corner of the living room playing a handheld video game, but before they left the house, Judy had managed to engage the boy in an animated conversation about game strategy. She told Charlie on the drive back to Cobo that J.J. Simms was a strong, smart boy who would be a great help to his mother in the hard days and months to come.

"Yes, what is it, Carter?"

"You remember the Spectrum contractor I told you about? Dudiyn?"

"The guy who installed the retina system?"

"Yep. He's dirty."

"What do you mean?"

"I dug up a prison record, and from there his education documents. The guy's illiterate, never even went to high school. No way he can even spell retina let alone install a high-tech panel like that."

Charlie puzzled over the information. A person didn't need a degree to install electrical systems or be a skilled technician. At least that had been the case only a decade ago, but now technicians were specialists who had to read and write training manuals, keep up with federal regulations, and analyze systems information.

"Are you sure?"

"I don't know what he's doing, but I doubt that it's building ocular security systems," Carter said.

"Okay. Let's fill Gil in on this. And I'll speak with Cynthia about Dudiyn. Give me any notes you have on the guy."

Carter handed over a file containing handwritten notes, transcripts, and a photograph from Interpol of a bald and bearded Bernard Dudiyn. Charlie thumbed through the contents and realized Carter was still lingering at her desk. "Is there something else?"

"My contact at the Federal Bureau of Prisons said they had another request, not so long ago, for information about Dudiyn."

"Is that important?"

Carter slid a sheet of paper toward Charlie. "It's a copy of a request for records form."

Charlie studied the signature at the bottom of the form, leaned back in her chair, and folded her arms. "That *is* odd, isn't it?"

Lin Fong had been playing the Madden game on his Nintendo DS for four hours when he realized he was starving. He poked his head into Charlie's refrigerator, grabbed two cherry tomatoes, and shoved them into his mouth. He picked up a few jars, looking at the labels—pickles, capers, chutney—and returned them to the shelves. No lunch meat, no leftovers. There were eggs, but he didn't like to cook. He checked the cupboards and opened a half jar of creamy peanut butter. He scooped a glob onto his finger and put it on his tongue. Lin checked for bread. "Damn, only English muffins. Who eats those things?" He spotted restaurant menus tucked between two cookbooks, and spread them on the counter. One menu was for Grant's lounge downstairs. They didn't deliver, but they had chicken wings and fries.

The lounge was dim, and it took a moment for his eyes to adjust. He took a corner stool at the bar and ordered a dozen wings and cheese fries to go. While he waited for his food, he played the next level on his handheld game. He'd scored another touchdown when the light from the street flashed across his screen, and he glanced in the mirror to see two men entering the lounge from Jefferson Avenue. Lin was about to return to his game when he realized one of the men was Geoff Heinrich, so he swiveled his stool away from the door and hunched over his game. He instinctively knew he shouldn't be seen by his boss, and he peeked up at the mirror as Heinrich and his companion passed the bar to sit at the far end of the room near the condo entrance.

The man accompanying Heinrich didn't seem the right type.

He was large, bearded, and wearing black jeans, a long-sleeved black T-shirt, and Doc Martens. A chain hung from his belt, and he wore a green knit cap stretched low to his earlobes where ostentatious gems, probably zirconia, sparkled. Even though it was freezing outside and raining, the man didn't wear a coat.

When Lin's food arrived bagged for a carryout, he pulled on his hood and headed for the outside door rather than the entrance to the condo. The wind cut through his thin layer of clothing, and he walked quickly to reenter the building through the front door. Lin hadn't expected his espionage duties to continue on his day off, but seeing Heinrich in this out-of-the-way location with an odd-looking man might be something Ms. Mack would want to know.

Charlie paused in the threshold of the office. Cynthia had her back to the door with her feet elevated on the credenza behind her desk. A large-format watercolor, similar to Monet's Water Lillies, covered the wall. The rest of the office was decorated in light woods and gray fabrics accented with lavender pillows, ceramics, and a green accent rug. Charlie knocked on the jamb, and Cynthia lowered her legs and spun her chair in one fluid motion.

"Hi, Ms. Mack."

"Please, call me Charlie. Can I sit?"

Cynthia moved to her sitting area and pointed for Charlie to take the sofa. "Can I get you some coffee, juice, or spring water?"

"I wouldn't mind an espresso. I'm surviving on caffeine today. I didn't get much sleep last night."

"I'm really sorry about Mr. Simms."

"Judy and I visited his wife today. She has to raise three kids by herself now."

Both women paused to reflect on that information. Charlie took a sip of her coffee.

"Cynthia, we've been checking the Spectrum personnel records, and we have questions about one of your employees."

"Which one?"

"Bernard Dudiyn."

Charlie locked eyes with Cynthia, looking for any sign of discomfort or surprise, but there was none. She found herself thinking Cynthia was a woman she shouldn't take for granted.

"What about him?" Cynthia asked.

"He's only been with the company for six months, is that right?"

"Isn't that what it says on his employment documents?"

"Yes. But I thought maybe he'd had a previous relationship with the company, or maybe with Mr. Heinrich."

"Why do you think that?"

"Our researcher has found that Dudiyn has a criminal record. He was incarcerated in Chechnya for two years, and his employment application references a company in Tel Aviv where he alleges he worked, but we don't think he's ever been employed with that company."

"Mr. Heinrich personally approved Dudiyn's employment, so he bypassed our regular hiring process. He supervises the technicians who installed, and now maintain, our retina-scanning systems. I found out about his prison record, but my hands are tied."

"Why on earth would Heinrich do that? Hire a criminal to work on security systems."

"He's often up to his own devices."

Charlie took another long sip of the hot, strong coffee, feeling the immediate jolt of the caffeine, and let her eyes slip to the cup as she placed it in the saucer. Over the years, she'd learned to allow silences to do some of her work. But Cynthia was a formidable opponent.

"You did your own check of Dudiyn's background, didn't you?" Charlie asked.

"Yes."

"Did you tell Heinrich?"

"Of course. This feels a bit like twenty questions."

"We've done some checking on you, too."

"And I, you," Cynthia parried. "Look, Charlie, what is it you want to know?"

"Do you think Dudiyn might be a threat to the show?"

"Possibly."

"What about Heinrich?"

"What about him? Look, this is getting us nowhere. Maybe we need to put our cards on the table."

"Okay, you first," Charlie challenged.

"I know that Lin Fong works for you. I think that's a very smart tactic, embedding him within Spectrum. But you better let me look out for him if you want to keep him out of harm's way."

"The new cameras require us to make some adjustments," Kwong said into the mouthpiece of his secure burn phone. His technicians had just completed the nightly electronic sweep of his five-star hotel suite, but he didn't dare use the room phone. "We've already taken care of that. We have an alternative space in a warehouse, and our people will work from there."

Kwong hated having to go through the Chicago handlers to receive orders, but it wasn't practical to convene the committee for minor operational decisions. Despite the death of Chenglei and the increased scrutiny that had followed, the work was going well. His technicians had already procured vital information through the computer networks of two General Motors contractors, and his people thought the breach had not yet been discovered. This was a strange new business for Kwong, but the experience of moving people, equipment, and information in the army of the People's Republic of China had prepared him for the work. The difference: His soldiers were called hackers and were armed with laptops and hard drives, rather than guns.

Kwong picked at the room-service salad. The greens were crisp and the tuna tartare well prepared, but he had little appetite. He sipped at his scotch and stared at the manila folder on the desk. The report inside was disappointing but not unexpected.

Kwong had ordered a surveillance of Geoff Heinrich a few months ago after Amy Wu's tearful account of his sexual advances toward her. Kwong suspected him of being a sadistic manipulator of women, and the report confirmed that Heinrich used his townhouse like a brothel, with an array of women visitors of all ages, races, sizes, and some with unusual attributes.

"The woman in the wheelchair, he has been with her before?" Kwong directed his question to the man perched on the edge of the side chair.

"Yes. She arrives in a van. A helper takes her to the garage door and Heinrich wheels her into the house. The driver and the helper wait in the van, one time almost two hours. She's been there at least three times," the operative said, reviewing his notebook.

"Have you been able to see into the house?"

"I was able to place a small camera outside a side window, but there was no time to test it, and it has failed. It hasn't been easy to return because I must enter a neighbor's yard to get to the rear of his house."

The hired man sweated, and his head bobbed up and down to avoid prolonged eye contact with Kwong. "One of his frequent visitors is a man dressed as a woman," the man said revealing his contempt. "Should I continue my surveillance, sir?"

"No. I don't think so. Do you have the pictures?"

"I have them on a CD. Should I leave it?"

"Yes."

Kwong placed the disc in his laptop and double-clicked the icon. He watched an edited version of arrivals to and departures from Heinrich's small corner house. The youngest woman looked like a girl really, maybe seventeen. The oldest, a stylish woman wearing a full-length fur coat, appeared to be in her late fifties. The woman in the wheelchair arrived four times. When she arrived her head was uncovered, but when she departed she wore a scarf. The transgender woman always arrived on foot, wearing heavy makeup and a flamboyantly coiffed blond wig. Even in the long-distance footage, her Adam's apple was prominent. There were four other women on the tape, and Kwong half expected to see Amy. The last scene on the tape was of a woman he had seen with the Mack investigators.

He ejected the CD, and poured a large scotch. He stretched out on the sofa. *This furniture is too soft. No wonder Americans are undisciplined and lazy.* He had taken to sleeping in the sitting room. The bed was too large, empty, and only made him more homesick. Before long the drink and his empty stomach made him pass out. The glass fell from his outstretched hand with a dull thud, and the diluted liquor seeped into the expensive carpet.

Charlie sat with Scott Hartwell and Cynthia Fitzgerald in a booth in a Rochester Hills bar, with a line of sight to the front door. They each had two fingers of Glenlivet, a pitcher of water, and a small ice bucket; the remainder of the bottle took up the center of the table. The bar was exclusive and far enough from downtown to minimize chance encounters with Cobo staff, auto show exhibitors, or Spectrum personnel.

Cynthia had joined Spectrum a few weeks after the company received the prestigious North American International Auto Show security contract. She had impeccable credentials as a project manager for the defense and auto manufacturing industries, and had managed university research contracts. Geoff Heinrich hired her after two interviews. He liked her obvious intelligence, understanding of hierarchy, her political connections, and her pewter gray eyes.

In the ensuing months, Cynthia had fended off Heinrich's occasional advances, and gained his confidence by providing various tidbits of information about DADA, staffers at Cobo, and her former auto industry clients. Much of that information had been fed to her by Hartwell who, Charlie had learned twenty minutes ago, was married to Cynthia's mother.

"So you already had doubts about Heinrich?" Charlie whispered even though the nearest diners were several booths away.

"There were too many red flags," Hartwell said.

"Like what?"

"Off-the-calendar meetings, being too cozy with the Chinese, ignoring protocols," Cynthia offered.

Charlie directed her attention to Hartwell. "And that's why you put Cynthia in place. And why you brought me and my team in at the last minute, because you don't trust your own man."

"We had doubts about him soon after we gave him the contract, but didn't know how to proceed," Hartwell said.

"Why not just fire him?"

"We'd made a huge investment in Spectrum, and we didn't have evidence of anything he'd done."

"Do you believe he's involved in the threat to Cobo?"

"I really don't know, Ms. Mack."

Charlie was annoyed. She curled her fingers around the sweating scotch glass, and scowled first at Hartwell, then at Cynthia, who took a long sip of her scotch. Charlie didn't like being manipulated. In a case she'd had last year, an undercover FBI agent's interference had put her at a disadvantage. She felt the same kind of duplicity at work now.

"This is more than a hindrance to the investigation, Mr. Hartwell. Heinrich already resents our being around, and if he thinks we're getting close to something, we'll be at the top of his list of problems. This could be the scotch talking, but I'm trying to figure out why my team and I shouldn't just walk away from this job."

Hartwell flipped to high-anxiety status. "Ms. Mack you can't . . ."

"I've lost a colleague on this case. The show opens in a few days, and we're still tiptoeing around each other. Either you trust me or you don't. We're all in, or you can go it alone."

"She's right, Scott," Cynthia said in a tone she'd used before to bring her stepfather around to her point of view.

Hartwell put up his hands in resignation. "I know. I know. But we're neophytes in this kind of thing. We sell cars. We're way out of our depth."

"Charlie, there's more. Because Heinrich was giving so much attention to Guí Motors, we recruited a person on the inside of their operation to provide information."

"Let me guess," Charlie said, the irritation rising in her throat. "The receptionist?"

"Right. Amy Wu."

"She struck me as a smart girl. Observant, discreet. I assumed she was loyal to Mr. Kwong."

"Yes. But also to me," Cynthia said. "Look, Charlie, we do trust you. You can have complete control. And you'll have me, Lin, and Amy to help with Heinrich."

"And Mandy Porter," Charlie added.

"Oh, so that's what it's all about," Cynthia said.

"Who's Mandy Porter?" Hartwell's eyes darted between the two women.

"Just another spider weaving a trap for your security chief," Charlie said, draining her glass. "All right, we'll stay. But from here on out, I'm calling the shots."

Cynthia lifted her glass in a salute. A still-conflicted Hartwell nodded his agreement.

"I promise you this, Mr. Hartwell: We'll make it as hard as possible for anyone to do harm to your show. We're clearer than ever about the seriousness of the risks, and we understand what's at stake for the city."

Charlie retrieved a pen and a package of orange Post-it notes from her leather tote. "Let's talk about Kwong and Heinrich. If they're involved in any harm toward Cobo, I'm sure they're just middlemen."

Cynthia slowly shook her head. "Maybe Kwong. I'm not so sure about Heinrich."

"The guy likes to strut, but my gut tells me he's not a mastermind."

Cynthia pointed to Charlie's colored sticky notes. "That's some high-tech system you got there."

"It ain't retina scanning, but it gets the job done," Charlie said with a confident smile. "By the way, I heard from Lin today that he spotted Heinrich and an odd fellow at the lounge in my condo building. He described the guy as looking like a skinhead."

"That might be Dudiyn," Cynthia offered.

"You think it's a coincidence that Heinrich was in your building?" Hartwell asked.

"To tell you the truth, I didn't consider it strange. A lot of people go to that lounge because it's close to downtown, but still sort of out of the way, you know?"

"Considering the secret meeting we're now having, yes, I get your meaning," Hartwell said.

"We should probably try to get a tap on Dudiyn and Heinrich's phones," Charlie said, writing.

"Dudiyn's a contractor. He's mostly off-site, and Heinrich is the only one with a number for him," Cynthia said.

"What about Heinrich?"

"That'll be tricky, too. He has a mobile number for work, but he has another, private, mobile phone. I don't have that number either."

Hartwell loosened his tie and removed his glasses to rub the bridge of his nose. He was beginning to lose focus. He looked at his watch and signaled for the bill. He signed an open-ended tab.

"I should leave. I've reached a point of diminishing returns. If you want anything else just order it. Are you going back to the office, or home?" His question was directed to Cynthia while pulling on his coat and a wool scarf.

"After we're done here, I'm heading home. Tell Mom I said 'hi,' and not to worry."

The two smiled at each other affectionately, and Charlie thought about giving her mother a call tomorrow. Then she considered something else.

"By the way, I need one more thing, Mr. Hartwell."

"What's that?"

"Fifteen thousand dollars for Josh Simms's widow. There are funeral costs and such. This isn't the kind of work where we have a pension plan."

"Ms. Mack, I'm truly sorry about your man. Just call my office and leave the name and address. I'll have a check delivered to her tomorrow."

"Where you been, Mack?" Don demanded.

The conference room was dark, and the exterior office illuminated only by the four desk lamps. Don hadn't shaved since yesterday, and his stubble was becoming a beard. He had a Burger King bag in front of him, and the largest soft drink Charlie had ever seen. It was almost midnight, which, for a private investigator, could be the peak of your day.

"You didn't answer your phone. You forget the rule?" Judy said.

"I'm sorry. But I had an impromptu meeting with Hartwell and Cynthia."

"Did you eat?" Judy held up a cheeseburger wrapped in paper.

"Yep, I got a free dinner. I also got carte blanche with this case."

"What does that mean?" Don asked.

"Hartwell was still holding cards up his sleeves, but we reached an understanding."

Don studied Charlie's face. She was a fourth-degree black belt in Tae Kwon Do. Once, he'd witnessed Charlie reach an understanding with a child molester that left the man in traction for six weeks. "Is he still standing?"

Charlie laughed. "It's nothing like that. He's our client. But I threatened to walk off the case because he and Cynthia haven't been completely honest with us. By the way, your instincts about Cynthia were right, Judy. She *is* spying. But she's spying for Hartwell."

"Wow. I didn't see that coming."

"Right, huh? And here's something else that will blow your mind. Hartwell is Cynthia's stepfather."

"No shit," Don said, grabbing the gigantic soda and taking a ten-second pull on the straw.

"And get this. They've suspected Heinrich was a bad guy all along."

"Noooo shit," Don repeated with an I-told-you-so smirk on his face.

Charlie moved to her desk, gathered up a few files, and pulled a variety of Post-it notes from her purse and desk drawer. "We're moving in a new direction. There's a lot to fill you in on. Where's Gil?"

"He's sleeping in there," Judy said, pointing to the conference room.

"Well, we're going to roust him. Grab your giant drink, Don, and follow me."

Heinrich spotted the boy when he left through the front door of Grant's Lounge with a carryout bag—the Asian kid, Lin something or other, that they'd hired for his programming and Mandarin skills. He was suspicious of coincidences, and when he returned to his desk, he accessed the boy's file on his laptop. Lin Fong's address was in Ann Arbor, not Detroit. But he had been wearing those flannel pajama pants, like maybe he was staying at one of the condos atop the lounge. Perhaps he was visiting a friend. Heinrich punched a series of buttons to begin a search in his database. When he got no hits, he expanded the search to include Cobo personnel. The office was dark except for his Tiffany desk lamp, and he worked the remote that opened his vertical blinds halfway. The three techs in the monitoring booth were intently watching the scenes in front of them. The desk lights of another half-dozen employees punctuated the work floor. He wondered if the staff were as diligent when he wasn't on site. He pressed the remote once more to close the blinds, and stood to stretch. He took six long strides to his pantry area, flipped on the overhead light, programmed the espresso machine, and waited patiently while a perfect blend of hot milk and coffee flowed into a blue cup with matching saucer. He dripped steamed milk into his cup in a medallion design. He was admiring the brew when his computer pinged a match. He darkened the light and balanced the cup to his desk. Staring at the screen, he found the information he needed. Charlene Mack lived above Grant's Lounge, on the seventh floor. Heinrich studied Fong's file again, then picked up his private cell phone.

Chapter 7

Wednesday, January 4, 2006
Auto Show: 4 days

"Tony. I need some answers."

Tony Canterra looked at the clock, and then to the woman sleeping next to him; she hadn't stirred from the phone's intrusion. He spun his legs to the floor, cupping his hand to his forehead for a moment, then walked to the bathroom, looking over his shoulder as he closed the door.

"Charlie, do you know what time it is?"

"It's come-to-Jesus time. What's Heinrich up to?"

The pause between them might have been uncomfortable, except they knew each other so well. Charlie held the phone tautly and turned the hotel room's desk chair so she could prop her feet on the coffee table. Her neck was stiff from tension and studying files. They'd completed their brainstorming about 2 a.m. That's when Carter came back on duty to make his overseas calls, Gil and Don went on patrol, and she and Judy returned to the hotel for a few hours' sleep. But she couldn't sleep.

"Why do you think *I* know?"

"Come on, Tony. It's too early in the morning for bullshit. What can you tell me?"

There was another long pause. Charlie took a swig of water.

She had to be careful not to get dehydrated. It happened when she wasn't exercising, wasn't sleeping, and, like yesterday, drank way more scotch than water.

"Guí Motors' presence at the auto show is just a cover for the cyber-espionage stuff I told you and your partners about, and Heinrich is helping the Chinese."

"He's helping? How?"

"Logistics. Supplies and staffing support. He's basically been part of their advance team."

"I'm confused, Tony. You're telling me that DADA's head of security is aiding a foreign automaker to spy on American manufacturers? Why would he do that?"

"Money. Plain and simple. It's an elaborate scheme, and has the full force of the People's Republic of China behind it. That's all I can tell you now."

"Does Hartwell know?"

"No. He just suspects something's fishy with Heinrich."

"Why not just tell DADA so they can fire Heinrich and ban Guí from the show?"

"The State Department doesn't want to strain their relationship with the Chinese."

"What are you doing about the spying?"

"I can't talk about that. I need you to keep this between the two of us, Charlie. You can't even tell your partners."

"Aww, Tony. I can't promise that."

"That's just it. I need you to promise."

Charlie had been sleeping fitfully. The new information about Heinrich and the Chinese was troubling enough, but an unnamed distress was pushing at her subconscious, and she was too tired to make sense of it. A sound in the hallway made her sit upright. She leaned forward to look at the broken seam of light at the bottom of her door, then reached over to the nightstand and pulled her revolver from the holster. The tapping came again not with authority, but persistent.

Through the peephole, Charlie saw a tousle-haired Mandy. Charlie lowered the gun, put it on the closet shelf, and released the deadbolt. Mandy eased through the door, and Charlie controlled its closing so it wouldn't slam at the annoying hour of 4 a.m. When Charlie turned toward the room, Mandy moved into her, encircling her waist and sobbing onto her shoulder. They held each other in a tight embrace for several minutes—heart to heart, their chins nuzzled on the other's shoulder. When Mandy's tears subsided, Charlie pulled her over to the bed, and they perched on the edge, entwined.

"It hit me all of a sudden that Josh is gone," Mandy said. "I was overwhelmed. Just two days ago, I was on patrol with him, Charlie, and now he's gone."

Charlie fell back onto the bed. "That's it." She opened her arms and Mandy nestled in the hollow of her shoulder. "It's what's been gnawing at me, too, but I was too tired to piece it together. When Don told me about Josh being killed, I was angry and stunned, but I wouldn't allow myself to think about my grief. I made sure to get money for Josh's family, but I haven't shed one tear for him."

Mandy rolled tightly into Charlie's body, rubbing her palm across responsive nipples and then gently kneading the fullness of her breasts. Charlie pulled away.

"No, honey, not tonight. Too tired."

"Your nipples don't seem to agree."

"They don't know how exhausted I am."

"Well, how about a massage. It'll help you relax."

"You know what your massages do to me."

"Shhh. Just shut off your brain for a while. Concentrate on my touch, how your skin feels," Mandy whispered.

Twenty minutes later, Charlie felt a convulsion begin at her center and glide simultaneously to her chest and her legs. Her toes spread and reached for the ceiling, and her right arm jerked involuntarily. Mandy still between her legs, Charlie remained open and perspiring. Her murmurs and after-shocks mingled together. She clasped Mandy's hands, completing the circuitry of a love that grew stronger each time they were together. Finally, Charlie pulled Mandy up to lie on her shoulder, where she burrowed her face in auburn hair and wept a long time for Josh Simms.

The activity level at Cobo had intensified threefold. Word had come that morning that Commerce Secretary Carlos Gutierrez would visit the auto show on its opening day. Exhibitors were putting final touches on their stages—testing lights, animation and sound systems. Food and other vendors were assembling elaborate aluminum structures and erecting signage. Forklifts, bucket cranes, and equipment carts crisscrossed every corridor. Charlie had deputized, so to speak, a half-dozen Cobo staff: Elise Hillman, the outspoken director of food services, as well as the loading dock and engineering supervisors. They, along with Tyson and Cynthia, made up the Mack team's internal eyes and ears.

With the death of Josh Simms, the status of the investigation had changed from search and surveil to question and detain. There were also new protocols in place for the patrols. The teams had been increased to three men, or, in the case of the group Don led this morning, two men and a woman. He, Hoyt, and Mandy were parked in a golf cart overlooking the loading dock. Just below their position, two eighteen-wheelers filled with carpeting were being unloaded, and another thirty people were involved in various activities. A half-dozen trucks were parked in the bays, and another ten idled on the access road.

"This is where the real vulnerability is," Mandy said. "Look at all these people moving in and out of Cobo. We don't know who they are, and we don't have enough people to monitor their activities."

"We've vetted the three loading dock supervisors, and that gives us twenty-four-hour coverage down here," Don offered.

"That's good, but there's just too much going on to see everything," Mandy said, then pointed. "For instance, see those six containers over there marked spotlights? They're large enough for any kind of contraband. I bet you could move a camel through here without anyone taking much notice."

"Any suggestions?" Don asked.

"We could put two of our people down here on twelve-hour shifts," Hoyt said. "But, that means you and Gil would have to be added to the regular patrol rotation."

"We can do that," Don said.

"Also, Spectrum has cameras on the dock. Let's ask Cynthia what she suggests about improving the monitoring down here," Mandy suggested.

"Okay, let's get to the office and figure out who we want to move down here," Don said, backing up and turning the golf cart. "Someone who can spot an out-of-place desert mammal."

Tyson sat across from Elise Hillman at her amazingly neat desk. He'd arrived in response to her call, and she closed the door behind him.

"Ty, I wanted to speak with you first, because maybe this is nothing."

"What is it Mrs. Hillman?"

"I think something's going on with Garry."

"Garry Jones?"

"Uh huh. In all the years I've known him, I can only remember him taking two days off. That was right after his wife died. Well, I was looking through vacation requests, and last month he requested time off for next week, but I told him he couldn't be off during the show. He knows that. All hands on deck during the big show."

"Right. He inspects the food vendors, doesn't he?"

"Not exactly. He's a compliance officer. He makes sure everyone is doing what they said they'd do in their applications. He's a good worker; he's been here as long as I have."

"So what's the problem?"

"He called in sick yesterday. I didn't think too much of it. A few people have taken a day or two off to nurse colds and flu.

But today I got a call from a woman who claimed to be from his doctor's office. She said Garry had been in an accident and had a fracture. She said he would be out of work for a week. When I asked for documentation, this is the fax I received."

Elise handed Ty a sheet of paper. The letterhead had the name and address of a clinic on Detroit's northwest side. Several doctors with African surnames were listed under the address. The body of the fax listed Garry's ailments with several obvious misspellings.

"When I called the number on the letter, I got an answering machine. When I tried to reach Garry at home, the phone rang with no answer and no option to leave a message. The whole thing feels wrong to me."

"I agree. I'll get this to Ms. Mack."

She paused to put Garry's folder in the pile of neatly stacked folders in her outbox. She peered at Ty a couple of times, and he knew this meant she had more to say. He sat patiently with his hands folded in his lap.

"I have to tell you, folks are starting to feel a little edgy. I'm not a nervous woman, but this thing with Garry has me rattled. This is just the kind of thing you all told us to look for. Are we in trouble? Tell me the truth, son. I need to know."

Elise Hillman had known Tyson since he was a baby. She was friends with his parents, and they all attended the same church. Her son had been one of Ty's classmates in high school. He looked at her with an unflinching stare. He would not lie to this woman.

"Yes ma'am. The trouble is real. But, the people who are working on this are smart. I trust them. They're doing more than the police can do, and they're working around the clock."

"Well, you know me. I'm not gonna be running scared. Even if I am scared."

"I know that."

"But this terrorism stuff is different." Elise interlaced her fingers as if she were about to pray. "I don't pretend to understand why someone would hate this country so much that they would kill innocent people. But I'm glad that Mack woman is in charge of this. Because in America, I know black people have way more experience with terrorism than white people."

"Yes ma'am."

"When do we come clean with Charlene Mack and her partners?" Tony Canterra paced Routledge's office, making a crisscross on the rug's Homeland Security insignia.

"Why? Has something changed?" James Routledge asked, moving papers around his desk.

"No, but do we want to wait until somebody else is killed?"

"You know as well as I do, Tony, the Secretary isn't going to jeopardize diplomatic relations with the Chinese without an imminent threat. We'll just have to continue along the path we're on."

"We only have forty-eight hours before we have to call a no-go on the Washington VIP visit."

"Tell me something I don't know." Routledge stood, leaned on the side of his desk, and watched the agitated pacing of one of his most experienced agents. "What was in the surveillance report this morning?"

"An intercepted communication between the Chinese Consulate in Chicago and Kwong. They're watching Heinrich too."

Routledge considered the information. "That's not so unusual. The Chinese don't trust anyone, let alone a German national."

"I can't help but think this cyber-espionage business might be a red herring."

Routledge trusted Canterra's gut. He'd been recruited from the CIA after he uncovered a terrorist sleeper cell operating in Seattle, and he'd been assigned for a year at Guantanamo. He wasn't an alarmist or a cowboy.

Routledge pointed to the conference table. "Okay, Tony. Stop your pacing and lay it out for me."

∽ ∽ ∽

"I need backup," Charlie said into the car's phone system.

"Oh, really. Is that what they're calling it, these days?"

"No. Really. I need to check out a couple of addresses, and I don't want to go solo."

"Where's Don?" Mandy asked.

"He and Gil are on patrol. Judy just called with information on a Cobo food inspector, and I have to check it out."

"Okay. I guess I got my two hours of sleep for the day. Pick me up in ten minutes in front of the hotel."

Charlie spotted Mandy, dressed in skinny jeans and a peacoat, as she turned onto West Larned Street. Mandy's jeans were tucked into black leather boots, and a navy knit cap was pulled over her hair with only a splay of red bangs showing. She was a stylish pirate. Mandy slipped one long leg into the Vette and pulled in the other—then leaned over and pressed her lips briefly onto Charlie's mouth. Charlie looked around in panic, shifted into first gear and gunned the Vette.

"You should see your face." Mandy laughed. "I didn't know black people could turn that red."

They arrived at the first address on Charlie's list, the one printed on Garry Jones's makeshift doctor's note. The storefront clinic on Hamilton Street near Highland Park stood amid a half-dozen blighted buildings.

"I think I'll put the Club on the Vette," Charlie said, pulling into a strip mall parking lot adjacent to the clinic.

Those tightly gathered inside the waiting room paused in their activities to look at Charlie and Mandy as they entered the door. Both women looked out of place, but particularly Mandy. Used to being stared at, Mandy just smiled at the men, women, and children who eyed her from their places of repose.

Charlie joined two people who were hovering over the office counter and staring down at the beleaguered receptionist. She hadn't looked up in five minutes.

"Excuse me, ma'am," Charlie said to the young woman, who was sorting through insurance papers.

The woman didn't acknowledge her, but the couple at the

counter gave her a side glance that said "Wait your turn." Charlie smiled at the pair, who looked away. She decided to skip over the subtleties and go to what was usually a last resort tactic. She planted her forearms on the counter and spoke directly to the receptionist in her "authority" voice.

"I'm a private investigator, and I need to talk to the doctor about this." Charlie placed her license and the shady medical report on the desktop in front of the girl.

The young woman stared for a moment at Charlie's likeness on the ID card, and then up at Charlie. The old couple looked at Charlie again and shifted over to give her more room. Those within earshot, which was everybody, stopped talking, fidgeting, texting, looking at magazines, and providing child care to stare at Charlie's back and again at Mandy who leaned casually against a magazine rack near the front door.

"What?" the receptionist asked, as if she hadn't understood Charlie's words.

"I need to ask the doctor a couple of questions. It'll only take a few minutes, and it's very important," Charlie stated.

"You're a private investigator?" The woman repeated, looking again at the license.

"Yes. And I need to speak with someone about the patient listed on that fax," Charlie said, pointing at the letter.

For the first time, the girl looked at the letter. She handed Charlie her license and stood up with a wobble. She exchanged a hapless look with the elderly couple and glanced at the wall clock.

"Okay, just a minute. I'll need to see if the doctor is available."

"Thank you," Charlie responded.

The girl reached under the counter, pulled a backpack over her shoulder, and walked, paper in hand, to a curtain that led to the examination rooms. After five minutes, Mandy joined Charlie and the couple at the counter.

"Where'd she go?" Mandy asked.

"I don't know, but I'm going to find out. Hello . . ." Charlie shouted over the counter. "I need a little help here," she said in a louder voice.

Mandy turned the knob on the door separating the waiting room from the doctor's area, but the door was locked, and her banging didn't elicit a response. By this time, a few patients were standing up and getting vocal about their own long wait. Charlie lifted herself onto the counter and climbed over. She unlocked the waiting room door for Mandy and then pushed aside the curtain to the back rooms. Mandy on her heels, Charlie passed through a narrow hallway lit by the daylight pouring in from three vacant examination rooms and the open backdoor. They stepped out into a garbage-strewn alley, which led to the parking lot. The car spaces reserved for the doctors were empty, and the receptionist nowhere to be seen. After a quick search of the parking lot and the nearby gas station, and a return to the clinic where the waiting room was in chaos, they determined the receptionist and any medical personnel at the clinic had beat a quick retreat.

"Well, I deduce the doctor's note for Garry Jones was fake," Charlie said, securing her seatbelt and starting the engine.

"Good thinking, Sherlock. Where to next?"

"To Garry's home. Ty says the man has worked at Cobo for twenty years and in that time has taken only two sick days."

"Maybe he's had a midlife crisis and is off to the islands with a twenty-year-old pole dancer he met at a strip club," Mandy mused.

"Or maybe he took a bribe to look the other way on a vendor application, and he feels guilty," Charlie added. "He could also really be sick. But I further deduce he wouldn't jeopardize what's left of his health by going to *that* clinic."

"True."

Charlie sighed. "If it turns out Jones *is* our weak link at Cobo, it means we'll have to recheck all the food vendors with a microscope."

They drove north on Hamilton to Six Mile Road, which was actually West McNichols Road, but nobody really called it that. It had begun to rain. In Charlie's opinion, it was a toss-up whether January or February was the ugliest month in Detroit. Day after day, the endless gray covered the streets and sky, and only the occasional fresh snow seemed to brighten an otherwise dreary landscape.

"God, I'll be glad when it's Valentine's Day," Mandy said.

"Why? You want me to buy you a box of chocolates?" Charlie said, batting her eyes.

"No, it's just this damned, gloomy weather. I need to see some pink and red."

"I was just thinking," Charlie said, staring ahead. "This will be the first Valentine's Day in a long time that I can say I'm in love."

Mandy stared at Charlie's profile and smiled. Their relationship wasn't easy, but Charlie's strength, her pragmatism, even her veiled vulnerability had been just what Mandy needed to feel hopeful again, after years of depression. She'd grown up in a tight-knit family with a stay-at-home mother and an accountant father who had encouraged her and her older brother to be their best selves. Her parents had supported all her explorations, applauded her accomplishments, and put up with her rebelliousness. When, in her freshman year in college, her brother brought a girl home to meet their parents, Mandy did also. Other Irish-Catholic families might have freaked out about their budding lesbian daughter, but her declaration of same-sex orientation had been accepted with love.

Her brother had been working as a financial analyst in the South Tower of the World Trade Center when the second plane hit on 9/11. For hours the Porter family waited for his call. For weeks they waited for the discovery of his remains. And for months her parents postponed the burial of their firstborn until their daughter could face life again.

"I think we should do something special for Valentine's Day," Mandy said.

"Maybe a trip?" Charlie suggested.

"Maybe. If we're still alive by the end of the week, let's start making some plans."

Charlie looked at Mandy, who tried to hold her earnest look as long as she could. Then they both giggled as if it were already April.

Garry Jones's modest house was bordered by four-foot hedges. Christmas decorations were still attached to the front porch railing, and long grass peeked through patches of dirty snow. A week's worth of papers lay on the porch, and envelopes and magazines bulged from the mailbox. As soon as Charlie stepped to the door, she was assailed by the telltale scent of death. She gave Mandy a questioning look, and Mandy nodded.

"You smell that?" The question came from behind them.

They turned to see the mail carrier. He was coming from across the street and stopped at the stairs of the Jones house.

"When did you first notice it?" Charlie asked.

"A couple of days ago. I know Mr. Jones, and I knew his wife when she was alive. I was a little worried when I saw he wasn't pulling his mail in at night, and then, I guess it was Monday, I noticed the smell. He's dead, isn't he?"

"We don't know," Charlie said.

"Well, why did it take you so long to get here?" the postman asked with agitation.

"I don't know what you mean."

"I called you guys yesterday. Told you about the smell and to send somebody out here to investigate."

Charlie shared a glance with Mandy, who turned and walked down the steps. "I'm sorry, we didn't get any call."

"Well I called. When somebody calls the police, you're supposed to come."

"Oh, you got us all wrong. We're investigators, not the police," Mandy said. "Some of Mr. Jones's coworkers were concerned about him; that's why we're here. But I think we better call the police again."

The metro police sent out two squad cars. Charlie and Mandy stepped aside as they broke through the front door. As a courtesy to a fellow officer, the police allowed Mandy into the house and

117

she pulled Charlie in behind her. When they stepped into the living room, they saw a man lying face down on the floor with two bullet wounds in his back.

The postman, holding his cap to his nose, identified the man as Garry Jones and fled to the porch steps. He was still sitting there in the cold rain when the coroner arrived.

"I thought you said I wouldn't see you this week," Ernestine said, stepping aside for Charlie and Mandy to enter her apartment. "It's good to see you girls, but I'm getting dressed to go walking with my group."

"Where are you walking in this rain?" Mandy asked.

"Oh, we walk indoors when it's raining or too cold. In the malls, around the airport terminal, we even walked in the Greektown Casino one afternoon. Anyplace with wide corridors."

"The building's driver takes them in the van," Charlie explained to Mandy. "I think it's about a dozen people, right, Mom?"

"Sometimes we have as many as twenty. We had that many when we went to the casino, but some of the people were doing more gambling than walking."

Ernestine paused to look at Charlie. She always knew when something was on her daughter's mind, because Charlie would talk less and listen more. She'd also hold a fake smile.

"What's wrong?"

"Nothing really," Charlie said. "We had to go to a house near Six Mile, and we were heading back to Cobo, so we just thought we'd stop in and see how you were doing."

Ernestine headed for the couch and sat down. Charlie and Mandy followed, sitting in the comfortable easy chairs. The assisted-living building offered one- and two-bedroom apartments with formal dining rooms and eat-in kitchens. Her mother's sixth-floor apartment was bright and airy, and also had a small balcony that had a side view of West Grand Boulevard.

"I thought you were running short of time," Charlie said.

"It's okay. We have a few minutes. I was going to fix my hair, but I'll just wear a baseball cap," Ernestine said matter-of-factly. "Now, tell me what's going on. Did you two have a spat?"

"No, nothing like that. We went to this older man's house today, and we found him dead. His wife had died, and he lived alone, and . . ."

"How did he die?"

"Uh, well." Charlie squirmed. Sometimes she discussed her cases with her mother, giving her the executive summary version, always leaving out confidential details and certainly excluding the violence and danger involved.

Mandy found a way to describe the situation. "Well, let's just say it wasn't from natural causes."

"I don't know how you girls can handle your jobs. I just couldn't do it," Ernestine said. "This case you're on is dangerous, isn't it?"

"Yes. But you don't have to worry."

"Tell you what, if you don't worry about me, I won't worry so much about your work."

The phone rang, and Ernestine moved energetically to answer. "Okay, I'll be right there," she said into the receiver. "The van's here. You two can ride down with me."

Ernestine grabbed her keys and her baseball cap from a hook on the clothes tree. She stopped for a moment, then went into the kitchen and returned with a bottle of water.

"Gotta stay hydrated."

The partners were gathered at the conference table, along with Carter, Tyson, and Cynthia. Charlie knew morale was low, and it was important to guard against losing focus and making mistakes. They could use a breakthrough.

"What I'm passing out are copies of Mandy's notes taken at the Garry Jones crime scene. Police found a packed suitcase in his living room, a sizable amount of cash, and two tickets to the Dominican Republic. This evening, Ty and Elise Hillman searched Garry's office, but found nothing unusual. With the murder of Mr. Jones, my sense is we need to revisit all the food vendor applications. That should be our focus. What do others think?"

"Garry could sign off on any number of requisitions. I think the only thing to do is pull any records with his signature," Gil said.

"But how far back do we go? Three months? A year?" Carter asked.

As they bounced around ideas, theories and concerns, Charlie kept an eye on Tyson. Mandy's notes contained graphic details of the scene, the condition of Garry's body, and the conversation with the postman. Despite what's seen on TV, she knew the murder of a human being wasn't an easy thing to process, and the emotional reactions could range from anger to fear to severe depression.

"When was it the Cobo food vendor was offered a bribe for his permit?" Charlie asked. "Remember, Hartwell told us about it. Ty, do you know? Tyson?"

"What?" he jerked his head up to the eyes of those around the table. "I'm sorry. I didn't hear your question." He looked tired. His eyes were puffy, and his skin sallow.

"That was September," Gil said, looking at his laptop. "The guy was offered a hundred grand for his permit by a man who appeared to be Asian, or Asian-American. The food vendor took ten grand for his exhibitor packet, but later thought better of it and reported it to Cobo officials."

"Does Garry issue all the food permits?" Charlie asked Ty.

"Yes. He's a compliance officer, so he issues permits based on his review of a vendor's application form."

"Let's pull his records, starting from last September," Charlie said.

"I'll take care of it," Carter said.

"What else?" Charlie asked.

"Some of the staff in food services are really shook up," Tyson reported.

"I can only imagine," Cynthia said.

"Would it help if I came up and talked to the group?" Gil asked.

"I'm sure it would help a lot," Ty said, managing a half-smile.

"Okay, let's talk about the loading dock." Don introduced the next piece of business. "A few of us discussed this earlier. It's a real point of vulnerability, and I think we need to put a couple of our people down there."

"The problems at the loading dock probably won't be solved by adding people," Cynthia said. "But I've been thinking that maybe we can add more steps to the receipt and delivery process."

"What do you mean?" Don asked.

"Well, each delivery has a shipping order or purchase requisition, which must be submitted to the loading dock supervisor. The document must have the name of the employee, vendor, or exhibitor who has requisitioned the freight or goods, and a corresponding name of a Cobo manager. For instance, one of the auto exhibitors might have ordered a special item for their display. I don't know, it could be a . . ."

"A camel?" Don offered.

Don's comment caused a brief pause. Cynthia blinked, taking in the suggestion, and Judy rolled her eyes.

"Okay, let's go with a camel," Cynthia said. "That kind of delivery would have to be signed off on by the events executive. Every exhibitor has an account manager, and they all report to the head of events."

"Okay, and does that executive sign off on every delivery?" Charlie asked.

"Not usually. If it's something ordered by a Cobo employee, the loading dock supervisor or department supervisor could sign off. But we could add the requirement that if a delivery has been requisitioned by a vendor or exhibitor, the account manager must come down to the dock to examine the client's deliveries against the inventory sheet on the purchase order. You see what I mean?"

"Sure," Don said.

"How much time will that add to the delivery schedule?" Gil asked.

"God, it could be as much as a half hour. Most of these account

121

managers have never seen the loading dock. They wouldn't be able to check, say, every container, but maybe they could do a spot check. You know, the kind you'd do for quality control."

"That's a good idea," Charlie said.

"Don't you x-ray packages?" Don asked.

"We do, and that works great for our local delivery carriers, you know, FedEx, UPS," Cynthia said. "But that wouldn't work for the camel or any of the other unusual deliveries we get during the auto show."

"We'll get a lot of complaints," Ty spoke up.

His voice was so low everyone leaned toward him. There was none of the bravado and confidence he'd shown the first day they'd met him.

"Tyson's right. We'll get complaints all along the process chain," Cynthia said. "The loading dock supervisors and drivers won't be happy with the delays and backups; the account managers won't be happy that they will need to leave their desks and venture down to the bowels of Cobo to reconcile inventory; and the exhibitors, vendors, and department heads won't be thrilled that there is another bureaucratic hoop to jump through."

Ty nodded. "I'll need to give the GM a heads up on this one. That level of complaining comes directly to his office."

"How did the GM respond when he heard about Garry?" Charlie asked.

"He was shocked. Elise and I were the ones who told him, and she was crying. I know he called Mr. Hartwell after we left."

"It's a sad situation," Judy said to Ty.

"Mack, I want to get back to the loading dock situation. I still think it's a good idea to include Novak and Carter in the process," Don said.

"Oh, right, Don. Thanks for getting us back on task. Don and I talked about this earlier today. Carter, we think you'll be great at spotting a questionable manifest or purchase order. And as I understand it, you can use your laptop to do on-the-spot checks if you need to."

"That's right," Carter said.

"We'll want you to give extra scrutiny to any deliveries to the Chinese contingent. And Judy will be there to spoon out the 'be patient' stew."

Judy nodded. "I can do that."

"Okay. I'll let the dock supervisors know," Ty said.

"I've got one more thing," Cynthia said. "The police commander who came to Cobo after Josh Simms was killed stopped by to see me this evening. I dealt with him during the Chenglei investigation."

"Let me guess: He wants to know what the hell is going on. Garry makes three suspicious deaths associated with Cobo Center in two weeks. He'd be a fool not to be upset," Charlie said.

"Believe me, he's no fool."

"Did Hartwell call the police commissioner?" Gil asked.

"Yes. I know he's spoken to him," Cynthia said.

"Well, I know Hartwell is against it, but it's time for me to work the informal channels with the police," Don said.

"Okay, Don. Make your calls," Charlie said. "But that doesn't mean bring in reinforcements. We're still trying to keep this thing in-house and off the public radar. Let's get back to work."

Chapter 8

Thursday, January 5, 2006
Auto Show: 3 days

Lin Fong had overslept. Too much fried food and too many gaming hours. It was already eight o'clock and he had to be at Spectrum at nine. Ms. Mack's shower was large with a rainfall nozzle, and it felt good. He grabbed the container of shampoo and poured a glob on his head. It smelled girly, but made great suds. After towel-drying his hair, he spent some time working gel into it until it formed a small peak. He looked a long time in the mirror, and thought his hair looked better than usual. He pulled on khakis, a white T-shirt and a long-sleeved, plaid dress shirt. It was cold today and more rain was expected, so he settled for a gray hoodie and a jacket. He stuffed a PowerBook into his backpack and gave the apartment a last scan before exiting. He'd have to throw out the pizza box and carryout bag when he got back from work. He took the stairs down rather than wait for the elevator.

The guy at the front desk directed Lin to a cab stand a half block away. When the chill hit his still-wet hair, he pulled his hood up and picked up his pace. From across the street, a silver van made a U-turn, sped toward him, and screeched to a halt. Lin was about to give the driver a dirty look when the rear door shot open, and a big guy grabbed him and his backpack in one meaty fist and threw him into the backseat. Fong felt the pressure of an arm around his neck and he began to struggle. He thrashed and fought back and was able to kick out the window on the driver's side before lack of oxygen sent him into darkness.

Kwong arrived at the appointed address. He'd slipped quietly away from the hotel, evading his driver and asking the doorman to hail a taxi to pick him up at the side entrance. There was another call with the executives tonight, so his morning schedule was open, and it would be a few hours before anyone took note of his disappearance.

He was escorted to the third floor of the nondescript building, where he was met by a diplomatic attaché, Homeland Security Agent Tony Canterra, and two other DHS staff assembled around an imposing conference table. The agents wore dark suits and stern faces, and they opened portfolios and rustled the papers they contained.

Kwong had worn his navy suit and red tie. He was a student of history, and thought now about the many images, captured in old paintings, of defeated generals in formal dress offering their surrender. Kwong poured a glass of water with shaking hands.

"Mr. Kwong. We've looked at the photographs and other documents you've provided. Your evidence against Mr. Heinrich is very compelling," Canterra said.

"He is a depraved and dangerous man. I could not be a party to whatever he is plotting. I am . . . a patriot," Kwong paused, looking in the eyes of each person, "but I am also a family man. I want my sons to be able to live free of terror."

"We understand."

"Were you able to secure my wife and children?" Kwong asked.

"Yes, sir," Canterra answered. "Last night your family was driven to the U.S. Embassy in Beijing. Early this morning they were flown, unofficially, to the embassy in Seoul."

Kwong sat back in his chair with a sigh. Yesterday morning, Jiaying had called to say she'd had a visit from the state police, an anonymous tip they said, about negligence of her children. The uniformed men had interrogated her, searched their home, and frightened their sons. Kwong believed his bosses were sending a message.

"Thank you," Kwong said with sincerity. He didn't fully trust these Americans, but sometimes it was necessary to sleep with the enemy. He stared at his shaking hands on the table. Not since he had asked permission of his father-in-law to marry Jiaying had he felt so anxious.

"I wish to defect." Kwong spoke the words that would initiate a series of protocols within the State Department.

"You are aware, of course, Mr. Kwong, that your involvement in industrial espionage is a violation of the 1996 Economic Espionage Act," the State Department staffer stated.

Kwong nodded. He took another long sip of water. "Spying is one thing. Killing another."

"We quite agree," the attaché said. "That is why we're willing to entertain your request."

"But," Tony interrupted. "First, there's something more we need from you, Kwong."

"I'm sorry for the delay, sugar," Judy said to an impatient truck driver. "I know it's been a long wait but we've got to be extra careful this year, and it's either deal with me or with the Secret Service over there with their black suits and earpieces. I think I'm nicer, don't you?"

Judy's tap dance was effective. She and Carter had been at the loading dock since 7 a.m. implementing a strategy of "disarm, charm, scrutinize, and feed." While she asked questions about the driver's trip, family, and the predictions for next month's Super Bowl, Carter's fingers pranced over his keyboard to check the veracity of the driver's identification and paperwork. When Carter flagged something unusual, he slid a card marked "C" to Judy. "Okay, we're going to have you queue up at Ramp 4. There will be a little wait but we'll keep you posted. Meanwhile, grab yourself a doughnut and a cup of coffee over there before you move your truck."

Trucks lined up at ramps 1-3 were turned over to a shipping

staffer for business as usual. But the paperwork for vehicles at ramps 4-6 was handed to a loading dock supervisor who summoned an account manager. If the threat to the auto show involved smuggling contraband into Cobo, Judy and Carter were determined to be the front line of defense.

"Have you heard from Lin?" Cynthia stood in the doorway of the Mack suite, aiming her question at Charlie.

Charlie was manipulating Post-it notes at her desk, concentrating on the red notes—the questions. She had a column for the vulnerability in food services, one for the Chinese, and a long line of notes for Heinrich.

"Hi. Come on in."

"Lin hasn't reported to work. He was due at nine, but nobody's seen him, and he's not answering my calls or texts."

"We have a way to reach him. He has a proprietary phone with a tracking device. I'll call Judy."

"Hi, Charlie," Judy answered.

"Hi. Can you give me Lin Fong's location? He hasn't reported to work. Cynthia's looking for him."

"Okay. Hold on a sec. I'm looking at the app. That's strange," Judy said.

"What is?"

"The tracking device shows Lin is here at Cobo, or at least the Berry is," Judy said.

"Wait, I'm putting you on speaker; Cynthia's with me. Repeat what you said."

"My app shows Lin's unit is at Cobo. Did you check his desk?"

"I didn't open his drawer, or look under the desk, but I will," Cynthia said.

"Okay, Judy, thanks. I'll call you back."

Charlie picked up her Berry, and punched in a number. The other phone rang until the voice mail was triggered. "Lin, it's Ms. Mack. I need you to call me. It's very important." After disconnecting, Charlie glanced over her shoulder at Cynthia and for fifteen seconds touched her fingers to her face, imitating Mr.

Spock's mind meld. Charlie then shoved her notes to the side, stood, and paced to the conference room door, and back to her desk. Cynthia watched.

"What are you thinking, Charlie?"

"What if something's happened to him? I got him into this."

"Let's not jump to conclusions. I'll check his cubicle again and the studio control room. Maybe he left the BlackBerry behind after the teleconference, and he's just running late."

"No. I've talked to him since then. Remember? He called me about seeing Heinrich."

"You don't think it has anything to do with that?"

Charlie sat again. "Wait. Have you talked to Heinrich about Lin being late?"

"No. I can't reach him either."

Judy's phone rang. Another call from Charlie, and Judy had three drivers waiting impatiently for her to stamp their paperwork.

"Will you check Lin's location again?"

"Charlie, remember, he's just a kid. Maybe he overslept," Judy offered. "Maybe he went to visit a girlfriend last night and couldn't pull himself together. Maybe he went to his aunt's house."

"He would have called me," Charlie said emphatically.

"Okay, I'll look at the program again, but I'll need to get back to you."

Judy sorted the paperwork in front of her. Two deliveries were on hold; the other had been cleared by Carter. "Okay, you're good to go, young man," she said to a baby-faced driver as she stamped his shipping order. She smiled at the other two. "I'm sorry, but we're still waiting for a manager to come and sign off on your cargo. I promise it'll just be a few more minutes."

Judy turned away from the drivers, and typed into her laptop. When she didn't see what she expected, she called BlackBerry technical assistance. "I'm calling about our unit 3567. Is there any way to get more detail on location, like what floor? Or what quadrant of the building? Okay. Please call me with the information as soon as you have something."

※ ※ ※

Amy Wu arrived at the Guí Motors suite at noon. The exterior door was locked, which was not unusual, but the door to the inner office was ajar. She listened at the door for the murmur of Mr. Kwong's voice in a meeting or phone call. Sometimes Kwong slept at the office on the black leather couch at the rear of the room, but there were no signs of his occupancy. The suite was eerily quiet, and his office was immaculate as usual. He did not rely on Cobo janitors to clean his suite; instead, he used a company that had been recommended by the consulate. Amy had seen the cleaners only once when she'd returned to the office late to retrieve her gym bag. The three-man crew had worn white, starched coveralls and white coverings on their heads and shoes. They were carefully dusting Kwong's prized dragons and other office fixtures with long-handled feather dusters. They'd acknowledged her intrusion only with blinking eyes above their dust masks.

This morning, Kwong's desk was wax-polished to a hard shine. Amy checked the cabinet that held the expensive liquor. There were two full bottles of Dewar's, and a half-dozen bottles of other kinds of spirits. There was another teleconference with Beijing that evening, so she opened Mr. Kwong's presentation to begin the editing and formatting.

Lin regained consciousness in a semi-dark room with high ceilings and a cement floor. His hands were cuffed behind him to a metal chair, and his ankles affixed to the legs by plastic ties. He wore only his T-shirt and khakis, and no shoes. His head ached dully, and his tongue felt like sandpaper. The cold from the floor made his teeth chatter. In front of him was a pull-down aluminum door where a sliver of outside light streamed in from the bottom edge. A narrow metal door was on the wall to his left, and the right wall was lined with six-foot storage cabinets. He couldn't move the chair enough to see behind him without knocking it over. He listened intently and made out a distant whirring sound like that of machinery. He spotted the blinking red light of a camera in the rafters. "Hey. Let me out of here," he hollered. He waited, heart pounding through his chest, but there was no response. *That car with the two men. One guy grabbed me and forced me into the back seat. Too close to fight, but I gave him a head butt. Then he put me in a choke hold,* Lin remembered.

Lin considered overturning the chair. He wouldn't be able to brace himself, and it would hurt like hell, but he might be able to inch toward the door. He eyed the camera. Whoever was watching might get their jollies from letting him squirm to the door for twenty minutes before they intercepted him. The blinking light dared him to try. He was suddenly aware of something in his back pocket. *The BlackBerry. How could they have missed that?* The men had probably focused on his jacket, his backpack, and the cell phone on his belt and didn't notice the bulge in his back pocket. For once his skinny ass came in handy. For the next half hour, he tried subtle maneuvers to reach his phone. By lifting up on his toes, his fingertips brushed the tip of his pants pocket. He almost tipped over the chair when the instrument vibrated against the base of his spine. He looked up at the camera. Only Ms. Mack and her team had this number; it meant they were looking for him. Lin heard a door behind him open and close, and then the thud of hard soles on the cold floor. He tilted his chin against his chest so his eyes wouldn't give away the hope he felt. Legs in black jeans and boots stopped in front of his chair, and when Lin looked up, he saw the man who had been with Heinrich last night.

Heinrich watched the interrogation on the monitor. The contents of Lin Fong's flash drive were inconclusive, but his phone contacts clearly showed a connection to Charlene Mack. The logs indicated a half-dozen calls that began five days ago and ended when Fong was employed by Spectrum. Dudiyn was being tough on the kid because the head butt had broken his nose. After two hard slaps, the boy was crying and admitted he was staying at Mack's condo. Dudiyn hit the boy again.

"That's enough," Heinrich said through the console.

Dudiyn sneered at Lin Fong. He was only a few years older than this soft boy, but he had grown up in Chechnya's impoverished countryside where crying was a sign of weakness met with harsh beatings. Some people mistook him for a skinhead, but his real allegiance was to a fat paycheck. He lifted his boot and kicked over Lin's chair, leaving the boy stunned and shivering on the cold concrete.

"You didn't have to do that," Heinrich said. "I told you just to scare the boy."

"He *is* scared."

Dudiyn was a man for hire, who got jobs based on word of mouth. He was considered efficient and methodical in carrying out orders. He had worked with a variety of criminal types throughout Europe: small-time crooks and syndicate bosses, even paramilitary groups in Syria. Heinrich studied him a moment.

"How's the work going at the warehouse?"

"Those Chinks are working around the clock with their faces pressed against their computer screens. They don't talk or eat; I haven't even seen one of them take a pee break."

"It'll only be a few more days," Heinrich said. "The new components will be in tonight. Once we've done our work, the Chinese will have to fend for themselves."

"What about that Kwong guy?"

"I'll worry about him. Blindfold the boy and take him to the warehouse. Make sure the others see you bring him in. It'll make a good impression." Heinrich's tone was icy.

Lin sucked on his upper lip; it was swollen but no longer bleeding. He was afraid and ashamed. The bald man's blows hurt like nothing he'd ever felt before, but his tears were more from fear than pain.

Dudiyn cut the ties on Lin's ankles and then unlocked the handcuffs, leaving one dangling from his left hand. He yanked Lin from the floor and pressed his fist into the small of his back, shoving him through the narrow side door to a graveled lot where Lin saw the van used to kidnap him.

131

"Get moving."

It was raining hard, and when they reached the van, the man Lin had decided to call Baldy pushed him aside roughly and moved close to the rear of the vehicle to manipulate the combination lock. Lin swiftly stuck a hand into his back pocket and out again. The man snatched open the van door.

"Get in and turn around," he ordered.

Lin lifted himself into the van and swiveled to face forward.

"Put your hands behind your back," Baldy said in an accent Lin didn't recognize. He clicked the handcuffs closed, and covered Lin's head with a pillowcase. "Lay on your side, and put your knees together."

Lin braced himself with his elbow as he lowered himself to the van floor. Then new plastic restraints were tightened around his ankles until he was trussed like a steer in a rodeo. As the van moved, Lin felt the gravel surface turn into a solid roadway. He was wet and freezing cold, and his ankles and shoulders hurt with every hole the tires found. In no more than ten minutes, the surface under the van returned to gravel and stopped. When the double doors opened, he was dragged out by his ankles. He couldn't keep his balance, and landed face first on the crumpled rock. The binding was removed from his ankles and he was jerked to his feet, and the pillowcase snatched from his head. Lin looked into the sinister eyes of his captor.

"Did you hurt yourself, crybaby?" Baldy said before undoing the handcuffs and retying Lin's hands in front with a plastic band.

A warehouse was in front of him, and Lin had only a second to glance at his surroundings before he was pushed from behind. "Get going."

Inside a massive room, at a span of work stations, three dozen Chinese men and a few women worked furiously at keyboards. Natural light poured through high windows, and Baldy pushed Lin, dripping water, along a carpeted aisle next to the desks. If Lin hadn't known better, he'd have said the fifteen-minute van ride had taken him across the Pacific to mainland China.

A few of the workers glanced up at him, and Lin's eyes pleaded for help, but they quickly looked away. "Help me," Lin said first in Cantonese, then Mandarin.

"Shut up," Baldy said, pulling his arm. "Just keep walking."

They reached a door on the right wall of the warehouse, and Lin was shoved through. They passed through a dim anteroom to a larger room awash in fluorescent lights, which held a long, heavy table with a half-dozen chrome chairs around it. Boxes and palettes were stacked everywhere, and along the far side of the wall was an old-fashioned drinking fountain. Lin touched his tongue to his lower lip.

"Can I have a drink of water?"

"Sit down." Baldy pointed to one of the chairs.

"Where am I? What do you want with me?"

The man rubbed at his nose, which had a wide bandage across it, and stared at Lin. "Don't be stupid. You want me to smack you again?"

Lin sank into the nearest chair. His left ear, nose, and mouth hurt where he had taken blows. He was tired, his throat was parched, and he was cold. The room's heat began to warm his feet and legs, and he longed to rest his head on the table, but he didn't dare sleep.

Baldy sat at the end of the table looking at his phone. He wore all black, as he had when he and Heinrich walked into Grant's Lounge the day before. He used a sausage-like index finger to punch a number into his phone, pushed his chair back from the table in a noisy display, glared at Lin, and rose, striding to the open door to the anteroom. Lin couldn't make out his conversation, but was glad for the chance to be away from the man's attention for a moment. The fingertips of Lin's bound hands grazed the BlackBerry. He prayed that Ms. Mack would find the clue he'd left behind.

Charlie, Don, Gil, and Tyson had convened for the noon meeting. In just a few days, six thousand journalists from around the world would descend on Cobo, taking pictures of the best design, technology, and innovation of the world's automakers. Meanwhile, their problems were piling up. A secret service advance team was on-site; the Metropolitan police were insisting on an increased role in the investigation of Josh Simms' murder; and now Lin Fong was missing.

"This is a no-brainer for me," Charlie said. "My priority has to be to find Lin."

"DADA won't see it that way," Gil said.

"I don't care about that. I think Lin's in trouble, and I think it has something to do with him seeing Heinrich yesterday."

"Heinrich wouldn't actually harm Lin," Gil said. "He doesn't strike me as the type."

"Yeah, but what about his henchman, this Dudiyn guy?" Don said. "Didn't Lin say he looked like a tough guy?"

"Yeah. Dressed all in black, boots. No coat. A knit cap over a bald head."

"I know who you're talking about. I've only seen him a couple of times. Muscular guy, cold eyes. He tries to give the stare-down," Ty said. "I'd say he's a guy who could hurt someone."

"If they've touched Lin, I'll hurt *them*," Charlie announced.

Ty's eyes grew wide. He heard the resolve in Charlie's voice and saw the look on her face. He turned toward Don and Gil for a determination on her ability to carry out the threat.

"Charlie's a fourth-degree black belt," Gil responded.

Ty's eyes grew wider, then squinted as he gave Charlie another appraisal. Finally, he smiled his admiration, which Charlie responded to with a grim face.

"So, what do we do about finding him, Mack?" Don asked.

"I'm going back to my apartment and start there. Maybe somebody saw something. Judy is still working with the Black-Berry techs to get a fix on Lin's phone. For a variety of reasons, a phone can be shielded from satellite detection, and it will ping to a recent location." Charlie stood. "I'm going to get started. I'll call you in about an hour."

ං ං ං

"You really think Heinrich might have taken this Lin Fong kid?" Ty asked Gil and Don. "I don't understand. Why would he do that?"

"We haven't been able to share everything with you, Ty. But, we put Lin in Heinrich's office to keep an eye on things for us inside Spectrum," Gil said.

Ty looked at the two men for a few seconds, and then nodded. "I get it. It makes sense to have someone like him embedded in Spectrum since Heinrich is tied to the hip with the Chinese delegation."

"I told you he was a smart cookie," Don said to Gil.

"Does Cynthia know?"

"It's a long story, but yes, she knows now," Gil said.

"Okay. Well, if you're sure he's not just AWOL, I know one place Heinrich might keep the Chinese kid."

"What do you have in mind, Pressley?" Don asked.

"Spectrum has a storage space not more than five minutes away. Heinrich had it built."

"What do you mean? Why didn't you show it to us before? What's in there?" Don barraged Ty with questions.

"It's an out of the way place, and I don't know for sure what's in there. None of us has access. It has a retina-scanning system for entry. I always imagined Heinrich had a tank or something in there."

"We better take a look," Don said, leading the way out of the conference room.

They traveled by golf cart to the loading dock area, and then down a ramp to the access road. Don and Ty snapped down the plastic rain guards, and at the end of the road they continued along an unmarked street going west.

"So Ms. Mack really has a black belt?" Ty asked.

"She does," Gil said. "I was there when she took the test."

"I saw her break a man's leg once," Don said with no attempt to hide his pride. "She had knocked him down, and when he got up he picked up a pipe and came at her. Before I could get to her, she had already taken the pipe from him. I had to pull her off the guy." Don smiled at the memory.

"Wow. She doesn't look the type."

"You really don't want to make her mad," Gil said matter-of-factly.

"Charlene Mack," Charlie answered, using her car's hands-free system.

"Hi. It's Cynthia. Where are you?"

"On the road. I want to backtrack Lin's movements from this morning."

"Heinrich is definitely involved in his kidnapping."

"Kidnapping?"

"Or abduction. Whatever's the right term. Look, I've been video recording Heinrich's office. I probably should have mentioned that to you."

"Yeah, you probably should have."

"I had a small camera and microphone placed in his office. It records nonstop. I usually check the footage at night, but I looked at it just now, and he was in this morning. Early. He was using his private cell phone and told whoever was on the other end to put the kid in storage and he would meet him there."

"Where's Heinrich now?"

"I don't know. He's not here."

"Don just called, and said Spectrum has some sort of off-site storage area. Could he have taken him there?"

"That's our weapons vault, a garage really, near one of the overflow parking structures. Assault-type weapons are stored there, along with ammunition and bulletproof vests—to be used in the case of a riot situation at Cobo. You want me to check it out?"

"Ty is taking Don and Gil there now. Is there a way to get in?"

"I've been working on that for a while. It has one of those retina scan units, and I'm not allowed access. If push comes to shove, you could just cut the power and ram through the door. There are security cameras that Heinrich monitors from his phone, so if Tyson takes your partners there, he'll spot them."

"Got it. I'll warn Don. Is there any other place Heinrich might take Lin?"

"Maybe his house; it's in the New Center area."

"Right. Mandy told me about that house."

Another dark feeling came over Charlie. She put both hands on the wheel and took a deep breath.

"Charlie, are you still there?"

"I was thinking about killing Heinrich."

"Hmm."

"You warned me, Cynthia. You said Lin could find himself in danger . . ."

"You can't blame yourself . . ."

"Oh, but I do."

Charlie pulled the Corvette up to the garage entry in her condo building, pushed the opener mounted on her windshield, and watched the door slowly glide upward. She drove one level up to her reserved parking space and took the stairs. Lin had left food boxes on the coffee table, and her expensive shampoo was overturned and oozing onto the shower floor. But everything else seemed normal.

She rode the elevator to the lobby, but the front desk guard was away. She sat on one of the gray leather couches and stared at the wall of large black and white photographs of the world's iconic landmarks. Clearly, the building's interior designers thought the Golden Gate Bridge, Big Ben, the Eiffel Tower, the Empire State Building, and an aerial view of Detroit's riverfront area flanked by the Renaissance Center and Cobo invoked sophistication, prestige, and power. Charlie was impatient and stood hovering over the security desk. A small radio behind the counter was turned on low volume. The meteorologist from WWJ, the all-news station, was giving the weather report. Today's temperatures would reach the upper thirties and, like yesterday, it would rain much of the day. Tonight and tomorrow would be colder with snow.

Charlie leaned over the counter to look at the five monitors.

One showed the parking garage entry she'd just passed through; another, the small shipping dock in the rear of the building. There was a full view of the rooftop; another camera rotated between the building's eight hallways; and the final monitor showed the front sidewalk of the building, including the doors leading into Grant's lounge.

"Hi, Ms. Mack. Can I help you?" The guard had come through the lobby door of the lounge with a brown paper bag in his hand.

Patrick Dresher was a middle-aged white man working a second-career job after being laid off fifteen years ago from his assembly-line job at Ford Motor Company. He wore the blue blazer, white shirt and black tie that, like the wall posters, announced the affluence of the building.

"Hi, Mr. Dresher. Were you on the desk this morning?"

"I sure was," he said, settling into his desk chair and looking up at Charlie with a pleasant smile. "I started duty at 7 a.m."

"Did you happen to see a houseguest of mine this morning? A tall, skinny kid. Asian-American?"

"Sure. I saw him. He left about eight-forty-five, eight-fifty. He was looking for a cab and I pointed him in the direction of the cab stand."

"Did you see him after that?"

"No."

"Maybe on one of the security cameras?"

"No. I just watched him leave and head down the street."

"Do you keep the footage from your cameras?"

"We recycle it every thirty days. You want to look at this morning's video?"

"I sure do. Do I need permission from somebody?"

"In this case, only me. Let me call the building engineer. He stores the tapes in his office downstairs."

Twenty minutes later, Charlie was peering over the shoulder of the building's maintenance supervisor at time-stamped surveillance footage from the front entrance. At 8:47, Lin Fong stepped outside of the condo building, covered his head with his hoodie, and adjusted his jacket collar. He wore khakis and had on a back-

138

pack. He leaned into the wind as he strode down the street and out of range of the camera.

"Was that him?" the engineer asked.

"Yes. Do you have a camera that shows the street corner?"

"The camera mounted in front of the parking garage does a one-eighty scan. Maybe we'll be lucky."

They were lucky. Although from a bit of a distance, the camera clearly showed the hooded Lin at the corner as a light-colored van stoped abruptly in front of him. Then a bearded man in dark clothes leaned out the side door, yanked Lin into the back, and the van sped off.

"Damn," the engineer said with an open mouth. "Should we call the police?"

"I'll call them," Charlie lied. "Can I see that one more time?"

Don steered the golf cart down a one-way paved road. After days of rain, the snow had been pummeled into grotesque black knolls resembling a terrain you might see in a Harry Potter movie. The rain was coming down hard, but the plastic curtains on the front and sides of the cart protected its passengers from the blowing volley. Following Ty's directions, Don ended up on West Jefferson.

"When did Heinrich have this storage area built?" Gil asked.

"It must have been within a few months of Spectrum getting the security contract. I remember there were arguments about the cost, and people wanted to know if Cobo staff would have to maintain or service the site. But Heinrich said his people would do all the service work, and DADA approved the budget and paid to have the garage built, so once that was settled nobody thought much more of it. I only know as much as I do about the place because Spectrum paid to lay in underground wiring, and I know all the major electrical contractors in town through my dad," Ty explained.

"Who at Cobo sees Spectrum's expenses?" Gil asked.

"As far as I know, Cobo only bills Spectrum for utilities and the costs associated with cleaning their office space. Our regular janitorial staff does their cleaning. Everything else is paid for by DADA."

The golf cart handled the wet road surface well. They were running parallel to Fort Street and passed the main post office, and then the distribution center for the Salvation Army. "I bet they don't get many tourists back here," Don said. When West Jefferson turned into Rosa Parks Boulevard, Ty led them south along a chain-link fence separating a parcel of undeveloped land from a set of railroad tracks and the Detroit River. The Ambassador Bridge stretched out ahead of them. "It's just ahead, over there." Ty pointed to a gravel access lane. The bunker-like building had a single, galvanized steel door. The 30-by-30-foot structure was concrete with no windows and a flat roof, trimmed in razor wire. Globed cameras were mounted on each corner. Don pointed out another camera mounted on a pole inside the fence line of the train track. The knob-less door operated with an ocular-scan entry system. The reader was enclosed in a plastic cover that opened with a key.

"Hmm. Doesn't look easy to break into," Don said after walking the perimeter of the structure.

"I suppose you could climb to the roof, go over the wire, and cut through," Gil said. "But I bet there are pressure sensors up there that set off some kind of alarm."

"I wouldn't take that bet," Don said.

"Look at this," Tyson called out. He was holding up something he'd found near the front tire of the golf cart.

"What is it?" Don asked, looking quizzically at the black wire dangling from Ty's hand.

"It's part of a phone headset," Gil said. "Is it for a Berry?"

"Yep," Ty said, slipping the tip of the broken earpiece into his own BlackBerry.

"It looks like Lin has left us a bread crumb," Gil said.

While Tyson and Gil stooped to look for the other end of the headset, a stony-faced Don walked again to the rear of the building. Four shots, first two and then quickly another two, startled Gil and Tyson. Gil drew his gun and ran fast toward the building. He stopped short when Don came into view.

"It's all right, Acosta," Don shouted before firing four more shots, two into each of the cameras mounted on the front of the building. "I'm just scattering some bread crumbs of my own."

"Glad you phoned," Don said. "We're at Heinrich's weapons garage. Fong was definitely here, but he's not here now."

"How do you know he was there?" Charlie asked excitedly.

"He left a piece of his phone headset for us to find."

"Smart boy."

"Gil used a favor with a judge friend to get a search warrant, and we broke through the door. We found weapons and ammunition, boxes of disposable cell phones, lithium batteries, and a shitload of bleach."

"Bleach?" Charlie asked.

"Yep. Where are you?"

"I'm leaving my condo. I just saw a video of Lin being snatched into a white van. Any sign of a van?"

"No."

"Okay. I'm on my way back, and I'm calling Cynthia to meet us there."

"She's already here, Mandy is too, and also Spectrum security folks."

"And that means Heinrich knows the place has been compromised," Charlie said. "I'll see you in ten minutes."

"There's been a breach of the weapons vault, and I can't get a visual," Heinrich said into the mouthpiece.

"I know," Cynthia responded. "I'm here now. I've been trying to call you."

"What happened?"

"The police forced the door; they had a court order."

"A court order? For what?"

"A search. The Mack team thought Lin Fong might be in the garage."

"Fong? Why are they interested in him?" Heinrich fished, testing Cynthia's loyalty.

141

"It turns out he was spying on us for Charlene Mack. And he's missing."

There was a momentary pause while Heinrich sorted a couple of thoughts.

"Why aren't the cameras working at the vault?"

"They were shot out," Cynthia hesitated. "By one of the Mack people."

"Which one?"

"Don Rutkowski."

"Ah. Ms. Mack and her people are becoming quite the nuisance. Where are they now?"

"Back at Cobo, I suppose," Cynthia lied. "Are you coming to the office?"

"I may be in late this evening. If not, first thing in the morning. Keep me posted on the situation with the weapons vault, and get someone out right away to repair the cameras and any other damage."

"Okay, but what about Fong?"

"What about him?"

"Charlie, uh, Ms. Mack thinks maybe he's been the victim of foul play."

"And what do you want me to do about that?" Heinrich dripped disdain.

"Well, he works for us, so I thought you'd want to know."

"Actually, he works for the Mack people. If he shows up, fire him."

Charlie watched Cynthia put her phone in the pocket of her coat and shove her hand in after. Then she lifted the other hand to the back of her neck. Charlie walked over to her.

"Does Heinrich suspect we're on to him?"

"I don't think so. I did what you said and told him Lin worked for you."

"Did he seem surprised?"

"No, annoyed. He said if I see Lin, I should fire him. Maybe he has nothing to do with the boy's abduction after all."

"No. You were right the first time. He has everything to do with grabbing Lin. That's why we need to check his house."

142

"Get over to the weapons storage. Someone has broken into the place. Pack up the phones and the other materials we need," Heinrich said. "And bring them to my place."

"How could anyone break in?" Dudiyn asked.

"That doesn't matter now. We only need two more days to keep things from unraveling. Go get the stuff and bring it to the house."

Dudiyn considered Heinrich the strangest man he'd ever worked for—hard to get to know, and even harder to like. He was ruthless, but with refined tastes. There were also rumors he was some kind of sex freak.

"What about the Chinese kid? Should I take care of him?"

"Let me worry about him. He's not going anywhere. Go. We need those supplies."

Heinrich grabbed his workout bag and his keys from the kitchen counter. At this time of day, the gym would be busy, but he needed to release the tension building in his core, and he didn't have time for his usual pleasures. On an impulse, he picked up his phone.

"I'm headed to the gym, and I thought you might want to join me for a workout."

"Uhhm. I'm not sure I have time. We have a crisis . . ."

"Yes, I've heard. I don't know about you, but a good workout usually helps to clear my head. I get some of my best ideas doing a weight routine, and it helps to have a good spotter."

While Heinrich talked, Mandy waved Charlie and Cynthia over and mouthed, "Heinrich. He wants me to meet him at his gym." After whispering to Cynthia, Charlie nodded a "yes" and gestured a thumbs-up.

"I guess a good sweat couldn't hurt. Okay, I'll meet you, but I have to retrieve my bag. Where's the gym?"

"So, what's the plan?" Mandy asked, after disconnecting.

"If you're with Heinrich at the gym, it gives us a chance to check his house. Try to keep him busy for at least an hour," Charlie said.

Charlie also wanted to tell Mandy to be careful, not to go too far with this unpredictable man in the name of duty. But Mandy read her thoughts.

"No worries, Sherlock. I'll keep everything on the queer and narrow."

Cynthia stared at the two of them, making no attempt to hide her curiosity about their locked eyes and veiled conversation. Charlie turned to Cynthia.

"Can you come with us?"

"What? Oh, to Heinrich's place. Uh, no. I have things to do here."

Charlie consulted quickly with the assembled team, and they went off in three directions: Gil and Tyson back to Cobo, Mandy to meet Heinrich, and Charlie and Don to Heinrich's New Center area townhouse.

At four o'clock, Amy called Kwong's personal cell again, and left her third voice message. Kwong was a methodical man. He would never be late for a call with his bosses, and he would never ignore calls. She returned to the inner office and flipped through the Rolodex on his desk looking for the emergency number she knew was there. She hesitated only a moment to organize her thoughts and determine what she would say before picking up the phone. A male voice answered in Chinese. "*Wéi*."

"Uh, hello. This is Amy Wu. I'm calling from Mr. Kwong's office in Detroit."

"Why are you calling, Ms. Wu?" The answerer quickly slipped into perfect English.

"Well, Mr. Kwong hasn't come into the office today, and he's not returning my phone calls. So I didn't know what I should do. We have a teleconference with the directors tonight."

"You did the right thing to call, Ms. Wu. I'm transferring you. Hold on."

Dudiyn rushed back into the room and glared down the table at Lin. He cut the plastic tie on his hands and handcuffed Lin's right wrist to the back of the chair.

"Stay put and be quiet, or I'll kill you," he said with feeling.

Dudiyn searched his pockets for his keys, and hurried through the anteroom to the outer door. He looked back, stepped through the door and doused the fluorescent lights in both rooms. Lin was shrouded in total darkness and shaking with fear. He waited only a minute, to make sure the man wasn't returning, before standing. He began dragging his chair in the direction of the door before he banged into another chair, knocking it over and falling on top of it. He was frantically untangling from the chair legs when he rubbed against the BlackBerry in his back pocket. He sat upright and with his free hand retrieved the phone, but immediately dropped it. He heard it skid. He groped at the floor, the chair scraping along beside him, but he couldn't find the phone. His heart raced. *Why hasn't the phone rung? Maybe they aren't even looking for me. Maybe I turned off the Berry when I was sitting on it. I need to find it.* He flopped around a bit more in the dark, scooting on his butt, the chair scraping along the floor with his movements, his head occasionally hitting something—the table leg or another chair or a box. Frustrated and hurting, he held his head. It had been at least an hour since he last cried. Now seemed like a good time.

Don passed the two-story houses, driving slowly. The complex had done a pretty good job of snow removal, and the streets were ashy with salt. "I think it's the corner house," Charlie said, looking back. "It's hard to see the house numbers."

"I'll turn around."

"Wait, that's the one. The number is on the garage. Do you see any way to get to the backyard?"

"No, but maybe there's some kind of alley access."

Don turned the corner to circle the block. This was a housing development that mixed new homes with existing stock. In the section where Heinrich lived, the houses had attached garages.

"No car in the driveway, and I don't see any lights," Charlie reported. "Let's go up the street, park, and walk back."

They parked a couple blocks from Woodward Avenue and approached the house on foot. It was a quarter after four and freezing. Charlie tightened the scarf around her neck and was glad for her boots. Don wore his old trench coat, with no hat, scarf, or gloves. His only concession to it was winter was wearing corduroy pants instead of khakis.

"Aren't you cold?"

"Nope."

The temperature had dipped to near freezing, and the wind was gusting. There were no other pedestrians, but a dog taking care of his business in his fenced yard spotted them and couldn't wait to finish before charging the fence, barking ferociously. Charlie saw the dog's owner peek through the curtains to see the source of her pet's agitation.

"I wish we had a dog to walk; it would help us blend in better."

"If I'd known, I could've brought Mitch in on the case."

Mitch was a fifty-five-pound boxer. Don and his wife had purchased him as a companion for their eight-year-old, special-needs son, Rudy. The dog had Don's body, Rita's soulful eyes, and Rudy's temperament.

Charlie laughed. "It would be good to have Mitch around now. Some dog ears to rub would be good for the mood in the office. Don, what if Lin is dead?"

Charlie had finally put into words her worst fears. She'd had no right to bring Lin into a dangerous situation. She had underestimated the stakes in this case. Heinrich, Dudiyn, and whoever else was involved didn't care about human life.

"They've got no reason to kill the boy."

"Maybe not before, but they do now. He's seen his abductors and maybe he's even seen what they're up to."

"We have to stay optimistic. Lin may have been at the storage garage, but we didn't see any signs of foul play. Heinrich doesn't like us, and we don't like him. He knows that. It wouldn't surprise him that we put Lin Fong in place as a mole. He's got Cynthia watching us."

"If he's hurt that boy . . ."

"I believe you, Mack. But, let's stay positive."

They reached the corner across from Heinrich's house, and slowed their pace. Charlie pulled out her phone and pretended to make a call so they could stand still for a minute while Don scanned the house.

"I don't see any movement. There's a window on the side of the garage, and the newspaper's still on the front porch."

Charlie put the phone away, and they walked along the side of the house to see if they could get a look at the rear. The fenced yard abutted the backyard of the house on the next block. When they got to the corner, they turned and walked back. At the garage, they paused.

"If you're looking for the guy with the Saab, he's not home."

Don and Charlie had not seen the woman get out of her car in the driveway behind them. She was carrying a small grocery bag in one hand and keys in the other. She hastily zipped up her parka to her chin and reached into the jacket to pull out gloves. She crossed the street to join them.

"He left about twenty minutes ago. I passed him on my way to the drugstore."

"Oh." Don said.

The woman glanced curiously at Charlie, but gave her attention to Don.

"There were two Chinese men here this morning looking for him, too. Or maybe they were looking for the other guy. The one with the van. What's going on?"

"There's not much going on," Charlie said. "It's funny you should mention the Chinese guys. We're here to meet a friend of ours, a young Chinese kid. Did you happen to see him?"

The lady shifted her position to square up between the two, assessing them both before answering Charlie's question.

"No. The guys I saw were older. There was no kid. But they were looking in the garage window, just like you were doing." Her eyes glided toward Don.

"Wow, you don't miss much," Charlie said, holding out her hand. "I'm Charlene Mack, and this is Don Rutkowski."

147

"Kathy Talbot," the woman said, shaking hands. "That's my house over there." She pointed behind her. "Say, you two are police, right?"

"Something like that," Don said.

"Private investigators," Charlie corrected, showing the woman her P.I. license.

"I thought so," the woman said, staring at Charlie's ID.

"Look, it's freezing out here. Why don't you come in for a cup of coffee? I need to take my medicine," Talbot said, holding up her bag.

Talbot's house was neat. OCD neat. She went to the kitchen to put on a pot of coffee and waved Don and Charlie to her living room. Within five minutes, Charlie's eyes began to water, and she sneezed. When Talbot came through the kitchen door holding a tray with three mugs of coffee, the source of Charlie's allergies followed with tail bobbing in the air. The cat immediately jumped on the couch next to Charlie.

"You don't like cats?" Talbot asked.

"I'm allergic to their dander."

"You know, they say that can be psychosomatic."

"Or, maybe just psycho," Don quipped, followed by, "This is good coffee."

"I'm glad you like it. I put a bit of cinnamon in it."

Don lowered the cup, looking into it as if Talbot had said strychnine instead of cinnamon. Charlie took a sip of coffee and watched the cat climb over her leg and jump to the floor.

"When did the two men move in across the street?" Charlie asked, clearing her throat.

"The older guy, the good-looking one, moved in about a year ago. I've only seen the other one for a month, maybe two. There's something fishy about the two of them. At first, I thought they were gay. Don't get me wrong, I got nothing against gay people. But, you know, you hear about the parties and stuff. So, anyway, the older man, the good-looking one, isn't gay because he has women over to the house all the time. The other one—the big guy—works in the garage a lot, late at night. He has a van with those loud mufflers. I hear him coming and going at all hours. I bought my house seven years ago, but these guys are renters, and sometimes renters don't care about the homeowner's association rules."

"What rules have they broken?" Charlie asked.

"Well, for one thing, people are always watching the house and loitering."

"Somebody other than the Chinese men and us?" Charlie asked.

"Well, sometimes, there's a car that sits right over there." The woman pointed at a space diagonal to Heinrich's house. "They use binoculars to look at the house."

"Binoculars," Don said. "Are you sure?"

"I'm sure. I have a pair myself."

When Don and Charlie left a half hour later, there was still no sign of occupancy at the house. Just for good measure, Charlie jumped over the back fence and knocked at the back door. She wasn't sure what lie she'd tell if Heinrich opened the door, but she wanted to rule out his house as the place where Lin might be. She peered into the kitchen window. There was a light on over the sink and nothing looked out of place. She knocked again and listened, then hopped back over the fence.

"Mandy just called," Don said. "Heinrich is on his way home."

"Okay, let's get back to the car."

"Where are we going?"

"Over there," Charlie said, pointing across the road to the nosy neighbor's house.

It was almost dusk. The headlights of a speeding vehicle swung across the gravel path, throwing rocks from the rear wheels. The white van stopped abruptly in front of the garage, and the two Spectrum guards, with guns drawn, aimed at the driver as he stepped out of the vehicle. Cynthia recognized Dudiyn and gave an all-clear sign. She intercepted him in mid-stride.

"You almost got yourself killed."

"What the hell happened here?" he demanded.

"I already told Mr. Heinrich what happened. The police broke down the door. They had a search warrant."

Cynthia was in mid-sentence when Dudiyn stepped around her and headed to the garage. He stopped to look at the scanning box, which hung from loose wires. In the light over the door, Cynthia saw the look of contempt he shot at her before entering the garage. From the doorway, she watched Dudiyn examine a few of the disposable phones. He knotted the bag, stepped over to the cases marked bleach, and began counting them. Cynthia stepped into the garage, and he turned.

"I'll need someone to help me load these boxes into the van," Dudiyn said.

"Okay. What's all the bleach for?"

Dudiyn stared at Cynthia for a few seconds. Then lifted the bag of phones over his shoulder, like Santa's sack of toys.

"You'll have to ask Mr. Heinrich. If he hasn't told you, it's not for me to say. I'll pull the van closer so we can start loading the boxes," he said, brushing past her.

Cynthia watched from the rear of the vehicle as Dudiyn and the guards loaded seventeen cases, each with eight plastic bottles of bleach, into the bed of the van. Dudiyn paced from the garage door to the van and back, and counted the remaining cases a couple of times. When he wasn't looking, Cynthia shined her flashlight inside. Along with the bleach and the phones there was a clear bag containing plastic ties. When the cargo was loaded, Dudiyn locked the van, fumbling with the keypad.

"Our guys will have the cameras repaired before I leave tonight. We'll also put in a keyed door. Will you take care of the repairs to the ocular scanning system?" Cynthia asked.

"What?" Dudiyn was preoccupied.

"The security system. Will you arrange to have it replaced, or should I?"

"Oh. I'll speak to Mr. Heinrich about that. We'll take care of it."

Without another word, Dudiyn was behind the wheel of the van and drove off. The Spectrum staff returned to supervising the camera repairs, and Cynthia sniffed her fingers. Surprised, she used the flashlight to look at her hand. She had punctured one of the bleach bottles with an ink pen and smeared a bit of the contents on her hand. Instead of the scent she'd expected, her fingers were coated with shiny, odorless granules.

Lin began a slow ascent from a restless sleep. It was so dark he wasn't sure he was really awake until he moved his arm and the chair resisted. He might have been asleep a few minutes or a few hours, but the stiffness of his body where it touched the cold floor suggested hours. He was disoriented, no longer even certain of the direction of the door, until he heard the hum of the water dispenser. He pulled himself to a sitting position and turned toward the sound. Scooting on his butt and dragging the chair along, he bumped into cardboard boxes and wood pallets until he finally reached the wall and pulled himself up to lean against it. He took a deep breath; his face hurt, and his tongue was heavy and dry. He extended his free arm, searching, until his hand touched the metal water fountain. He slurped water for a very long time, then let the water drip onto his chin without catching it and put a palmful on the back of his neck. He reached, again, for the wall and nuzzled against it like a lover. The coolness against his cheek turned the sharp ache into a dull one. Finally, he righted the chair on the floor and sat in it with his back against the wall. He could use the wall to work his way to the outer door, which he now knew was to his right. But, even when he got to the door and even if he managed to get it open, he wouldn't know what lay on the other side.

The BlackBerry was his best chance for survival. It was somewhere on the floor in front of him. He would be systematic about it, scooting on his butt toward the middle of the room, keeping the chair directly behind him and using his free hand and legs like antennae to keep from bumping into anything. Then he'd shift over a yard or so and reverse his course.

His system worked, but it took what felt like almost an hour to find the phone. When he did, he cradled it like a baby. He used his thumb to touch the keyboard, and the backlight sprang to life. He carefully punched in the seven numbers he'd memorized.

"My God, Lin. Where are you?" Charlie shouted into the phone's speaker.

"Ms. Mack . . ." Lin gasped.

"Are you alright? Where are you?"

"I'm not sure. In a warehouse where there are a bunch of Chinese workers. They had me in another place at first, and . . ."

"Are you all right?"

"I'm bleeding some. It's the guy I saw with Mr. Heinrich in your apartment building. The bald one with the beard. He beat me."

"Oh, Lin. I'm so sorry. I never meant for you to get hurt."

Lin let out a sob, then gathered himself. "I'm okay."

"We're coming to get you. Right now. But you've got to help us find you. What kind of a room are you in? Are there any windows? Did you see any kind of landmark outside?"

"Uh, no. There are no windows, and it's too dark to see anything. But this place isn't far from where they had me at first, and when we got out of the van we were almost directly under a freeway."

"Okay, Lin, that's a good start. Can you hear any kind of noise from outside?"

"No."

"Okay. Hold on. We're coming."

Charlie and Don were sitting in the neighbor's living room across the street from Heinrich's house. He'd arrived a half hour ago, entered through the garage, and left the door open. Forty minutes later a white van pulled into the garage and the door was closed.

Don and Charlie waved their goodbyes to the neighbor and bolted through a rear door to the car. Don turned it around to head east toward John R, where he careened south to the Fisher Freeway service drive. Charlie held onto the Buick's door handle.

"He said the building was under a freeway overpass, but he's got to be closer to Cobo," Don said.

Charlie nodded, and took her phone off mute. "Lin, can you get out of the room you're in?"

"I don't know. I'm handcuffed to a chair, and it's so dark I keep bumping into things."

"You're handcuffed?"

"He cuffed my wrist to the arm of the chair. But I can pull the chair."

"Okay. So one hand is shackled, and one is free?"

"Yes."

"Are your feet free?"

"Yes."

"Okay Lin, listen carefully. Just keep moving, as best you can, in the direction of the door. Keep your phone on, and we'll stay on the line. We're searching for you, and we'll find you. Okay?"

"Okay, Ms. Mack."

Charlie put the phone on mute and turned to Don. "He's scared."

"He's got a right to be. Let's call Novak, maybe now she can track his phone."

"That's right. Pull over, Don. There's no use just driving around."

Don idled at the curb and called Judy while Charlie continued to reassure Lin.

"Yes, Don," Judy answered.

"Charlie and I have the Fong boy on the line, and we need you to trace the call," Don said.

"He's on the phone? Is he okay?"

"That's what I said, isn't it," Don said gruffly.

"Put the call on speaker," Charlie ordered. "Judy, we don't know where Lin is. He's in some kind of warehouse with no windows. He can't see to find his way out, but we don't think he's very far from Cobo. Anything you can do to trace his call?"

"I'll try."

Crawling on his knees and dragging the chair beside him, Lin had managed to reach the narrow door to the anteroom. He was still trying to inch his way over the threshold when he heard the turn of a doorknob ahead of him and watched a swath of light from the warehouse spread across the room. A slender silhouette broke the light, and with the slam of the door the room was once again dark. Lin held his breath. There was no further movement at the door, but he knew someone had entered.

"Hello?" a small voice sounded.

Lin didn't dare answer or move.

Then Charlie's voice squawked through the phone. "Lin, are you still okay?"

Suddenly, the overhead fixture washed the room in light. Lin stared toward the door, willing his eyes to adjust to the change. When they did, he met the gaze of Amy Wu.

The handler at the emergency number had spoken briefly to Amy, asking her a few questions and advising her to go to a nearby facility operated by Guí Motors, where she was to wait until she was contacted. She'd heard Mr. Kwong, Heinrich, and the directors in Beijing speak of another location, but her duties had been exclusively at Cobo Center. She'd retrieved her car from the Cobo garage and used her GPS to get to the location, but ran into a dead end. So she turned on the interior lights to read the directions she'd carefully written. She found the one-level industrial building at the end of a long rock driveway. Her headlights swept across the number "5017" affixed to a red sign above the double doors. There were no other cars in the shallow parking area, and no one in sight. Motion lights illuminated the front door as she approached. She knocked, and when there was no answer, opened the unlocked door and stepped in.

A large, open room was abuzz with the activity of laptop keyboards. Five rows of desks were manned by workers, both men and women, all young, all wearing white earbuds, and all appearing to be Chinese. Some of them stared at Amy as she entered the room, but others only glanced up for a second before returning to their tasks. She walked slowly along a vinyl runner toward the rear of the room. Six round fluorescents were strung from metal beams in the high ceilings, but every work station also had a gooseneck lamp glowing onto the desktop. She expected someone to greet her, but no one did. When she got to the last row of desks, she stopped.

She stepped off the runner and leaned toward the young woman nearest to her. "Hello, can you help me?"

The worker looked at Amy, and then back to her keyboard. When Amy didn't move, and continued to hover, the girl removed her earbuds.

"Can you help me?" Amy said again.

The worker placed her index finger to her lips. Amy stepped closer to her, and whispered, "I'm here to meet someone."

The girl gave a nervous look around, and quickly gestured with her head and eyes toward a door on the wall behind her. Then she immediately replaced her earbuds and like those seated around her, began tapping her keyboard as if her life depended on it.

Amy had approached the door tentatively, then put her ear close to listen. The light from the room behind her momentarily flooded the dark inside, and she quietly slipped around the partly open door. The room was silent and black. She'd groped at the wall near the door for a light switch, and when she couldn't immediately find it, she spoke a timid "hello." With no answer, she was about to return through the door when a tinny voice rang out. Scared, Amy's hands slapped frantically for the light fixture, and when she'd illuminated the room she immediately recognized the skinny boy on the floor. He was crouched near another door, a chair linked to his arm, and his face was bruised and puffy. She rushed to his side and put her hand on his shoulder. Lin wrapped his free arm around her. "*Xié xié*," he'd said over and over.

Amy and Lin stepped from the door. "Let's go," she said.

155

They walked purposefully on the vinyl runner toward the door, carrying the chair between them. No one tried to stop them as they passed the rows of workers and when they reached the exit, Amy stepped out first and held the door for Lin. They made it down the driveway to the rear of Amy's car and out of view of the warehouse. Amy spoke to Charlie on Lin's phone and gave her the address of the warehouse, then returned the Blackberry to Lin who clutched it to his chest. There was nothing to do but wait, so Lin sat in his attached chair. He didn't have a coat, and it was beginning to snow, so Amy draped her jacket around his shoulders, then sat in the driver's seat with the door open and turned over the engine to get some heat. Beyoncé's voice blared from the radio before Amy adjusted the volume, then looked at her own phone. There was a missed call from Mr. Kwong.

"Amy, where are you?"

"I'm very close, Mr. Kwong. I've been calling you all afternoon."

"I know, I know. I'm at the office now. I need you to send my notes to the directors before our call."

"Yes, sir. I'll be there very soon."

Amy stepped out of the car to check on Lin. The boy was still cold and shaken, and his eyes stared up at her with barely veiled shame. She wished she had a blanket to put around him.

"Do you like Beyoncé?" she asked.

"No. But I could hear that you do."

"I like her because she's a woman who makes her own decisions, and knows how to make her own way."

"Is that the kind of woman you are?" Lin pried, forgetting his predicament for a moment.

"You'd be surprised."

"Maybe I would," Lin said and offered a weak smile. "But, when I've seen you at Cobo, you seemed so, so traditional."

"I have to. For my job."

"How did you know where to find me?"

"I didn't know you were here. I was meeting someone. It was just a lucky break that I found you."

"More like a blessing," Lin said.

Charlie and Don arrived quickly and rushed to Lin's side. He tried to stand, but collapsed into the chair.

"Take it easy," Don said. "I'll get these cuffs off."

Amy grabbed her coat from Lin's shoulders, touched him on the arm and prepared to leave, but Charlie intercepted her.

"What is this place?"

"I was told it is a facility of Guí Motors. Our emergency contact told me to report here when Mr. Kwong didn't come to the office."

"There doesn't appear to be any security."

"I didn't see anyone in charge. There are a bunch of young computer workers inside. I'm sorry, Ms. Mack, but I have to go now. Mr. Kwong needs me."

"Thank you, Amy," Charlie said.

"May the ancestors bless you." Lin used Mandarin for the formal farewell greeting. He looked up at her from his perch on the driveway.

Amy smiled at him. "You're welcome. I was pretty sure you spoke Mandarin."

Charlie leaned into the window of the car. "Cynthia Fitzgerald said you would be a friend."

"Miss Fitzgerald also spoke to me of you. I don't know what's happened here, but I'm glad I could help."

Amy drove off to the strains of Beyoncé's "Me, Myself and I" and was probably too far away to hear the shot that separated Lin from the chair that had been his companion for hours.

"Let's go in and find out what's going on," Don said.

"We'll come back later and do that. I want to get Lin to the emergency room."

At the hospital, Lin answered the curious questions of the medical staff by saying he'd been mugged, but didn't want to report it to the police. Lin's x-ray showed no broken bones. He received a couple of stitches near his ear and swallowed a couple of heavy-duty painkillers. While they waited for his discharge papers, Lin gave Don a BlackBerry tutorial. At eight o'clock, Charlie heard from Mandy.

"Where are you?"

"Don and I are at the hospital with Lin."

"How is he?"

"He was beaten up, but he's okay now."

"Did you find anything at Heinrich's house?"

"No."

"You still think he's involved?"

"Yes. Lin said the man who beat him was the one he saw with Heinrich, and the description fits Dudiyn. The guy beat Lin until he admitted he was working for me, and he also asked Lin if he was spying for the Chinese."

"All Heinrich seemed to want to talk about at the gym was the Chinese. He didn't even try to make a pass at me. He just kept driving home the idea that the Chinese delegation was up to something, and we should keep an eye on them."

Charlie looked at her phone when she heard the buzz of another call coming in. "Hold on a minute, will you?"

"Charlene Mack."

"You forgot my phone number already?" Tony Canterra asked jokingly.

"Believe me, I've got all your numbers, Tony. What's up?"

"We need to talk."

"About what?"

"It's too much to discuss on the phone."

"Well, as a matter of fact, I have a couple of things I need to discuss with you. We may have a lead. A warehouse on Morrell Street. Where Guí has a bunch of computer workers. One of our people was held there tonight, against his will."

"Can we meet somewhere? Away from Cobo?"

"Sure. Why don't you come to my hotel room?"

"Oh, how long I've wanted to hear those words."

"I'll have the team there."

"I see. Okay, I'll be there in about an hour."

Charlie switched calls. "Mandy?"

"I'm still here."

"That was Tony; he wants a meeting. I'd like you there. It's at my hotel room in an hour."

"Okay, but I've got to make myself presentable for the famous Tony Canterra."

"You're always presentable."

"Not after a patrol shift, a fitful nap, and a weight workout. I'm a sweaty mess and I need a quick shower."

"Don and I are dropping Lin back at my place, and then we'll see you."

"I'm really sorry about the boy getting hurt, honey."

"So am I. And somebody's gonna pay."

"Drink, Canterra?" Don asked, answering the knock at the door.

"Only if you're having one."

"I am. Just one. I'm back on patrol in a couple of hours."

Tony entered the room and smiled at Charlie. "Where's Gil?"

"He's on the way over."

Then Tony locked his gaze on Mandy. "I don't think we've met."

"No. We haven't. I'm Mandy Porter." She had been sitting on the edge of Charlie's bed and rose to extend a hand. "I'm working with the Mack team; good to meet you at last."

Tony feigned embarrassment. "Oh, so you've heard about me? Well, these two have known me a long time." He stared again at Mandy, remembering something. "I've heard your name. You're with one of the local forces, aren't you?"

"Grosse Pointe Park," Mandy said. "I'm on leave to work this case . . . as a favor to Charlie."

Tony paused, remembering other things he'd heard, his brain forming a question.

"There's been another casualty, Tony." Charlie abruptly changed the subject.

"Oh?"

"Mandy and I found one of the Cobo food inspectors dead at his house. He'd been shot."

"You're rechecking the documents for all the food vendors?"

"We've got two people on it."

"I have some news, too," Tony said, leaning against the wall near the door and taking a sip of his vodka.

Charlie understood how these so-called briefings from federal agents worked, and so did Don. Tony would parse out facts to maintain control and to protect the interests of Homeland Security. The Mack team would need to ask pointed questions if they wanted any real information. So Charlie got into the game. She walked over to the minibar and retrieved a tiny ten-dollar Glenlivet. They all watched as she upturned one of the glasses, dropped three cubes of ice, one at a time, into the glass, then slowly poured the scotch.

"You want one?" she asked Mandy.

"No. I'm sticking with water."

Charlie clinked glasses with Don as she passed him seated at the desk, and again took her perch next to Mandy on the bed. "So, what's *your* news, Tony?"

A knock at the door was Gil. He rushed into the room.

"Did I miss anything?"

"Tony has some news," Don said dryly. "Drinks are in the minibar."

"Don't mind if I do," Gil said. "What's going on? More trouble?"

"Heinrich is your bad guy," Tony announced. "The director informed DADA of that tonight."

"I think we already figured that out," Charlie said.

"So you're saying the Chinese delegation isn't the threat?" Don asked.

"They have their own agenda, but no they aren't a threat."

"Guí Motors has a warehouse full of Chinese workers at an off-site location. One of our freelancers, a kid who just started shaving, was beaten up badly and taken to that warehouse where he was handcuffed to a chair." Don's voice was working its way to an angry pitch.

"We know about the warehouse. Heinrich leased it for Kwong.

160

They're working together, but not. It's complicated, and I can finally tell you more," Tony said, looking at Charlie.

"Let's hear it. What're they after?" Charlie asked.

"It's a Matryoshka ploy."

"Like the nesting dolls?"

"Very good. You remember your Russian briefings. Only this time it's more like Chinese boxes. On the surface, the Chinese are stealing trade secrets from U.S. automakers. We know that's what Guí Motors is engaged in. But, within that scheme is a power struggle between the Chinese government and a billionaire from Hong Kong. It's that box we're worried about."

"Is that where the terror threat comes in?" Mandy asked.

"Yes. We've tracked activity—weapons purchases, some real estate deals—back to this businessman who seems to be playing out his own agenda. We think *he* may own Heinrich."

"What's this guy after?" Gil asked

"He's a former member of the legislative branch of the People's Republic of China and was ousted four years ago. It diminished his family's standing among the inner circles of the government and undercut his business. He's been planning a retaliation against China's central committee for years."

"And this is the year the North American International Auto Show is honoring China for accomplishments in auto manufacturing, with a recognition from the U.S. secretary of commerce," Charlie said.

"Right. And if a disruption to the auto show can be tied back to Guí, it will be a huge political and economic disaster for the Chinese. What better way to retaliate."

"What's in it for Heinrich?" Mandy asked.

"A very fat paycheck. Millions of dollars. He's been employed by Guí Motors to help with the cyber-espionage and he's working for the billionaire to disrupt the auto show. He's being paid by both teams on the field."

"And he's on Spectrum's payroll too. It's a triple-cross," Mandy assessed.

161

"How did DADA take it when they got the news?" Charlie asked.

"Not well. It was a hard blow to finally know they'd been the first link in his chain of deceptions. Still, they understand the situation they're in now."

"What's your evidence that Heinrich is at the center of things?" Don asked.

"A first-person account."

"What first person?" Charlie asked.

Tony paused to take another sip. Charlie could see the wheels moving as he contemplated his response. She shared a look with Don as the silence extended, and put a hand on Mandy's knee to unnerve Tony. Taking note, he shifted his weight and then resumed his pose against the wall.

"I'm not sure that's relevant. But we're certain the information we have is valid." Tony hedged.

"How is Dudiyn involved?" Charlie asked.

"The same billionaire hired Dudiyn to assist Heinrich."

"Is anyone else involved?" Gil asked.

"We don't know for certain. We don't think so, but we can't rule it out."

"Okay. So, what do you suggest we do?" Charlie played along.

"Continue working with Heinrich. The next twenty-four hours are critical. He's thinking maybe his plan is in jeopardy, but he's not sure. Don't pressure him."

"What *is* his plan?" Charlie asked.

"We don't know the details, but maybe an attempt to detonate explosives."

"He wants us to think the Chinese are the ones we should be watching," Mandy said.

"I'm sure he does. So go along with that. Let him think you believe him."

"And what will DHS be doing?" Charlie asked.

"We'll be working the back channels. Monitoring communications, keeping the secret service informed. We'd like to embed a couple of agents into your security patrols. You can tell Spectrum you brought on more freelancers. We don't want Heinrich to know Homeland Security is formally involved."

"How big is this threat?" Charlie asked.

"We think we're looking at a bomb. Not nuclear, thank God, but something big enough to cause fatalities and debilitating damage," Tony said.

"So, we are talking terrorism," Gil stated.

"It's serious business. That's why I convinced the director to let me fill you in."

"If it's that serious, why not just shut the show down?" Mandy asked.

The room was silent for nearly a minute. Don drained the last of his drink, and Mandy stood up and shoved her hands into the pockets of her khakis.

"It's a damn good question," Don agreed.

"China's president is visiting the U.S. in April. It's a big deal, because it's his first official visit. The White House doesn't want anything to interfere with that visit. Then there's the State Department. They're in some tricky diplomatic negotiations with China on human rights and playing a role in ensuring a nuclear-free North Korea. The U. S. wants to maintain a good relationship with China, and a part of that is playing up China's role as an international auto manufacturer. That means the Detroit Auto Show will not be canceled."

Charlie imagined her notes on a table, shifting and sorting them into a logical pattern. Facts, what-ifs, players, and questions. "Is Kwong your witness?" she asked.

"No," Tony said quickly.

"We'll take that as a yes," Don quipped.

Chapter 9

Friday, January 6, 2006
Auto Show: 2 Days

Charlie looked at those jammed around the conference table: the Mack partners, the Cobo insiders, and the freelancers, which now included two DHS agents, one a senior agent who had already been badged. Charlie, Don, and Gil had talked long into the night with Tony, deciding what to share with whom. Two things they'd agreed not to share with the larger group were any mention of bombs, and Tony's warning about Heinrich.

"People walking the Cobo corridors who are not recognized are to be stopped and questioned. Delays at the loading dock are going to be even longer, because now one of the Mack group will personally inspect incoming deliveries flagged by Judy and Carter," Charlie reported.

"Ms. Hillman, all food vendors have been rechecked, but each will need to provide to you the documents of their employees, from dishwashers to chefs. No exceptions."

"I understand, Ms. Mack."

"I'll need each of you supervisors to provide me with your department activity schedules for tomorrow. I want to know what work is being done, who's doing it, and what time it's happening."

"I can collect those," Ty offered.

The staff trusted Tyson. He was one of them. They understood the added duties being piled on, but shaken by the death of Garry Jones, none of them complained.

"Good idea. Get those to Ty as soon as possible today."

As a concession to Heinrich's red herring, security personnel would be stationed near the offices and exhibit areas of Guí Motors. However, the warehouse where Lin had been held captive was off-limits. Tony had informed them that the land and building were registered to the People's Republic of China.

Hoyt Timberman had some concerns about integrating the new freelancers into the patrol groups. Charlie had introduced the two women to the other freelancers as "highly experienced." The agents were supposed to be undercover, but their first-day outfits shouted, "Hi. I'm a federal agent."

"You'll still be managing the logistics of the security patrols, and I think the best thing to do is to put at least one of our regulars with the newcomers."

"Well, alright then," Hoyt said, flipping through his schedule.

"We have another new protocol," Don said. "Each patrol team, and supervisors in each of the Cobo service areas, will receive two-way radios. Pressley, you'll have one too," Don said, catching Tyson's eye. "We'll use channel three for all our communications."

"Anybody can listen in on those," the senior agent noted.

"That's true. But our BlackBerrys aren't perfect and, if for some reason Cobo's communication systems go down, we'll need the redundancy," Charlie explained.

"We've already had a snafu with the Berrys," Judy added. "The walkie-talkies will give us a lot of coverage; they have a range of thirty-five miles. The frequency is already set. You press this button to speak, and that's all there is to it."

"Look," Charlie said, scanning the eyes of each person in the room. "What we've discussed today is proprietary information. I know you'll be tempted to tell your key managers or husbands, wives and significant others, but don't. Your discretion is critical to thwarting what we know is a credible threat to the auto show, and we want to keep everyone safe."

The somber faces that looked back at Charlie were response

enough. The Cobo supervisors began to gather their materials and the radios Judy had distributed. Ty arose from the table.

"We got your back, Ms. Mack," he said, leading the staff out of the conference room.

"I appreciate that, Ty. Judy, you and Carter should get back to the shipping dock."

"We're on it." Judy was already moving out of the conference room, followed by Carter.

The rest of the group remained to plan an overnight search of the building. They were looking specifically for components that could be used in a bomb. Searchers would inspect every door, wall panel, drawer, container, closet, and corner in the areas of the building where the public had access. The search, which would begin that night, would be a huge task.

"I suggest we go floor by floor," Gil said. "We could leave one group on patrol, a few people at the Guí Motors sites, and the rest of us focus on the search."

"Can we pull a half-dozen people from Spectrum to help?" Charlie asked Cynthia.

"Sure. I'll put together an overtime work shift."

"Will you need Heinrich's approval?" Mandy asked.

"Yes, but I'll tell him we're using our guys for the Guí surveillance."

"Actually, if we can use your people at the Chinese delegation spaces, I can free up four of our people to participate in the search," Hoyt said, looking at his assignment grid.

"Consider it done," Cynthia said.

Charlie, Cynthia and Mandy came up with a disinformation strategy to use on Heinrich. Mandy would text Heinrich asking if she could meet him again, but this time at his house. They hoped Mandy's show of interest would lull Heinrich into thinking they were not on to him.

"Okay. Let's meet here at the office at six o'clock," Charlie told the group. "Go take naps. We're up all night tonight."

∽ ∽ ∽

Heinrich watched Dudiyn, seated at the garage workbench. The man had no formal education, but was one of the most talented technicians he'd ever worked with—equally adept at wiring electrical circuits, cutting pipe, and mixing chemicals. He had the nimbleness and touch of a heart surgeon. But there was another side, a commonness that was repulsive. For one thing he never seemed to wash his uniform of black jeans and black T-shirt. Heinrich stepped through the door connecting the house and garage and opened the small window facing the narrow backyard. He looked over Dudiyn's shoulder at the hand-drawn schematic he was using to guide his assembly.

Binary explosives were the easiest to construct. Most used common components readily available at a big-box hardware store, a drugstore, or on eBay. They could be packaged in small containers and easily transported and concealed. Of course, there was always the danger of an accident, and Heinrich wasn't pleased the bomb assembly had been moved to his house, in a densely residential area, versus the out-of-the-way storage building.

"How's the work going?"

"No problems so far. Except I wish I had more room and more ventilation. The garage had air conditioning."

"I'll bring in some floor fans. Will that help?"

"Yes, but I could also use a respirator."

"Okay. You're being extra careful, right?"

"I'm always careful. Speaking of which, what do we do about that kid?"

"You're really dying to get rid of him, aren't you?"

"Not really. He's just a loose end. Like that Chinese guy, and the black guy who worked at Cobo."

"Are you forgetting the Mack team member in the parking garage?"

"That was different. He was one of the soldiers; he died in a firefight."

"The kid's not going anywhere. In a day or two, the programmers will be recalled to Beijing and somebody will find him."

Dudiyn turned on his stool and locked eyes with Heinrich for a few seconds, then returned to his wiring task. He was being paid a substantial amount of money for this job, but he also cared about the reputation he'd gained for being reliable and thorough. He didn't like loose ends.

"You think we should move the timeline back a day or two?" Dudiyn asked. "The security breach at the garage is troubling."

"No."

"If everything is quiet for a few days, the Americans will be lulled back into complacency."

"The client still feels an incident during the press preview will garner the most national and international attention."

"Maybe. But if we wait, we can do more damage. There will be more people, more loss of life. It'll scare the shit out of them."

"No. We're sticking to the original plan. How much more time do you need to finish up?"

"I'll be at it the rest of the day, and into the night. I still have to pack the shrapnel and connect fuses to each tube. I've got forty of these to build."

"When do you add the explosives?"

"Mixing the powder and ammonium nitrate is the last task. I'll do that in the Cobo garage. It wouldn't be too smart to drive through town with that stuff already mixed."

"I've got to go into the office. I'll bring the fans when I come back. Don't blow the place apart."

Dudiyn watched Heinrich cross the garage and step into the house. With his designer clothes and fancy tastes, he was as soft as the kid. He knew for sure he'd never work for, or with, this crazy German again.

It was the final day for major deliveries. The deadline and the new rules for check-in were putting drivers, vendors, exhibitors, and Cobo departments on edge. The Mack team spot-checked every delivery of food and restaurant supplies, and gave special scrutiny to cargo containing electronics, any organic materials, or chemicals. Judy and Carter were in charge of this daunting task, and by 11 a.m. they had processed only twenty trucks.

168

That morning, an eighteen-wheeler filled with floor plants had been held up for two hours while three bomb-sniffing dogs provided by Homeland Security put their talented noses to work on each plant. A refrigerated food truck with four hundred pounds of hot dogs, forty cases of buns, five thousand packages of frozen barbecue spare ribs, and one hundred gallons of potato salad idled in one of the bays. The driver was pissed off and had threatened not to return the following Friday for her scheduled delivery, but Judy talked her down from the cliff ledge. A third cargo truck carrying popcorn machines, 500 pounds of popcorn, 50 boxes of oil, and 10,000 popcorn bags had just been processed by Carter, and now the driver was being interviewed by one of the DHS agents. Most of the time, it was a driver's credentials, unusual cargo, or incomplete paperwork that raised a flag for Carter. He had two laptops open and two mobile phones to check in with his far-flung sources, which included the FBI, Interpol, the Secret Service, and even the Teamsters.

Judy spotted a lanky guy in fitted jeans and wearing a Stetson swinging down from his cab. He threw a half-finished cigarette into the snow, stomped it as if it were a campfire, and marched toward the loading dock booth. Judy grabbed her jacket, jumped off her stool, and stepped through the door of the booth to intercept him.

"Sorry for the delay, cowboy; we got a lot of security today, and we're trying to keep 'em rolling but our hands are tied."

"I'm on a tight deadline here, and I been cooling my heels for forty-five minutes. I could have unloaded and been back on I-75 by now."

"You headed north or south?"

"I'm going to the U.P., and with this cold and snow I'd like to get there before nightfall. How much longer is it going to be?"

Judy glanced over her shoulder to Carter for help, but he was studying his laptop screen. She looked up at the six-foot-two driver and gave him her best "I know you know I'm stalling but play along with me" smile.

"Come on. Let me have your paperwork. I'll see if we can get you on your way."

Judy returned to the booth, hopped onto her stool, and unfolded the driver's manifest. She rested an elbow on the narrow countertop that was doubling as a desk, and flipped the first page of the inventory list.

"What are Three-Stream stations?"

"They're a set of waste containers. Three of them, stacked side by side for recyclables and trash. My helper and I have a hundred stations to unload."

"And they cost $50,000? Those must be some fancy trash cans."

The driver pushed back the tip of his hat with one lean finger, and stared at Judy. His scowl turned to a small grin as he realized she was just killing time. So he decided to flirt.

"What's your name, young lady?"

"Judy. Judy Novak."

"No kidding."

"What?"

"Novak. That's my name too. No, really. Look at the last page of the freight order where I signed for receipt of the cargo."

"Jerry Novak. Well I'll be damned. Polish?"

"Born and raised. The cowboy hat just gives me something to talk about."

"Well, hey cousin."

"So, what about it, cousin. You think you can get me out of here?"

Judy called one of the agents over to the booth, and they walked with Jerry to the back of his big rig. Judy checked out the identification of the helper, and they all watched as a black Labrador retriever gave the truck's contents a once-over. The aluminum and corrugated cardboard receptacles were shrink-wrapped. Blue for cans and bottles, dark green for paper, and a black container marked trash. Each unit was stenciled with the initials NAIAS, for North American International Auto Show.

"Those are some good-looking containers, cowboy," Judy said.

"We got the exclusive deal this year to provide these beauties. Well, are we good to go?"

Judy looked at the dog handler who gave a nod, jumped from the ramp of the trailer, coaxed down the Lab, and then gave the dog a treat. Judy watched for a few minutes while Jerry and his helper loaded twenty units onto a flatbed hand truck. A maintenance supervisor came down to sign for the delivery, and in a few trips all the recyclable units had been wheeled through the cargo doors. Jerry flashed a smile and threw up a wave as he lifted himself into the cab of his truck. He backed the vehicle as if it were a grocery cart and exited the one-way access road, leaving giant tire marks in the snow.

"Everything good for this next truck, Carter?" Judy asked.

"Yep. They have design pieces for the Jeep display. They're doing an indoor waterfall, so they have tubing and pumps and what not. I've got the engineering supervisor coming down to sign off on the paperwork."

"Well, we've got another fifty deliveries to go. Do you need a cuppa and a doughnut?"

"Yeah. With sprinkles, please."

"So, they *are* increasing their surveillance of the Chinese," Heinrich said with satisfaction.

He leaned back in his chair, sipping an espresso. Cynthia perched on the sofa across from his desk with clipboard in hand. Her task was to disclose some insider information to distract Heinrich, but not scare him off. It was a ploy she'd used before to gain, and keep, his trust.

"That's what Ms. Mack reported this morning," Cynthia said. "There will be around-the-clock security at the delegation's offices, in display areas, and at their hotel. Apparently, she has some tip she's following."

"A tip from who?"

"She didn't say, but I might be able to get her to tell me."

"You're getting along with her pretty well."

"I think so. I've tried to be helpful. She's been pretty frantic about finding Lin Fong, and to tell you the truth it's compromised her work. By the way, I've deactivated his ID and closed his remote access to our server."

"What? Oh, the Chinese kid. Good." Apparently, Heinrich didn't know about Lin Fong's rescue. He was distracted and looked at his phone for the second time in ten minutes. "Coincidentally, Ms. Mack's associate has contacted me. She says she wants some advice."

"You mean Mandy Porter? I'm not surprised," Cynthia said reeling in Heinrich.

"No?"

"No. She's sort of filling in for her. They're . . . lovers, you know?"

"Lovers?" Heinrich said, louder than was necessary.

"Based on what I've seen and heard."

"What have you seen?" Heinrich's tongue darted momentarily from his lips, and he leaned forward.

"Long stares. Hands touching, and I've seen them together in Ms. Mack's car."

"You think they're lesbians? Both of them?"

"Well, my gaydar is pretty accurate. I know there's something between them that's more than professional."

This time, Heinrich looked at his Rolex. He drummed his fingers on the desk and began stacking papers. "What's happening with the Secret Service?"

"I've met with the head agent, and gave him all the files they asked for. So far, our security protocols have checked out okay. Oh, and the police want to talk to us, about Lin Fong."

"Right. Well, you take care of that, unless they insist on seeing me." Heinrich stood to signal the end of the meeting. "I have some schmoozing to do this morning with a few of the exhibitors, and a few calls to make before that."

"Okay."

"And, we should do a full-staff briefing tomorrow morning; make sure everyone's here. Invite the Mack team, if you like."

"I'll schedule it for 10 a.m."

"Fine."

Amy made the tea as instructed, and carried a tray with the ceramic teapot and cups Mr. Kwong said had been a gift from his wife, to the door. She knocked.

"Come in. Please put the tea on the table."

"Is there anything else you need, sir?"

"Please, Amy, sit with me," Kwong said, rising from his desk.

He was dressed as usual in a blue suit and red tie with a crisp white shirt, but his demeanor was different. Not all business, with rapid-fire instructions given in English, nor with a leering stare induced by the scotch. He slumped over the low reception table, and opened his hand toward the bench across from him.

"Please pour the tea, and one for yourself."

Amy poured the gold liquid from the pot, holding the top gently with her index finger. She handed a cup across the table to Mr. Kwong. He took the saucer with a shaking hand and quickly secured it with his other hand; Amy pretended not to notice. She sipped her tea while Kwong looked into his cup as if reading messages from his ancestors. Amy decided to break the uncomfortable silence.

"Mr. Kwong, are the people working at the warehouse Guí employees?"

Kwong's head jerked up and he took a moment to answer. "Yes. They are doing research and development."

"Why was Lin Fong being held captive there?"

Kwong took a long sip of tea, then placed the cup gently into the saucer. The shake in his hands had subsided. "He was thought to be a burglar. It was just a misunderstanding."

It had been clear to her from the beginning of her employment that the company was involved in secret activities in which she was not to be involved. It was only the providence of Mr. Kwong's absence that had enabled her to help Lin Fong escape. She had never asked Kwong where he'd been all day yesterday, and she didn't ask any questions now.

"Have I been a good supervisor?"

With the abrupt change of subject, it was Amy's turn to refocus. She placed her tea on the table and crossed her hands on her lap. Last evening, during the Beijing teleconference, he had been mostly quiet, allowing the engineers and design team to answer the bosses' questions about the exhibit. The company president and vice president would arrive in Detroit tomorrow, and he had read the logistics document she'd produced, verbatim, to give his report. It was only after he was asked about the continued scrutiny of the company's activities that he became more animated. At that point, she was dismissed from the conference.

"I have found it easy to work for you, Mr. Kwong. You are very clear and organized."

"I appreciate that, Amy. I have built my reputation on the efficiency of my work."

He seemed to want to say more, so Amy picked up her cup and took a long drink. Kwong squeezed the crease of his trousers with his fingertips, then placed his palms on his knees, assuming the position of an obedient servant. Amy resumed her crossed hands posture.

"I love my wife and children. My family is my life. You may be too young to understand what I mean about family. You are, after all, American Chinese."

Amy wasn't quite sure why she was offended by his remarks. She might not be blindly loyal to the Chinese government and the bosses in Beijing, as Kwong was, but she was acutely aware of the significance of family ties. It was never far from her mind that her family's influence had gotten her this temporary job, and it was her parents' continued generosity that allowed her to take a year-long break from her university studies before she attended medical school in the fall.

"I do understand, Mr. Kwong. The multi-strand twines of family form an unbreakable bond. You work so hard I would have guessed your allegiance to Guí Motors was the most important thing."

Kwong looked down at his ceramic cup and lifted it, but the trembling had returned, and he quickly replaced it on the table.

Then, without a hint of his change in mood, he dipped his face into his hands and wept. The sadness spread until it filled the corners of the room. Amy stood and began collecting the cups and pot onto the tray. When she met Kwong's eyes, they were filled with his longing for home.

"When I was your age, it was easy to know what was right. In today's world, right . . . and wrong come in degrees, and each man must define his own boundaries of loyalty."

"Is there anything else, Mr. Kwong? May I order you some lunch?"

"No. I'm not hungry. You can go ahead and get your own lunch. I'll be fine."

"With the executives coming in tomorrow, I'd planned to eat at my desk today in case you had any last-minute needs."

"Thank you, Amy; that was very thoughtful of you."

"I'll just go to the ladies' room and be right back," Amy said, closing the inner door.

She unlocked her desk drawer and retrieved her purse. The two security guards watched her as she walked down the hall, but they maintained their vigil across from the suite's front door. When she returned to the office, the door of the cabinet behind her desk was partially open, and a bottle of Dewar's was missing.

"We probably shouldn't be doing this," Charlie said, chucking her boots and ripping her jeans down to her ankles.

"Stop being so responsible."

"But, I am responsible. I've always been."

Across the bed, Mandy was undressing with equal intensity. "Well, there's only one thing I want you to be responsible for right now."

Unclothed, they fell together on the bed, giggling.

"I feel like we're playing hooky from school, or grabbing a quickie at lunch," Mandy said, pulling the covers up to her neck.

"That's exactly what we're doing."

"And that's the fun of it, Charlie. Allow yourself to have some fun."

Charlie dipped under the covers to part Mandy's legs. Neither said another word, but their moans dueled as they made love with the enthusiasm of teenagers. Mandy placed her hand on the lump under the blanket formed by Charlie's head and pulled her deeper inside. Charlie was not only a martial artist, but she had equal skill in oral pleasuring. She knew how to apply just the right amount of pressure, when to be the aggressor and when, and how to, absorb a passionate response. When Mandy's butt levitated from the bed, and her thighs became taut, Charlie raised her arms to hold Mandy's hips, rhythmically alternating between licking, sucking, and plunging her tongue until she brought Mandy's passion to the surface with a prolonged eruption. When the quakes quieted, Charlie crawled up Mandy's body, gripped her wrists, and lifted them above the pillow. Slowly, Charlie began rotating against Mandy's mound, until they moved in tandem. When Mandy tried to lower her arms, Charlie held them fast. "I need you to touch me," Mandy said. Charlie released one wrist and reached down to massage wet lips. Mandy groaned in appreciation, and used her free hand to grab a hunk of Charlie's ass. She parted Charlie's cheeks and splayed her finger along the crevice. "Oh," Charlie gasped, humping harder. Mandy came again. This time with small whimpers, and Charlie's name on her tongue.

Charlie rolled onto her back and reached out for Mandy, who curled into her arms.

"I guess I was pretty horny," Mandy said.

Charlie didn't respond; she just pulled Mandy tighter against her heaving chest. They lay silent for a couple of minutes sharing the satisfaction of damp skin and growing love.

"I started feeling territorial when Cynthia described Heinrich's reaction to our being a couple."

"Umm. Hmm."

"You knew?"

"I saw your jaw tighten."

"I don't want anyone but me thinking about you that way."

Mandy lifted onto her elbow to look at her lover. She caressed her face, then laid her palm on Charlie's chest.

"I know it will happen all the time," Charlie added. "It's the downside of dating an amazingly beautiful woman."

"Stop your talking. I'm doing you now."

Charlie smiled. "I bet other lesbians do more sweet-talking and kissing in bed."

"Oh, I see. First, you pin me down and now you want to be romantic. Okay. How's this: I adore you. You're my very own brown beauty. I don't care how many other people look at me. I only have eyes for you. Now, I'd like us to stop talking so I can explore you from your curly head to your pedicured toes."

"Where's Charlie?" Don asked, standing over Judy's desk.

"I don't know. After our noon gathering, she went to Cynthia's office, then phoned to say she would be out a couple of hours."

Judy watched Don's scowl, then she looked over at Gil who gave her a squint and tilt of the head. Judy closed her laptop, and prepared herself for a session of Don control.

"Do you want me to try to reach her?" she asked.

"No. But I'm thinking of having a meeting with Heinrich."

"Why do you want to do that? I thought we were supposed to keep hands off," Judy said.

"I'm having second thoughts about that. If he's the bad guy, why give him the chance to blow something up?"

"I don't think it's a good idea to work him up." Gil picked up the pacification.

"Canterra didn't say we shouldn't talk to the guy," Don argued.

"That's true, but what would you say to him? What do you think he'll tell us?"

"I bet I can beat some information out of him."

"The goal is to make him believe we're focusing on the Chinese now, that we've bought into his deflection. Then maybe he'll put his guard down and lead us to the trouble," Gil explained. "We're keeping an eye on him, and so is DHS."

"And don't forget, Mandy's meeting with him this evening to keep him on the hook," Judy piped in.

"I know, I know all that. But I'm damn sick of just waiting around for this asshole to make a move."

Don shook off his sports jacket and stomped into the conference room. He opened the mini-refrigerator, stared in, and slammed the door. He started sorting through the basket of snacks on the table. "Don't we have any doughnuts or something, Novak?"

"Look in the credenza," Judy hollered back.

"You better call Charlie," Gil whispered to Judy.

In the last few days, the Mack partners had established a routine of meeting between 6 and 8 a.m., at noon, 6 to 8 p.m., and midnight. They were usually joined by a varying combination of the freelancers, Tyson, Cynthia, Tony, and sometimes one or two Cobo managers. It was a way to share information and stay encouraged. Tonight's search for bomb components in Cobo's public areas would replace the midnight meeting. Judy had brought in food from Mexican Village and at 7 p.m. the group gathered snugly in the conference room, including all the freelancers, the two DHS agents, and Tyson, who had come around to propose an idea.

"We should put our janitors on the team," he said. "They're here early in the morning, late into the evening, and are constantly in and out of every level. They already use two-way radios, and if they know what to look for, they could be invaluable to us."

"That would mean letting more people know we're looking for explosives," Charlie said. "Could we count on their discretion?"

Ty shrugged.

"How many are there?" Gil asked.

"Forty."

"Wow. That would give us some real manpower," Don said

"But only twenty-five or so would be around to help with tonight's search. The rest don't have shifts before Sunday," Ty noted.

"That's still a lot more help. What do you think, Mack?"

"The downside is, we can be sure someone among them will

178

reveal that we have a bomb threat. But at this point, we have to take that chance. Anyone see any other problems with the notion?" Charlie asked the table.

"Have they all been background checked?" Senior Agent Mann asked.

Charlie nodded to Carter to respond. He was working on a plastic container of chicken enchiladas with pico de gallo, beans, and rice. He put down his fork.

"Yes. We checked them out early," Carter began, "because it's true, they do have access to the full building. Cobo does a criminal check on the janitors, and everyone's bonded and drug tested."

"Are they uniformed?" the agent spoke up again.

"They wear navy work pants and blue shirts. But they have name and facility patches," Ty said.

"I see what you're getting at," Charlie said. She had chosen one of the taco platters, and wiped at the sour cream on the corner of her mouth. "It's easy to buy those kind of work clothes, isn't it?"

"Far too easy," Mann said.

"Okay, before we start the search, will you discuss it with Don, Hoyt, and Tyson?" Charlie suggested to the agent. "Figure out a system for identifying *all* the Cobo staff during the show."

"Anything else? Judy, Carter, any problems on the loading dock this morning?"

"No problems, just delays and angry drivers. A lot of the food deliveries came in this morning. I've never seen so many hot dogs, hamburger patties, buns, popcorn, hot pretzels, mustard, and bottles of water," Judy said.

"Or toilet paper," Carter added.

"Oh, that's right. The facilities supervisor signed for a lot of things today, too. There were deliveries of TP and hand towels, hand soap for the restrooms, and there was a delivery of recyclable bins and trash containers. I remember that one, because the driver's name was Novak," Judy said.

"Spare us the details," Don said, dipping chips into the guacamole container he had commandeered for himself.

"How did the bomb-sniffing dogs work out?" Hoyt asked.

"Just fine. They had their noses to the grindstone," Judy quipped.

Everyone groaned at the bad pun. The levity seemed to signal the end of the full meeting, and small groups formed to discuss individual issues.

"Are you good?" Gil asked, following Charlie to her desk.

"Yes. You?"

"Mandy's meeting with Heinrich tonight?"

"That's right."

Gil was a great reader of people. A skill he'd picked up at eighteen when he started a summer job as his uncle's part-time car salesman. Later, he'd joined the Marines, and when he got out, he and Charlie had met and bonded at the Detroit College of Law, where they were later recruited by Homeland Security. They'd both wanted to use their law degrees to help their people, but after witnessing the blatant racial profiling at DHS they had become less enamored with their work as federal agents.

"You worried for her?"

"Not particularly. She's a professional. Look, Gil, what's bothering you?"

"I'm not prying, Charlie. Tio wants me to pull out of the case."

"You've been talking to your uncle?"

"I know you're supposed to be the one communicating with DADA, but he called last night, and I gave him an update."

"He's worried?"

"Very."

"We all took this job aware there would be risks. In fact, your uncle was the one who first warned us."

"I know. It's just that the stakes have gotten higher. I mentioned it to Don and suggested he should be thinking about Rita and Rudy."

"What'd he say?"

"You know Don. He gave me his Marine look. But maybe it would be a good idea to send Judy home, or at least back to the office. She's done a good job with the background checks and the loading dock work, but I don't see what more she can do here."

The stench of sweat, chemicals, and solder fumes hung like smoke in the garage. A couple of times, Dudiyn used the remote to open the overhead door. But gawking neighbors and their nosy dogs forced him to seal the small space again. He'd built twenty-seven PVC pipe bombs that could be detonated with a phone signal. Each would weigh about five pounds once they were loaded with nails, and the compact size would make them even more lethal.

He needed a break and some dinner. Heinrich's kitchen was useless, filled with chrome counter machines that made unappetizing food and drinks, and jars filled with grains, seeds, and nuts. The contents of his refrigerator were no better. Apples, limes, fussy little containers filled with stuff that smelled like shit. He returned to the garage and grabbed the keys to the white van.

For security, the van was parked a few blocks away in a church lot. The custodian had agreed to allow the vehicle to park for a month when Dudiyn forked over five brand-new hundred-dollar bills. Dudiyn walked once around the van with a flashlight to check for tampering. The only prints in the snow had been made by a stray cat. He drove north on John R and made a quick left. The McDonald's on Woodward Avenue would have to do for his dinner. He hated dealing with the mongrel workers, but tonight he didn't have many other options. He couldn't be away from the house too long. He had to keep an eye on the chemicals, and he still had a lot of assembly work to do.

"May I take your order?" the voice said through the speaker.

"I want a number ten," Dudiyn said.

"Do you want to add an apple pie or a milkshake to that?"

"No."

"What kind of drink do you want?"

"A Coke."

"Okay, that'll be $7.43. Pull up to the first window."

He handed ten dollars to a middle-aged Mexican woman. She pressed a button, which opened a cash drawer, and retrieved change and a receipt which she dropped into Dudiyn's outstretched hand.

"Have a good night," she said, smiling, to Dudiyn. When he didn't return the smile, she looked away. "Drive up to the next window for your food."

Tonight, Dudiyn didn't feel like leaving the van in the church lot and trudging back in the snow to the house, so he backed it into the driveway. Heinrich's car was already there.

"Where've you been?" Heinrich said coming out of the house.

"I needed some food. I can't eat that bird-food crap you have in your kitchen."

"I bought three fans. They're in here." Heinrich opened the trunk of the Saab.

Dudiyn carried the boxes into the house, through the kitchen, and into the garage. He took the fans out of the packaging and plugged them in facing the workbench. The circulating air was already working to dissipate the chemical fumes.

"That's better," Dudiyn said.

"I'm going to have some company tonight so this door will be locked," Heinrich said, pointing to the door between the kitchen and the garage. "Also, you need to move the van back to the church lot."

"Look, I still have a lot of work to do to keep to the deadline. If I'm walking back and forth, that means I'm not working."

"I don't want to take a chance on anyone seeing this van. Mack and her people may have been able to pull the security footage when you nabbed the kid, and one of them is coming here this evening."

"Let me guess. The redhead."

"Just keep your mind on the work. We need all the units completed and ready to be transported by tomorrow morning."

Dudiyn used the remote to open the garage door and close it again as he exited. The church parking lot was still empty, and he parked the rental van next to the blue church van where it would look less conspicuous. Then he placed the call he'd suspected he would have to make.

The Chinese client had hired him directly to work with Heinrich. But the Chinks were the same to him as the other mongrels. What had happened to the world? When had the white man lost control? He blamed the Jew-run media for the upheaval in the natural order of things.

"You said I should call if Heinrich became a problem."

"What is the nature of your concern?" the voice said in perfect, unaccented English.

"He's letting his personal habits affect his judgment. Plus, we've had a security breach, and I think we should push the operation back a few days."

"What kind of breach?"

"Someone broke into the place where we were keeping our supplies."

"Was anything stolen?"

"No, but . . ."

"Delaying the event is out of the question," the voice said.

"Okay. But Heinrich has become a liability. I can complete the operation alone."

"Give me a minute," the man on the other end of the call said.

Dudiyn exited the van and walked around it, checking each door. The flashlight picked up a glint on the bumper he hadn't seen before. He unlocked the back and directed his light onto the floor. He saw a shiny line from the rear of the van to the bumper. Holding the phone to his ear, he walked quickly back to the house, passing a couple of people who gave him curious looks because he wore no coat.

"Are you still there?" the voice asked.

"Yes. What do you want me to do?"

"We don't want anything to interfere with our timetable. But on the other matter, use your best judgment. Is that clear?"

"Yes. Very."

A second car was in Heinrich's driveway, a late-model Corvette. So Dudiyn used the remote to let himself into the garage. He looked around to assure himself that nothing had been disturbed, then remembered the silver residue he'd seen in the back of the van. One of the containers of aluminum powder must be leaking. He squatted next to the phony bleach bottles and examined the bottoms of the cases until he found one with a small puncture at its base. *Odd.* He got the duct tape, tore off a small piece to cover the opening, and replaced the container in the case. He turned on the light at the workbench and hunkered over it, adjusting surgical loupe glasses behind his ears and turning on his soldering iron. The sound of a woman laughing wafted into the garage. *Have your fun while you can, Casanova.* In the morning, he would swap the van for the church vehicle, and Heinrich would help him load the shrapnel-filled PVC tubes. By this time tomorrow, he would be mixing the chemicals and attaching the phone circuitry; then right under the noses of the security people at Cobo, he'd plant the bombs. He had to give Heinrich credit for the idea of a diversionary tactic: They would place small amounts of the chemical mix in the planters around the visitor areas at Cobo. That would keep the police, feds, and the investigators busy late into the night while the Spectrum staff unwittingly helped put the plan into motion.

He'd been working a half hour when he got the tickle behind his ear. Over the years, he'd come to trust the signal that someone was watching him. He looked over his shoulder toward the curtained window in the kitchen door and thought he saw a head bob out of sight. He removed the heavy-lensed glasses he wore and spun his stool to face the portal, remaining in that position for two minutes, listening and watching, before he turned back to the bench to finish his work.

Heinrich's townhouse was decorated in a contemporary style, much like his office. The first time she'd visited, they'd had a casual breakfast at his kitchen counter. But this time, he beckoned Mandy into his sleekly furnished dining room, where he offered white wine sheathed in a monogrammed stainless steel cooler. A two-tiered tray of hors d'oeuvres sat on the glass table.

"Wow, I guess I didn't dress for the occasion," Mandy said.

"Food and drink should always be a special event," Heinrich said, bringing in two long-stemmed glasses. "These are chilled to forty degrees."

"How did a security guy get to know so much about fine dining and fashion?"

"I've not always been able to indulge my tastes in the finer things of life, but now I do at every opportunity."

"I can't imagine you as poor."

"I was never poor. My family, my parents, were academics. They worked hard to make sure I had an exemplary education. But they were never particularly, uh, interesting. At school I mingled with the sons of Europe's elites. That's where I got my introduction to life's pleasures."

Heinrich leaned closely over Mandy as he poured the wine. His cologne had the musky scent of nutmeg and brandy, and his umber cashmere jacket brushed against her shoulder. He emanated the power of a dangerous, albeit elegant, predator. Heinrich sat in the white leather chair across from hers, and Mandy relaxed her back, letting her spine feel the weight of her holstered police special. She reached into her tote and pulled out a file folder.

"I have the notes and recommendations from the Secret Service. You've probably already seen them," Mandy said.

"Yes."

"I thought it would be useful to coordinate our efforts to meet the recommendations."

"I agree. Why didn't Ms. Mack join us?"

"She's been detained on another matter that requires her attention."

Heinrich's smile was almost indiscernible. But Mandy saw it before he covered his lips with a tilt of his wineglass. Mandy took a sip of wine and studied the bite-size delicacies on the tray.

"Please. Try some. I made them myself. Simple appetizers, really. Ceviche, some dates in orange zest, and foie gras."

Mandy laughed. "You make your own foie gras?"

"Cooking is only one of the ways I choose to express myself."

185

Mandy started with the lime-cooked red snapper, chewing slowly and then giving her top lip a quick flick of her tongue. Heinrich liked watching women eat, and he'd noticed Mandy's habit of licking her lips when they shared breakfast. Next, she bit into the goose liver on toast, her eyes closed for a second in appreciation. Heinrich felt himself stir.

"These are really tasty."

Mandy slid a typewritten paper across the table. Heinrich glanced down at it, but didn't pick it up. Finally, he reached into his jacket and pulled a Montblanc ink pen from its recesses. He unscrewed the cap and drew the page toward him with the tips of his fingers. He checked a few items on the list and pushed it back to her. He recapped the pen and returned it to his inner pocket.

"Those things are being handled by Spectrum," Heinrich said matter-of-factly.

"Fine. We'll take on the other items," Mandy said, checking the list. "We've doubled our security on the Chinese automaker. Their company executives are coming in tomorrow. So far, their work seems to be business as usual, but we've also put a guard at their hotel."

"That seems prudent. I've worked closely with Mr. Kwong and his bosses. They're up to something, but I can't imagine it's anything violent. Kwong is such an obsequious man. Whatever they're up to, I'm sure it troubles the Detroit auto dealers. That's why I've put up with their meddling."

"Including us?"

"Well, I have to admit, your team has been more competent than I gave you credit for. The food and wine are sort of a peace offering. So I hope you'll put the paperwork aside and enjoy what I've prepared."

Mandy didn't hear Heinrich's phone ring, but it must have vibrated because he looked annoyed as he reached into his pocket for the instrument. He looked at the number and rose from his seat.

"Excuse me. I have to take this call. Please, enjoy the hors d'oeuvres."

Heinrich answered with a "hold on," then disappeared into his den. His face was pinched in irritation as he closed the sliding doors to the dining room. Mandy waited only a couple of seconds before bouncing to her feet. She headed to the kitchen and dumped her wine into the sink. She'd heard the sound of the garage door opening shortly after she'd arrived, and wondered if someone else was in the house. She peeked into the window, then heard Heinrich's muffled voice rise in anger, and his footsteps, so she quickly stepped back into the dining room. She was standing at the table, examining the appetizers, when the sliding door opened. Heinrich gave her a quizzical look.

"I hope you don't mind. I was about to pour myself another glass of wine," Mandy said, smiling and feigning a slight buzz.

Heinrich's sophistication didn't include the talent of distancing his emotions from his face. The irritation of being disturbed by the call was quickly eclipsed by lust, and he moved to stand very close to Mandy. She deftly moved back to her seat, leaving him to pour the wine.

"You're afraid of me," he said, handing her the glass

"We've been through this before," Mandy replied.

"Why did you ask to meet me?"

"Charlie and Don aren't your biggest fans. But I can tell you're a professional, and it doesn't make sense for our teams to be adversaries."

Heinrich hovered over Mandy. Anticipating. His scent now the fragrance of smoldering ash. He noted the contrast between the pale skin of her forehead and red hair, and the way her shoulder-length locks brushed the fabric of her black turtleneck. He returned to his chair and poured himself more wine.

"How long have you known Ms. Mack? Have you worked with her before?"

"Don't you already know the answers to those questions?"

Heinrich smiled. "Well, as you say, I am a professional. I know you're a police officer. So how is it you've come to work with private investigators?"

"Charlie is a friend."

"A friend?"

"Yes. And colleague."

"Not a lover?"

"Where'd you hear that?"

"Word gets around." Heinrich took on a smug look. "You two, uh, don't seem the type."

"What type is that, Mr. Heinrich?"

"I didn't mean any insult. It's just that my idea of American lesbians is a bit more corduroy than cashmere."

"I'd think an erudite man like you wouldn't be so narrow-minded." Mandy reached for her tote. Now, she really *was* beginning to feel the effects of the wine. "I'm leaving."

"As you wish. I didn't mean to drive you away with my questions. Too personal, perhaps?"

"Perhaps."

Heinrich walked into the den, returning with Mandy's coat and scarf. He assisted her with her jacket, and Mandy stuffed the scarf in her tote.

"Speaking of erudite, I thought I understood your inference when you called saying you wanted to meet at my home. I was very clear with you last time about what I want."

Mandy paused in the doorway. She'd thought of a half-dozen ploys to extricate herself from tonight's one-on-one. Fortunately, Heinrich's smugness and insults had made it an easy proposition.

"I guess I'm just not as sophisticated as either of us thought. Thanks for your time and cooperation."

Mandy walked carefully on the slick walkway to Charlie's Corvette. The engine fired up right away, and she backed out of the driveway and away from the house. She saw the light glowing through the small window on the side of the garage. She was pretty sure the man she'd seen was Lin's assailant, Dudiyn. He seemed to be doing some wiring, she was almost certain she'd seen the hot tip of a soldering iron.

At 9 p.m., the Mack Partners, Mandy, and Cynthia Fitzgerald were around the table. In an hour, an all-hands-on-deck search would begin of any location where the general public would have access. Twenty Cobo facilities staff would participate in the search while Spectrum staff would monitor all cameras as usual, keep an eye on the overnight construction work at the Jeep display, and guard the areas controlled by Guí Motors.

Mandy had returned to Cobo with a slight headache. She described Heinrich's maneuvers with appetizers and white wine, and reported on Dudiyn's presence in the garage.

"That sounds like him, all right," Cynthia said.

"Did you see any other vehicles?" Gil asked.

"No. Just Heinrich's Saab."

"You couldn't tell what Dudiyn was doing?" Don asked.

"No. Like I said, I thought I saw a soldering iron on a stand. He had on some kind of glasses and was sitting at a workbench."

"Could be making bombs," Gil stated.

"Damn. Why can't we get a search warrant and go see for ourselves?" Don asked.

"It might be a good idea to check in with Tony tonight," Charlie said. "Maybe DHS will tell us what's going on at the house. But first I've got one more piece of business. Gil thinks some of us might need to pull back from the case."

"Pull back?" Judy asked.

"Yes. Because of the danger," Gil said. "Judy, I thought you might want to move back to the office. The only fieldwork left to do is tonight's search. After that, we wait and watch."

"I can help watch."

"That's not a bad idea, Acosta," Don agreed.

"Wait a minute; regular deliveries will be coming to Cobo tomorrow, and there's still the communications to monitor," Judy argued.

Charlie observed the dynamics. Judy looked hurt. But things *were* getting too hot to keep the civilians around. In the waiting and watching game, it was good to have as many eyes and ears as possible, but it wasn't fair to ask people to face risks they weren't getting paid to take.

"What do you think, Cynthia?" Charlie asked.

Cynthia had been studying the room, too. She'd spent almost a year keeping an eye on Heinrich and assessing the danger to Cobo. She knew he was close to acting; that's why she'd flagged the situation for Scott two weeks ago. Chenglei's murder had been the final warning for her.

"I think Judy should go home. I think we should warn Tyson and the department heads. And if it were up to me, I'd close the show."

Tony's information on Heinrich's house had come from the secret eyewitness, who he still wouldn't identify as Kwong. When Charlie called him, Tony reported a white van coming and going from the house for over a week. And the man they knew as Dudiyn had been walking around the neighborhood and entering the home and garage at all hours.

"Are they assembling bombs?"

"No one's been able to get inside the garage to confirm if explosives are being assembled there."

"Cynthia saw phones and phony bleach bottles filled with some silver powder in the weapons garage. Dudiyn took those things away."

"Those could very well be bomb components," Tony said. "I'll check that out. There's also been another kind of activity going on at Heinrich's house. I've seen a tape of various women visiting. One of the women was your friend, Mandy."

"I know. We sent her in, to see what she could find out from Heinrich."

"How did that work?"

"It didn't."

"So how long have the two of you been seeing each other?"

"For a while."

"That's why there's no interest in fanning old flames?"

"I'm only looking forward, Tony. Only forward."

"Is that all you're saying?"

"No. Thanks for the information. Bye."

The search on level one was the easiest. Half of the ground level was parking, which was regularly patrolled by Cobo security. There was a stage area and exhibit space in the Michigan Hall rooms, but the rest of level one was taken up by Spectrum offices, back-of-house storage, a TV studio, and the loading dock area. Those areas were unavailable to the general public during the auto show, with the exception of the broadcast operation, which would get a lot of use during the upcoming three-day press preview.

Gil's search partner was the junior DHS agent. They hopped out of their golf cart and pressed the buzzer at the door of the TV facility. The chief engineer, a no-nonsense guy who had built the operation from scratch, knew everything about the space.

"During the press preview days, I have more than a hundred confirmed bookings for shoot/edit/satellite packages; we're working around the clock. A half hour of time costs two thousand dollars, so I'm dealing only with local network affiliates, the international media, and the major print publications, not the guy who writes a newsletter about cars. The broadcast and cable networks bring their own production trucks to the show."

"What do you get for two grand?" Gil asked.

"An editor, a single-camera shoot, studio space if you want it, and uplink time on our satellite. Most people are doing five-minute segments for their newscast or website. A lot of it is on tape, but some are doing live shots."

Gil and the agent searched a half-dozen edit rooms, two black-box studios, and a prop room, and did a thorough sweep under desks and chairs. Finally, they examined the master control room.

"You have an impressive amount of equipment," Gil said.

"Our equipment costs are hundreds of thousands of dollars a

year, and it's all under lock and key," the chief said, patting his jeans pocket, "and I'm the one with the key."

Gil and the agent returned to their transportation. It was almost midnight. "He's got a close eye on the TV facility. I doubt anyone will bring something in he doesn't see," Gil said.

"We need more people like him. Where to next?"

"Michigan Hall, but there's a lot to cover, I counted almost thirty racing cars in there. We didn't really talk about how we would inspect the cars. Let's check in with Charlie."

"Yes, Gil?" Charlie shouted into the two-way radio.

"How are we handling the vehicle searches? We have two dozen or so on display in Michigan Hall."

"We were just talking about the cars. Come on up to level two. Let's figure it out."

Chapter 10

Saturday, January 7, 2006
Auto Show: 1 Day

The two-person search teams on level two were following a concentric-circles pattern, working their way into the center of each floor. They were checking window ledges, balconies, entrances and exits, alcoves, public restrooms, vendor spaces, seating areas, the information booths, ticket kiosks, and coat-check rooms. Next, they'd moved inward to search hallways, vertical transportation—the engineering name for elevators and escalators—and benches and planters. They'd been at it for two hours, using rubber gloves to reach into corners, under surfaces, and inside holes and crevices. On the second-level concourse, the search teams circled their golf carts in what looked like the defensive tactic of a 19th-century wagon train against an Indian assault. In the center were the Mack partners.

"I've got a motorsports setup downstairs. There are a bunch of racing cars, NASCAR simulators, and several other exhibitors," Gil said.

"We should be looking under each vehicle," Don noted.

"We better save that for the bomb sweep," Charlie said. "ATF will be bringing in dogs tonight, and that's when they'll check the interiors of the vehicles. We'll make sure they also use the undercarriage inspection mirrors. For now, let's just focus on things like mirrors, locks, the windshield, and bumpers."

"One thing we should be looking for are transmitters," senior agent Mann said. "They can be used to trigger an explosion. They can be very tiny; some are magnetized and can be easily attached to a vehicle."

"Did everyone hear that?"

Heads nodded.

"We'll need some cotton gloves," Mann said. "Gliding your hand along the surface of the vehicle is the best way to find any bugs. Rubber gloves are going to stick."

"Can we get the gloves we need?" Charlie asked the janitorial staff honcho who Ty had described as the best supervisor in the building."

"No problem," she responded.

"Sounds like the showroom search could take three or four hours," Don noted. "Maybe we should do that now and save the perimeter checks on the top levels for last."

"Okay, we'll do it that way," Charlie agreed. "Does anybody need food yet?" Charlie looked at Don.

"I could use some coffee," Gil said.

"And maybe some sandwiches," Don added.

At 4 a.m., the search of the vehicles in all the exhibit, concourse and showroom spaces was completed. The gloved inspections had worked perfectly, and soon the teams had the car exterior searches down to ten minutes, a bit longer for the SUVs and trucks. Nothing out of the ordinary had been discovered by the searchers, and with thanks Charlie had released the janitorial staff to resume their other duties.

The Mack team came together again before tackling the upper level perimeter searches, including the People Mover station and the rooftop parking area.

"I think we can divide up again on the top levels," Charlie announced, looking at the floor plan. "We'll have an inside group and an outside group. Four teams will check the rooftop parking and search the People Mover areas. The interior teams will search the meeting rooms on levels three and four. You'll likely finish first, and you should go back to the hotel and get a few hours of sleep when you're done. I'm volunteering me, Gil, Don, and Hoyt for outside duty. Do I have four more volunteers?" Everyone raised their hand, and Charlie smiled. "Okay, I appreciate your diligence. Don, I'll ride with you. The rest of you figure it out among yourselves. We'll head up top in fifteen minutes; those of us going outside will need coats. It's snowing again."

Charlie, Don, Gil and Hoyt were checking the third-floor access to the People Mover. The doors leading to the Congress Street stairway were locked, but would reopen again at noon. The group checked along the inside window frames, along the textured walls, and around signage. They crouched to rub gloved hands along the underside of the escalators and to inspect the tripod arms on the waist-high rider turnstiles.

"Are we done here? My knees are killing me with all the crouching I've done tonight," Don complained. "Let's go up and look at the passenger platform."

Like all the People Mover stations, the Cobo station had unique artwork. The glass mosaic of vintage cars adorning the walls and a stretch of the tunnel was a tribute to Detroit's long-time dominance in the auto manufacturing business.

"That turquoise car is a '55 T-bird convertible," Don said with admiration.

"I wouldn't mind having the real thing," Gil responded.

"What's behind those doors?" Hoyt asked, pointing to an unmarked door in the wall behind them.

Charlie looked at her blueprints. "It's marked storage. Probably cleaning supplies. The carpeted areas must get pretty dirty from foot traffic in and out of the station."

The Detroit Transportation Corporation had already increased the security cameras on the People Mover system in anticipation of next month's Super Bowl. The Cobo Station was just one of thirteen along the 2.9 miles of elevated single-track. Charlie

195

counted four surveillance cameras on the third level entry, and now she noted another four in the passenger waiting area. The station platform was cold because the narrow tunnel, which cut through the northeast section of Cobo Hall, allowed not only the automated train, but winter's cold gusts, to enter.

"It wouldn't be impossible to climb down onto the tracks and plant an explosive device," Don said, pointing. "How long is this tunnel?"

"I don't know," Charlie said. "Tomorrow, let's make sure to check in with DTC's office. I assume they do a regular check of the tracks, but we'll ask them to do a special walk-through tomorrow. We'll need to get DADA involved for that."

When they were finished at the People Mover, they joined the search group on the rooftop. Slowed down by the snow, the other teams were still painstakingly checking the walls, entrances, and vents. The rooftop could accommodate twelve hundred cars, but at 5:00 a.m. on a Saturday, only six cars were parked on the rooftop, close to the west elevator entrance.

"They're probably monthly renters," Charlie speculated as they passed the cars.

"We only have this side to complete," Mandy reported to the partners. "We've searched all the other sides, but we haven't checked any of the cars yet."

"Okay, we'll take the cars," Charlie said. Don made a wide turn in the accumulating snow, followed by Hoyt and Gil in the other cart.

The group stopped and gathered around a Dodge truck. Charlie used her glove to wipe away snow on the driver's side windshield.

"Yep. It's a monthly parker. Look, there's too much snow to pat these vehicles down. Let's just do a visual check and take pictures of each one and the monthly parking permit. We'll have Judy get the names of the owners and call them later today."

"I'll take pictures of the license plates too," Hoyt said.

"Good idea."

Gil used his BlackBerry to take a close-up of the parking permit, making sure to get a clear view of the permit number. Hoyt used his scarf to clear the rear plates to take pictures. Don and Charlie stood together watching the snow fall. The flash of the phone cameras made the flakes look like winter lightning bugs.

A couple of hours before daybreak, Dudiyn drove the white-paneled van to the church. A fresh layer of snow had fallen overnight, and the van's tires made the first tracks in the lot. He removed the tags and wiped down the handles, mirrors, seats, and steering wheel. He popped the lock on the blue van and hotwired the vehicle. The parking lot camera would record his activities, but it didn't matter. By the time someone reviewed the church's security tape, he and the stolen van would be long gone. He left a second set of tire tracks as he exited the lot, turned left away from the house, and drove toward the freeway so the tire treads would blend in with those of other vehicles. He turned north on Woodward Avenue and then doubled back to the house. The early weekend hour and the snow kept the nosy neighbors indoors as he backed the church van into the garage.

The pipe bombs were neatly stacked in boxes on the far side of the garage. Each plastic casing had a stick-on logo of a well-known pest control company. When planted, the bombs would look like industrial-sized rat traps. The chemicals had been measured, placed in quart bags, and labeled. That would make them easier and faster to mix. The rewired circuits were in a bag. It would take only a few hours to pack the pipes with the explosives and shrapnel, and attach the fuses.

Dudiyn looked at his watch; he had at least four hours before Heinrich returned to help him load the vehicle. He entered the house, relieved himself in the fancy toilet, and stared into the mirror. He hadn't slept in twenty hours. He gauged whether he was hungry enough to go out for food, but settled for orange juice, which he drank from the plastic container. He returned to the garage and climbed into the roomy backseat of the church van. Within minutes he was sleeping soundly.

∽ ∽ ∽

Last night's search had been exhausting, but useful. It gave them a baseline for noticing any modifications to the public landscape of the building. It was one thing to study the blueprints of Cobo, another to have, literally, touched the surfaces of the building.

The wind howled outside Charlie's hotel room, and she watched the flurries dance in front of the window. She was checking out today. There would be no more breaks for phone calls to her mother, meals away from Cobo, or sex. In the next twenty-four hours, they had to discover—and prevent—the threat to Cobo. If they couldn't, Detroit would be a sad footnote in the age of terrorism.

"We need to leave soon," Charlie called out. She looked at Mandy's black turtleneck, jeans, boots, and ski parka on the side chair. "You're all packed, right?"

"Yep. I basically packed two days ago, I'm just wearing what I had on last night. Are you finished?" Mandy asked, sticking her head out of the bathroom door and holding a string of floss.

"Almost. I have some toiletries to get when you're through."

"Okay, I just need to brush; then I'll get dressed."

"You don't mind Heinrich seeing you in the same clothes?" Charlie hollered to the open bathroom door.

Mandy came to the threshold with a toothbrush in her mouth, wearing only panties and a bra. She held up her index finger to signal the additional time she needed, then reappeared. "Nope. What can you expect from someone who's more corduroy than cashmere?"

Charlie and Mandy knocked on Judy's door. She hadn't taken easily to the order that she return to the office. She'd pouted, and rationalized why she shouldn't be sent home. But Charlie, Don, and Gil held fast to their decision. It wasn't until Judy invoked a Broadway show tune that Charlie began to have a change of heart. Like Judy she was a sucker for musicals, believing they were the source of all practical wisdom. As a last resort, Judy had belted out a few bars of the show-stopper, "And I Am Telling You I'm Not Going" from *Dreamgirls*. That's when Charlie knew

198

she had lost the fight so she pulled rank on the partners, and proposed a compromise. Judy would spend minimum time at Cobo, but would continue to monitor communications and coordinate the Mack partners' needs from her hotel room. Judy answered the door with an enormous smile, which Charlie mirrored.

"All ready to go?" Judy asked, stepping aside to allow Charlie and Mandy to enter.

"Yep. We have a meeting with Spectrum staff, and then with Tyson's boss. I'll come back for you around one o'clock."

"Wow. You've already got this place laid out like a command center," Mandy said admiringly.

Judy had, undoubtedly, worked with the hotel staff to accommodate her room's new function. She'd negotiated for two phones and two desks, which were cleared for her array of laptops, file folders, and phone chargers.

"I'm already coordinating with Carter on today's last-minute deliveries. I'm speaking with the drivers if they need to be appeased while he's checking out their paperwork. I can monitor the radio transmissions from here, but I need to get the rest of the BlackBerry equipment and set it up."

"Got it. We'll see you later. I'll call if I need anything," Charlie said.

Spectrum staff meetings were held bullpen-style. Chairs were grouped in an orbit of the company's self-proclaimed celestial object—Geoff Heinrich. He remained on his feet, the better for his audience to see his tailored black wool slacks and black linen tunic. Today his boots were made of some dead reptile. Department heads had given their reports, and were now listening to Heinrich trivialize the auto dealers' concerns about a threat to the show.

"Nevertheless, we want to be at the top of our game for the next ten days, ladies and gentlemen. The North American International Auto Show is why we exist. Questions?"

"When the Secret Service is here, do we follow their orders?" an employee asked.

Heinrich pirouetted to face the young man, who began to shrink under his angry glare. Veteran staff shifted uncomfortably and stared at the floor. Cynthia was mortified that this new weapons technician didn't understand the unspoken rule that Heinrich's call for questions was just for show.

The Mack team sat together, Charlie between Don and Mandy. They were there to give Heinrich the impression that they carried no suspicions of him. Charlie felt movement at her right arm and was too late to object as Mandy rose to make a point in support of the hapless employee.

"My experience with the Secret Service is they will give us a wide berth to protect the show. Their primary concern is the protection of the commerce secretary. But, if the needs of the show conflict with their protection detail, they'll pull rank."

Heinrich stared at Mandy. His countenance changed from anger to amusement. The staffer looked at Mandy and smiled; she smiled back, shot Heinrich a look of disdain, and sat down. She wouldn't return Charlie's glare.

"That's very useful, Ms. Porter. Do you or Ms. Mack have any further observations or helpful information?"

Charlie spoke up before Mandy could. "No, we don't. We appreciate being included in your staff meeting, and this is also a good time to thank you for the extra people you've assigned to us. I know you have protocols to follow for the first-day activities, and we'll try not to get in your way."

"What was that all about?" Don asked Charlie. They were taking a golf cart to the fourth level to meet with Cobo's general manager.

"What?"

"That interaction between Porter and Heinrich. She can really push his buttons, huh?"

"I guess so. He's a creep."

"I see you've come around."

"We're going to take him down."

"*Before* he blows up something?"

"That's definitely my preference."

"When you think about it, Mack, all we still have is a lot of speculation that something bad will happen if we can't stop it. Gil said it reminded him of his first year in the Special Forces. He'd be in the outskirts of some country hunting down bad guys, but didn't always know what the bad guys looked like. So, all he and his company could do was get up in the morning and drive around, waiting for a reason to shoot at somebody."

"That's a pretty good analogy. The difference is, we know the identity of the bad guy."

"That's the part that stinks. We should just grab him and the other guy."

"How do we know there's just *one* other guy? Maybe there's a whole bunch of bad guys. There was more than one man when Josh was shot. Maybe some of the bombs are at Heinrich's house and some are somewhere else. What if we raid the house, and he blows up the neighborhood?"

"You're doing that Post-it thing in your head again."

Don and Charlie were met by Ty outside the office of Mike Mathers, Cobo's General Manager. When Ty had called to set up the meeting, he had discovered there was a problem.

"He's mad as hell."

"About what?" Charlie asked.

"I don't think he really believes there's much of a threat to the auto show. He thinks it's just DADA being paranoid. But a couple of the department heads have called in to say they're afraid for their safety and are not coming in to work. Now, he's worried about the possibility of damage to Cobo and potential lawsuits. If there's a real threat, he's obligated to inform our insurance company and board of directors."

"Holy Jesus, and he's just thinking about all of this stuff now?" Don asked.

"Like I said, he and DADA have been going back and forth about auto show security for years. He reluctantly agreed to bring in Spectrum, and he thought bringing you guys in was just another precaution. But now he's freaked out."

Mike Mathers was built like a fullback. His shirt strained to contain his shoulders, and he stood six or seven inches above Don. He had a firm handshake and would have been handsome had he allowed his barber to completely shave his head rather than trim the swaths of hair on either side of his dome. After shaking hands, he landed in his chair in a thud and leaned over the desk.

"Jesus Christ, Ms. Mack, what the hell did you say to my staff yesterday?"

Don recognized a kindred spirit and didn't give Charlie a chance to respond. He stood and leaned over the desk. Even so, he had to look up at the man.

"Look, Mathers, don't make us play guessing games. Time is too short. What the hell is the problem?"

The two men assessed each other. Players face-to-face on the line of scrimmage. Charlie and Tyson watched, not knowing quite what to expect. Finally, Mathers leaned back in his chair and entwined his fingers over his massive chest.

"I'll tell you the problem, Rutkowski. I've had three department heads call in sick today. The day before the auto show begins. That's never happened before, and it's a huge pain in the ass for me."

Don lowered himself back into the chair and rubbed his hand through his thinning hair.

"Well, I can see that would be a big problem, Mathers. We told your staff what we believe. There's a chance that tomorrow, or the next day, or the next, some fool will try to set off explosives at Cobo to disrupt the auto show. I understand your people are scared, but we can't stop this thing by being afraid. We're committed to stopping it, but we're going to need your help."

Mathers looked at Don, then over to Charlie and Tyson, and offered a wry smile. The tension in the room plummeted.

"You're right, Ty; he's a pistol."

"I told you, boss."

"What is it I can do to help keep us safe?" Mathers asked.

ของ ของ ของ

Ty walked Charlie and Don to the golf cart and took the backseat. Mathers had agreed to approve overtime for staff in food services, facilities management, engineering, and parking management rather than bring in temporary staff. Bringing in new people meant doing more background checks, and there was no time for that. Mathers would also call Hartwell for advice on how to handle his board and the insurance company.

"So, what's his story? Is he an ex-football player, or something?" Don asked.

"He played two years with the Packers before he busted up his knee. He's run convention venues in Sacramento and Toledo, and was the number two in Dallas. He knows what he's doing, but he's very practical, not much out-of-the-box thinking. One thing I'll say about him: He doesn't run scared. I once saw him make Heinrich blink."

"Good man," Don said matter-of-factly.

"Is Elise Hillman one of the people who called in sick, Ty?" Charlie asked.

"Yes. I was a little surprised. Her husband probably insisted she stay out of danger."

"Well, I'm not blaming her," Charlie said. "Who's second-in-command in food services?"

"Bill Fox. He's been around a while, knows the ropes. Team player. He'll be okay."

"What about facilities and parking?" Don asked.

"Now, that's a different story. I'll need to check to see who's filling in, in those departments."

"Where to?" Don asked, starting up the electric cart.

"Can we check in with facilities?" Charlie asked.

"I don't see why not," Tyson responded.

"I'm surprised you have a full-time facilities staff. I thought most organizations outsourced that kind of work," Don said.

"Maybe the smaller guys do, but we have a constant need for maintenance services. Besides the general cleaning staff, we have specialty cleaners for our elevators and escalators. We have a landscaping and green-space crew, and a few others."

Ty took the lead when they entered the facilities office. "Hey, Amanda. I know the boss is out today, but who's in charge when he's away?"

"Dennis Calhoun. He's been up and down all day. He's probably at the loading area. They were finishing up the inventory and doing a schedule for the week. You want me to call him?"

Ty looked to Charlie for direction on the question, and Don and Charlie stepped out of the office to confer.

"We could go down to the dock and see Calhoun in action," Charlie suggested.

"Let's do it," Don said.

Calhoun and three others stood over a makeshift table in one of the storage rooms near the loading dock. The three men and one woman looked up when Tyson and his companions entered, but quickly returned to their heated conversation. Charlie told Ty not to interrupt, and she used the opportunity to examine the room and its surroundings. In the hall were several mini-loaders, two small tractors, and a half-dozen golf carts. Two walls of the room were covered with industrial-sized metal shelves holding all manner of materials and supplies needed to operate a convention facility. In the center of the space were huge palettes holding shrink-wrapped crates and boxes marked as paper goods, light-bulbs, floor mats, glass cleaner, and floor wax. A gigantic roll of red carpet secured by several chains was on one wall, and a canvas cart was filled with hard hats.

"Is this space normally locked?" Charlie asked Ty.

"Yes. There's also always somebody here to answer the phone."

Charlie recognized Calhoun from the first Cobo meeting. Although he wasn't the department head, he seemed to have the attention of the others and command of the table. The group wore dark work pants and blue shirts—some short-sleeved, some not. A Cobo patch was on the shoulder of the shirts, and each person had a name patch. Charlie moved closer; she wanted to hear what he was saying.

"No, that's not going to work. I need you for at least ten hours on Monday. The walk-through with the Secret Service is in the morning, and you have to be there, Rachel. I'll make it up to you."

Charlie led the way out of the room. "I think I've seen enough, Ty. Calhoun seems to have things well in hand. I don't think we need to interrupt him. Invite him to our six o'clock meeting, will you?"

"So that's how we'll use the new security bands," Tyson completed his report to those assembled around the Mack conference table.

"It's a good plan—simple, but effective," Don said. "A different color-coded band for each day ensures that we know who belongs and who doesn't."

"I have to give credit to your new freelancer for the procedure," Ty said, pointing to agent Mann. "We distributed the bands last night to the janitors on the search team. We'll use another color for today. Fortunately, we have enough bands in-house to make it work. Only staff that need to be in the auto show areas will wear them. I've typed up the color codes for the rest of the week, and the affected departments will receive the bands this afternoon."

"Does Judy have the codes list?" Charlie asked.

"Yes. I've already faxed it over to her at the hotel."

"Good. We still need to talk with parking management about how they plan to search their facilities ..."

"I've done some checking on that, Ms. Mack," Carter Bernstein said. "Cobo outsources the work to a local company, and their main job is to collect tickets and fees."

"That's true," Ty said. "But we have an office that negotiates the contract with the company and also coordinates VIP arrivals and special valet services. That office interfaces with Spectrum on parking security."

"But Spectrum's security of the parking areas consists mainly of patrols, which we're now supplementing, and the cameras, right?" agent Mann asked.

"That's right," Ty agreed.

"We should probably do a meeting with the parking company," Don said.

"I'll go with you, Don," Gil said. "Ty, can you come along to make introductions?"

"Sure," Tyson said.

"Where is he now?" Charlie asked, making herself comfortable on Cynthia's office couch.

"Not sure. After the staff meeting, he met with IT. He went to Guí Motors to see Mr. Kwong, then came back to the office, got his coat, and said he was going to lunch."

"He hasn't been staying around Cobo very much in the last few days."

"Odd, isn't it, when you're in charge of security for the auto show."

"Has he mentioned Lin?"

"No. Not a word."

"Have your people noticed anything unusual?"

"No. Everything's been fairly routine. What about the warehouse where Lin was found?" Cynthia asked. "Who's checking up on that?"

"Our Homeland Security liaison, Tony Canterra, is following up on what's going on there. I'm pretty sure he already knows, but he's keeping some things to himself."

"How is Lin?"

"Fine. Still resting at my place. I ordered groceries for him yesterday. He'll be there a couple more days. I don't want to send him home until he has fewer bruises."

"He's a brave kid."

"I agree. But he may not think so. He was kind of embarrassed that he was so scared. How's Amy doing?"

Cynthia shifted in her chair, and her eyes darted away from Charlie.

"What?" Charlie asked.

"I know I shouldn't have, but I warned Amy she should stay home."

"Did she?"

"No. She said she couldn't leave if Mr. Kwong was staying."

"It's hard to know the right thing to do. Have you considered leaving?"

"No."

"Duty and obligation?"

"Something like that."

"Okay. Give me a call if you see or hear from Heinrich, will you?"

"You think we'll be able to stop him, Charlie?"

"We'll stop him. Know why? Because he's not nearly as smart as he thinks he is."

Dudiyn heard the front door open, and he stirred. He looked at his watch. He had slept four hours. When he emerged from the van, Heinrich was standing in the garage.

"Are you ready?" Heinrich asked.

"Yes. Any trouble at Cobo?"

"Everything's under control. You worry too much. I'll change clothes and be right back."

Dudiyn took out the van's comfortable rear seat to make room for the cargo and to give him space for the assembly work he would do later. It took a couple of hours to load the van. Even though the chemicals weren't yet mixed, they shouldn't be unnecessarily jostled and required careful packing.

"I have to change clothes again and get back to the office. Give me at least an hour before you arrive at Cobo."

"Okay. I'll get something to eat before I come over. I should probably park on level four. I need all the ventilation I can get."

"No. Park on the ground level; it will give you more options if something goes wrong. There'll be more vehicles and foot traffic, and you won't stand out to the Mack patrols. After you pack the components, you'll need to find a place to change into your uniform."

"Okay."

Dudiyn wondered if he should kill Heinrich now, or wait until things were underway at Cobo. He should probably wait. It might raise suspicions if no one could find the head of Spectrum the day before the auto show. Dudiyn tucked the pistol in his waistband and put the bagged uniform and his shaving kit on the front seat of the van. He positioned the small briefcase with his passport, cash, and a change of clothes behind the seat before taking a last look around his makeshift workroom. Then he used the remote to open the garage, and pulled out. It was snowing again. As the garage door closed, he threw the remote control into the snowbank next to the driveway.

"What is it, Mr. Kwong?"

"My bosses are here. I think they may be suspicious of me."

"Why would they be suspicious? Our commerce secretary is coming here on Wednesday to present a commendation to the president of your company. Isn't that a demonstration of your good work?"

"Yes, Mr. Canterra, but I thought ... maybe ..."

"What's bothering you?"

"Heinrich."

"What about him?"

"He came by to see me today. He had a changed demeanor. Have you heard anything?"

"Nothing definitive. We did intercept a call, and we know whoever hired him may be trying to get rid of him. But that shouldn't jeopardize your situation."

"Okay."

"Anything else?" Canterra stared at his desk phone. He didn't want Kwong to get cold feet. He would need him to help prosecute Heinrich.

"You're sure my family is still safe?"

"Yes. They're safe."

The six o'clock team meeting was larger than the borrowed conference room could hold, so at Cynthia's invitation they'd moved the gathering into the Spectrum bull pen. The full contingent of freelancers were joined by Cobo representatives from engineering, food services, administration, and the parking management company. Judy had rejoined Gil, Don, and Charlie for a few hours at Cobo to make sure all the information anyone needed could be gathered and shared. Everyone was surprised when, fifteen minutes into the meeting, Geoff Heinrich joined the group and pulled up a chair next to Cynthia.

"Did I miss anything?"

Everyone looked toward Charlie, who had stopped talking in mid-sentence when she saw Heinrich advancing. She gave a glance toward Cynthia and continued.

"No. Not really; we're basically at status quo. We've got our full contingent here tonight and throughout the day tomorrow to do patrols. We've done another scan of the press corps invitees to see if anything has changed in the last couple of days. We've had a few dropouts, but we have no new names on the list."

Heinrich nodded. He was playing it very cool, didn't show any sign of nervousness or his usual indifference. He was appraising the DHS agents and assiduously avoiding eye contact with Mandy, who had been wearing a scowl since his arrival.

"Ms. Mack was just bringing us up to date on a new plan to identify staff who belong on the floors. It's a technique used by Homeland Security," Cynthia said.

"Oh?" Heinrich said, returning his attention to Charlie. "How does that work?"

"It's a color-coded wristband. Simple really, and it's not going to be used by everyone. For instance, your Spectrum staff and our team won't have them."

"Who will?"

"Maintenance people, engineering, janitors, food services employees, Cobo's communications and events team. Any staff who will be in the concourse, showrooms, hallways, and exhibit spaces."

"What about exhibitors?"

"That'll be hit or miss. We're providing the bracelets to the exhibitors, but we can't police their compliance. We only came up with the idea yesterday," Charlie said with a glance toward Ty and agent Mann, who had devised the plan.

"It's a good idea," Heinrich said. "May I have the code sheet?"

"Judy, please provide a copy to Mr. Heinrich."

Charlie and Judy shared a look. Judy pulled the code sheet from her portfolio, rose from her chair, and walked it over to Heinrich.

"Thank you. Ms. Novak, isn't it?" Heinrich smiled and gave Judy a hazel-eyed wink.

For a moment, her knees grew rubbery from his attention until she remembered who she was dealing with. She offered a weak smile and returned to her chair with another glance toward Charlie.

"What precautions are being taken for the exhibitor previews tonight?" Heinrich asked.

"We're leaving those events to the exhibitors. We have a list of the VIP attendees, and we'll have ID checks at the front entrance. The exhibitors will provide escorts to their displays. Cobo security will be wearing their yellow parkas, but our patrols will be inconspicuous. Is there something more you think we should do?" Charlie asked.

"No. That seems quite adequate."

"We've put together a master schedule, which includes each department's activity, and the exhibitors' agendas, as well as the required Secret Service activity. It's a timeline of what's happening at Cobo, as we know it, for the next twelve hours. We're passing it around now. Take a look at it, and then we'll take questions," Charlie said to the group.

6 p.m.
Planters watered and visitor seating areas cleaned
Loading dock closed to deliveries

8 p.m.
VIP Advanced exhibition receptions:

210

Detroit Auto Dealers Association, General Motors,
Hyundai, Bavarian Motor Works, Ford Motor Company,
Guí Motors, Honda, & Toyota
 Valet parking staff on duty
 Restricted security patrols

9:30 p.m.
All visitors cleared from Cobo

10 p.m.
Valet parking closed
Cobo Security patrols resume in all areas
Non-permanent fixtures placed: smoking area ashcans,
waste containers, rope & stanchions

11 p.m.
Alcohol, Tobacco, and Firearms (ATF) Bomb Squad
sweep 1

Midnight
Washrooms cleaned and stocked
Red carpet installations completed
Elevator & escalator cleaning
Auto Show banners/signage installations

4 a.m.
Carpet vacuuming

6 a.m.
Metropolitan Police/Secret Service Briefing. Level 3
conference room
 Valet Parking set up & Special Deliveries (Larned
Garage)
 Street Sweeping and sidewalk cleaning
 Press Credentials delivered to security area

A general discussion ensued about the schedule, staffing needs, and assignments. Carter Bernstein would rotate between monitoring security cameras and the loading dock special deliveries. Hoyt and Don had constructed a two-person patrol schedule so they could cover more ground. Spectrum security guards would assist Cobo's facilities staff in distributing rope, stanchions, and recyclable containers. Judy would stay around until midnight to set up phone charging stations in the office and to help Cobo security with tonight's VIP IDs. Two members of the Mack team would accompany the ATF bomb squad in their sweeps. Charlie and Cynthia would prepare the documents and reports for the MPD/DHS/Secret Service briefing in the morning.

Most people in the room still weren't aware the new freelancers were DHS agents. Heinrich certainly didn't know as he unabashedly flirted with Agent Mann. When the schedule was being discussed, he moved his chair to sit next to her.

"Ms. Mack, maybe it would be wise to supplement our camera monitors with some of your team members," Heinrich offered. "We'll be keeping eyes on tonight's VIP receptions. We're diverting cameras to keep at least two of them in proximity to their display areas. It would help us to have more people watching. As you know, the Chinese automaker is hosting a reception tonight."

Heinrich made it clear, by his attention, that his choice for one of the invited team members was the woman sitting next to him. He threw a see-what-you-missed glance at Mandy.

"We'll send over two or three people to help. It's a good idea," Charlie said, appeasing Heinrich in his attempt to both impress, and throw further suspicion on Guí Motors.

"Don and I spoke to the parking management company president today," Gil said. "He was very cooperative. They'll be using their most experienced employees for the show, and they're putting an extra supervisor on duty beginning tonight. All their staff are bonded and will wear special auto show insignia on their uniforms."

"When will the security bracelets be distributed?" Heinrich asked nonchalantly.

"Those on duty tonight already have their bracelets. Others will receive their bands for each day as they come on duty. Isn't that the plan, Don?" Charlie asked.

"That's the plan, Mack."

"I didn't expect him to show up," Cynthia said.

"Well, you said it before, he's always up to his own devices. What did he do after the meeting?"

"He walked around the office talking to staff, made a couple of calls on his private cell phone, then left."

"Will you be able to check your videotape while he's gone?"

"Not now. He didn't take his coat, so I assume he's still in the building."

Judy had brewed a pot of coffee, and Charlie and Cynthia worked around the conference table preparing the law-enforcement briefing packets. It would be another long, sleepless night and Charlie had opted for comfortable clothes—a turtleneck under a wool sweater, jeans, and sneakers. Cynthia had discarded her Spectrum jacket and shoes.

"You said something at the meeting that was interesting," Charlie said. "Why does Spectrum help the facilities staff set up equipment for the auto show?"

Cynthia shrugged. "It's something Heinrich agreed to do. He announced it at a staff meeting a few weeks ago, that a few of our guys would help Cobo staff rope off restricted sections of the building, and set up public areas. Why? Is something wrong with that?"

"I don't know," Charlie said, but her sixth sense was tapping her shoulder.

"I thought Judy was working out of the hotel?"

"She is. She's just hanging around long enough to help us package these reports, and then she heads back to the hotel. All we have left is the report on the exhibitor previews. We'll drive by the exhibitor spaces in a half hour and make sure their events are winding down, then come back here and finish up."

෧ ෧ ෧

Judy stood at the conference room door, leaning on the jamb with a determined look on her face.

She was preparing for another round of fighting about staying at Cobo. But Charlie was just as determined that Judy would not be spending the night at Cobo.

"You'll come with me and Cynthia to check in on the exhibitors' receptions. We'll leave in thirty minutes, and then come back here to finish up the briefing books. After that you're going back to the hotel."

Judy stood straight to make an argument. She glanced at Cynthia, looking for support, but Cynthia had decided to remain neutral by leaning over to zip up her boots. Judy crossed her arms, glaring at Charlie.

"Don't be 'Iowa Stubborn,'" Charlie said, glaring back.

"*Music Man*. Meredith Wilson." Judy replied, recognizing the reference.

"Correct. No more arguments, okay?"

"Oh, hell," Judy said, turning toward her desk.

"You two are hilarious," Cynthia chuckled. "You quote Broadway musicals at each other?"

"It's a guilty pleasure we share," Charlie smiled. "She can also match me lie for lie, another gift we share."

"You see that as a gift?"

"It is in our game. You must be pretty good at it yourself. You've been fooling Heinrich for months."

"He frightens me, Charlie. I think it was Nietzsche who said 'convictions are more dangerous foes to truth than lies.' It's the kind of warped thinking that allows terrorists to do the things they do."

"According to Tony, Heinrich's only conviction is about money. DHS has tied him to an overseas account with a recent deposit of three million dollars, and Tony thinks that's just a down payment."

"That's a lot of money. I spoke to Scott tonight. He's terribly embarrassed about not seeing through Heinrich from the beginning. He blames himself for the murders of the food supervisor and your friend Josh," Cynthia said, shaking her head. "I've never heard him so despondent."

"I understand the instinct to own the responsibility for things gone wrong. That's certainly the way I feel about getting Lin in trouble. But until we're out of danger, self-blame is a waste of energy."

Using his Spectrum ID, Dudiyn had encountered no trouble entering the Larned Garage, and he'd parked in the last row, next to the food trucks marked with the names of Cobo eateries. It had taken several hours to blend the chemicals, pack the mix into the pipes, and connect the phone detonators. He'd worked in the well of the church van, sitting behind the passenger bench, with the back vents open to get a bit of air. The windows were tinted, but he'd used only a headband-mounted penlight to illuminate his handiwork.

He was sweating and irritable from hunger. Earlier in the day, the activity in the garage had been impressive, with the deliveries of catered food, a group meeting of valet parking staff, and regular rounds of security patrols. But it was almost 7:30 p.m. and quiet now. He donned the green Spectrum jacket over his T-shirt and jeans, stepped out of the van, and hefted two bags onto his shoulder. He scanned the entry lock with his card and walked confidently into the Cobo service circulation area, then entered the back lobby and stepped into the nearest men's room. He made sure he was alone, then propped open the lavatory door with an orange cone. With the set of master keys Heinrich had provided, he unlocked the janitor's closet and retrieved a cart with mop and bucket, blocking the entry to the restroom.

He had to do something about his body odor or it would attract attention. He put the plastic bags into a stall and, shirtless, stepped up to the sink, then pumped a handful of soap from the dispenser and lathered his armpits. He soaked a stack of paper towels, and wiped his underarms, face, head, chest, and the back of his neck, then used another stack of towels to wipe himself dry. He used scissors to cut clumps of his beard, leaning over the commode to let the hair fall. He opened the bag with his janitor's uniform, and pulled out a long-sleeved, light-blue shirt with a name tag that read "Albert." He paused to listen for any noise from the open restroom door before sitting on the commode and removing his shoes and socks. He pulled off his black jeans, careful to slip them over his ankle holster and the Kel Tec P32. He used a few of the discarded paper towels to wipe his pubic hair and groin, then donned the blue cotton work pants. He put his two cell phones into the pockets and clipped his key ring onto the belt loop, then slipped on the black socks and work shoes. He stuffed the empty plastic bag with his jeans, boots, and scissors, retrieved the safety razor and left the stall to stand before the mirror. Within fifteen minutes he was clean-shaven. He buttoned his shirt, tucked it, and gave himself a once over.

Heinrich had messaged a few minutes ago to meet him near the loading dock. Dudiyn messaged that he was on his way. He shoved the bag with his dirty clothes and Spectrum gear into the supply closet and locked it, then draped a handful of black trash bags over the janitor's cart and pushed it down the hall.

Dudiyn paused at the north stairwell of level one. Continuing along the hall would lead to the meeting rooms, so he took a left at the corridor leading toward the dock area. He lifted the mop and bucket combo from the cart, and placed a small bag into his back pocket. There was activity all around him, but he proceeded with the invisibility of a uniformed man doing menial work. A Mack security patrol rolled toward him. Head down, he busied himself with the mop against an imaginary, stubborn stain on the baseboard. The patrol gave him only a fleeting glance. As a teenage inmate, he'd swabbed miles of floors in one of Chechnya's most notorious prisons. There, he had also continued his education in how to execute a kill in close quarters and how to build a pipe bomb.

Dudiyn wheeled the bucket past the facilities storage hangar where staff were using chain hoists to unload giant reams of red carpeting. He pushed through the plastic barrier of the loading dock. Out of a shadowy corner, twenty feet away, Heinrich emerged on foot.

"You look different without the beard," Heinrich said.

"That's the point."

"We shouldn't be seen talking."

"You called me."

"Yes, but something has come up. The Mack team is using a color-coded band system to identify staff on the floor. If you don't have the bracelet, you'll be noticed."

"So get me a band."

"I'm working on that. But for now, you should stay out of sight. If you're nabbed before you plant the bombs, the whole thing falls apart."

"So, how do we set up the diversion?"

"Give me the mix; I'll plant the chemicals." Heinrich said holding out his hand.

Dudiyn was still itching to kill Heinrich. He imagined shooting him right now. His small weapon would make only a minor noise. He'd prop Heinrich in the golf cart and return it to the shadows of the loading dock where it might not be found for hours, maybe not until tomorrow. He could plant the chemicals in the seating areas himself, and then hide out until he could place the bombs. Of course, if he were spotted without the bracelet, he'd increase the risk he wouldn't complete the job or escape Cobo.

"Are the receptacles in place?" Dudiyn asked.

"They'll all be in place by ten or eleven. There's still plenty of time."

Dudiyn looked at his watch. It was almost nine now. "Any chance of getting me some food?"

"The exhibitor receptions are going on. I'll see if I can pick up something."

"Okay. I'll lay low until I hear from you. But don't take too long."

Heinrich watched Dudiyn's departure, then stepped into the facilities room where a dozen workers were moving crates, loading lifts, and rolling out red carpet. Those who noticed him nodded or turned away to avoid a greeting. He knew the staff at Cobo didn't like him, and some feared him. He liked it that way. He watched their activities for a while, leaning on the manager's desk. His real reason for being there was to get one of the yellow bracelets the men were already wearing. Believing no one was paying attention to him, he opened the top drawer, looking for the bands.

"Can I help you, Mr. Heinrich?"

Facilities supervisor Dennis Calhoun had entered the storage area and was standing behind him. Heinrich wasn't startled. He just turned and gave the man a blazing stare.

"I wanted to see if we were on schedule for the overnight activities," Heinrich said. "I see the men are using the wristbands. That's good."

"Yes, it seems like a good plan."

"Can I see one of the bands?" Heinrich asked.

"Sure. They're in that envelope on top there," Calhoun said, pointing.

Heinrich pulled a few of the bands from the envelope and dropped them onto the desk. He lifted one, pretending to examine it. "A low-tech solution."

"Right," Calhoun said. But he was already looking at his clipboard, and counting the crates of velvet roping his men were pulling from the walls.

Heinrich slid the bands across the desk into his palm and replaced them in the envelope. All but one. He walked over to the crate Calhoun was examining and watched a few minutes more. "Keep up the good work," he threw out, before he turned and walked out of the storage areas.

Calhoun stared at the man's back a few seconds, glanced at his desk, and returned to his inventory count.

Heinrich drove his cart near one of the visitor seating areas on Cobo's second level. The new furniture was contemporary— leather and chrome with sleek plastic cubes that served as tables. The three planters, made from the same material as the tables, held large palm fronds, which provided aesthetic balance to the hard furniture. Dudiyn had put the chemical mix into pill bottles that could be easily opened and poured. Heinrich stopped at one of the planters, opened a vial, and tipped it into the soil. The entire action took less than ten seconds. He put the golf cart into gear and moved to the next area.

Dudiyn retraced his steps to the main corridor, swabbing with his mop along the hallway. When he reached the janitor's cart, he spotted another cart outside the toilet where he'd changed clothes. He walked the fifty yards to the restroom, carrying his mop, bucket, and a handful of trash bags. Inside the door, a uniformed lady janitor gathered paper products into her arms. She was short, Hispanic, and wore a yellow paper band on her wrist. The woman looked up, startled, when he entered the room. She formed the beginnings of a smile, which disappeared quickly when she realized she didn't recognize the uniformed worker. Dudiyn kicked aside the cone that held the open door, and the woman dropped the bathroom tissue. Her scream was cut short when his strong hand pressed one of the plastic bags hard against her face. Now he had the colored bracelet that would ensure his safe access through the halls of Cobo.

He recovered his own cart from the corridor, pushed both carts into the restroom's vestibule, and affixed an "out of order" sign on the external door, then locked it. The restroom would be his headquarters until he could begin positioning the bombs. He removed boxes, brooms, dust mops and gallon jugs of cleaning fluids from the supply closet, placed the dead woman in the rear, and rearranged the supplies to hide her body. Dudiyn then piled paper and rags together into a makeshift pillow. He was hungry, but since he couldn't eat, he would sleep.

Amy maintained a discreet distance from Mr. Kwong. Close enough for him to signal if he needed anything, but far enough away to honor tradition and assuage the sensibilities of the business and government officials attending the Guí Motors VIP reception. They had flown from the Chinese mainland to Detroit, Michigan, to witness the acknowledgment of Chinese auto manufacturing on the world stage. On Wednesday, Guí Motors would receive a citation for their work from the U.S. secretary of commerce, the governor of Michigan, and the Detroit Auto Dealers Association. Amy understood the importance and symbolism of the honor.

Before she'd entered high school, her parents had related numerous times the story of the beating death of Chinese-American Vincent Chin. Chin had died at the hands of two Detroit autoworkers disgruntled by the influx of Japanese automobiles to the U.S. The killers had mistaken Chin for Japanese.

Amy saw her boss beckon. "Yes, Mr. Kwong."

"Please escort Mr. Zhéng and his translator to the smoking area."

"Yes, Mr. Kwong," Amy said, tilting her head in a bow.

She led the way to the semi-enclosed balcony designed to accommodate smokers. It was still snowing, and a brisk wind blew from the nearby Detroit River. A few other smokers on the other side of the balcony huddled in a tight group. Mr. Zhéng, wearing only his suit and a scarf draped around his neck, stepped away from the others to light his cigarette. His translator, a tall bespectacled man, joined Amy under one of the patio heaters.

"Is it always this cold in Detroit?" he asked.

"It is cold a lot of the time," Amy said.

The translator shoved his hands into his jacket pockets and shivered. His client was pacing, smoke following him. Zhéng lit a second cigarette.

"You seem a modern woman," the translator said, assessing Amy.

"Does that surprise you?"

"Yes. Although the businessmen we work for are intent on finding honor in the work of the future, they remain steeped in the traditions of the past."

"Well, you seem a man of modern sensibility. How did you come to have this job?"

"My family has worked for Mr. Zhéng for a long time."

"I have my position through family connections also."

Mr. Zhéng discarded his cigarette butt in the ashcan and

made his way to the door. The translator and Amy fell in line behind him. Zhéng wiggled his finger, and his employee stepped up to walk with him.

Seven other automakers were holding preview parties on Cobo's second level, and a few of their departing guests ambled along the displays of cars to the elevators. As Amy followed her charges back to the Guí exhibit, she saw Geoff Heinrich in a golf cart parked near the visitor seats. She thought he might be waiting to have a conversation with Mr. Kwong. Mr. Zhéng returned to his colleagues, and Amy fixed a stare on her boss until he noticed and approached her.

"What is it, Amy?"

"Are you meeting with Mr. Heinrich tonight?"

"No. Why do you ask?"

"He's waiting over there," Amy said, pointing behind her. But when she and Kwong turned to look, Heinrich was gone.

Heinrich had been able to plant six vials of chemicals on level two. It had taken no more than twenty minutes and would have gone faster, except he consciously tried to avoid the location of the security cameras. He had two vials of chemicals left. He contemplated where to put them, then had an idea. He paused in the corridor near the Guí Motors exhibit. The party was well underway. He turned his cart in the direction of the south service elevator, rode up one floor, and pulled his cart into the main corridor of the third level. It was quiet. This floor had mostly administrative offices. Only the communications staff, preparing for tomorrow's press day, and maybe staff from the general manager's office would be working this late. Heinrich turned toward the administrative offices, but before he reached the east-west corridor, a Mack patrol turned the corner and headed his way. They stopped side by side; Mandy Porter sat in the passenger seat.

"Are things quiet tonight?" Heinrich asked the driver.

"Yes," Hoyt said icily.

"And how are you tonight, Ms. Porter?" Heinrich said with the smile of a cartoon cobra.

"Perfect," Mandy said with her own venom.

"Well, carry on," Heinrich said, and continued down the corridor.

"He's a piece of work," Mandy said, looking back over her shoulder.

"More like a piece of shit," Hoyt responded.

The facilities staff were positioning the waste/recyclable stations across from the food vendor stations and lavatories on all levels of Cobo Center. The shrink-wrapped packages were made up of three connected containers for paper, trash, and bottles. Each level was to have a minimum of twenty stations. Later, janitors would come by to line the containers with oversized trash bags, and Spectrum staff would place stand-alone recyclable bins next to the trash stations on levels one and two.

Charlie, Cynthia, and Judy were near the BMW display, monitoring the preview activities and doing an informal count of the guests. They'd already stopped by the receptions at General Motors, Hyundai, Guí, and Honda.

"I count about thirty guests," Judy said.

"Right," Cynthia said, jotting on her clipboard. "So far, that's the smallest gathering. All we have left is Toyota and Ford Motor."

Charlie turned the key in the ignition of the golf cart and proceeded down the hallway. Ahead, they saw a Spectrum team placing recyclable boxes next to the waste stations. The boxes were the standard white cardboard containers marked with the ubiquitous recyclable logo and the iconography of a man discarding paper debris into a U-shaped basket. One of the team members waved for Cynthia to stop, and Charlie slowed down. When Cynthia hopped out for a discussion, Charlie asked Judy a question. When she didn't respond, Charlie turned toward the back seat. Judy was concentrating on something across the corridor, her brow furrowed. Charlie had learned to trust Judy's advice, as well as her silences.

"Something wrong?"

"I'm not sure."

Before Charlie could question Judy further, Cynthia returned to the cart, and they continued to the Ford exhibit, which took up a large portion of the exhibitor floor.

"Are your guys on track?" Charlie asked Cynthia.

"Yep. They're almost done with the recyclables distribution. They're headed next to back-of-house storage to pick up stanchions and rope."

Judy and Cynthia did an eyeball count of the Ford guests and made a few notes. Next was the Toyota exhibit. Although the Ford exhibit space was larger, the Toyota gathering had more people. Over one hundred visitors were laughing, drinking, and admiring the cars, in particular the new Lexus LS460. Over the last year, U.S. car sales were weakening while Toyota was becoming the leader of the pack.

"Well, it's a quarter of ten; Cobo's security should be coming around in a few minutes to make sure the exhibitors are clearing out their guests," Charlie said, looking at the schedule. "Let's get back to the office and finish the briefing book so Judy can get back to the hotel."

"Okay," Judy said stubbornly. "But I'm coming back in the morning for the briefing."

A half-dozen golf carts were lined up in the hallway in front of Spectrum's main door. Charlie, Judy, and Cynthia hopped down from their cart.

"Looks like we have a full house," Judy said.

She was right. Don and Gil were sitting around Don's desk, with the patrol schedule in their hands, looking up at an enlarged copy of Cobo's four levels taped to the wall. Carter Bernstein was perched at Charlie's desk, charging his Black-Berry and busily tapping away at his laptop keyboard. In the conference room, Tyson and the two DHS agents were sorting color-coded bracelets into manila envelopes. The top of Judy's desk was filled with bags of White Castle burgers and chicken sandwiches, and the aroma of steamed onions and beef grease had taken up residency.

"Who's out catching the bad guys?" Charlie asked loudly.

"We all are, Mack," Don bellowed. "But an army travels on its belly. Have a few sliders."

Carter leaped from Charlie's desk with apologies, pulling the cords of his laptop and phone from the outlet next to the desk.

"Don't get up, Carter. We'll go into the conference room. What are you working on?"

"I'm leaving in a few minutes for the monitoring room, but I'm still following up on some Dudiyn information."

"Anything new?"

"Not yet, but I'm waiting for a couple of things. I'll get it written up for you as soon as it comes in."

Cynthia passed on the White Castle, but Charlie and Judy grabbed a couple of sandwiches apiece, and moved toward the conference room. Ty and the two freelancers shifted to one end of the table, leaving space for the work on the briefing book. Don and Gil stopped at the door of the conference room as they prepared to return to the patrols.

"They should be starting the bomb sweeps soon, so we're heading out to the floor," Gil announced.

"We're coming, too," Agent Mann announced.

"You buy these, Don?" Judy asked, chewing a slider.

"I did. I even got extra dill pickles for you. I also have my receipts."

"Good man."

"Stop it," Gil said, smiling. "Things are confused enough without the two of you being nice to each other."

Judy and Don offered snorts, and Charlie chuckled. The others didn't know what to make of the levity with the clock ticking down to a terrorist attack. But the Mack team had learned from experience that humor could often make a dangerous, even bleak, situation bearable.

By 11 p.m., Judy had completed binding the briefing books, Cynthia and Ty had returned to their offices, Carter Bernstein was monitoring cameras in the Spectrum glass office, Don and Gil were keeping tabs on the scheduled work, and most of the freelancers were back on patrol.

"Almost done?" Charlie asked Judy.

"I'm done. Just doing a quality-control check."

"Okay. Stack the books in the conference room when you're finished. You need any help carrying the chargers and radios to your car?"

"Aren't you driving me to the hotel?"

"No. I better stick here and prep for the team meeting."

"I could stay."

"No. You can't."

"I could give Carter a break from the monitoring."

"He'll be fine."

"Fine," Judy said with resignation. "Then I guess I *could* use a hand taking the equipment to the car."

Charlie had her feet atop the desk and had begun to right herself when the two-way radio squawked loudly.

"Mack. Get up here, level two. The bomb squad has found something," Don's urgent voice crackled.

"What is it, Don?" Charlie shouted into the radio.

"Explosives. North side of the GM display."

Charlie grabbed her jacket and unlocked the desk drawer. She reached in and pulled out her revolver. Judy stared wide-eyed at the gun, but grabbed her purse and followed Charlie to the door.

"Where do you think you're going?"

"Well, I'm not staying here," Judy answered on the run.

When they reached the second level, Mandy and Hoyt were parked in the concourse near the Chevy Camaro concept car.

"We just got here, and the bomb squad ordered us to stay back," Mandy said.

"Where's Don?"

"Over there," Mandy said, pointing to the stairwell on their right.

"Okay. Let's go. Leave the carts," Charlie ordered. "Judy, you're staying put. No arguments."

As they approached, Don and Gil were talking to Agent Mann. She broke off the conversation and made her way through the maze of cars to four men huddled together near the General Motors display.

"They found explosive materials," Don said quickly. "But so far no bombs."

"Where?" Charlie asked.

"There," Don said, pointing a hundred yards away to a seating area where one man, wearing an ATF jacket, held the leash of a Labrador retriever. "Apparently, the dog found something in the planters."

"Where's Mann off to?" Charlie asked.

"She's trying to get us more information. She flashed her DHS credentials, and they said she could hang around. They told us to stand here." Don was miffed.

Suddenly, the radio crackled again. "We got explosives spotted on level three," the voice said. "ATF just told us to get back."

"This is Charlie Mack. Who is this?"

"Vince, from the facilities staff, ma'am."

"Where are you?"

"Level three, outside of the Ambassador Ballroom."

The Mack team's three-cart caravan streaked through the hallway to the service elevator. Charlie, Judy, Don, and Gil went up first while Mandy and Hoyt waited. As soon as the door opened, Don gunned the cart out of the elevator. Two facilities staffers flagged them as they approached the turn to the ballroom.

"We were tacking down carpet, and one of the bomb dogs found something near the benches across from the ballroom. We were told to back off."

"We're going in," Don announced and shot down the hallway.

Charlie was about to follow when she remembered Judy. Mandy and Hoyt had just pulled up.

"Judy, you wait here with Mandy," Charlie said, jumping from the cart. "Hoyt, I'm with you."

The lovers brushed shoulders in their exchange of seats. Mandy stood next to the vehicle, and she and Judy watched in exasperation as they were left behind.

"Are you as pissed off as I am?" Judy asked.

"More."

"Charlie took her gun," Judy remembered.

"I should hope so. The people we're dealing with aren't going to give themselves up."

"You think it's more than Heinrich and Dudiyn?"

"There could be others. We have to assume there *are* others."

"So what do we do now?"

"Like we were told: We wait."

Ten minutes later, a modified Jeep, topped with an armored dome, passed the cart. Two men in the front seat wore caps with the ATF insignia.

"Please wait here until we give you the 'all clear,'" the agent in the passenger seat shouted to Mandy, who waved a half-hearted acknowledgement.

Dudiyn had slept inches away from the dead cleaning woman. At one point, someone had knocked at the outer door, and he'd sat upright, putting his hand on his gun, prepared to kill anyone who discovered him. When the knocking subsided, he drifted back to sleep. His internal clock awakened him at 11:00 p.m., and Heinrich still hadn't called. As he relieved himself, he mentally reviewed the work he'd do in the next few hours.

There were more than thirty restrooms in Cobo, and he had forty bombs. He would place most of the bombs outside the first and second level restrooms, including one with the dead cleaning lady, to aid in his escape. The others he'd plant at the vendor booths where long lines of people would linger and eat. If the diversion had worked, security would already be swarming around the visitor seating areas examining the explosives components in the planters and searching for explosives in the other plant containers.

His phone vibrated. Heinrich was finally calling. The text said he was waiting. Dudiyn removed one bomb from the heavy bag, then carefully placed the bag into the well of his janitor's cart. He covered the well with a full package of white rags. He gathered the towels and rags that had made his makeshift pillow, and placed them, along with another single bomb, into a bag with the dead lady janitor, then locked the closet door. His phone vibrated again. Dudiyn taped the ends of the yellow band around his wrist, and as an afterthought he retrieved the blue baseball cap the dead woman was wearing and adjusted the fit. Clean-shaven, his baldness covered, and disguised as a janitor, he would casually move about the hallways of Cobo. He blocked the storage closet with the cleaning lady's cart, unlocked the outer door, and removed the "out of order" sign before he left. The restroom was open for business again.

Chapter 11

Sunday, January 8, 2006
Auto Show Press Day

The second positive on explosives set off an urgent response, and dozens of people converged on the third level. Mandy and Judy had been waiting in the corridor to the Ambassador Ballroom for a half hour. They watched a Detroit Metropolitan Police commander, a team of FBI agents, Ty Pressley and his boss, and four ATF agents with bomb-sniffing dogs pass them by. Three other Mack teams had also taken up position next to them, waiting for word. Mandy picked up the walkie-talkie.

"This is Mandy Porter requesting a status report. Should we stay in position?"

A few seconds later came the reply from Don. "Hold your position, Porter; we're on our way out."

The Mack partners, Hoyt, and Mandy were in animated conversation fueled by adrenaline and a carafe of coffee Judy had made. The rest of the freelancers were back on patrols, or doing other duties. Tyson joined the group in the conference room with the latest information from Mike Mathers.

"They've found explosives on level three and in four areas on level two," he reported. "Now that they know what to look for, they'll spend the next several hours sweeping all the exhibition areas, the showroom floor, and the meeting rooms on all levels of Cobo."

"Do they know how the chemicals got there?" Don asked.

"Not yet," Ty said, slumping in his chair.

"What about Heinrich? Where's he?"

"That's what my boss wants to know. We just came from his office. He isn't there. Ms. Fitzgerald said he left hours ago. We tried calling him, but he didn't answer."

"We saw him earlier," Hoyt said. "On the third level."

"What time was that?"

"I don't know, maybe eight."

"Judy, please go talk to Carter," Charlie ordered. "He's monitoring the security cameras. If Heinrich is at Cobo, we want to know where."

"I'm on it," Judy replied.

"When will we know if we've beaten the threat?" Ty asked.

"Maybe not until morning. Meanwhile, we can't let down our guard. We'll keep up the patrols, as best we can, without impeding ATF work," Charlie said. "Oh, and I better give Tony a call."

Charlie was leaning in through Cynthia's doorway. The Spectrum offices were quiet. Most of the staff would return to work tomorrow at six. Except for the light pouring from the monitoring room and glowing from Cynthia's desk lamp, the hallways were dark. "I asked Judy to sit with Carter in the monitoring room."

"Yeah, I saw her go in. This whole thing is pretty nerve-wracking, and the staff is antsy. They're watching the bomb teams moving around the place, and they want to be part of the action."

"I know what you mean. Mandy's mad at me for holding her back and, as you can see, Judy's still here."

Cynthia nodded, then cupped her brow in her hands. "My head is aching."

"You should take something."

"I already did. It hasn't kicked in."

"We're doing some brainstorming. You want to join us?" Charlie invited.

"Sure. It might help me to focus." Cynthia stood and walked toward the door, grabbing a couple of apples from the bowl on her coffee table and flipping one to Charlie, who caught it neatly. "Here's some brain food. My contribution to your thinking game."

Passing empty cubicles, they moved stride for stride on the carpeted walkway toward the temporary Mack suite. Then Cynthia suddenly stopped in her tracks.

"Oh, damn, damn. With all the bomb stuff, I forgot to tell you. Amy called. She saw Heinrich earlier tonight."

"She did? Where?" Charlie spun around.

"Near the Guí VIP party."

Charlie ran to the monitoring booth and gestured for Judy and Carter. "I need you two to get the tapes from the Guí Motors display and bring them to the office."

"How many days of tape do you need, Ms. Mack?" Carter asked.

"Not days, just from the last four hours. Bring them as quickly as you can."

The Post-it notes were already mounted on the white board in the conference room. Don usually liked to run the team meetings, but he deferred to Charlie when it came to her sticky notes sessions. Nevertheless, he stood at the board serving as a human pointer. Gil and Cynthia had made themselves comfortable at the table— Gil with his third cup of coffee, and Cynthia with shoes off and a foot propped on her chair. In the outer office, Judy and Carter were viewing security footage on Judy's desktop.

"Let's go back to the first note, Don."

Don obediently pointed to the Post-it that read: *Did Heinrich plant the bombs?*

"Do you really think he'd be the one to plant explosives?" Cynthia asked. "It just doesn't seem to fit him."

"I agree," Don said.

"It may seem out of character. But we don't really know his character," Charlie reminded them.

"I wouldn't underestimate this guy. Just because we don't like him doesn't mean he isn't smart or tough," Gil said. "It's odd though, isn't it?"

"What's odd?" Charlie asked.

"That ATF found explosive chemicals, but nothing else. How were they to be detonated?"

Charlie shrugged.

"That would be one red and one green note in your system. Right?" Cynthia asked.

"You catch on fast," Charlie said, handing two new notes to Don, who placed them among the others.

Charlie stared at the board for a moment, then poured a cup of the too-strong coffee and sat with her back to the board. "I think we should clean up the board. I'm getting overwhelmed with the number of notes. It's hard to think."

"It doesn't help that you've hardly slept in thirty-six hours," Gil said.

"Which notes should we take down, Mack?" Don said, positioning himself in front of the board.

"Maybe we don't take any down, just rearrange them." Charlie turned her chair toward the notes. "Like that one in the questions group about Jones."

Don pointed. "Who killed Garry Jones?"

"Yep. Move that to the bottom. That's not important."

"Not important?" Gil asked.

"You know that's not really what I mean, but who killed Mr. Jones probably isn't as pertinent now. The same with who killed Chenglei. When we started the case, figuring out how his death was connected to a plot against Cobo was a primary question, but now it's not."

"Following that reasoning, I guess we should move the note about Josh below the line, too," Gil said somberly.

Charlie stood, and walked to the board. Don stepped aside as she placed the three notes, asking who killed Josh Simms, Garry Jones, and Chenglei, in the middle. "Point taken, Gil."

"How about moving all the facts and questions about the Chinese together?" Cynthia suggested. "There must be more than twenty of those. Let's see what's left then."

Cynthia was catching on to the techniques of this game, and Charlie helped Don reorganize the notes. It wasn't unusual for Charlie to arrange and rearrange individual notes until she had an insight. Sometimes she connected the notes in ways that were expected, and other times placed them in a random order. It was a way to trick the brain into a different way of thinking.

"Okay, good. Now let's move all the notes about Heinrich off to the side, including the ones we just put up," Gil offered.

After more manipulation of the notes, the board had a lot of white space. Don had taken a seat and found a stale doughnut to go with the over-brewed coffee. Charlie stared and pondered, carefully lifting and then replacing the remaining notes into two columns—one for questions, one for facts and conjectures. Then she shifted them again. Don and Gil had seen her in this reverie before, and waited and watched silently. Cynthia took the hint. When Charlie was done, there were only five notes front and center, all questions. The first two were personal and pertinent: *Who kidnapped and hurt Lin Fong?* and *Who killed Josh Simms?* Next were the three, currently relevant, questions: *Where is Geoff Heinrich?*, *How are the explosives to be detonated?* and *Is anyone else involved?*

Don took the red marker and boxed the personal questions. He then wrote the word *payback* above it. Don had demonstrated this kind of dramatics on a white board before, and he always meant what he wrote.

"Ms. Mack, we've found something," Carter said, rushing into the conference room.

"You have to see it," Judy said, out of breath.

Everyone peered over Judy's shoulder at the laptop on her desk. A not-so-clear video was in pause mode, and she rewound it for a few seconds before she pushed the play button. The security camera's vantage point was of the Guí Motors display, but included one of the visitor seating areas in the background. They all watched as a golf cart entered and stopped; the driver's back was to the camera. Then the cart moved again, to a planter holding a small palm bush where the cart paused a second time. Finally, the cart pulled away from the area and out of view.

"Now, wait a second, here's what the camera from the concourse shows," Judy said, deftly navigating the security footage thumbnails and joggling through the timeline. "Here."

The Chinese delegation party was in full swing in this footage. Businessmen and elegantly dressed women milled around the cars, holding champagne glasses. Mr. Kwong stood awkwardly off to the side, chatting when he was approached, but not mingling with the others. From the right a golf cart moved into view and turned into the visitor rest area. The vehicle paused at the large palm plant for a few seconds then continued down the corridor. Judy paused the video, and Charlie looked quizzically at the others peering at the screen. But Judy was already moving her mouse over the picture.

"Wait. Wait for it," she said, and punched the keyboard.

The close-up of the man in the golf cart looking back toward the Guí Motors party was grainy, but conclusive. The time-coded video at 9:10 p.m. showed Geoff Heinrich loitering at the planter where explosives had been discovered.

"And . . . we have another video showing him loitering at another planter near the Ford exhibit," Carter explained excitedly.

A brief silence preceded a barrage of simultaneous suggestions and questions, and Charlie gestured for quiet. "Hold on. Let's coordinate what needs to be done next," she said, hurrying back to the conference room followed by the others.

"First, Carter, get hold of any camera footage that shows the planter areas, on all levels, in the past few hours. The feds will want that."

"I'll help with that," Cynthia volunteered and, without waiting for acknowledgement, left the office with Carter.

"Mack, we need to find this guy. We should put all patrol teams on alert to locate him."

"Right, Don. Get in touch with Hoyt."

Don rushed to retrieve his walkie-talkie while Judy and Gil waited for assignments.

"Wait. Don't call Hoyt yet," Charlie said, dropping into a seat. "If one of our people finds Heinrich, what do we want them to do?"

"They should detain him," Don said.

"What about the explosives?" Charlie asked.

"What do you mean?"

"What if he detonates a bomb when we try to take him?"

"That's a chance we have to take."

"No, Don. Charlie's right," Gil said.

"At least if a bomb goes off tonight, fewer people will be hurt," Don argued.

"True, but we don't know how many bombs he has, or how many he may have planted, or where. What if he has more accomplices? If we detain him, that may not be the end of things."

"Okay. I see what you're getting at," Don said. "So, we don't grab him, just keep tabs on him, see where he's planting the stuff, and get at the explosives later."

"Exactly. Right now, Heinrich thinks he's moving about with a certain amount of impunity. Maybe we can beat him at his own game."

Heinrich looked at his watch; it was 11:30 p.m. The walkie-talkie he'd taken had been squawking every thirty seconds, so he turned it to the lowest setting. He'd planted the last batch of chemicals close to the Ambassador Ballroom so they could be easily found. As he had guessed, when a bomb-sniffing dog recognized the signature of explosive components near Cobo's executive level, the alarm went out. And, as he had hoped, most of the security patrols swarmed to the third level. He'd returned to the loading dock area to stay out of sight and to rendezvous with Dudiyn, but his messages had been ignored.

That asshole, if he fucks up this plan, I'll kill him.

He heard the sound of rolling wheels and then a low whistle. Heinrich peeked through the plastic strip curtains and waved

Dudiyn over. "Where've you been? I sent you a message twenty minutes ago."

"I was busy."

The two held each other's stare in the dim light. Heinrich tried to read the thoughts behind the man's cold, gray eyes, wishing they weren't partnered on this dangerous task. Heinrich's client had insisted he use Dudiyn. Although he was quite competent on the technical side of things, his proclivity for violence and poor hygiene would have exempted him from being hired if Heinrich'd had the final say. Finally, he took a step back and offered Dudiyn the item in his hand.

"Here's your security band."

"I already got one."

"How'd you manage that?"

Dudiyn didn't bother to answer. He just stepped deeper into the loading area, then turned to face Heinrich. "Did the diversion work?"

"Like a charm. But law enforcement is all over the building. They're concentrating on levels two and three, where I put the bait."

"Okay. Did you find me any food?"

"No. I was avoiding the cameras. Sorry," Heinrich said as an afterthought, "You have the bombs?"

"I have them."

"Fine. The receptacles are in place, so you should be able to start placing them in about an hour. We're behind schedule. How long do you think you'll need?"

"Maybe two hours. I'll take my time. I don't want to arouse suspicion. If the feds have some areas roped off, I may have to place fewer bombs."

Dudiyn kept looking back at the door and shifting his weight from foot to foot. He jumped when the muffled sound of the two-way radio sounded.

"What's that?"

"I got my hands on one of the two-way radios."

"Maybe I should have it."

"No. I'm leaving Cobo now, and it's the only way I can keep up with what's going on."

Dudiyn removed his cap and wiped his head and face with a paper towel from his back pocket. He tapped his foot.

"What's wrong with you?" Heinrich asked.

"No problems."

"Meet me when you're done. And for God's sake, respond to my messages. We both want to be paid, so don't fuck things up."

The two locked eyes again. Heinrich felt the man's hatred pulse toward him, along with his unbearable stink. Heinrich turned away to retrieve his golf cart. He was about to enter the cart when the acrid body odor pulsed over him. When he turned, Dudiyn, visible only in silhouette, was slowly approaching him.

"What do you want?"

"I think I should have the walkie-talkie."

"I already told you "no."

Dudiyn was close enough now for Heinrich to see his face. His eyes were wide, two pinpoints of concentration. His lips were twisted in a sneer. Heinrich looked down to see the gun in Dudiyn's hand. Held steady, and pointed at his gut. Heinrich's second of fear was replaced by bold arrogance and he squared his body to Dudiyn. He locked on the man's eyes and swept the gun aside with his hand. That's when Dudiyn grabbed his arm, raised the pistol, and shot three bullets into the back of Heinrich's neck. Dudiyn smiled as the German's eyes registered confusion, and when he tried to speak, Dudiyn pushed him against the golf cart, and Heinrich fell in a slump into the seat.

The VIP reception had been a success, and the Guí executives were pleased. Mr. Kwong had released his suite at the hotel to one of his bosses and had insisted on sleeping in the office. Amy had volunteered to stay, but hadn't been allowed, and after the preview party Kwong escorted Amy to her car in the Cobo garage.

"You have been a loyal worker."

"Thank you, Mr. Kwong."

She'd noticed tears in his eyes when she started up her car, and in the side mirror view he stood like a burdened man.

She called Cynthia when she got home, reporting Mr. Heinrich's sighting and Mr. Kwong's state of mind. Cynthia told her of the found explosives, and Amy called Lin Fong. They had spoken a few times since his escape from the warehouse. When she'd first seen Lin at the teleconference, pretending to help the technician but clearly spying for Mr. Heinrich, she'd thought he was a little too sure of himself. But since the abduction, she'd learned he was just a second-generation Chinese-American trying to fit in.

"They found explosives in Cobo, and there are police dogs everywhere."

"Do they know who planted the explosives?"

"I don't think so."

"I bet it was Baldy."

"Who?"

"The guy who beat me," Lin said. "He was just plain mean. I think he meant to kill me."

They were both quiet for a few minutes. The only light in Amy's suburban bedroom came from her cell phone and the laptop she had open on her oversized bed.

Lin was sprawled on Charlie's couch in the living room where he'd paused his PlayStation 2 to listen to Amy's soothing voice. She was a modern girl who listened to rap music and read fashion magazines, and was smart and caring.

"Amy?"

"I'm still here."

"I want to go back to Cobo to help."

"What could you do?"

"I don't know. But I want to be there."

"That's not a good idea. Cynthia says the situation is dangerous. She warned me that I should stay away."

"Did I tell you Ms. Mack taught me Tae Kwon Do?"

"Yes. That's how you met her."

"Uh huh, that's right. She used to say something in our class.

She would say, fear isn't the opposite of bravery. When Baldy was beating me, I was afraid, but I'm not a coward."

"I know that, Lin. I don't think you have anything to prove."

"You know we have something to prove every day."

"The model minority," Amy said woefully.

"I want to help Ms. Mack. That's what she hired me to do, and I want to show her that she can still count on me."

The janitor's cart was heavy, and Dudiyn struggled to push it in the direction of the first-level service elevator. He looked at the five-pound PVC pipes in the well of his cart. It had been his idea to put pest control labels on the pipes, so that even if they were spotted, they wouldn't cause immediate concern. As Dudiyn moved toward the TV studio, a man outside the facility was looping camera cable. Holding one end of the cable between his thumb and index finger, he rolled the cable across his elbow and back to his hand. He displayed an enormous smile as Dudiyn approached, and paused in his task.

"Getting things spiffy for the show tomorrow, I see."

"Yep," Dudiyn said.

"First thing tomorrow morning, I've got two dozen live feeds coming out of our studio. The Europeans love these car shows even more than we do." The man laughed.

When Dudiyn didn't share in the cheerful banter, the man changed the subject. "I hear there's some kind of trouble in the showroom. The security guys came charging through here a few minutes ago," he announced.

"Yeah. I heard." Dudiyn began pushing his cart. "But I've got a schedule to keep so, I'll just steer clear."

"Okay. Well, don't work too hard."

Dudiyn didn't answer or look back.

Tony Canterra had come to Cobo after calls from Charlie and the ATF. He joined the Mack partners in the conference room where Cynthia, Scott Hartwell, Tyson, Mandy, Hoyt, and Dennis Calhoun, the facilities supervisor, were discussing the bomb threat. Judy and Carter were in the outer office still screening video from the security cameras.

"What are we talking about here, Tony?" Mandy asked. "Are we looking for a big bomb like Oklahoma City?"

"No. It took an enormous cache of explosives to pull off something like Oklahoma City, and we have new safeguards to monitor transactions involving large quantities of bomb-making materials. FBI, ATF, and global agencies use a database to keep up with that stuff. This is more in line with an IED: that's an improvised explosive device. But, that being said, perhaps a car bomb isn't out of the question. I'll alert ATF to sweep the parking areas when they're finished inside." Tony made a note on the writing pad in front of him. "Maybe we should also consider additional barriers in front of the doors."

"I've had some experience with IEDs in Afghanistan," Gil said. He rose and began writing on the white board. "They require a switch, a fuse, some kind of container, the explosive, and a power source."

"That's right," Tony said.

"What will they look like?" Mandy asked.

"Well, they probably won't be very large, to make them easier to smuggle into Cobo. IEDs can be made into a suicide vest, or they could be pipe bombs or pressure devices."

"Do we have any idea where Heinrich is now?" Hartwell asked Cynthia, who shook her head no.

"We're still looking for him," Charlie said. "We have footage of his comings and goings a few hours ago in a half-dozen areas of Cobo, but our patrols and cameras haven't spotted him in the last couple of hours."

Tony interrupted the conversation about Heinrich with an update on ATF's work. "Sweeps of the public areas on levels two and three are completed, including the administrative offices on three," he said, looking at his phone. "They're using canine units and handheld detectors. They'll focus on level four now."

"When do they sweep our level?" Gil asked.

"They're saving level one for last."

"Why?"

"I know the answer to that one," Hartwell spoke up. "The fourth level is a higher priority. It's adjacent to the People Mover station."

"Yes," Tony responded. "Also, they've already done preliminary sweeps of the seating areas and exhibits on this level, and found no explosives components."

Charlie knew from experience to be skeptical of the information federal agents gave to civilians. Even when they offered facts, they often withheld the truth. She, Don, and Gil had been trained in that nimble game of deception during their own days at DHS.

"What do you make of that, Tony?" Charlie asked.

"Make of what?"

"Why ATF has found only a smattering of chemicals, but no real bombs?"

Every head turned toward Tony for his answer. But before he could speak, Hartwell offered an excited opinion.

"Could the explosives have been in the planters for a while? When were the seating area improvements done?" Hartwell asked the facilities supervisor.

The man searched his memory. "I believe they were finished just before Thanksgiving. Our landscapers would have put the palm plants in then."

Hartwell's unintentional deflection had, momentarily, taken Tony off the hook. Don and Charlie exchanged a look, silently agreeing Don would play the bad cop role he loved so well.

"You didn't answer the question, Canterra. Why aren't we finding any bombs, no blasting caps, that sort of thing?"

"Heinrich has help," Tony answered.

"We know that. Dudiyn," Don said.

"Right."

"So, we're not out of the woods until we find both of them," Hartwell said more than asked.

"What do you have on Dudiyn?" Charlie asked. "We intercepted one of his calls," Tony said cryptically.

"And?" Don asked.

"And he's probably the person we should be looking for now."

"I think he was the one I saw working with a soldering iron at Heinrich's house," Mandy stated.

"And he was definitely the one retrieving the fake bleach containers and phones from the weapons building," Cynthia added.

"Wait a minute," Gil said excitedly. "Maybe that's where Heinrich is hiding—the weapons garage. Maybe that's where they're both hiding."

The conference room became electric. Hoyt was already rising from the table when Tony's words slowed him.

"Wait. Heinrich's not at the Spectrum storage building."

"How do you know?" Don asked.

"We know."

"What about Dudiyn?" Gil asked.

Tony shook his head no. "We don't think he's there either."

"Oh, stop the bullshitting, Canterra. Either tell us what you know, or let us get on with our stumbling in the dark," Don yelled.

Charlie watched Tony. He was a good man, but an even better soldier. She watched as he mentally weighed the pros and cons of disclosing the information he was holding close. Finally, he looked at Charlie and held her gaze. He was prepared to tell more.

"Dudiyn is still on the loose, but we've already located Heinrich," Tony said.

"What? Where is he?" Hartwell shouted.

Tony let out an audible sigh. "He's dead. His body was found a half hour ago, and we're pretty sure Dudiyn is the one who killed him."

Don, Hoyt and Mandy were the most shaken by the news of Heinrich's death, primarily because they each wished they'd been the one to kill him. Tony confessed that Agent Mann, the one Heinrich had cozied up to at the Spectrum staff meeting, had planted a tiny tracking device on his expensive slacks. Since then,

DHS had been following his movements throughout Cobo. Tony then recounted the relevant points of the intercepted phone call in which Dudiyn promised an unknown person he would get rid of Heinrich and execute the plan against Cobo himself.

Charlie retrieved the folder Carter had prepared on Bernard Dudiyn, and as she thumbed through it passed the contents around the table.

"This is him?" the facilities supervisor asked, looking at an eight-by-ten photograph. "He looks like a skinhead."

"Yes, and he's a pro. As you'll see from the Interpol report, he's known to a few police agencies around the world," Charlie said.

"His Spectrum ID gives him access to most of the areas in Cobo," Cynthia stated.

"Can his ID be deactivated?" Tony asked.

"Yes. I'll take care of that right now," Cynthia said, and left the room.

"I've a theory," Charlie said, walking around the conference table to the white board, where she ripped one of the notes down and laid it in the middle of the table. "And it helps to explain this question: How were the explosives found in the bomb sweep to be detonated?"

"What's your theory?" Gil asked.

"Maybe what the dogs found aren't any part of the bombs. Maybe those chemicals were put into the planters to keep us all busy."

Charlie took her seat while the others stewed on the notion. Around the table, eyes grew wide as the plausibility began to set in.

"Damn," Mandy finally said. "A diversion."

"I think you're onto something, Mack," Don said.

"Think about the timing," Charlie said. "Heinrich had tonight's schedule. He knew the bomb sweeps wouldn't occur until the preview parties were done, and he was aware there'd be fewer security patrols. He took a chance he wouldn't raise much suspicion by moving about the public areas while VIPs were in the building."

Gil picked up the theory. "And then, while we all flocked to the areas where he planted the chemicals, and ATF was frantically taking chemical samples, Heinrich was off . . . doing what?"

"Being killed," Tony said wryly.

"Maybe Dudiyn is the one who was to place the real bombs all along," Gil said.

"We should get this picture to the facilities staff," Calhoun said.

"Right," Don said, and turned to Hoyt. "And let's get copies of his picture to all the patrols."

"Tell them he's armed and dangerous," Tony said. "In addition to killing Heinrich, it's likely he killed the food services employee, Chenglei, and maybe your friend Josh."

"He was also the one who beat up Lin Fong," Charlie said with anger.

Dudiyn moved slowly, purposefully, along the perimeter of the second level. His objective was to place the pipe bombs in as many of the recyclable containers as he could access. So far, he'd positioned ten of the units. The bombs were powerful enough to cause structural damage, and serious injury or death to anyone within a twenty-foot radius. A few areas were cordoned off with police tape where ATF bomb teams, wearing what looked like green space suits, were still sifting through planters.

As patrols rode by, they gave Dudiyn a cursory glance. When they did, he shook open a garbage bag, making sure his wristband was visible. His only close call was an encounter at a restroom where an actual member of the Cobo cleaning crew was working.

"How's it going? You got this area too?" The man eyed Dudiyn curiously.

"How's it going?" Dudiyn repeated. He felt the man's stare, but kept his head down so the bill of his cap would cover his face. He lifted a PVC section out of his cart, making sure the dead rodent sticker was in full view. "Doing pest control. Damn rats are everywhere," Dudiyn mumbled.

"I hate rats," the man said, swiftly pushing his mop and bucket into the restroom.

Dudiyn placed a bomb into the bottom of the recyclable box, then pushed one of the thick black bags in next to conceal the device, and stretched the ends over the corners of the box. He gave a quick look around and studied the schedule. Some workers were on scaffolding in the ceiling, changing lightbulbs and adjusting spotlights. Others were still polishing the concourse escalators. Ahead he could see another box next to a vendor stand. Dudiyn pulled the baseball cap firmly down on his head and moved slowly along the corridor.

"Where'd you find Heinrich's body?" Charlie asked Tony.

"In one of the alcoves off the loading dock. He'd been shot, three times. Want to take a look?"

They walked the hall of level one. Cobo staff, delayed by the activities of the bomb sweeps, were hanging some of the auto show signs. Using hydraulic lifts, they worked from buckets a hundred feet high, affixing the flexible signs with cable. Sign erection had become less and less important in recent years as sophisticated computer-operated LED displays had replaced the old-fashioned banners. But there was still something very impressive about a gigantic banner, spanning the width of the concourse, welcoming visitors to the most well-attended auto show in the world.

When Charlie and Tony reached the corridor to the loading dock, they saw Calhoun moving some of the heavy machinery in the hallway.

"How's it going?" Charlie asked.

"Okay. But our maintenance schedule has pretty much gone to hell. A bunch of police are in the dock area, taking photographs and asking a lot of questions. I told them the same thing I told you, Ms. Mack. My guys didn't see nothing. Heinrich came in here and watched us work for a few minutes and then left. But I remembered something I forgot to tell you."

"What?" Charlie asked.

"When I first noticed him, he was standing by my desk and had opened the drawer. I think he was looking for the wristbands. You know, the security bracelets. I caught him at it. I showed him where they were, and he picked up a few of them, then put 'em back."

"Where are your bands?" Charlie asked.

"In the desk. I'll show you."

Calhoun climbed down from the John Deere lifter and trudged in heavy work boots into the storage room. His desk was covered with blueprints, various tools, clipboards, and a coffee-stained calendar. He reached into the top drawer and laid a manila folder on top.

"They're in here."

Charlie dumped the contents of the envelope onto the desk. Five yellow bands fell onto the calendar.

"Is this all you have?"

"Yep. Those are left for the guys coming in at four to do the vacuuming. That's the last thing we do before we open the doors."

Calhoun picked up one of the clipboards. His brows furrowed and he dropped the clipboard onto the desk. He looked up at Charlie with a mix of concern and embarrassment. "Only thing is, there should be six of those bands, not five."

A white cotton sheet was draped over Heinrich's body. The police and FBI agents conferred in a tight circle on the far end of the dock. The coroner and his assistants were packing up samples and tools. Tony identified himself and introduced Charlie to the medical examiner, then leaned over the stretcher to lift a corner of the sheet. Heinrich's face was a stony mask, his mouth contorted in a teeth-baring grimace.

"Shot at close range," the coroner said. "A small-caliber pistol. Possibly a 32. Missed the carotid artery by a half inch. That's why there's not much bleeding."

"Time of death?" Charlie asked.

"Two hours ago."

"Pull the sheet all the way off, Tony," Charlie said.

Tony drew the sheet from Heinrich's body down to his Italian loafers. Charlie leaned over to examine his wrists.

"No security band," she said.

"He probably got it for Dudiyn, so he could blend in," Tony said.

"Blend in as what?"

"Could be anything. A valet parking guy, a security guard . . ."

Charlie interrupted Tony and pressed the talk button on her radio. "Our person of interest may have a security band," she said into the mouthpiece.

Don, Mandy, Hoyt, and Tyson replied to her transmission with questions. The squawking radio got the attention of the Detroit police commander on duty. He was the one in charge of the Chenglei murder investigation, and the one Charlie had met with when Josh was killed. The veteran cop was African-American, probably six-foot-five, and, so far, a survivor in the investigations of police misconduct within the city administration. He ambled over to Tony and Charlie with a countenance of irritation.

"Another body, and here you are again, Ms. Mack."

"Hello, Commander."

"And this time it's the head of Cobo's security." The officer's stare of accusation took in both Tony and Charlie. "Can you tell me anything about what's going on here?"

"Not really," Charlie said. "I'm as surprised as you about Heinrich. You know Tony Canterra of Homeland Security," Charlie deflected.

"Yes. I remember," he said, looking down at Tony. "We got a terrorist situation here, Canterra?"

"Very likely. But I think we're on top of it."

The lieutenant's scowl showed his complete disbelief. He looked at Charlie and smirked.

"If you call three bodies in three weeks being on top of it, who am I to argue," he said, sucking his teeth and turning away.

"We appreciate MPD's help with the canine units," Tony shouted to the man's massive back. The commander gave a dismissive wave as he exited.

"I need to get back to the office," Charlie said.

Charlie thumbed through Dudiyn's folder again and found the note she'd seen earlier.

"Carter. I have a question for you," she shouted toward the outer office.

"What can I do for you, Ms. Mack?" Carter said, entering the conference room.

"Did you get the additional information on Dudiyn that you mentioned?"

"I've been so focused on looking at the security footage, I haven't checked my email in a while. I'll check now."

"I'm interested in this note about multiple passports. That's been verified?"

"Yes, it has."

"Can we get photocopies?"

"That's what I've been waiting for."

It was 2 a.m. One of the few times in the last twelve hours that Charlie had been alone to do her thinking exercise. Her eyes burned and her concentration was shot. She turned to the white board. She removed the *Where is Heinrich* note, then wrote and placed a new green note onto the middle of the board. It read: *What is Dudiyn up to?* The question stared back at her.

"What do you think his next move will be?" Hartwell startled her. He was leaning on the door jamb, jacket off, shirtsleeves rolled up.

"I'm not sure."

Hartwell took the seat next to Charlie. They both gazed at the board for a full minute in silence.

"Cynthia and I decided it was best not to tell the Spectrum staff that Heinrich is dead."

"I think that makes sense. Despite what Tony says, there could be another accomplice we don't know about," Charlie replied.

"This is quite the system you have," Hartwell said, pointing to the board.

"It usually works well for me."

"And this time?"

"In this case, we started with more questions than facts. Facts that would be at the very core of most of the investigations I take on."

"We're very grateful to you, Ms. Mack."

"You might as well call me Charlie, since we might die together tonight."

Hartwell recognized the black humor and chuckled. The anxiety that came with the unknown had stripped the others of calmness, but he was more casual than ever. He popped up from the table to pour coffee.

"Can I get you another cup?" he asked.

"No. Caffeine stopped having any effect on me hours ago."

"You've done a good job, Ms. Mack. Uh, Charlie."

"How can you tell? I sure can't."

"Cynthia's been giving me regular reports."

"She's been a huge help to us," Charlie responded with a weak smile.

"Believe me, you and your partners were the right people for this job. We know all the ambiguity has been a hindrance, but we didn't know any other way to handle things." Hartwell shifted in his seat. "But the bottom line is, none of this would have happened if I hadn't hired Heinrich."

The two sat in silence. Hartwell was looking to Charlie for a response. Since there was none, he hung his head.

"You fucked up, all right."

Hartwell's eyes were large as he looked up, startled by Charlie's frankness and profanity. She offered a tired smile.

"Feel better now?"

Carter and Judy stepped into the conference room with gloomy faces, Carter carrying a handful of papers. Hartwell was still recovering from Charlie's tough love.

"We've got another problem," Judy said.

"Come on in. What is it?"

"These are photocopies of three other passports used by Dudiyn. He has a few different aliases," Carter said.

"That's not so unusual, is it?" Charlie asked.

"No. But this is." Carter put four photographs in front of her.

Charlie and Hartwell leaned over the documents. Each showed a different person, with only the barest resemblance to the man they knew as Dudiyn.

"Are you telling me, all four of these photos are of Bernard Dudiyn?" Hartwell asked.

"I'm afraid so," Carter replied. "The photo you distributed earlier may not be what he looks like."

"Don, where are you?" Charlie said into the walkie-talkie.

After a few minutes, Don responded. "We're on the rooftop. ATF is just about finished with their sweep."

"I need you back down here. Bring Gil, Hoyt, and Mandy with you."

"What's up, Mack?"

"You've got to see for yourself."

Dudiyn had been monitoring the radio and was aware the color-coded security band no longer gave him a free pass. The patrols came by every thirty to forty minutes, but they were looking for something unusual or out of place, and the janitor disguise continued to give him invisibility. It also helped that he wasn't alone in the corridors of Cobo. Scores of workers were polishing glass windows, hanging drapery, erecting signs, installing carpet, replacing light fixtures, and cleaning the various surfaces of the building. But his task was taking longer than he'd expected.

He'd completed placing twenty-five pipe bombs in the recyclable boxes on level two, fewer than planned, because many areas were still blocked off. He was heading next to level three where, according to the radio chatter, the ATF had completed their bomb sweeps. He'd take a break after that, and sometime around 6-8 a.m., he'd plant the last bombs near the level one exhibits.

Dudiyn became alert as a patrol team approached. He'd transferred his gun to the tray on the mop cart where he could easily reach it. As he'd done before, he stopped and lifted his dripping mop to scrub away at the nearest baseboard. As the patrol vehicle passed, he looked up from his fake chore. The pair glanced at him. The male driver quickly looked away, but the woman shifted in her seat toward him as they passed. It was Heinrich's redhead. He continued his scrubbing and, for effect, whipped a rag from his back pocket, stooping to dry the water-splashed wall. He rode a service elevator up to the third level and moved deliberately to the nearest restroom. His cart was getting lighter as he removed another of the five-pound units from the bag. The detonations tomorrow on multiple levels of Cobo within minutes of each other would create a whirlwind of chaos and carnage.

Amy had dressed quickly in the dark. She understood Lin's need to demonstrate loyalty. That's what she'd felt when she offered to stay at Cobo. She wanted to help Mr. Kwong. He was in trouble, even if she didn't know what kind of trouble it was. She disarmed the security panel and closed the front door gently. Her parents were asleep on the other side of their sprawling home, and the live-in housekeeper was also likely asleep in the small cottage attached to the rear of the house. When she reached the car port, she rearmed the house with her remote fob. Her father had all kinds of security gadgets, cameras, alarms, motion detector lights. Even now, he might be watching on his mobile phone as she started her car and backed out of the driveway with the lights out.

At 2:15 a.m., Amy picked up Lin outside of the downtown condo building, where last night's snow coated the curbs or had been windswept against the corners of the building. Lin made a long silhouette in front of the well-lit lobby window as he shivered in a thin gray hoodie and a knit cap. He carried a laptop in his ungloved hands.

"It's cold," he noted as he slid his lean torso into the front seat.

"This is Detroit. You need to wear a coat," Amy chastised, then followed with, "Sorry."

"I like it that you care about me," Lin said with a sideways glance and a grin.

"Don't flatter yourself. I just can't stop channeling my mother when it comes to dealing with people who need help."

"Seriously, Amy, thanks for coming to get me."

"I think we're both making a mistake."

"Both?"

"Yes. I'm going back with you."

"You don't have to do that."

"Why not? Because I'm a female?"

"I didn't say that."

"I can be brave, too."

"I knew you were brave when you walked into that warehouse to save me."

"I wasn't there to save you, remember?"

"I know, but most girls wouldn't even have opened that door and stepped into a dark room. And when you saw me handcuffed to a chair, you could have left me there."

Amy made a U-turn on Jefferson Avenue and headed to Cobo. At the front drive, a police car with flashing lights blocked the passenger drop-off lane. Two armored cars with ATF markings idled at the curb. At this time of night, they'd need to go to the employee entrance near the Civic Drive security station to be buzzed in by the guard. Amy drove to the Larned Garage and used her access card, lifting the gate. The garage was empty, except for the last row against the wall where staff cars and restaurant trucks were parked. Amy pulled to the end of the line of cars and turned off the engine. She removed her keys from the ignition, then turned to Lin, leaned over, and pressed her lips against his mouth. Lin was momentarily unable to move, but it took only a few seconds before he returned the passion of Amy's kiss. A strange noise gave them a start, and together they stared through the windshield as a man pushed a cart with a mop toward the other end of the lot.

"Come on, let's walk around to the front," Amy said, grabbing for the door handle.

"No. Wait. *Don't open that door*," Lin said in a panicked whisper.

"Why? What's wrong, Lin?" Amy said, looking into his terrified eyes.

"The way he walks and moves. I know that's him. That's Baldy."

The group around the table peered at the photo montage Judy had mocked up. Tony had returned, and Cynthia and Hartwell stood against the wall. The photo array showed Dudiyn dressed as a businessman with a three-piece suit and a neatly trimmed mustache; in athletic wear, with long hair and a backpack; as a beardless, bespectacled geek; and in the uniform of a law-enforcement officer, complete with a cap and aviator glasses.

"It's hard to believe all these are the same guy," Hoyt said. "So now we're looking at anybody in the building, even if they're wearing the security band?"

"Any *man* in the building," Don said. "I assume he can't dress up to look like a woman."

"I don't think we can underestimate this guy," Gil said.

"Have any of you seen anyone suspicious?" Charlie asked.

Heads shook "no" around the table. Hoyt took a sip of coffee and quickly put the cup back on the table, hoping no one saw the trembling of his hands. Tyson's sad-sack demeanor made him seem ten years older. Gil stood and offered his seat to a tired Cynthia.

"It's possible Dudiyn is staying out of sight tonight. Wouldn't it be easier to plant the bombs tomorrow when the press corps is here?" Gil asked.

"Maybe," Tony said. "But the call we intercepted mentioned keeping on a schedule, and there was some kind of deadline tonight. We still haven't ruled out a car bomb scenario. Let's assume whatever he's doing, it's happening now."

"There must be a couple of hundred people at Cobo, and more coming in the next few hours," Mandy said. "Lots of workers, Spectrum staff, administrative staff, a few of the exhibitor design teams just moved back into the showroom. It wouldn't be difficult to go unnoticed."

The Mack patrols were circulating on every level of Cobo, still working in two-person teams. They'd been instructed to check in with their status every half hour. Charlie was splitting her time between crisscrossing Cobo to provide general supervision, and having a presence in the office.

"What's our communications status?"

"We're good," Judy reported. "The BlackBerrys are still working fine for regular communications. I'm rotating the two-way radios to keep all of them charged, and I've recharged each of them except the one we gave to Cynthia. I already called her about it," Judy reported.

Carter had returned to the Spectrum monitoring room, and Judy was bugging Charlie for an assignment beyond the communications tasks. So when Charlie was called to the third level for a conversation between Cobo's GM, Scott Hartwell, Tony Canterra, and the ATF head, she allowed Judy to ride shotgun.

"We've done an extensive search tonight. We've checked every sitting area, done sweeps of every exhibitor space, and checked every room accessible to the public," the ATF agent said, checking his notes. "Two restrooms were out of order and locked, so we still need to check them. We also did sweeps of the balconies and exterior smoking areas. But what I really want to talk about is our change in assessment of the bomb threat. I've been speaking with agent Canterra about this. I agree with him that an IED of some sort is the most plausible threat. From what we've been seeing in other parts of the world, suicide vests and vehicle bombs are terrorists' weapons of choice these days."

"Correct." Tony picked up the argument. "Suicide bombs account for more fatalities than other IEDs, and their main purpose is to instill fear. One of Ms. Mack's team members mentioned vehicle bombs earlier, and I've given it some more thought. I think we should gear up for potential auto bombs. They wouldn't cause as many deaths at Cobo, but they'd get a lot of attention."

"Can you imagine it?" Hartwell said with a pale face. "The photographs of plumes of smoke rising above Detroit? It would look like the '67 riots all over again."

"So I'm recommending we concentrate our efforts on the parking areas, on Cobo's perimeter, and on individual searches tomorrow as people come in. If we agree on that strategy, I need to send my people home for a couple of hours' rest and then get them back here around daybreak."

"What do you think, Ms. Mack?" Mathers asked.

"I'm not a bomb expert, but I do have some experience with brutal, dangerous men, and we have one on the loose." Charlie looked each man hard in the eyes, and then softened her face when she glanced at Tyson and Judy, who were wide-eyed and scared. "We're not out of the woods until we can account for Dudiyn. Heinrich had knowledge of our schedules and protocols tonight. There's no reason to doubt that Dudiyn now has that information."

Judy raised her hand, and cleared her throat. Heads turned toward her. Charlie knew she wouldn't interrupt unless it was important, and nodded for her to speak.

"I just got a message from Cynthia. She can't find the two-way radio we gave her. She left it on her desk earlier today and hadn't even noticed it was missing. She thinks Heinrich took it."

Heads swiveled back to Charlie for an interpretation of this latest news. She splayed her hands on the table, and the tasteful chocolate-diamond ring Mandy had given her gleamed under the fluorescent lights. She raised her gaze to the expectant eyes.

"I believe our dangerous man has been monitoring our communications for hours. He knows everything we know, including that we're looking for him."

When Judy and Charlie were clear of the GM's office, Judy passed on Cynthia's second piece of information.

"She said we should meet her at the guard station at the Civic Center drive entrance. There's somebody there to see you."

"Is that all she said?"

"Yes."

Tyson hurried out of his boss's office suite and flagged down Charlie as she executed a three-wheel turn.

"Ms. Mack. I have a thought. If Dudiyn has a walkie-talkie, maybe we can send a message that will lay a trap for him."

Charlie smiled at Tyson. "That's very good thinking. We're going to meet in my office in a bit. I want you there. Judy will call you about the time."

Charlie and Judy idled in front of the service elevator in their golf cart. Charlie watched the LED number change from one to two and finally three. Judy gave Charlie a wry look and pursed her lips.

"Are you ready to admit Don was right?"

"What's got you giving credit to Don?"

"Tyson."

"Okay. He had to prove himself to me, and he's done that. He's a smart kid with good common sense. You happy now?"

"I guess so. If you can be happy and scared at the same time."

"Believe me, we're all scared." Charlie looked at her watch. "Wow, it's almost three o'clock. Send a message to the others to meet us at the office in a half hour."

When Charlie and Judy exited the elevator, they headed south through the concourse. Cynthia was standing at the door of the security office as they approached. She waved them over.

"What's up?" Charlie asked.

"These two showed up, asking for you. The night guard called me when he couldn't reach you in the office." Cynthia pointed inside the room, and Charlie stepped through the door with Judy at her heels. Two clearly irritated guards initially blocked their view, but when they moved aside, Lin Fong and Amy Wu looked up at Charlie like two puppies who had eaten a package of doughnuts.

"Hi, Ms. Mack," Lin said.

"Lin. Why aren't you at my apartment?"

"I heard about the trouble. With the explosives. And I came to help."

"And . . . I want to help, too," Amy said.

Charlie stared at them in disbelief. Cynthia and Judy stood nearby, each with a stern face and crossed arms. Charlie consulted briefly with the two guards, and the conversation ended with both Charlie and Cynthia signing a form that transferred responsibility for the unannounced, middle-of-the-night visitors to Spectrum and the Mack partners.

"Let's not talk in the hall," Charlie instructed. "Cynthia, will you drive Amy?"

Lin and Amy shared a look of solidarity as they parted ways. Lin took a seat in the back of Charlie's cart.

"Why did you come back to Cobo, Lin? It's too dangerous for you to be here."

"I feel like I let you down, Ms. Mack."

"No. You did not let me down. If anything, it's the other way around. How did Amy get involved?"

"I asked her to drive me, and she said she wanted to come back too, to help her boss."

"Well, I don't have any control over Amy, but you're not staying. I'm going to have someone drive you back to my condo."

"You can't do that. I saw him. He's here at Cobo."

"Who's here?"

"Baldy. The guy who beat me. Amy and I saw him in the parking garage."

Once more in this long night a set of grim faces stared back at Charlie. Lin had seen Dudiyn in the employee parking garage, beardless and dressed in a janitor's uniform.

"You sure it was him, Fong?" Don asked.

"I'm sure. I watched him walk around when he had me tied to that chair. I'll never forget his eyes, or the way he moves. Tonight he had on a baseball cap, and his beard was gone, but that was Baldy all right."

"Wow. I think I may have seen him, too," Mandy said. "On the third level. He had a janitor's cart."

"We probably all saw him without seeing him," Gil pointed out.

"Okay, we're going to regroup quickly and get after him. We're pretty sure he has a walkie-talkie, and Tyson has an idea for smoking him out."

The plan was simple and perilous. They would concoct some communication over the two-way radios to draw the man out of hiding and then, somehow, put him out of commission before he could detonate a bomb. New color-coded bands would be distributed immediately, which would make him easier to spot. Don and Gil would dress like members of the crew who would soon begin vacuuming the miles of red carpet that had been laid overnight. When they spotted Dudiyn, their disguises would enable them to get close enough without arousing his suspicion.

Tyson was dispatched to retrieve uniforms for Don and Gil and to make sure the next set of wristbands were quickly distributed to the facilities and cleaning staffs. Cynthia and Lin Fong joined Carter in Spectrum's monitoring room to view video of the parking garage where Lin had seen Dudiyn. Hoyt rounded up the six patrol teams to update them on the new procedures, which included limiting radio communication and returning to the BlackBerrys as the main tool of communications. Mandy's task was to chauffeur Judy around with fresh batteries for the BlackBerrys. Charlie, Don, and Gil remained in the office with Scott Hartwell.

"The fact remains, even if we locate Dudiyn and manage to capture him, it doesn't guarantee that we can get our hands on the bombs," Gil said.

"I know. I know," Charlie said.

"You heard what the ATF supervisor said," Hartwell reminded Charlie. "He's convinced the threat to Cobo will be from suicide vests or car bombs."

"I don't care what he said, Scott. Think about it. What was the purpose of the diversion? If not to distract us from something that was going on *inside* Cobo tonight? Our main objective is to locate Dudiyn and track his movements. Then, maybe, we can save your auto show."

Hartwell nodded.

258

"And if we find bombs," Don added. "We'll call in the ATF."

"What if he figures out you're onto him and panics, and blows Cobo to smithereens?" Hartwell asked.

"Then, at the least we'll have minimized the loss of life," Charlie said soberly.

"Wait, Mandy. Stop here," Judy shouted.

Mandy applied the brakes hard. The electric cart lurched, and the tires screeched. Judy was turned in the seat looking back. Then she bolted from the cart.

"What is it, Judy?" Mandy asked, leaping from the cart and following.

"Look," Judy said, standing across from the entrance to the ladies' restroom. "That extra recycling box. That's not supposed to be there."

"What do you mean?"

"I processed the driver who delivered the waste containers. Those three right there," Judy pointed to the left. "He told me he had the exclusive contract for all the trash and recyclable containers. But I saw some Spectrum staff setting up those boxes earlier."

"Well, there's your answer."

"No. Why would Spectrum be setting up trash containers?"

Charlie had told Mandy about Judy's many gifts. She was a people person, a world-class weaver of lies, a Broadway musical geek, and a compulsive file maker. "She has a perception of things others don't have," Charlie often said.

"Let's take a look," Mandy said, crossing the corridor. Judy lined up behind her.

Mandy lifted the recyclable box with one hand. "It's not heavy." Then shook it, and heard something moving in the bottom of the box. She stuck her hand in the empty bag and tilted it to feel the bottom where she grasped something heavy. Startled, she quickly removed her hand. "Something's in there." She peeled off one of the tight corners of the bag, and lifted it from the container. On the bottom of the box was a white tube with a rat-control label. "It's some kind of rat bait."

"I hate rats," Judy said, drawing back.

"It's just the pesticide, not a rat," Mandy said, reaching in for the tube.

The container was smooth and heavy. She hefted it in her hand. *Feels like four or five pounds.* The sticker showed a dead rodent under a red *X*. Mandy examined the tube, some kind of pipe made out of PVC material. One side was closed tight, but the other end had a small opening. *Must be where the rat breathes in the poison.* Suddenly, Mandy stood erect. She leaned forward very slowly and backed away from the box.

"What's wrong?" Judy asked.

"C'mon. Let's go back to the cart," Mandy said pulling Judy by the hand.

Mandy almost lifted Judy into the vehicle, before she darted to the driver side and shot down the hall to the Spectrum suite. She jumped from the cart, darted into the suite, and ran down the corridor into the office. The Mack partners and Hartwell were startled as Mandy and then Judy burst into the conference room out of breath.

"We found a damn bomb," Mandy gasped.

Following Mandy's description of the pipe bomb, Charlie acted quickly. Her first call was to Tony Canterra, who was still at Cobo. Next, she called Carter and Lin Fong, telling them to concentrate their review of security footage on the restrooms. Before Mandy and Judy fled the area, Judy had had the presence of mind to use her phone camera to take a picture of the recyclable box. The photo had been distributed to the patrol team, with strict orders to locate the boxes on all levels—but to stay away from them. General Manager Mike Mathers ordered the facilities supervisor to find out where the boxes came from, and then convened the key players around the table in his office.

"The shipping receipt says fifty Universal recycling boxes were delivered to Cobo on November first," Dennis Calhoun said to the group as he rifled through his clipboard. The Mack partners, Hartwell, Tony, Cynthia, Mandy, Tyson, and an embarrassed ATF supervisor looked on. "The purchase order was signed by Geoff Heinrich and approved by . . ." Calhoun looked up at Charlie with a shudder. "It was approved by Garry Jones."

"The dead food services supervisor," Judy said.

"I didn't think anything of it when Heinrich told me we'd help to distribute the recyclable boxes," Cynthia explained in a shaky voice. "I just thought he was pretending to be helpful."

Hartwell and Mathers looked ashen, and the ATF agent was somber as Tony peppered Mandy with questions about the pipe bomb.

"Describe, again, the wire you saw. Was it a single wire or a coil?"

"A copper wire, but coiled with plastic or something on the tip."

"How large was the hole in the end of the pipe?"

"I'd say no more than a quarter inch."

"And how long was the wiring?"

"Maybe an inch and a half."

"That sounds like an explosive device," the ATF supervisor said despondently. "Was anything taped to the exterior of the pipe?"

"No. Just the rat label."

"Okay," Tony said. "Charlie, what have your people reported?"

"They've spotted all fifty boxes. They're on levels one, two, and three. Most are in front of restrooms, but a few are in the food vendor areas."

"I've got to get my people in to examine each of those containers," the agent said to Tony.

"I know, but Ms. Mack would like you to keep a low profile, so we can catch the man who planted them. Is there a way to do that?"

"That's not really our protocol," the agent said, shaking his head. "Now that we have a possible bomb, and we know what it looks like, we need to move fast. Those devices are set to be detonated remotely."

"Our suspect was last seen on level one in one of the garages; he might see the comings and goings of a large ATF squad. Would it be possible to bring your agents in through the front door or on foot or by using unmarked vehicles?" Charlie asked.

"We don't usually do that," he started objecting.

"Well, this time I need you to do just that." Tony's voice left no room for discussion or dissent. "How soon can your people get here?"

"I can have some of them here in a half hour with containment vessels. The rest in an hour, but the lab people will need their truck; that's how they control the robotic units."

"You can use the loading dock for your vehicles. The police have searched every inch of that place, and they still have an officer on guard. Our guy can't be hiding there," Tony said.

"Is there something we can do in the meantime?" Gil asked. "Cynthia says Spectrum has a half-dozen portable explosives detectors. We could use those to determine if all of the boxes have bombs."

"I don't know about that," the agent began. "We usually maintain a security perimeter for civilians."

"Mandy probably wouldn't be sitting with us now if the bombs were booby-trapped," Gil said matter-of-factly.

Eyes glanced toward Mandy, but she was staring at Charlie, who was staring back, oblivious to the others in the room.

"I think it would be a good use of our time, to identify the affected containers," Don said.

"I agree," Charlie said, returning her attention to the room.

"With our facilities uniforms, Don and I can just blend in with the other staff," Gil said.

Don, Gil, and Charlie had received cursory training in bomb disposal at DHS; Mandy and Hoyt had similar training from their police departments. Using the mobile detectors would save time for ATF.

"Okay. It's Don and Gil on the lead, with Hoyt, Mandy, and me as backup," Charlie said.

"And me," the ATF supervisor said.

Tony overruled the idea. "When your agents arrive, you'll need to give them directions and get them coordinated. You can pull my two people from the patrols and put them on this," Tony said to Charlie.

"Good idea, Tony."

Judy sensed the end of the meeting and asked the question she was holding. "Are we still planning on coaxing Dudiyn out of hiding?"

"No. Not anymore," Charlie answered. "Wherever he is, we want him to stay put. If he figures out we know the location of the bombs, he might detonate them early. We'll smoke him out after the devices are secured."

"Okay, but what do you want me to do?" Judy asked.

"You've done a whole lot already. After all, you were the one who located the bombs."

"Charlie's right, Judy," Mandy added.

"But I can't just sit around now," Judy argued.

"Okay, here's your assignment. Go to Spectrum now and work with Carter and Lin. Have them shift their attention to footage that shows the recyclable boxes near the restaurants. Also, make sure they're watching the live cameras for Dudiyn. We need to know if, and when, he's on the move."

"Judy, you can ride with me," Cynthia said, standing. "I'll get the detectors unpacked and make sure they're charged and ready to go."

Don and Gil would team up on level two, the two DHS agents would check level three, and Charlie and Mandy would scan the boxes on Cobo's first level. Teamwork and guts would be the drivers of this "Hail Mary" operation.

Chairs scraped as the players stood to take on their tasks, and when the office emptied, only Mathers, Hartwell, and Tyson were left. Mathers was still visibly disturbed.

"I know what you're thinking, Mike," Hartwell said. "It's nothing like the business decisions we have to make every day. The whole thing is too organic; there's no playbook or procedures manual."

Mathers nodded.

"But what you should know is I believe that team is scrappy, unorthodox, and brave enough to pull it off."

Mathers looked at Tyson. The young man had been around Cobo for two decades, and loved the place and its people more than most.

"What do you think, Ty? Can they save us?"

"I'm betting my life on it."

Amy had been secured in Cynthia's office for the last hour. In the Spectrum glass office, she could see Lin sitting before one of the security consoles. When Cynthia was called away, Amy waited fifteen minutes before leaving, unnoticed. She knocked on the outer door of Guí Motors, and when there was no answer used her key to enter the office. The room was dark except for the ceremonial candles that had been lit last night when the bosses arrived from the airport. Amy turned on her desk lamp and crossed the room to extinguish the candles. The tall glass containers were hot to the touch, and the air swiftly filled with the smell of smoky jasmine.

Amy tapped at the interior door several times before Kwong's raspy voice replied, and she opened the door.

"Is that you, Amy?"

"Yes, Mr. Kwong."

"Why have you returned?"

"They have found explosive devices inside of Cobo. Maybe you should leave."

"Where would I go?"

"You could come to my home. My parents would welcome you."

Kwong stared at Amy only a moment before he shook his head no. Then he buried his face in his palms and sobbed.

"I'll make you a cup of tea, Mr. Kwong. And there are also some almond biscuits left over from the party."

Judy peered at her laptop screen. Dudiyn, dressed as a janitor, had been pushing a mop cart all around Cobo. The 360-degree security cameras were programmed to videotape for three minutes in

264

one direction before switching views. In two of the tape sequences, Dudiyn could be seen busying himself near the recyclable containers in the middle concourse of level two.

"See, there," Judy said to Cynthia, Carter and Lin, pointing. "He puts the bomb in just before he ties down the bag."

Cynthia had moved the three to Heinrich's office where they could monitor the taped security footage and tie into the live cameras from their laptops. The presence of outsiders in the boss's office, especially Lin Fong, who had been fired from Spectrum, caused a few raised eyebrows among the staff. To those who asked, Cynthia explained that it was Heinrich's orders.

"I think the most efficient way to backtrack his movements is for each of us to take a floor and look at the corridor footage," Carter suggested.

"Starting about 11 p.m.?" Judy asked.

"That sounds right," Carter said

"Why eleven?" Lin asked.

"It's the time of death the coroner gave us for Heinrich," Judy said.

"Wait a minute. Mr. Heinrich is dead?"

Cynthia, Judy, and Carter reacted with embarrassment. Lin was trying to recover from his second shock of the night.

"I'm sorry, I thought you knew," Judy said.

Cynthia picked up the apology. "Lin, things are moving so fast now, it's hard to remember who knows what. There are still so many uncertainties. Some information is being shared and some not."

Lin was still trying to make sense of the news and the explanation. He bent his head from side to side to release the tension in his neck.

"Heinrich was found on the loading dock last night, shot, and we believe Dudiyn killed him."

"Okay," Carter said, wasting no more time. "Judy, why don't you take level three; I'll take the second level; and Lin, you concentrate on level one. We're focusing on vendor areas, and let's use the floor plans to mark every location where this guy went."

Carter was the first to strike gold. He rewound the footage to 12:05 a.m. on the time code. Dudiyn could be seen planting one of the white tubes in the recyclable box in front of a beverage vendor station. He circled the area on his map and continued his review of the videotape at double speed. Dudiyn stopped again at a restroom in the south concourse, and Carter marked the spot. He went on like this for a half hour and marked nine places. So far Judy and Lin hadn't had a single sighting of the man.

"It looks like he may have started on level two," Carter said.

Lin had been scanning the footage from the north atrium camera on level one. His first sighting of Dudiyn came at 11:30 p.m. when he emerged from the level one restroom near the Larned Street garage with his janitor's cart and disguise. Lin shifted to the camera facing south on that corridor and watched from the opposite perspective as Dudiyn shuffled down the hall and turned the corner.

"I'm starting back even earlier on this camera," Lin announced.

The on-screen time code read 8:44 p.m. when a cleaning lady entered the atrium from the meeting rooms and stopped outside the restroom before entering. Five minutes later, Dudiyn pushed his cart along the atrium corridor and entered the same restroom. After another five minutes, Dudiyn pulled the two carts into the restroom and reappeared briefly as he placed a sign on the door.

Lin sat back in his chair.

"What is it, Lin?" Judy asked

"At nine o'clock, Baldy went into that restroom by the parking garage and didn't come out until two and a half hours later."

"That's information we should get to Ms. Mack," Carter said.

Judy nodded her head in agreement. "Maybe that's his hiding place."

"But I saw him in the garage around two-thirty," Lin said.

"Right. But nobody's seen him since," Judy said. She punched Charlie's number into the BlackBerry.

"Oh, and tell Ms. Mack a cleaning woman went in the restroom too, but she never came out," Lin announced gravely.

Judy's call drew Tony, members of the bomb squad, Cynthia, and Charlie and Mandy to the first-level men's room. It was 4 a.m. The armed ATF supervisor was the first to enter the restroom, gun drawn, holding the Mack team, Tony, Cynthia and a half-dozen curious Cobo staff at a safe distance. He returned to the hallway to signal the restroom was empty and began to suit up in the bomb disposal gear that the rest of his team wore.

"What's the protocol now?" Charlie asked Tony.

"That's ATF's explosive ordnance disposal team, EOD for short. They've been disarming the devices your patrols have located. They have handheld equipment to determine the degree of danger each bomb presents."

"Why not use robots?"

"This is faster."

"How many bombs have been found?"

"ATF has retrieved thirty IEDs from levels one, two, and three, all from the recyclable boxes you alerted us to."

"You think that's all of them?" Mandy asked.

"There's no way to be sure," Tony said. "But we've been very lucky so far; all the bombs have been set up for remote phone detonation. Apparently Dudiyn's not aware we've found them."

The supervisor walked over to the group, removing his head gear. "We've looked in and around each urinal, behind the sinks and towel dispensers, and in each stall. This is one of the restrooms that had an "out of order" sign on the door. We hadn't gotten around to it yet," the man said, embarrassed for the second time that night.

"That's not important now," Charlie said. "Did you find anything?"

"We have a locked door in there. A closet or something. We need another key."

"I have a set of master keys," Cynthia said.

"Is it safe to open?" Tony asked.

"We'll know shortly. You can come and watch if you like."

Charlie and Tony watched from the restroom's exterior door as the EOD used handheld detectors, which looked like cordless drills, to determine whether it was safe to unlock the storage door. The detector maintained a green light, indicating the door wasn't booby-trapped. They applied a portable x-ray unit to the door, then paused in their work.

"We're going to open the door now," the head agent said over his shoulder, "but based on our analysis of the devices we've already retrieved, there's not much danger from a detonation in an enclosed space like this closet. That's why this guy has been placing the pipe bombs out in the open. When it blows, it'll blow front and back."

Tony and Charlie watched the bomb squad members, holding thick plastic shields in front of them, slowly unlock the door. When it was open, two of the agents turned on high-powered lights affixed to their helmets and stepped into the closet.

"We've got a red light sensor. Everybody move back."

Tony and Charlie rejoined those gathered behind the ATF tape marking the fifty-foot safety perimeter.

"What is it?" Mandy asked.

"They found something," Charlie replied.

Ten minutes passed while everyone waited, staring at the open restroom door, on edge for the sound of a blast. The ATF chief finally came to the door, waving Tony and Charlie over.

"We found another IED, just like the others. We've already deactivated it by cutting the copper fuse, and we're taking it to the containment chamber we've set up behind the loading dock," the ATF agent reported. "But we also found a woman's body. From the uniform, I'd say she's one of the janitors. A rag was stuffed in her mouth, and she was in the same plastic bag as the bomb. We also found two more bags with men's clothes and this." The agent held up a green Spectrum jacket.

Charlie, Cynthia, Mandy, Tony, and Scott Hartwell assembled around the stainless-steel coffee table in Heinrich's office. Judy, Lin, and Carter worked on the other side of the room, doing the tedious work of scanning the last six hours of activity in Cobo's public areas for any other signs of mischief.

"Using a Spectrum ID, Dudiyn accessed the rear lobby at 7:08 p.m. from the Larned Street garage," Cynthia reported. "He's been at Cobo all night."

"And we know from the security footage that he hid out in that men's room a couple of times tonight," Charlie said.

"But where is he now?" Hartwell asked.

"He had to have a vehicle to transport the IEDs. Did he scan his badge to get into the garage?" Tony asked.

Cynthia shook her head. "I don't know. There's an attendant at that garage until 8 p.m. and you only have to show your ID, but there are cameras in the garage. Maybe we can spot him coming in."

Lin cued up the security footage from the garage and began the search. In the Larned Street garage, three rotating cameras recorded in fifteen-minute intervals. It took about ten minutes before Lin saw a scene that got his attention. He looked at it twice before nudging Judy to take a look. Nearly ten hours earlier a blue van drove to the Larned garage gate, and the driver flashed an ID to the guard. The gate opened, and the van circled the garage before backing into a spot against the wall near the restaurant food trucks. Judy and Lin watched the van for ten minutes at fast speed, but the driver never got out. Lin toggled the footage forward at triple speed for almost ten minutes. A few security patrols whizzed through the scene, but there was no activity around the van until a man wearing a green jacket emerged from the shadows. Lin slowed the video to normal speed, and they watched him walk to the employee entrance, carrying two bags. At the door a bearded Bernard Dudiyn reached into the pocket of his jacket, swiped his badge against the keypad, and disappeared inside Cobo.

"We've got the vehicle," Judy announced calmly.

The conversation on the other side of the room stopped, and Charlie walked over to the conference table. Lin pointed to the screen.

269

"He got out of that van right there. He drove in and stayed in the van at least three hours before he entered Cobo with some plastic bags."

The others came to peer over Lin's shoulder. He pointed again at the video.

"Lin, find the footage of him returning to the van," Charlie said. "When you and Amy saw him."

Lin toggled the footage forward. At 2:26, Amy's car could be seen entering and parking along the back wall of the garage. A few minutes later, Dudiyn came into view in his janitor garb. He was pushing a mop cart toward the rear of the garage and entered the space between the blue van and the deli truck.

"Cynthia, can we feed the live camera of the Larned garage to the monitors in here?"

"Of course," Cynthia replied.

"Wait, I'll do it," Carter said, leaving the room.

In a few minutes, one of the screens over the seating area flickered, and the parking garage came into view. The van was still parked against the wall. Charlie sent a message on her Black-Berry and within minutes Don, Gil, and Hoyt entered Heinrich's office.

"What's up, Mack?" Don asked.

"Dudiyn may be in that blue van in the employee parking garage," Charlie said, looking at the monitor. "It's the one parked next to the deli truck. Lin found the footage of him driving the van into the garage."

All eyes shifted to the monitor. The room was eerily silent, as if Dudiyn might hear if someone spoke. Hartwell began pacing in front of the door. The calm he'd exhibited a few hours ago had given way to his usual edginess.

"I remember seeing that van when we made rounds. I thought it was one of the restaurant vehicles," Hoyt said.

"What's he doing in there?" Judy said.

"I think he's waiting until the show opens to the press," Charlie answered. "He's shown he's good at staying off the radar."

"What do we do next?" Don asked.

"First, we need to verify whether or not he's in the van, and do that without rousing his suspicion," Charlie said.

"Maybe this would be a good time to use ATF's robots," Tony said.

The ATF readily agreed to put one of their robotics units to work, and within fifteen minutes two agents placed their smallest unit, a five-pound surveillance robot, at the gate of the parking garage and retreated. A technician at the ATF command truck used a gaming toggle to quietly advance the thin, flat, square robot toward the van. Equipped with three micro-cameras and x-ray capabilities, the unit rolled silently up to and under the truck to take pictures and readings.

Gil and Don, still in their facilities uniforms, stepped out of the lobby door, chatted softly, and lit cigarettes. They had guns tucked against their backs and were prepared to take down Dudiyn if he exited the van. They watched as the robot reappeared from under the van and quietly rolled back through the parking gate to the waiting hands of the ATF agents.

Dudiyn woke from a fitful sleep. He wasn't sure what had awakened him, but he assumed it was the two guys taking a cigarette break outside of the employee entrance. Through the windshield he watched the men finish their smoking, drop the butts onto the sidewalk, and stub them with a twist of their boots. Then one of them swept up the butts into his handled trash pan while the other scanned the door, and they entered Cobo.

Dudiyn pushed the backlight on his phone. Only a quarter of five. The hardest part of any offensive was the wait. He'd learned to sleep when he could. Mostly on the ground, wedged into a craggy rock, or in a bombed-out structure where both stars and rain poured through the opening of a jagged roof. He'd joined the rebel forces in the Chechen war because his brother was a guerilla fighter and because, after his mother was killed, he didn't feel he belonged anywhere else. When his brother was captured and later executed, he had become one of the most ferocious fighters against Russia's militia.

The air in the truck was stale, overwhelmed by his body odor. He reopened the back vents on both sides to allow the cold air to circulate, then checked the battery on the two-way radio. There had been very few communications in the last few hours, only an occasional check-in. He stretched out again on the passenger seat and placed the radio next to his ear. In an hour or so, he'd return to his bathroom retreat, take a leak, charge his phones, and clean up a bit.

The ATF supervisor came to Heinrich's office with the news on his laptop. The robot's sensors had registered the existence of a large quantity of explosive materials. The robot had traversed the length of the van with the built-in x-ray equipment, and the negatives clearly showed the outline of a man lying prone on the back seat. On the floor of the van, a bag held eight or nine of the pipe bombs. The other interesting items were two cell phones in the man's pocket, one of the two-way radios near the man's head, and a small handgun in his waistband.

"Well, now we know what we're up against," Charlie said. "What do you think, Tony?"

"He still has bombs in the van, and I assume one or both of those phones can trigger the devices. If we rush him he could easily detonate those bombs, but more importantly, any that we haven't found in Cobo."

"Will the phone detonate all the bombs at once, or are they wired to respond to different signals?" Gil asked.

"That's a good question," the ATF agent said. "The devices we've found had two wiring configurations, which means two different signals could be used to detonate the units. For instance, he could detonate the IEDs on level two, and then later detonate the ones on another level."

"That would make the situation even more chaotic," Charlie noted.

"We've got to get him out of that van and find a way to get those phones away from him," Don said, stating what seemed impossible.

"Let's take one thing at a time," Charlie said. "Maybe now it's time to put Tyson's false radio communication ploy into action."

The group discussed various messages to draw Dudiyn away from the garage. It should be something that would not panic him, but would compel him to leave the van, and leave the explosives behind. There were lots of ideas, but none seemed to have just the right combination of urgency and opportunity to lull out of hiding a man who was hell-bent on blowing up the auto show.

"I've got it," Charlie said. "What if we announce that DADA is putting out a breakfast spread between 6 a.m. and 7 a.m. on the third floor, and all staff are welcome to get coffee, doughnuts, and breakfast sandwiches whenever their work allows?"

"You think he'll leave the van to eat?" Cynthia asked incredulously.

Charlie didn't say a word. She just let the thought percolate among the group. Soon, others became champions of the idea.

"When you think of it," Gil said, "it's the kind of communication that signals an all-clear at Cobo. He'll think the diversion has worked, that no one's yet found Heinrich's body and Cobo is back to business as usual."

"I like it," Mandy said, smiling admiringly at Charlie.

"It could work," Tony added. "But he might want to retrieve his janitor's cart, so we better put things back the way he left them in the men's room."

"And you better reactivate his ID, so he can enter Cobo," Gil added.

"God, I forgot about that. Good catch," Cynthia said.

"So, you think he'll just leave the bombs, grab some food, and bring it back to the van?" Don asked.

"I hope so," Charlie said.

"Or maybe he'll put the bombs in the men's room," Cynthia said.

"That's also possible," Don agreed.

"What do you think, Judy?" Charlie asked.

"I think his work is done for now, and he's got time. Even if

273

he brought food with him, he'd be interested in hot coffee and fresh eats. You wouldn't believe the number of times I've used doughnuts to get men to do what I want. I think it'll work."

Heads nodded. But Scott Hartwell was still pacing and had been unusually quiet.

"What's your opinion, Scott?" Charlie asked.

"All I know is, in four hours, when six thousand world journalists show up at Cobo, they have to be safe."

At 5:30 a.m., the two-way radio squawked near Dudiyn's ear. He recognized the voice as belonging to Cynthia Fitzgerald and turned up the volume. She announced that the auto dealers wanted to thank the staff for their hard work in preparing for the auto show and had set up a breakfast buffet on the third floor. She sounded cheerful and happy.

They think everything is fine.

The garage was still quiet, but in the next half hour the it would be buzzing with early-morning action. Shifts coming and going, valet parking setting up nearby, and according to the schedule the street sweepers would be arriving.

I'll clean up a bit and give everyone time to run for the food, then head up there, grab some coffee and a few sandwiches, and bring them back to eat.

Dudiyn laced up his boots and donned his cap. His pistol was snug at his back. He looked at the leftover bombs.

Better take one, just in case.

By ten of six, a dozen Cobo staff had entered or exited the employee door, and the parking spots near the lobby door were filled. Dudiyn watched as the parking attendant came out of the rear lobby door juggling a small tray of food and two cups of coffee before taking his seat in the booth. Dudiyn grabbed the bucket he'd brought to the van, and placed his gun and one of the pipes inside it, covered by a rag. He exited the van, looked around, and then tapped the lock button. The parking attendant was in an animated conversation with one of the Cobo security guards. Dudiyn took his time walking to the employee entrance, his entry card in hand. But before he got there, the man he'd seen at the TV studio last night came out the door. They locked eyes.

"You're still at it I see," the guy said, smiling and holding open the door.

"Yeah. But I'm almost done," Dudiyn mumbled, passing the man.

"Yeah. Me too. Well, like they say, there's no rest for the wicked."

Dudiyn surveyed the bathroom and checked the storage closet. The cleaning lady and the bomb were still in place. He grabbed the magnetized "out of service" sign and stuck it on the external door. He leaned over the counter and looked into the mirror. The eyes that reflected back brought an image of his brother's face, contorted in pain, eyes and mouth open, limbs mingled among the other dead bodies in the open grave. He closed his eyes against the memory.

He placed the two phones and his pistol on the sink, and removed his shirt and cap. He yanked a handful of paper towels from the receptacle, then lathered his armpits, neck, and the hair on his chest. His beard was growing back fast so he used the dull razor to clean up his face. He smelled and looked better, but his shirt and trousers were wrinkled from sleeping in the van— nothing he could do about that. He moved the trigger phone to his shirt pocket. At 6:20 a.m., he left the restroom and locked the door. His gun and a single pipe bomb were lodged in the bucket he carried; in the other hand he held a mop. He surveyed his surroundings, then moved to the service elevator.

Standing in front of the monitor, the group had watched Dudiyn's interaction with the Cobo worker. Cynthia switched views to the atrium camera, and they watched as Dudiyn paused in front of the men's room, then entered.

"He doesn't seem to have the bombs," Don said.

"There might be a couple in that bucket," Tony offered.

"Who was that man he spoke to at the door? They acted like they knew each other," Charlie asked.

"That's Ross, the chief engineer at the TV studio. He's okay," Ty said.

Ty had joined the group a half hour ago, looking fresh from a shower and a change of clothes, but still with the countenance of a man who knew the danger wasn't over.

"We don't have much time," Don said. "Gil and I are going to the van. Somebody warn us if you see him coming."

"Don, give it a couple of minutes," Tony cautioned.

As if on cue, the restroom's external door opened enough for Dudiyn to peek out and attach the "out of order" sign.

"He doesn't seem to be going for the food," Charlie said.

"Let's wait and see," Tony said.

All eyes were focused on the monitor. Two minutes passed, and there was no movement at the door. Don stood at the entrance of Heinrich's office, shifting from foot to foot, and Hartwell's pacing had reached manic levels. Suddenly the door opened and Dudiyn stepped into the corridor carrying the bucket and a mop. His cap was pulled low onto his head and he walked with a slow shuffle away from the men's room.

"We've got to assume he has the gun, the phones, and maybe a bomb or two," Gil said.

"Okay. Can we go now? I'm tired of waiting," Don said.

"Go, Don. Out the front lobby and around to the garage. We'll monitor both the garage and atrium cameras. Gil, make sure to use your earpiece and keep your phone line open," Charlie ordered.

"Right, Charlie."

Don and Gil flashed their Spectrum IDs as they exited the service door of the front lobby. It was freezing, but they didn't have time to register the discomfort. The garage was almost a quarter of a mile around the exterior of Cobo, and they had to move fast. The street sweepers were already at work on Washington Boulevard, and a few workers noted the two coatless

276

men running along the building, but no one tried to stop them. When they reached the garage, they slowed, walked to the parking booth, and again flashed their Spectrum IDs. "We're doing a patrol of the garage," Gil said, out of breath.

The parking attendant gave them a look. "Weren't you the guys who came to our headquarters to check us out? Why are you wearing those janitor uniforms?"

"Can't explain now. We're doing surveillance work."

They kept their eyes on the employee door to their left as they moved to the north wall of the garage. They stopped at the first vehicle in the long line of food trucks.

"It's the one after the deli truck," Gil whispered and pushed Don forward.

Gil, he's on the move, he heard in his earpiece. Gil touched Don's back again, and he stopped and turned.

"What is it?"

"Charlie."

But he's not heading your way. It's okay, Gil. He just got on the service elevator.

"Okay, we're clear," Gil said.

They counted ten trucks down, and stopped in front of the van. "Let's check the outside," Don said. "But don't touch anything."

They moved first to the driver's side of the van. The tinted windows made it difficult to see in, but the small penlight Gil pointed into the cab showed a couple of fast-food bags on the passenger seat. It was impossible to see through the side windows, but Gil flashed the light onto the ATF x-ray photos. "The bombs are in a bag behind the passenger seat, which ends here," Gil said. At the rear of the truck the window vents were open. Careful not to lean on the van, Gil pointed the light down toward the van's floor and tried to peer in, but the view was limited.

Don lay flat on the cold cement to look under the van, pointing a light up into the chassis. He noted no openings and no booby traps. He got to his feet and compared the photos to what he'd seen.

"It still looks good underneath."

"Okay, let's check the other side."

They repeated their inspection on the passenger side of the van. The wall at the rear of the vehicle stank of urine.

"The guy was in the van a long time. He got out to pee," Don said.

Leaning against the wall and aiming the penlight down into the louvered vent window brought better results.

"I can see the plastic bag," Gil said.

"Okay. Open the front passenger door," Don ordered.

Gil had experience with cars. As a teen he'd worked summers at his uncle's car lot in Alabama, sweeping, washing vehicles, learning to plug tires and do oil changes. He eventually worked his way up to sales assistant. And when his uncle moved his dealership to southeast Michigan and built it into a million-dollar business, Gil had been a top salesman. Along the way he'd also learned to break into cars. It took less than thirty seconds, using a screwdriver, for Gil to open the door.

"Good job, Acosta."

Gil climbed into the van, over the console, and opened the side-panel door. Don got in, perched on his knees on the bench, and shined his penlight over the seatback. Soon Gil's light joined in to illuminate the van's floor. The lights picked up spatters of a shiny substance. A contractor-sized plastic bag was against the wheel well. It bulged with content and was twisted closed. On the other side was a cardboard box with gallon-sized bleach containers, quart-sized baggies, a spool of copper wiring, and an open bag of nails. The compartment's odor of sweat and chemicals was assaulting.

"Let's look at the picture again," Don said.

They pointed their lights on the x-ray photo of the underside of the van. The photo clearly showed the bag containing a half-dozen or more of the pipe bombs, and the box. The bag had been disturbed since the photo taken by the ATF robot. Also, a bucket that had been in the back of the van was missing.

"Looks like he may have taken some of the bombs," Gil said.

"Let's open it up," Don said, pointing to the bag.

Gil climbed over the seat and sat on the floor. He pulled the bag between his knees and slowly emptied the contents.

"Eight," Don said.

Gil nodded. "Charlie, I've got eight of the IEDs in the back of the van. They look like all the others. Should we try to disarm them by pulling out the copper wire?"

That's a negative, Gil heard in his earpiece. It was Tony Canterra's voice.

Bring the devices out of the vehicle and to the outside of the garage. ATF will meet you there.

"We're supposed to bring them out," Gil said, putting each unit back into the bag.

Don opened the door and stepped out of the van, looking around. Gil handed the bag to Don and climbed over the seat.

Gil, he's on the move. He just entered the service elevator on the third level. If he's coming back to the van, you've got maybe three minutes. Charlie's voice was high-pitched.

"We've got to get out of here. He's coming back," Gil said.

The bombs weighed at least forty pounds. Gil held the bag in two tight fists, following Don carefully and deliberately to the garage exit. The parking attendant gave them his suspicious attention as they sidestepped the gate and headed north on Washington Boulevard. Before they got to Larned they were intercepted by two street sweepers.

"We're bomb squad," one of the men said, eyeing the bag. "Is that them?"

"Yes," Gil said, handing off the bag.

The ATF pair continued up Washington Boulevard where one of their vehicles was parked.

"Where is he now, Charlie?" Gil said into his phone.

He just got off the elevator, and he's heading your way. We're coming down.

"Let's go," Charlie said to Mandy.

"Tony, are you coming with us?"

"No, I better join ATF."

"Okay. Judy, call Hoyt for backup but tell him to stay out of sight until I call for him."

"Charlie, be careful," Judy pleaded.

A few employees remained huddled near the coffee urn in the third-floor concourse. So Dudiyn grabbed a couple of the small juice boxes, stuffed a few breakfast sandwiches into his bucket, and before anyone could engage him in conversation moved quickly back down the hall to the elevator. At level one, he stepped out cautiously, looked both ways, and shuffled toward the restroom. He glanced at the locked door of the restroom, then continued to the garage. At the door, he paused to stuff his gun into his belt and stepped through, holding the bucket and mop in one hand. The garage was quiet. He walked slowly and alertly to the van. He was within five feet when something on the ground caught his eye, a streak of a shiny substance on the floor to the left of the vehicle. He stopped, then stared at the windshield. The hair on his neck tingled. He slowly bent, placing the bucket and mop on the floor, and took two steps back. Just then the door behind him opened loudly, and he swiveled his head.

"Charlie, look out," Don called out from the direction of the parking booth.

Dudiyn dropped to his knees and fired two shots in the direction of the voice. Charlie and Mandy scrambled to their right and dived between two cars.

"Did he go to the van?" Gil looked sideways at Don as they ran, crouching.

"I don't know," Don answered.

The bomb's noise was thunderous in the confined space. The force of the explosion sent Don and Gil to the ground in a slow-motion roil. Nails shattered windshields, ripped into sheet metal, and sounded an orchestra on the cement floor. The heavy odor of black powder hovered in a smoke cloud that spread through the garage.

In a couple of minutes the parking attendant ran to Don, who was closest to him. "What the hell was that?" he shouted, arms flailing. "What the hell," the man said again, crouching next to Don, who was just beginning to move. "Are you all right?"

"Where's Acosta?"

Gil was a few feet ahead, and answered for himself by groaning and turning over onto his back.

"You all right, Acosta?"

"I think so. Just let me lie here for a second."

"Mandy?" Charlie tried to lift herself from the ground but Mandy was on top of her. "Mandy?" she said again because her ears were too shocked to hear her own question.

At the sound of the explosion, Mandy had instinctively thrown herself over Charlie, and the back of her jacket was covered in glass splinters.

"I'm okay," Mandy said, sinking onto her butt. "I may have some glass or something in my thigh. Something's there, and it hurts like hell."

"Where did Dudiyn go?" Don screamed.

"You mean the guy who ran into Cobo?" the parking attendant asked.

"C'mon, Gil," Don said, pulling himself up on rubbery legs. "Can you stand?"

"Yeah, I think so. But you sound like you're under water."

"Mack, are you guys okay?"

"We're okay, Don. Let's get after that bastard."

"Careful," Don said, opening the door. "He might be on the other side."

Dudiyn was not in sight, but as they turned the corner, guns raised, Hoyt was slumped over the steering wheel of his golf cart.

"Are you hurt, Timbermann?"

"He told me to get out of the cart. I told him to go to hell and took a shot at him, but he got me," Hoyt said. "I thought he was going to run into the restroom, but instead he headed through that service door. He had a key."

"On foot?" Charlie asked.

"Yeah."

"Are you sure you're okay?"

"I'm fine. Don't let him get away."

"Mandy, stay here with Hoyt." It was an order, and no time for an argument. Only a moment for a seconds-long shared glance through the closing service door.

Don took the lead, followed by Charlie and Gil. They held their guns in the two-handed position, pointed down, as they moved at a trot through the brightly lit service circulation area. Gil was still a bit wobbly and trying his best to keep up. They paused and swung their weapons toward each door they passed just in case Dudiyn tried an ambush.

"Do you think he ducked into one of these rooms?" Charlie shouted. "He's got keys."

"Nah. I think now he's just running," Don answered.

"Look," Gil shouted, pointing to the floor near the wall. "That's blood."

"Good old Timbermann," Don said. "He nicked the son of a bitch."

When they reached the corridor turning west toward the loading dock, they picked up speed. Dudiyn was leaving a steady blood trail now, and they followed it right to the door marked "VIP parking." Don grabbed the knob, and it turned. He crouched low, and pushed the door open forcefully. When no shot rang out, he ducked inside the semi-darkness of the small parking dock. There were no vehicles, no sound, and only the shine of the streetlights pouring into two high windows in the pull-down grate.

"Let's try the door leading to the access road," Don said, leading the way.

It was an hour away from daylight, but Gil's penlight picked up the blood on the doorknob.

"He definitely took a good hit," Gil said.

"Outstanding," Don replied, opening the door slowly.

Don stepped out onto the small iron landing and down the stairs that led to the loading dock access road and a line of commercial dumpsters. Gil swung the penlight back and forth on the snow.

"Here. More blood."

They moved slowly, Gil slightly in front now because he had the flashlight, Charlie and Don on either side. Charlie occasionally looked back to make sure the rear was clear. When Gil stopped and crouched, Don and Charlie followed.

"Come on," Gil said, standing and moving quickly down the access road. When he reached Washington Boulevard, he stopped again and pointed the penlight.

"He's doubling back. I think he's headed to the garage."

When the Mack team reached the garage at a run, several groups of people were milling around the area, including the ATF supervisor, who was having a heated argument with two police officers. The parking attendant was holding court near the employee door, pointing excitedly. Gil moved quickly to the back wall. The van was still there, but the panel door was open.

"Look, there's blood on the seat," Gil said, pointing the penlight.

"He was probably trying to retrieve the other bombs," Charlie said. "Now he knows he's screwed."

"Where the fuck is he now?" Don yelled. "Where would he go?"

"The weapons building. He has Heinrich's keys," Gil said.

"You're right, Gil. It's the easiest place for him to hide now. He's figured out by now all his bombs have been disarmed. But that damn place is loaded with weapons. Let's get a cart and go after him."

Dudiyn pressed a rag into his side. He was losing blood and needed to stop running soon. Someone had removed the bag of bombs from the van, and his detonation signals weren't working. He'd wired the bombs to respond to two sets of numbers, and neither number had triggered any additional explosions. Only the bomb he'd had in the bucket had done its job.

It didn't make sense to try to escape Cobo. He'd failed to use the IEDs to cause chaos at the auto show, but maybe he could still salvage his reputation. The assault weapons, tear gas grenades, and stun grenades stored in the weapons vault could still do the job the old-fashioned way.

The chaos in the garage had allowed him to come and go without attention, and he'd gathered his escape bag on the chance that he could still walk away from this mission. But if he couldn't, it didn't matter. He would die as a soldier just as his brother had. Dudiyn made his way on foot over to Congress Street and then past the Lodge freeway entrance. Traffic was relatively light, but yesterday's snow thaw, plus this morning's below-freezing temperatures, left a lot of slick spots on the dark street. He was doubled over from the pain of the gunshot wound, and he didn't have a jacket, but to the few pedestrians he passed he probably just seemed drunk. He crossed over the berm, just below the People Mover, when he heard a sound behind him. He climbed up into one of the structural walls of the freeway and tucked himself into the dark. Right after the cart passed, he lost his footing.

"Shit," Dudiyn hissed under his breath.

"Stop, Don. I heard something," Charlie said, jumping from the back seat of the cart and running back to the overpass.

"Wait for us, Mack," Don said.

Charlie had run a few yards when she saw Dudiyn unfold from the shadows of the concrete underpass. He held his right hand to his stomach. He and Charlie stood face to face like two gunfighters. Charlie had her gun extended. Dudiyn's lips contorted into a teeth-baring smile. He slowly raised his left hand out in front of him. Charlie shot once, spinning Dudiyn sideways. When he righted himself, he took a step forward and lifted his .32 revolver again. Charlie fired a second time. Dudiyn slumped in a heap onto the icy concrete.

"The bomb only damaged a couple dozen cars in the garage, mostly employee vehicles, and three of the restaurant trucks," Scott Hartwell said, smiling. "DADA will take care of all the damages."

The others gathered around the conference table of Cobo's general manager's office weren't quite as cheerful. Scott read the silent cue from Cynthia to ratchet down his enthusiasm. For a moment there was silence.

When the bomb exploded, the group monitoring the garage footage in Heinrich's office had responded. Hartwell, Ty, and Carter raced from the Spectrum office where they intercepted and assisted the injured Mandy and Hoyt. Cynthia and Judy grabbed Lin and ran with him up the stairwell to Cobo's main security office on the second level; that's where they found Amy.

"I'm sorry about your man being shot and about your other team member's injuries. I trust that both of them will be all right," Scott said to Charlie.

"Hoyt will be in the hospital for a while. He took a bullet to his hip, but he's come through the surgery well. Mandy had some injuries from shattered glass, and she caught a piece of shrapnel, but she sent a message that she was all patched up. She's probably on her way home."

"That's what you think," Judy said, pointing to the door.

Mandy entered the room wearing a set of hospital scrubs and a trench coat, and carrying a cane.

"I hope you didn't think I'd miss the wrap-up meeting," she said, grimacing.

"Way to go, Porter," Don said. "How's Timbermann?"

"I saw him before I left the hospital. He was awake and talking to his wife."

"Glad to hear it," Hartwell said.

"So, what did I miss?" Mandy asked.

"Charlie shot and killed Dudiyn," Gil said.

Mandy stepped to the table and touched Charlie's shoulder. "I'm sorry, babe."

"It couldn't be helped," Charlie said.

Gil picked up the story. "Hoyt had put a bullet in him, but he made a run. He went back to the van, we think to get the rest of the bombs, but when he couldn't find them, he retrieved a bunch of money and some passports. Then he ran again. We think he was on his way to the weapons garage."

"That's a good guess," Tony said. "We ran Dudiyn's fake passports, and interestingly he's been in proximity of a number of terrorist incidents around the world. The best we can tell is he was a freelancer. I don't think he had any connection with Heinrich before this job."

"With both of them dead, I guess that's something we'll never know," Cynthia said.

"But who put them up to this?" Mathers asked.

"A Chinese industrialist from Hong Kong hired them both. This businessman has a beef with China's central government, and he wanted to embarrass them by making sure China's first involvement with the Detroit Auto Show was tied to terrorism," Tony said.

"And the espionage piece?" Gil asked. "What role did that play?"

"Kwong had been told that part of his job was to organize the covert gathering of automotive trade secrets. Heinrich was recommended to Kwong by someone in the Chinese embassy with ties to the industrialist, to help with the logistics of the espionage operation. What Kwong didn't discover until later was that Heinrich was also involved in plotting violence against the auto show."

"So, Kwong *is* your witness?" Don said.

Tony nodded. "He doesn't have a stomach for murder, and when he learned that Heinrich, or at least his hired man, had abducted Lin and was probably behind the terror plot at Cobo, he came to us."

"Did Dudiyn kill Garry Jones?"

"We think so, Ty," Charlie said. "ATF will do ballistics tests on the gun Dudiyn had on him tonight to be sure."

"What about Chenglei?" Don asked. "This whole thing seemed to start with his murder."

"Well, there's still a lot we don't know," Tony said. "Chenglei was part of the group of Chinese at the warehouse trying to hack

General Motors' computers. We think Heinrich, or maybe it was Dudiyn, paid Chenglei to get a vendor's license, but when it didn't work, they got rid of him because he knew too much."

"Why'd they want a vendor's license?" Mathers asked.

"Probably to bring in the materials they needed to make the bomb scheme work. When they didn't get the license, they went directly to the food supervisor with a bribe," Tony said. "You'll probably uncover a few other deliveries that will raise flags."

"Tony, do you know any more about who killed Josh?"

"It was one of the men who kidnapped Lin. We recovered the gun that killed your colleague. Both assailants have been caught and detained. It appears that Heinrich hired them. His fingerprints were on the cash band found in the back of the van."

"I'm just glad the whole thing is over," Cynthia said.

"Me too," Tyson agreed.

"Well, ladies and gentlemen, it's almost time to open the show doors," Hartwell said, standing. "You're all welcome to stay and watch the media events. They're very exciting."

Judy stood, gathering her files and purse. "I'm heading home to the excitement of eight uninterrupted hours of sleep."

"Not me, Novak," Don said, yawning. "I'm going to get another look at that new Dodge Challenger. What about it, Charlie? Gil? You with me?"

"I'll tag along," Gil said. "I'm interested in seeing the Lincoln concept car."

"Not me," Charlie said. "I'm driving Mandy home."

Charlie insisted Mandy stay at her condo so she could be waited on during her recuperation—until Mandy reminded Charlie that she already had a houseguest.

"Oh, darn, Lin. I forgot about him. Where is he?"

"Cynthia said Amy took him back to your apartment right after they allowed her back into the garage. Fortunately, her car wasn't damaged. Why don't you stay at my house?"

"I'd like that."

Charlie drove Mandy's sedan, because the bandage on Mandy's

leg wouldn't allow her to get in and out of the Corvette. They rode in quiet for a while, each holding their own thoughts about the last few days. Charlie sped along East Jefferson Avenue, passing Belle Isle, and then the small and not-so-small eastside townships and cities that flirted with the Detroit River.

Charlie reached for Mandy's hand. "You threw yourself over me when the bomb exploded."

"To tell the truth, I'd do that for anyone. I'm just wired that way."

"I know that about you."

Charlie had been formulating a question, and finally asked. "Have you ever killed anyone in the line of duty?"

"Yes. And I know how it feels. When the adrenaline has worn off, and the thought comes out of nowhere that you've taken away someone's life, even if that someone was a scumbag, it feels awful."

They arrived at Mandy's place in the full brightness of the morning.

"We may as well have some breakfast," Mandy said, unlocking her front door. "When was the last time you ate?"

"The White Castles."

"Oh God. I'm scrambling some eggs and cutting up some fruit."

"No. *I'm* scrambling the eggs. I'm waiting on *you*, remember? Go, get off your leg."

Fifteen minutes later the eggs were ready, served with sliced cantaloupe, strawberries, and whole wheat toast. No coffee was offered. Mandy appeared at the kitchen door wearing a soft yellow teddy and matching boxer shorts.

"That's a sexy bandage you're wearing."

They ate at the kitchen island so Mandy could dangle her injured leg from the stool without it bending.

"I love you," Charlie said, and shoved a chunk of toast in her mouth.

"I know."

Charlie stabbed a piece of cantaloupe with her fork, and

before eating it made another pronouncement: "I think we should move in together."

"Your place or mine?"

"Neither. We should live somewhere that we pick as our together place."

"I wonder what your mom will say?"

"Let's ask her tomorrow. Right now, I want a bath, a cry, and to stay in bed until sunset."

"You want to be alone?"

Charlie shook her head.

"Not even for the cry?"

"No, not anymore."

About the Author

A Detroit native, Cheryl A. Head now lives on Capitol Hill in Washington, D.C., where she navigated a successful career as a writer, television producer, filmmaker, broadcast executive, and media funder. Her debut novel, *Long Way Home: A World War II Novel*, was a 2015 Next Generation Indie Book Award finalist in both the African-American Literature and Historical Fiction categories. Her first Charlie Mack Motown Mystery, *Bury Me When I'm Dead*, was a finalist for the Lambda Literary Award. When not writing fiction, she's a passionate blogger, and she regularly consults on a wide range of diversity issues.

Coming March 2019

Catch Me When I'm Falling
A Charlie Mack Motown Mystery
Book 3

Prologue

Detroit, April 2006

April was a precarious month in Detroit, offering the promise of an impending spring or the surprise of an ice storm. Palm Sunday was mild, and Carla walked several blocks to the bus that brought her near Saint Gabriel's Catholic church. She sat on a stoop to marvel at the pretty dresses worn by the little girls, and the tiny suits that made boys look like the men they would become. The line of worshipers entering the front doors brought a brief wave of nostalgia for her own childhood, a faint memory of family and home. She picked up a small piece of palm dropped by one of the children. Cradling it in her fingers, she crossed herself and then shuffled back to the bus stop. She retrieved her belongings from the shelter, and then ate a meal of flavorless chicken with plain white rice, and broccoli.

Later, she drifted to sleep with dreams of pink dresses, stained glass, and steaming bowls of arroz con pollo.

Carla rolled over on the hard bench, tugging her outer coat's collar tighter to cover her exposed neck. She'd heard a sound. A clink and a snap. Another clink, like metal on metal when sharpening a knife, then a tinny snap. Sensing someone nearby, she opened an eye. On the next clink, there was a scratching sound followed by the telltale smell of lighter fluid. It was not yet morning, and a figure stood in silhouette near the streetlight. She watched a flame gyrate against the black clothes of what she already considered her assailant. She pushed against the wooden bench with her elbow to sit upright, the other hand instinctively reaching for the bag near her feet. As the lighter snapped closed, the figure was again shrouded in shadows, and her heart registered an irregular beat. The strains of a Spanish ballad sung by a wounded male lover floated toward her, and her mind flashed for a second to a distant memory of lost love. She heard the clink and snap again. She rolled onto her thick hip to lift herself from the bench, but the pressure of a hand on her shoulder pushed her back onto the seat.

"Where are you going?" The man's voice was soft, melodious, as if his words were a lullaby.

He squatted next to the bench. He smelled of garlic and reefer. Another clink-scratch was followed by a wave of intense heat, and she flinched. The flame illuminated both their faces. His eyes were dark and feral—then his face contorted in fear and he flung himself backwards, scampering like a sand crab until he managed to gain his footing.

"Bruja," he hissed. "You witch."

The man ran to a dark-colored car at the curb, its wheels trimmed in blue lights. He flung open the door, assailing the night with plaintive lyrics, until he closed himself in. The car sped away, and the squeal of the tires matched Carla's scream.

"Diablo," she shrieked, fleeing the wooden bench. The plastic bag she carried was heavy with her life, and the quickness of her retreat thwarted by the weight of the clothes she wore. After walking several blocks north, she leaned against a concrete berm. The last two swallows of dark liquid returned her heart to a duller

292

pace, and she threw the empty bottle onto the gravel behind her. "Diablo," she muttered again as she shuffled into the receding darkness of the corridor.

Chapter 1

Charlie was awakened by a familiar sound outside her window, and she slipped out of bed to stand at the floor-to-ceiling glass, watching a shipping barge glide through the silver waters of the Detroit River. The peach-hued sunrise colored the façade of a dozen modern high-rises on the Canadian side of the river. She observed the enormous vessel for a while, imagining it carried mounds of sculpted steel, rows of windshield glass, gigantic towers of treaded rubber, engine and plastic components, perhaps even the shiny, new finished products. She got back into bed, pulling her knees and covers up to her chest.

People told her she had everything. This high-end building, along the city's expanding riverfront, was supposed to be her nesting place—a symbol of her success and freedom from the expectations of others. But, that was before she knew there could be no space for nesting without Mandy. In two weeks, they would wake up together in a new home. Mandy's excitement at the prospect of their shared life was contagious, and Charlie had begun to think her personal fulfillment could, finally, match her professional accomplishments. But, she was also aware of her own subtle resistance. It had been building with tiny complaints, minute flashes of doubts, and the recasting of priorities. She had sabotaged her happiness before, and didn't want to repeat the mistake, so she had stopped by her mother's apartment for a chat about the upcoming move.

"How's the packing going?" Ernestine had asked as they sat with cups of tea at the dining table.

"I hate it."

"Hate's a strong word."

Charlie scrunched her face in defense. "Mandy has us on a schedule. We're rotating between our two houses. So far, we've packed up both living rooms, and my kitchen. I hadn't realized I'd accumulated so much."

"We all have a lot of stuff. A major life event like moving gives you an opportunity to sort, and purge, and organize."

"I remember watching you pack up Daddy's office. It was a whole year after he died, and you were sitting on the carpet in front of his desk, in the middle of the night, putting things in boxes and crying."

"I never knew you saw that."

Ernestine cupped her mug of tea and sipped a few times, while Charlie used her finger to make a series of circles on a napkin. John Mack, invited by their vivid memories, momentarily took his place again at the head of the table.

"I kept a big box of your father's things that felt important to me at the time. But, I also gave a lot away—his papers to the law library, photographs to your uncle, and his suits to charity."

"I'm glad you kept the desk for me. I love using it."

"He would be so proud of you, Charlene."

"I'm not so sure. He never appreciated whining, and Mandy says lately I've been doing nothing but."

"Are you afraid?"

Charlie had tilted her head, manipulating in her mind imaginary Post-it notes on an imaginary white board. It was her technique for solving puzzles. The green notes were facts: She loved Mandy. She'd never been happier. She'd put her condominium on the market, and Mandy had sold her apartment. They had a house closing in two weeks, and a deposit paid with a moving company. She then lined up a row of red notes—the questions: Would she lose her independence? What if Mandy didn't really love her? What if this new lifestyle wouldn't make her happy?

"You're right. I *am* afraid," she had admitted to her mother.

That admission had been a week ago, and she was still holding onto doubts. She'd always shunned the labels: lesbian, bisexual, and hadn't made a choice because the lines were never sharply drawn. But Mandy presented a bright, clear line. She could continue her life punctuated by an emptiness she couldn't explain, or she could embrace the chance for a whole life. Charlie again slipped out of bed and moved to her river view. Now the sun splashed the Windsor skyline in brazen hopefulness. "What's wrong with you?" she said to her reflection in the window. "This is a no-brainer."

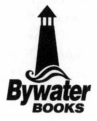

At Bywater Books we love good books about lesbians just like you do, and we're committed to bringing the best of contemporary lesbian writing to our avid readers. Our editorial team is dedicated to finding and developing outstanding writers who create books you won't want to put down.

We sponsor the Bywater Prize for Fiction to help with this quest. Each prizewinner receives $1,000 and publication of their novel. We have already discovered amazing writers like Jill Malone, Sally Bellerose, and Hilary Sloin through the Bywater Prize. Which exciting new writer will we find next?

For more information about Bywater Books and the annual Bywater Prize for Fiction, please visit our website.

www.bywaterbooks.com

CPSIA information can be obtained
at www.ICGtesting.com
Printed in the USA
LVHW01s1000150418
573534LV00001B/1/P